Marazion

Thursday Market

Julie Kabouya

Copyright © 2024 JK Publishing

All rights reserved.

No portion of this book may be reproduced in any form without written permission from the publisher or author, except as permitted by copyright law.

The characters and events portrayed in this book are fictitious. Any similarity to real persons, living or dead, is coincidental. And if you believe that, you'll believe anything.

Character glossary

Efreet: Devil. Large and destructive. (Arab)
Djaal: The lying, one-eyed false messiah. (Islamic)
Jann: Shape shifters that live in deserts and usually appear in the form of whirlwinds or camels. (Arab)
Jinn (Djinn) An intelligent, powerful spirit of lower rank than the angels mentioned in the Quran and other doctrines. Able to appear in human and animal forms, disperses into light or smoke. (Arab)
Marid: Rebellious of Jinn. Native to the elemental plane of water. Perceived as the most powerful. Shifting moods rapidly, as quickly as a storm upon the sea. Considered dangerous to imprison. Marids enjoy hunting in the oceans for sport, and because of the devoted self-worth, they collect pearls and other treasures. Water-based magic is utterly useless. Fire is their weakness. Flattery and compliments are the only thing that can beat them into submission, and remain on your side (Arab)

Mustatil Vipers: Guardians of the ancient burial grounds. Needs heat to emerge. Hates wind. (Author)

Naga: A form of intelligent Jinn that are snakes beneath a different disguise. (Author, inspired by Indian mythology)

Nagini: Half Cobra, half human. Proud and semi-divine. Associated with bodies of water. (Hindu)

Shiqq: Lower form of Jinn. Half creature, with a monstrous appearance. (Arab)

Siren: Mermaids/Mermen (Greek)

Translations

Arabic

   Asalaamu alaikum -Peace be upon you

   AstaghfiruAllah – Forgive/Excuse me

   BismiAllah – In the name of God

   Binti – My girl/woman

   Du'a – Prayer/supplication

   Kalb – Dog

   Khubz - Traditional bread

   Kuffar - Disbelievers

   Habibi – My love

   Hamduillah – Thanks to God

   Inshallah – God willing

   Jazak – Thank you

   Kohl – A black powder, usually antimony sulphide or lead sulphide, used as eye make-up and sun protection, especially in Eastern countries.

When the human race learns to read the language of symbols
A great veil will fall from the eyes of man

1

The Return

The narrow roads squeezed them into a holy haven. It had been forever, but the familiar welcome remained untouched - a medieval time warp you never wanted to leave. Roofs that dipped and leaned, laden with yellow lichen and robust seagulls. The old and the new in all shapes and sizes, crammed together to form a visual ode to the sea. The popular Cornish town abundant with Mediterranean planting and whitewashed granite, complimented the aqua sea peppered with dancing surfers. The golden sands brought on tears behind the Christian Dior's that obscured an old soul, Esme's heart almost stopping when they turned sharp right onto Draycott Terrace, gripping the seat while she kept her stomach in place.

The 'Sold' sign outside The Dolphin bed and breakfast set off a frenzy of butterflies. Now a terraced, four storey town house with sash windows, overlooking her favourite bay. The mechanical whirr of the handbrake on the white Range Rover jolted her into believing it was real, the surprise so large she had no option but to succumb, crumbling her wall.

Musa turned to face her, his black chinos juddering on the leather seats, trying his hardest to mask the anticipation of rejection. It was awkward between them, confined with unspoken words on a six-hour journey.

'Welcome to your new life, my dear.'

She looked at the keys in his hand. It would be fine, she thought, and this was the fix that needed to happen. A blessing in disguise, perhaps.

'Are you serious?' her greyish-green eyes wide, a little greyer of late.

He placed the keys in her clammy, trembling hand. Musa was looking his best today; manicured to perfection with his Arab dominance oozing all over her. Just a slow dip of his head confirmed the reality. Her heavy breaths raised a smug smile from him. It had been a while since he heard any voiced pleasure from her, knowing it was all his fault. Hoping the move would put a thicker sticking plaster over her wound.

'Come, we look inside.'

Distant bursts of children's excited screams and crashing waves cleansed her as she gracefully left the vehicle, everything unspoilt and beautifully preserved, even the unique smell of sea spray and hot tanning oil had remained. Her melancholy had no place here, and how would her anxiety fair amongst such a laid-back lifestyle? She stuck out like a sore thumb this time around, not as care-free or fitting in by default. Esme felt nervous about her hijab, sure people had stared a little longer with judgemental eyes. If she had known, she would have toned down her D&G outfit, which was attracting more attention. Her pastel linens and chiffon reflecting the façade to remain a cut above, the only way to earn respect and get people to over please, was Musa's ethos.

The street shielded from the sun with hardly any room for modern cars, held all the vivid memories in one place: the convoy of family friends arriving after a long journey, bleary-eyed and ready to blow the rat race away for two weeks.

Unsure her legs would carry her to the door, she still managed to respectfully greet passing tourists laden with beach towels as they took the steps to the bay, holding the same iron handrail she did. Blackened and pitted from thousands of foreign hands.

Standing on the top step of the Dolphin, a nostalgic glow broke her nerves as she paused to gaze at Porthminster bay below, her tears blurring the perfect view. She had come home. It was difficult to put the key in the door, pausing to tap her clavicle three times and giving her pink pearl necklace a tweak.

'Here, I help you darlink. I know it's big shock for you.' Musa opened the grey front door, both greeted by the smell of damp. Esme was dubious stepping into the cool entrance paved with Victorian floor tiles. It was an instant comfort, wishing she was crossing the threshold with her mother, accompanied with laughter amongst the welcomed chaos and plans for a traditional takeover of the beach huts. Dumping her Louis Vuitton bag on a small table at the foot of the stairs, Musa walked ahead admiring the cornices while she tapped the glass of the barometer hung near the door – the needle stuck on '**fine**'.

'Is a bit cold in here,' he continued, poking his head around doors and in cupboards, every room with its original features. The extended kitchen had a Belfast sink and overlooked next door's wall, the stale smell of cooked breakfast and stewed tea stirred her. The upstairs had additional short stairs leading to the various levels with two double ensuite bedrooms, plus a family bathroom. A roof space that creaked where the seagulls congregated outside the window. Musa had to stay in the middle so he wouldn't hit his head. She decided it would be her son's room, a bolt hole and essential isolation for his condition. Her daughter would be happy on the lower level.

'Habibi, there are better properties than this one. You do not have to accept it. I can sell it for a good profit. The agents gave it to us under market value.' Yes, because Musa would have haggled them under the table with promises of further purchases and overseas buyers. Properties were hot news after it was pinned for the G Summit's location.

'No, I don't want to let it go,' she choked, 'it was a wonderful surprise, thank you.'

He detected a glimmer of returned affection and that was a big enough stitch to pick at, he'd missed their heated embraces.

'You are too sentimental. We stay here for a few months only, okay? We move on, habibi.'

Esme wandered downstairs leaving Musa to inspect the passable bathroom with a roll-top bath. Her heels echoed off the oak floor as she entered the large sitting room. The whole place painted white imagining cosy throws, log baskets and her rock lamp placed in the cast iron fireplace. The high, ornate ceilings meant it was Musa's dream house and fast becoming hers. She remembered sitting in there having breakfast with her mother, swimming costume on ready for a sea-filled day. Esme was a bit of a water baby when she was young, 'one last minute' extending to several. She couldn't remember when her fear of water set in, certain it was projected from her mother.

Stopping to peer out the sash windows, the old, warped glass changed the shape of the picturesque town of Saint Ives, leaving her breath on the pane from the deep ache and dream come true. She moved on and studied the pictures left behind that hung from rails on golden thread. Arabic calligraphy in one, just making out the word **Allah**. Two others with artistic impressions of the Hamsa, or Fatimah's hand as it's commonly known. Five digits with an eye in the palm, said to ward off evil glances with pious protection. It wasn't common in Musa's culture, perceived as false worship. People had such a romantic and misguided idea of being married to a Saudi. Affluency had changed her, she often caught herself looking down her nose at people or places, conditioned into a lifestyle she depended upon. The return to Saint Ives crudely reminded her of where her roots lay.

A small room off the lounge looked out to the back yard. Esme remembered it being the room for cereals and toast, with little jam jars haphazard in wicker baskets. It smelt musty now and was in dire need of decoration, the depressing sage green just made the vibe worse. Taking a quick nostalgic look around, touching the walls flashes of white cotton tablecloths sprung to mind. It would be the perfect place for her art materials and unfinished projects if she ever returned to painting.

Another door off the lounge led to a stairwell and basement. She remembered there being a second set of stairs this end before the two houses were separated. The minimal décor continued as she descended, becoming eerily quiet. There wasn't much space at the foot of the stairs as she took each one gingerly, like she was invading someone else's space, with hooks for coats and a door to the left and an odd smell of tar, or maybe it was wood preserve.

She turned the handle, it was locked, pushing it to be sure. Checking the keys in her hand, it must be missing, putting her ear against it, trying the round, brass handle again. Knocking lightly, certain she heard movement. There were deep scratches in the frame, she touched them, getting a small splinter.

'Moose! Do you have another key?!' She called up the stairs, sucking the tip of her forefinger.

He appeared, booking a flight to Riyadh on his mobile.

'What habibi?'

'This door, it won't open. Did they give you any other keys?'

'Are you happy?'

'I am, thank you. Hamduillah. Is there another key?'

'I have another surprise!' beaming.

'Another one? I don't think my heart can take it.'

'Would you like, eh, your tea? Red tea, and cake?'

'I would, but can we talk about this door first?'

'Good, come, we have a café.'

'Moose, the door!'

'Sorree, sorree. I mean, I have bought you a Café, not a coffee, my love,' his smile broad, framed by his perfect goatee.

'A Café? Another one?'

'Correct. Ya hamduillah, it's perfect. On the harbour. Come, we see it.'

'You are crazy!'

'Yes, for you. Come, forget the door, is just spare room for boxes. Not important. Leave it.' Waving his hand dismissively.

She regarded the door that seemed to look back; an invisible life in the weathered grain. Trying the handle with a little more force, before being pulled away by Musa's manicured spin.

His visits to England were few, faced with desperate individuals on return. The hostile demeanour his guard against prying and protection of his skill, for he never performed it alone. The blur of the white thobe was all she remembered, a fateful rescue from a handsome bachelor.

She became untouchable in the community. He was real-life marriage material, with an inescapable clause.

***

2

Riyadh

Architectural high risers dominated the cloudless skyline, their mirrored structures the prisms of the city and landmarks of the world. Everything had a luxurious finish, even the tunnels. Palm trees lined the flat streets where southern California met the Arab world, with a Starbucks in every direction. Musa checked his Rolex when the call of the Athan penetrated the heat for midday prayer, heading to his café where he wouldn't get the door closed in his face. Diesel fumes from dust-covered taxis suffocated him as he headed to the heavier populated areas that were out of sight. Where local males adorned steps and shop frontages beneath the shade of palms, stray cats among them playing at their feet hoping for a morsel of dry bread or discarded bones.

His legs were heavy walking the dirt road, having left the comfort and opulence of the malls and hotel. His shoulder-length black hair sleeked into a coiffured man bun hidden beneath the red and white head dress, with Raybans that framed the beautiful face. The crisp, white cotton thobe that reached the top of his Birkenstocks stuck to the middle of his back, a stark reminder he had adapted to a colder climate. It was always good to come back home and reside on the top tier of society. There were no distractions in Riyadh, things were simple with everything you needed to nourish your faith and alter ego, as well as maintaining a deeper connection with his creator. Britain afforded a less arduous life during daylight hours, a compromise in addition to the profitable properties.

Navigating the underdeveloped areas wasn't so easy anymore, having to stride roadworks and barricades in long attire was proving to be a further obstruction in a bid to turn the arid areas into westernised attractions. The migrant workers looked uncomfortable in their high-viz gilets, with worn faces and tired hearts but what other choice did they have? Money was good, living not so and anything was better than back home and the lack of humility they would receive elsewhere. Families had adopted most, dutifully remaining on the bottom rung within society. Kept sweet and coerced for what they had to offer the Arab world: Agarwood and cheap staff.

He entered the shaded respite of ancient stone arcades, out of breath with an insatiable thirst. Outlets housed bored owners sat on foot stools checking the internet and smoking shisha, discussing the lack of tourists. The older residents congregated in the centre exchanging the same topics while they drank tea. Riyadh was a stop point for pilgrims on foot, before reaching every Muslims' ultimate mission and sacrifice in the city of Medina.

The smell of burning apple tobacco and freshly cooked khubz made Musa hungry, but his thirst needed satisfying first. People passed, some women in full covering, others not. Things had changed rapidly, and he wasn't sure he liked it. The liberated women had expressed their release by dying their hair in obscure colours and wearing what they wanted. A freak show, he thought. He felt all eyes on him, looking straight ahead to avoid the beckoning of desperate proprietors. Reaching the end of the arcade there was a young Asian boy selling bottles of 7-Up in ice boxes.

'Asalaamu alaikum. Wahad,' handing over two dollars for one bottle. The boy waved his hand, he was not happy with this currency, Riyals were preferred – foreign money was hard to change. Musa offered ten dollars, the boy smiled nervously, it was tempting and meant a short day, but his father would not be pleased. Musa put the money back in his wallet and walked away, his thirst intensified on seeing the boxes of cold liquid provocatively placed on ice. The boy pulled him back, offering him a free drink with a decaying smile.

'La. La,' Musa protested. But the boy insisted, the cap already off. Musa accepted with grateful gesture. The poor were poorer because of it, with less of a curse. He waited until he left the arcade, humbled from the blessing, stopping to drink the whole thing in one go – the fizz burning his gullet. He discarded the empty bottle with the others, releasing a large belch through his nose. The sugar rush had stirred the enzymes, and he was looking forward to a traditional meze.

His café still had gender segregation seating, there were only a few remaining after the liberation, he'd made sure of it. The carved wooden door sat in an equally ornate arched frame; the name written in Arabic above it - 'El Abadis' (*the eternal*). Dearest Ibrahim stood in the doorway, relieved to see him.

'As salaam alaikum brother! Hot enough for you?'

Shaking hands and kissing cheeks.

'Alaikum salaam Ibrahim, you wanna speak English today, eh?'

'It is good practice for me. How is the family?'

'Alhamdulillah.'

'Good, good. Allah be praised.'

'Is my table ready?'

'Of course.'

The man from Yemen in his seventies led him to the best table, his dark skin and origin meant he hadn't gotten far in the Middle East; just managing to stay afloat on favours and good manners. His close white turban and thobe from a different era, always with a small bunch of dried herbs behind his ear, told a tale of conflict with an Indigenous resistance. Musa noticed that his dark blue eyes were looking a little weary. He'd given him the position to watch over the café because of his unfaltering loyalty.

The background music grounded Musa as he entered. Lutes, tambourines and goblet drums filled his emptiness with 'home' as he thumbed the tesbih beads over his fingers; counting his blessings and repenting his sins.

Silver bowls were brought to his table by another nervous young Asian, with some extra bread and a coffee in a small cup with saucer, accompanied by a large jug of water which Musa immediately took.

'Shookran. I need water first. This heat is kicking my ass! AstaghfiruAllah.'

'Ha-ha! Ya'rub. Got used to western climate too much. You are looking more westernised every time I see you, brother, which is not that often. Have you forgotten your roots?'

'Maybe. I feel like a foreigner now. SubhaanAllah,' stroking his goatee in place.

'The day you left you became a foreigner, brother,' placing down small plate of dates and candied fruit, as he checked around for listeners. Musa tore the bread and dipped it in the humus with his right hand, offering it to Ibrahim.

'No, no. Hamdullah, you eat.'

Ibrahim had been anxious to speak to him face to face over his provocative question, continuing in Arabic. 'Is there a wife for me in Britain?' he whispered.

Musa snorted a quiet laugh and shook his head. 'Live the rest of your life without burden. Why not an Arab?'

'I can't afford one! If it weren't for you, I'd be living in the mountains with the rest of the sorry souls who can't afford them!'

'Who needs a woman who isn't happy sleeping on the floor? What are you looking for, a loan?'

'Please, don't insult me. What good is a loan?'

Musa didn't look up and tried a different dish, the one with fava beans. 'Desperation clouds judgement,' he commented, tearing the bread with his teeth.

'I am not desperate. I'm tired of this life. Look at me, I'm going to die in this place, no offense. I am grateful for your trust in me, hamduillah. What's the news back in ice capital?'

'We have moved to the south coast. Esmay's favourite place, a surprise.'

Ibrahim studied Musa. 'I see. Your means are stretching you?'

'Not at all. They have good investments in the south. How are the books looking?'

'The ends are no longer meeting, we need to move to the mall. Everybody is going there now, eating artificial food from the west. Bah!' he turned to face the door, 'they are poisoning our youth! Cine-mas. What has happened to us? Hmm? Have you seen them, coming from Lon-don now, bringing their western cars and music from the devils.'

Ibrahim tutted and crossed his legs, throwing his hands up in despair. Musa wiped his mouth with the checkered cloth, gulping down a glass of water.

'There's too much salt in these dishes,' giving his goatee another stroke. Squinting his hazel eyes at Ibrahim.

'Be grateful you have easy food on your table, Musa. We have lost our culture to the Amrikas, this I know. Like it's not fashionable to be Arab anymore.'

'We are laying traps,' Musa uttered, wiping bowls clean with the khubz.

'Listen, brother. I know you can help me. People talk.'

'People talk too much.' Musa said.

'I'm an old man, I need company. Company that's not going to cost me the earth!'

'You are seventy-five, brother. Too much company could give you a heart attack. The mountains may be a better option for you.'

Ibrahim chortled, 'I would die a happy man!' taking the oregano from behind his ear and holding it to his nose. 'Ya Allah. What does my lord want from me? The only life I ever wanted, taken by the hand of the same people I wash dishes for!' Dabbing a solitary tear from his eye with Musa's napkin. 'My beautiful wife and daughter...' he held composure '...like flowers!' in a sharp whisper, cupping his hands in front of him and looking into them with purpose.

'Women are a creation like no other. One that gives you scent and colour, withstanding anything and bringing a smile to the darkest of days. But once you betray that, ha-ha! They will become the *new* wife. Only it will be a bad new. Remember this. Your Esme is a good woman, don't ruin it by this ummah's need to compete with status and more genitalia than they can handle.'

Musa gulped his last mouthful. 'I gave you responsibility of this place, my friend. Is it not serving you?'

'Not anymore. Most are going to Mac-don-alds! Ya Allah. Eating hypocrisy for breakfast. Digging their graves with their teeth! Calling it Halal. Pfft! This is becoming the badge of irrelevance these days.' The piped music made up for the awkward silence. 'A good wife would turn this place around, brother. Turn me around. I pray for her every day.'

Musa stood, throwing a hundred dollars on the table.

'This will make up for the lack of customers today. Meet me at the Al Masaa, midnight, in the singles section.'

'The Al Masaa?! You will need your hundred dollars back if we are to meet there. Can't we discuss it here?'

'Midnight. Take the rest of the day off,' ruffling the boy's hair as he left. Thrusting some dollars in his hand. 'Midnight! Don't be late! Salaam!'

3

The Package

Midnight. Lit frontages reflected in the glossy paint of super cars, sparking enticement into the urban, traditional and the random. The Four Seasons Hotel the dominant landmark; the most beautiful piece of architecture that reflected its surroundings by day, becoming a beacon of light after dark. Its adorers dined beneath the bright blue which illuminated the skies, privatising the opulence and highly polished surfaces within. Its workers on hand to serve or assist. The migrants' accomplishment of pride and low self-worth, a mock paradise in its wake.

Musa left the hotel room in traditional dress, comfortable in his freshly laundered cotton with seams that indicated a pristine service. Each staff member he passed offered humble greetings or peaceful wishes of a good night hoping for a competitive tip. A Bengali door attendant tipped his hat with white-gloved hands, maintaining professionalism when Musa handed him twenty dollars. The heat took his breath away, gladly receiving the light relief of a tepid breeze.

The Al Masaa was a walk away, busy but never full. The largest Café in the world seating up to a thousand guests; at least you always got the seat you wanted. Waiters greeted him in the usual kiss-ass manner, escorted to the terrace overlooking the Four Seasons. Large, beige parasols collapsed for evening leisure shielded dressed tables with gold ashtrays, serviette holders and toothpicks. The background music gently playing popular covers in an Arabic fashion. They fussed around him while he waited for Ibrahim, unsure if he would show up, it was late for an old man used to living during the peak of the heat. A well-dressed waiter returned with a silver tray of dates on smooth, wooden sticks and a carafe of water with two glasses. Musa had ordered mint tea as the coffee was leaving a bad taste. He never spoke, just expressed his appreciation, too much interaction could spark off conversations like Ibrahim's.

Traditional tea pots and glasses were shone to perfection, Musa's spy glasses for his surroundings. Checking his watch, 12.10am, perhaps Ibrahim wasn't coming, and his sleep was more important than his need for a better life. Musa strained the sweet, minty liquid through his lips admiring the Four Seasons towering above him. Their worship of fake illumination had taken over and he thought about Esme as the nightlife filled his senses, just one huff escaped his nose when he thought of their nights in Saudi. Her intuition scared him at times, and he did his utmost to oppress it. She was his most treasured possession, his daughter a close second. But his son was the apple of his eye, the protector of the family and next in line. Bright, intelligent having won several Quran recital competitions.

Ibrahim startled him as he clumsily pulled up a chair, 'salaams. Sorry I am late, brother. No room for immigrants. Your name is the ticket of entry, eh?'

The waiter who had fought with Ibrahim waited for Musa's authority, leaving the table with a subtle bow when he was waved off.

'I thought you had changed your mind.'

'I was close, but something pulled me here. Curiosity, or the devil himself.'

Musa raised his chin as he pulled at the mandarin collar. 'Where is your faith, brother?'

Ibrahim winced as he eased himself onto the seat, patting his heart with his right hand.

'Right here.'

Musa offered him the aperitifs on the silver tray. 'Eat, you look like you need it.' Ibrahim ate the dates in a ravenous manner, checking the middles for any castaways.

'I hate this place. Everything is fake. So, what is this proposition?' Ibrahim asked.

'What makes you think it's a proposition?'

'Why else bring me here, under the all-seeing eye?'

Musa's skin goose bumped, 'you've been watching too many movies.'

'I don't watch teevee. They lie too.'

Musa shifted forward, checking around before speaking. 'I need your help, dearest uncle.'

'*Uncle*? Ya Allah, who knew this day would come?' he chortled. 'SubhaanAllah, how the tables have turned.'

Musa ignored Ibrahim's jab, sliding a gold amulet towards him making Ibrahim jump back.

'What is this?!'

'Your wish.'

'AstaghfiruAllah! I did not ask for wishes!'

'Let me rephrase that – your prayers answered in one little package.'

'You give me Sihr?!'

Musa held Ibrahim's forearm, 'keep your voice down, brother! Have I ever caused you harm?'

'No, never,' Ibrahim calmed, slurping the mint tea. 'Forgive me. But I know what that is, and I do not accept black magic. Aouthou bileh minna shaitaan a'rajeem.'

'You feel you need protection from me?'

'Maybe you are my devil, enticing me here for your own gain and Musa has been murdered.'

'Do you want to change your life, or not?'

'At what cost?'

'What do you take me for?'

'A man with dollar signs in his eyes that has lost all compassion and sense.' Ibrahim got up to leave, Musa grabbed him by the arm again.

'There's no getting out of it now, you came and that was the first part of the contract.'

'What contract? I did not agree to anything with you, and my bed is calling me.'

'Your empty bed, where you will die alone.'

'So be it. I would rather die alone than be part of this!' pointing to the Four Seasons. People were beginning to stare, the side of Ibrahim's face illuminated by the hue of coloured led lights that laced the balcony.

Musa clenched his jaw, 'you will share the benefits and get your wife, free of charge.'

Ibrahim sat, 'I am listening.'

Musa checked around, and in the tea pot.

'I trust only you, with my life…' he waited for staff to pass, lowering his voice '…I need you to help me with an undoing.'

'Undoing? Brother, why are you getting yourself involved with this at your age? You have a beautiful family, mash'Allah.'

'I was not prepared for this consequence. My daughter needs protecting,' he leaned back and stabbed the white tablecloth with a date stick. 'I need to close the gates I have opened. The prophecies are true. May Allah help us all.'

'Why has it taken you an inevitability to realise? Stupid, all of you. The unseen forces are having a field day with your inability to remain on the path of mercy. This is why your country is going to the dogs. The signs are as close as the clothes on your backs.'

Musa gulped the sweet tea, 'the dimensions are thinning, merging into one another. More are falling through, using corrupt souls to conduct their deeds and determination to lead us into the fire. Their resentment still exists in their black hearts, and they will stop at nothing, *nothing!*' he whispered, feeling his chest tighten.

'Ya rub, we all knew this was coming, the Dajaal's moment is close but we still blindly follow those in power,' Ibrahim smacked his lips from the sweet indulgence.

Musa kept snapping his head from left to right, catching dark movements in his peripheral vision.

'They have overpowered us, including political leaders. Silencing, coercing. I saw things that will live with me until this is all over,' continually checking over the clientele.

'I have never seen you this agitated, brother. It scares me. What is this help you need?'

Musa tapped the amulet, 'I need this taken to Lake Khararah.'

Ibrahim raised his wiry eyebrows. 'Elemental Jinn?! And this is too far for an old man to travel!'

'I will ensure you are taken care of. Let me explain.'

Ibrahim rested on the table, 'you of all people should know what happens to people when they get involved with the black magic.'

'I know very well. This is not for malice or revenge. I have become complacent and greedy in my work and now I'm paying the price.'

'Ya Allah, you are putting you and your family at great risk.' Ibrahim sorted through the sweetened fruit, mistrusting their perfection.

'If you are willing to help me, you can have the Café, I need it open, however many customers we lose. You will have more than enough from this.'

Ibrahim rubbed his fingers together to expel the date syrup, 'what is the *deal* here?'

'You take it to the lake. I will make it worth your while.'

'Why don't *you* take it to the lake?'

'No one knows you. You'll go unnoticed. Place it, and leave. No conversation, just go. Do you hear me? No conversation.' The old man held eye contact with Musa, processing the unease.

'Why don't you sleep on it. Uncle? Think about it and get back to me in the morning, inshallah. I will leave for the UK soon. But know this, if you still refuse, I will be selling the café. I need to erase my traces.'

Ibrahim toyed with the condiments and began folding a serviette. 'And my wife?'

Musa hesitated, drumming the table from the turmoil in his belly, 'one thing at a time. I will keep you in my du'as. You will get your wife, inshallah.'

'And I'll do it, God help me I'll do it. And I will keep you in my du'as, without anything in return. You take whatever is attached to this, this, hell in a shiny package,' he raised his palms. 'I have no strength to fight with you. Forgive my foolishness, I appreciate you, but I want no part. I am tired. Salaam young man, Allah's eyes be with you. I will have your favourite breakfast waiting for you, inshallah,' he left. Heaven would offer him his desires, without eternal consequence.

Musa wrapped the triangular amulet in a serviette. He needed a guardian he could trust, and Ibrahim was the only one worthy of such a position. Hoping the old man would come to his senses and throw caution to the wind at sunrise.

4

Lake Khararah

Dune bashing GMC's and Nissan trucks occupied the red-sanded attraction. A showcase for the onlookers, socialising under the shade of Acacia trees among grazing dark-furred camels. The air cleansed with the scent of Oud, taking ownership among the plumes from shisha and barbeques. Ibrahim arrived with aching bones, Musa was persuasive at breakfast and his longing for a companion was greater than his conscience. More instructions were to follow once the amulet was deposited. He wasn't sure he was in the right place, too weary to travel any further. His chaperone worked with Musa and was chosen for his experience in the detection and repellence of black magic.

Arriving later in the day came with a breeze that moved the lake into little waves, hurrying to its edge where the elderly rested on fold-away chairs to cool their feet. Families and brothers sat crossed legged on large rugs, silver tea pots brewing on clay bowls of hot coals and traditional music played from vehicle speakers. Frequented for its miracle.

He knelt at the water's edge filling his cupped hands and moving it over his head, around his neck and up his forearms, wiping the last over his face, repeating it before replacing his white turban. Resting back on his heels admiring the serene view and chaotic company, grabbing his white thobe and frantically feeling for the amulet around his neck. It was there, clutching it as he got to his feet.

'As salaam alaikum brother,' said a man in a heavy Indian accent sat near the edge, a tourist from Mumbai, using a red 4x4 as a wind break. Ibrahim acknowledged him with a nod.

'Come join us, please, sit.'

'No, thank you, I am not staying,' Ibrahim responded, hand over his heart.

'We have all night. Relax with us. I have brought a speciality,' the Asian smiled broadly. 'I'm sure you've had a tiring journey, uncle. I won't keep you, you are welcome.'

He agreed, his parched throat and rumbling belly overruled Musa's warnings. Two other men sat with them wearing similar designer clothes with a finely groomed image, smelling of high street colognes.

'We are here for the same reasons, eh?' the Asian jeered. 'I am Anwar,' holding out his hand.

Ibrahim reciprocated, 'Ibrahim.'

'Welcome Ibrahim. These are my cousins, Prakash, Gibril. We come here every year. Is nice place. You live in the city?'

'Yes. I am Café owner, in the city.'

'Sounds good brother. What's the name?' Ibrahim thought carefully, he wanted to say the Al Masaa but that lie may backfire.

'Just ask for me, they will know.'

The Asian handed him a piece of cake, 'eat, it's Aflatoon, we are famous for it – hmmm?' pushing the toffee-coloured rectangle in Ibrahim's face, taking a forced bite. Squashy and deliciously sweet.

'This is good, but not too much,' patting his stomach.

'So, what is your wish?' Anwar asked with a straight face.

'I just came for a change of scenery,' Ibrahim said with palms raised.

'As long as you are not like these fools, sir.' Anwar jerked his chin towards those around him, wobbling his head. Ibrahim touched the amulet having second thoughts, the favour for Musa increasing self sabotage. But he was the only Arab that had truly helped him.

'I came here for something else.' It was difficult keeping his word, Anwar had that kind of personality that would drag anything out of you.

'A woman?' Anwar pushed him gently with a wink.

'No, no – well, inshallah. I don't know.'

'I can see you are holding onto something. Give me, I look for you.'

'No, no. I must go. Thank you for your hospitality.'

Anwar pulled out an amulet from the front of his shirt, swinging it provocatively from a gold chain, doing the head wobble in an inflated manner.

'We are all here for the same thing. Depending on what you are desperate for my friend. I carry this one with me.'

Ibrahim began to sweat, he should just go home and forget the whole thing, thank Musa, and never speak of it again.

'I can take a look for you,' Anwar insisted with clicking fingers. His face rounded from the glow of the imminent sunset.

'Thank you. I am going to take a short walk to think.'

'Uncle, I am not here to rob you. Why would I? I'm just making sure you are in the right place. You don't want anything coming back to you in a negative manner, eh?'

Ibrahim reached into his shirt, pulling the leather cord over his head and reluctantly handing it to Anwar, receiving shooting pains from his sinister gaze.

He watched the Asian man study the golden case and engraved inscriptions, verses in ancient Arabic. 'You are in the wrong place for this, brother,' handing it back. 'This place is contaminated. You need the other lake,' his tone solemn. 'Look at these people,' he wrapped a cloth around the handle of the silver tea pot, removing it from the coals and pouring it into etched glasses.

'These people don't know what they are doing. Not all are here for the same thing. They come to watch and see what happens to the fools that have forgotten themselves. I can tell you have a good heart, my friend. You don't want anything ruining that.'

'What did you see?' Ibrahim begged.

Anwar turned down his mouth and shook his head, 'nothing I've seen before. Who gave you this?'

'I'm sorry, I cannot.'

Anwar offered him the glass, 'Here, drink. Cardamom to wash down the Aflatoon,' he smiled sympathetically. 'You must proceed, there is no going back,' straining the steaming hot tea through pursed lips.

'Where must I take it?' Ibrahim held the glass between the tips of his fingers, scrutinising the view and the people he dared not pass judgement upon.

'It's close to here. You turned too soon. Leave before dark, otherwise we may never see you again.' Ibrahim snapped his head round, Anwar chuckled.

'I'm joking with you dearest uncle. You have an amulet for the water spirits. The kind that does not come to this place. There must be hundreds of amulets in this water rotting on the bottom. Half of them of no use to anyone, taking people's hopes with them. Extortion, that is all. You must have paid a high price.' Handing his associates some tea.

'I think the price may be higher than I thought.' Ibrahim mumbled, looking into the water.

'We smoke Oud first, eh? Calm you down. You look like you are about to have a heart attack!'

Ibrahim raised his head above the bonnet of the Nissan, looking for the chauffeur. Spotting him sat with someone he knew.

'What brings you here, apart from this lake?' Ibrahim asked.

'The atmosphere. We like it, don't we brothers?' the other two raised their glasses, mouths full. 'Saudi treats us well.' He held two pieces of Oud to the glowing coals, raising the burning shards to admire the majestic trails snaking their way upwards.

'Here...' handing a piece to Ibrahim. But he had no intention of smoking it, instead wafted it over himself, reciting.

Anwar reached into his trouser pocket giving Ibrahim a small, brown paper package, 'Artificial is no good. Take this.'

Ibrahim opened the packet cautiously, afraid to see what was inside – little chips of genuine Oud.

'I cannot accept this brother,' handing the expensive package back.

Anwar pushed his hand away. 'Please, do not insult me. Take it.'

'Jazak Allah Khair. Thank you.'

'Wa iyyakum, welcome. Now, you should go before it gets dark.'

Anwar opened his vehicle, reaching in the side pocket for a serviette and pen. He leaned on the bonnet and made a rough sketch of a map, the pen catching in small folds of the delicate paper. 'Your driver will have a good idea. When you see the primates then you know you're heading in the right direction. It's about sixty-eight kilometres from here. You might make it. May the gods be with you, eh?' mockingly patting Ibrahim on the back.

He scanned the crowds for his driver, ignoring his gut. Feeling like a lost child as his poor eyesight made everyone look the same, tripping over feet and legs of chairs.

'Having trouble, uncle?' Anwar led him by the arm through the visitors.

'Can you see my driver?' peaking his hand over his eyes.

'Look, I will take you. We are losing light. We will be one hour maximum, insha'Allah. I will bring you back or take you back to your home.'

'No, no. I must find him.' Ibrahim was losing his fight, feeling duped.

'Nonsense, nonsense. Come, I know the way, it will be quicker.' Ibrahim continued to search while Anwar pulled him towards the four-by-four.

Reluctantly getting in the back of the vehicle, over thinking and over analysing, the amulet around his neck began to take on a presence getting heavier on his mind and burning his skin. The thought of fulfilling his duty, financial ease and promise of love were the only incentives keeping him in the stifling vehicle. He felt old and vulnerable, alone. Dropping the map out the window before Anwar skidded out of there. Ibrahim knew Musa wouldn't harm him, he had family and a good reputation. However, there was a flaw manifesting in the trust.

The straight road was sparse; one petrol station and a handful of run-down properties on the way. His throat was drying, he'd forgotten to bring essentials in his haste.

The rugged terrain was like a home coming, this is where his kind came to hide away from the westernised falsehood and unaffordable marriages. The roads had since been repaired, making driving easier with a pleasing noise from the tyres. Trees and greenery were visual wonders for an arid mind and soul, their barks weathered and split.

Baboons played chicken on the carriage way, carrying young on their bellies, and menacingly sitting in groups. They were vicious, attacking you if you dare stop to rest, luckily avoiding the larger vehicles. Ibrahim was never one to judge but calling these savages primates irritated him; as long as the earth was red, he would never associate himself with a monkey.

'Ah, our signal. We are close, uncle. Have you ever had an encounter with one of these creatures?' Talking over his shoulder. Ibrahim shook his head, feeling weary. 'You are lucky!'

Ibrahim pulled at the cotton shirt trying to get air to his skin, the radio an icebreaker along with his buzzing head and thoughts. He silently prayed for help and relief as his sugar levels plummeted, feeling foolish he had not come prepared travelling with a stranger.

'Here, you look like you could use it,' Anwar handed him a canteen of water. Ibrahim took small sips. On the shimmering horizon, something lay ahead – Ibrahim leaned forward, squinting between the front seats. A distorted vision of a man selling brightly coloured dates beneath two parasols became clearer as they reached the brow.

'There! Please sir, can we stop?' Anwar reluctantly pulled in.

Round baskets on a makeshift table filled with the red and yellow fruit; soft, plump, and sweet to counteract Anwar's rich indulgence. Baboons sat respectfully beside the table as they picked and sorted through the dropped fruit. The elderly man gave them a silent, toothless smile. Ibrahim asked for two mixed bags. The old man pushed himself up from the stool and hobbled over to the window. The man laughed, pointing down the road saying something Ibrahim couldn't quite understand, something in a native tongue - Aramaic. It was a long time since he heard the language. Dialects had taken over and ancient traditions had long gone except in the use of amulets and spells. He took the bags and quickly wound up the window halfway in case the Baboons descended upon them. The old man pushed his finger through the gap, speaking words of warning to Ibrahim.

'Shookran, Shookran,' Anwar said, rudely moving on, 'old fool,' he muttered, leaving the elderly man waving the dust away from his lungs.

Ibrahim shared the dates with him, biting away the nourishing flesh and throwing the stones out of the window. 'You should check the middle brother. You may have unwanted stowaways.'

Enjoying the free ride, taking in the passing views that triggered fond memories after being confined to the city. His permanent squint and sunbeaten face didn't possess sunglasses, Kohl always present on the tips of his eyelids anywhere he went. He felt like he was the only one hanging onto tradition and practical living. What would this new life bring? He wouldn't know how to deal with a dehumanising modern life.

Plateaus began to flatten, and occupation dwindled. Ibrahim gulped as he watched Anwar steady the steering with his forearms whilst unscrewing the cap of a water canteen, tipping his head back letting it overflow from the corners of his mouth. He was pleasant enough, but Ibrahim's gut hadn't stopped squirming since being in his company.

Anwar turned sharp right and continued along a twenty kilometre desert road to the hidden lake. Ibrahim's anticipation growing as well as his choking nerves. He was sure they were lost, and he had been fooled.

As the ride shook him over the uneven surface, in the blink of an eye, dunes began to rise. Some red as the ones he'd left, others purple and mauve framing a visionary wonder. The light became a soothing orange with hints of green dappling his poor eyesight – was he seeing things? An Oasis? Drawing closer, he stared in disbelief. All the years he'd lived in Riyadh and never knew this place existed, maybe it didn't and they had heat exhaustion. Anwar squeezed the brakes, causing a cloud of dust which rushed ahead of them, engulfing the vehicle.

Fallen palms arched above the surface of the lagoon, twice as lustrous from their abundant source. Ibrahim's eyes scanned the small lake sheltered by higher dunes, more greenery appearing through the sand. He got out, his mouth gaping, leaving the door open he kept his distance from the edge to study the plants that surrounded it. Shaking his head, he cautiously waded through a pathway of Nepeta, running his fingertips over the top disturbing its mint and sage scent. He'd missed that smell, pinching off a sprig and tucking it behind his ear. Succulents peeped through the sand and carpeted his way to the edge where he stood and considered the small fish that darted beneath the surface. Ibrahim snorted to himself and scratched his head.

'SubhaanAllah, are we dead?' he muttered, looking back at Anwar whose mouth bulged with dates. 'Did you take us without us knowing, Allah? Does this mean I am forgiven?' Looking up to check if there was still a familiar sky.

His knees popped when he crouched, placing his fingertips on the surface and licking them, jolting away in case the fireside stories were true. He did it again; it was slightly cool and far too tempting not to wash his face with it. The water was like no other, holy and he wanted to drink more, scooping the surface, and sucking up the contents from his palm. Certain the water was from paradise itself.

'Ya Allah, bless this water for I am a foolish, old man. Cleanse my tired bones and forgive me should you be displeased with me.' Taking the leather string over his head he held the amulet above the surface, his weary arm shook as he hesitated. Perhaps Anwar was tricking him and leaving the amulet here would be a fate worse than death. But this pool wasn't deep enough for anything else but little fish. No, no, this was the right lake. It was probably his forgetfulness and Anwar was a blessing.

Mesmerised by the amphibians' iridescent scales and neon eyes he was sure he heard drums, cupping his hand over his ear left ear. The middle of the lagoon began to form decreasing circles, the fish retreating to the palms' shade. He watched in awe and terror steadying himself as the ground vibrated beneath him, the drums getting louder beating out a battle cry. Looking back at Anwar who encouraged him with a shooing hand. Something caught the corner of his eye. A shadow lurked in the deeper part of the water, the atmosphere heavy with static. He knew it was time to drop the amulet and he did it without hesitation, there was no sound as it entered, reciting verses of the Quran as he did.

Ibrahim watched the amulet sink slowly, resting on the first level then sliding towards the deeper part, stopping himself from retrieving it. It disappeared, sudden movement on the surface startled him, scuffling away from the edge.

'Bismillah! Bismillah!' he cried shielding his eyes. His chest heaving as the surface bubbled in a frenzy, a female agony escaping the turmoil and then a sudden calm. Ibrahim trembled watching, waiting. Was that it? He checked around as he sat back on his hands, rolling onto his all fours to ease himself up, repeating comforting words as his heart near beat out of its place. Brushing himself off the water became active again, something was rising, he stepped back. Was it, a *head*?! Striking, odd-coloured eyes with a defensive stare visible above the surface. Ibrahim looked on in horror and intrigue.

'Jann,' he uttered breathlessly. He'd never seen one before but trusted they were real from the tales of torment to desert military. The creature grinned at its freedom; voluptuous in shape, pearls and precious stones falling from the torso as it writhed provocatively. He gave the creature a bashful smile, ecstasy lubricating his loins and old bones.

'No! Uncle! No!' the driver had arrived. Ibrahim was swooning, his eyes closing as she sang songs of old to him in an angelic voice, not noticing her mouth full of pointed teeth. 'Brother! Wake up! Brother!' the driver hollered, making his way to Ibrahim with his hands over his ears. He grabbed Ibrahim's slender arm, snapping him out of hypnosis and pulled him toward the vehicle. Ibrahim struggled to keep up, the driver went on and started the engine, with no sign of Anwar or his truck. Ibrahim's ankle was suddenly grabbed and pulled, he fell on his face, clawing at the sand as he was dragged backwards.

'Ya Allah! Ya Allah! Have mercy! I beg you!' the driver put the SUV into reverse, Ibrahim clutched at the Nepeta crushing it and tearing it from the roots as he was dragged with force. Sand entered his mouth and eyes, tears of panic allowing a brief, strained perspective. 'Ya Rub! *Please*! Forgive me! I will do anything! *Anything*!' the pulling stopped, his hands full of vegetation laying still with eyes shut, playing dead. He began to sob, afraid to look back, hearing the tyres slipping in the sand then coming to a halt.

'Uncle! Hurry! Now! Run! Ya Allah, run!' he scrambled to his feet, the resistance in his joints causing him to cry out. Clumsily and blindly searching for the SUV, 'this way! I am here! Don't look back! Come, *come*!' Ibrahim staggered with his arms outstretched, yelping when his hand was taken. The driver bundled him in the back seat, the old man barely breathing with his clothes dirtied and snagged.

Resisting the temptation to look back was immense, the driver squeezed his eyes shut, 'La! I will not look at you!' the Jann screamed in defiance, his muscles tensed as he broke into a sweat, 'Aouthou bileh minna shaitaan a'rajeem!! Leave us, devil! Or in the name of the almighty, I will return you to your entrapment!' There was hesitancy as his body turned, keeping his eyes closed he used his hearing for surveillance, opening one eye then the other.

The lake had gone, so too had the lush palms and rainbow dunes.

***

5

Going Max

Saint Ives harbour housed a small lighthouse that bled rust from its rivets, perched on the end of a small pier, with lobster baskets stacked neatly against the sea wall. Private, moored fishing boats bobbed and tipped on the tide, but when it was out, you could walk back to Porthminster beach by it, if you knew your tide times. Many had been caught out by risking it for a biscuit. A cobbled road lined with surf shacks, shellfish restaurants and ice cream parlours with a discrete amusement arcade nestled amongst them, complimented private artisan galleries that dominated corners, igniting Esme's creative streak.

She rubbed her callused hands together from the slight chill, her smile forced and nervous. The place was deserted, just how she liked it where you could appreciate the dreamy ambience.

Repositioning the fake flowers in small vases and straightening the chairs outside the cafe, bolts were being unlocked and wooden doors creaked open, feeling a little anxious about how her first customer would be received. The lifeboat station prepped for the enthusiasts and imminent rescues, she watched them intently; a Royal institute and well-respected charity run by volunteers. Risking their lives for the ill-prepared and stray Lilos.

Max, the family golden retriever, sat like a lion just shy of the picket fence barrier, sniffing the air and barking at seagulls raiding the bins. Esme fiddled with her hijab; perhaps the cerise peonies on a white background that covered her long auburn hair, was a bit too much. Picking at her fingers and biting her lip she watched people pass her by with that same look of blind prejudice. Deep down she wanted to challenge it. White convert Muslims slated by cultures and branded oppressed. Up north no one noticed, communities were larger and catered for, she knew Cornwall would be the compromise in that respect, but Musa said he had plans.

It all started at art college, meeting a group of convert Muslims and her first love interest in the faith. Joining a community whose paradigms matched hers, and where she declared her belief and devotion. Their engagement became the magnet for evil eyes. Jealousy ran through the places she once trusted, and she became strangely ill, and he became strangely distant. The heartbreak was almost too much to bear, causing a sudden onset of mystery ailments. Esme was missing classes, prompting a visit from a friend with gifts of divine protection. "You have black magic attached to you, sister." Was all she said, with a contact number for an undoer of cast revenge: Musa. The mystery man who came to her aid and rescue. Highly regarded, his ability to detect and eradicate the unseen was his expertise, with a price to match. The rest, as they say, is history.

The ring of a bicycle bell and squeaking brakes on the cobbles shifted her reminiscing, Max releasing a friendly alert.

'Morning. Bit chilly,' she said. Her stomach churning when the cyclist stopped at the café.

'Yeah, breeze comin' in from Penzance,' leaning his bike against the fence in his second skin lycra. 'You open?'

'Uh, yes! Yes, we are,' stepping aside to welcome him in. Max sniffing his legs and shoes, 'sorry, he won't hurt you, he's just a big softy.' The cyclist patted Max which he loved, turning in circles to make sure he got physical attention all over.

'Hey there boy! What's your name?'

'This is Max.'

'Is Musa here?' he asked, unbuckling his helmet.

'Oh, you two know each other?' The cyclist waited for his answer, 'right, he's not I'm afraid, he's in Riyadh but he should be home soon. Can I give him a message?'

The cyclist shook his head, 'is the coffee orn?' His accent local, not that strong.

'It most certainly is. Cappuccino?'

'Flat white, please.' She'd only just got used to the myriads of coffee tastes, the flat white proved to be a grey area.

'Sure. Cake? It's gluten free.'

'Got any normal cake?'

'Yes, of course. Carrot or Victoria sponge?'

'Surprise me.'

'Sure. Would you like to go 'Max' for an extra pound? We donate it to the lifeboat centre.'

He roughed up Max's head, affectionately amused, 'yeah, why not?'

'Great, coming right up.' She checked her Rolex, the waitress was late and the looks from others were setting off her anxiety, doing her tapping and breathing exercises. Masking it up with her newfound dream. The prep of coffee was always a noisy one; Musa bought the best barista machine there was, and she was still getting used to it. Her lack of dexterity an annoyance.

'Hello! Excuse me?' A larger-than-life woman called over the din, hovering at the door with a Chihuahua squished under her arm.

'Oh, sorry. Good morning, how can I help?'

'Are you dog friendly?'

Esme stalled, they weren't, Musa would have kittens. 'We are indeed,' she answered with a smile.

'Wonderful! Do you serve doggy treats?'

'Just waiting for stock, but they should be here by the end of the week.'

'Oh, what a shame,' the woman walked in, running her eyes over the blackboards. 'I'll have a Rooibos please, and uh...' Browsing the cakes under the glass domes on top of the pine counter, '... a flapjack. My poochy likes those, don't you darling?' Pouting as she tickled the nervous dog under its chin. Esme wasn't keen on the breed, too snappy and yappy. Although Max was extremely interested, trying to mouth its quivering back legs.

'I think you'll do well here. We're not used to, y'know, your...*type*. If you pardon the turn of phrase.'

'We're more than delighted.' Esme answered, trying to control her bitch face.

'No offense, of course. We needed something a little cultural, so to speak. Will you be doing any special dishes? The stuff you eat?'

'Umm, haven't really thought about it. We're not a restaurant per se. I didn't want the hassle. I'm sure my husband will be bringing back some of his traditional pastries.'

'How sweet. Perhaps you can do a night of it. What does the name mean?'

'Abadis? It means eternal.'

'How exotic! Can I sit inside?'

'Of course, I'll bring your order over,' Esme smiled tightly. Her heart fluttering and gut stinging. She served the cyclist first. Max deciding to stay inside, hell bent on pestering the lap dog.

The waitress, Suzie, arrived in a fluster, tugging at her clothes.

'Sorry Esme, alarm didn't go arf.'

'Ok, well, it happens to the best of us,' she pulled the girl away from earshot. 'We're dog friendly as of today, but try and direct them outside for now.'

'It'll be chaos if word gets out!' She whispered.

'Well, not necessarily. I won't put a sign up, and just say we're waiting for the treats to be delivered, okay?'

'Right. You sure you know what you're doing?'

'Yes, on my head be it. Oh, and don't forget the 'Max' offer. There *is* a sign for that, with Max on it. If I can get here every morning with him, at least he'll stay until you get here, otherwise I'll have to do a walk around town, hand out some leaflets, get familiar. All clear?'

'Crystal.'

'Good. Call me if it gets too busy but I'm aiming to be back. I must finish the blasted boxes! There's so many! I never knew how much stuff we had accumulated. Heavens!'

'Kay, but I'm still havin' trouble with the stock room door,' twisting the end of her black cardigan.

'What do you mean?'

'It won't open. I tried the key an' everythin.'

'What is it with this place and doors?! Okay, well, don't worry for now. I'll get someone to have a look at it. Do you know anyone?'

'And the red sand.'

'Red sand?'

'Yeah, there's like sand sometimes, patches on the floor, by the stock room.'

'Well, there's bound to be if people are not wiping their feet!'

'It ain't our sand. I know that sounds bloody daft, but it's kinda sparkly lookin.'

'Okay, look, don't worry yourself about it. Musa and I will sort it out when he gets back, God willing.'

'What if I run out of stuff?'

'Call me!' Esme left with Max following, bumping into punters with her head down, on a mission to get home and finish unpacking.

*

Relieved to be home, entering the cool hallway that greeted her with nostalgia each time. Max barely getting through the door before he sprawled himself on the tiles.

'Mum! Look at this!' Her son, Hassan, shouted from the top of the stairs.

'Not now Harvey. I have a mountain of boxes to unpack!' Harvey was his alias, one that gave Musa a twitch, and one that stuck. He gave her the toughest labour, and deepest bond. Bitter-sweet memories of star gazing with her mother as they counted the contractions that seemed to go on forever.

'Pleeeeese Mum!'

Esme dumped her bag in the usual place, 'this better be good. I'm ready to drop!'

Her fourteen-year-old son led her into his room by the hand; coarse black hair and deep brown eyes set on a soft face. He was kind-hearted and protective, rushing to help and in constant need of validation. The bottoms of his joggers were moving away from his ankles and he always had creased t-shirts on, reflecting his chaotic mind and inability to be tidy, and Esme wasn't really into ironing. He loved the room in the roof with the creaky floorboards, having to duck your head in certain places. Hassan given first choice because he was the golden child.

'Look! I can see the sea from my window! How cool is that?'

Esme looked out with him, always managing to raise a smile from her, 'I know right? I'm still pinching myself.'

'Here, I'm pinching you, it's real. Why are the windows wobbly?'

'Wobbly? You mean, warped?'

'Yeah, like, if you do this...' He bobbed up and down, laughing, 'everything looks weird! Like those funny mirrors at the fair!'

'They're just old, sweetheart.' She brushed his hair into place, her daily bond.

'Why did we buy a house like this? It's a bit, y'know, not like our other one.'

'Well, it does you good sometimes. Anyway, baba has his eyes on other places. We won't be here long, it's just a steppingstone. Ready for lunch?' Hassan loved lunch. Excited and nervous in his belly about their new life; it was a big leap for a worry-wart. Leaving his best friend was the hardest, having a little cry to himself when no one was looking. He missed acting out Marvel movies in their large rear garden, playing Black Panther. Layla, on the other hand was on her bed, Air pods in, blocking everyone out. A new place meant new boys, seaside boys – fresh and vibrant with sun kissed hair and tanned pecks.

'Layla? Lunch?' Esme called outside her door, her daughter on the level below Hassan's. She wanted his room so she could be out of her father's way where he couldn't listen in on her face timing. The sixteen year old tutted and turned up the volume.

'No, I'm fine.'

Esme rolled her eyes, 'we got an answer. That's something. Maybe the sea air will improve her personality.'

'I think I'm going to love it here, Mum. I mean, we live near the beach!'

'Say mash'Allah, please. I don't want any jinxes.'

'Sorry, mash'Allah. I just wish, you know, Grandma was here, too.'

She picked one of Max's hairs off his back, raising a deterring smile.

'We had some customers at the Café today. Fancy taking a walk round town after lunch, to introduce ourselves? Hand out some leaflets?'

They sat around the heavy pine kitchen table. Lunch was a rocket and salami sandwich on soda bread with beetroot crisps. Esme was on her phone while stroking Max's head with the other hand, occasionally looking around trying to accept the fact she was back.

'What are you looking at?' Hassan asked.

'I'm texting Baba, aanndd did you know how Saint Ives got its name?'

Hassan shrugged, scrolling social media.

'Saint Ia came here on a leaf and settled at the church in town. How cute is that? We'll see it later. My arty fingers have been itching since I got here. Must be the light.'

'I don't like it when you get arty fingers. Why do you have to paint all the time?' he sulked, 'baba pays for everything.'

'I like my independence, and my art is my therapy. Can't stand the thought of being a nothing. Anyway, it's not all the time, is it? You're exaggerating again. I haven't painted in a long time. That reminds me, we need a cleaner.'

'Baba just doesn't know how to do stuff like you.'

Esme stroked his cheek adoringly, 'did you take your pills?' Hassan nodded with a crooked smile, 'right, shall we take a walk after I unpack some boxes? We need to hand out our flyers, and get a hot chocolate.'

Max heard the word '*walk*' and clambered to get his toy rabbit, which used to belong to Hassan. It was still in one piece considering it went everywhere with him, having to prise it from his mouth sometimes. One ear was hanging off, the fur stank of drool and its eyes were chewed into squints.

Esme managed one box; the rest felt too overwhelming, did she have to do everything? The lower floor door was still unobtainable, with more excuses from Musa than she'd ever heard.

'You coming *walkies*?!' Max jumped with excitement as she pushed on her Crocs.

'Bunny has to stay behind. Put him down, there's a good boy,' she teased him first, both exchanging little growls of defiance as they tugged on the toy. Max was the last one left from a litter of equally adorable floof and loyalty. Esme's therapist suggested that a good-natured dog would help with the family's anxiety, especially Hassan who needed constant reassurance. Max seemed to know when it was time to comfort him, he could smell it. Anxiety was acrid, sometimes sweet.

Stepping out onto their fresh territory they were greeted with an abundant atmosphere. They felt like tourists as they walked single file along the path into town, all eyes on Esme. Max stopped periodically to smell posts and walls; his tail circling as he sniffed up new visions. The tonality light turned the sea the brightest turquoise, forcing them to stop and admire it over the wall.

Esme was jolted sideways as Max tugged on his leash, keen to explore further. Memories came flooding back and it took all she had to hold back the flood gates. It must have been the cry of the seagulls, they were such a completion of Saint Ives and any other British coastline, as well as the bane of everyone's lives.

The cove began to disappear as they got closer into town, the decline leading them into shaded warrens where the sea breeze disturbed your hair. Cottage windows were level with the road, a few with stable doors and nautical exterior decorations with plant containers bursting with annual colours. They passed two parish churches as shops and cafes began to appear. The quaint little town became part of them as they trod the cobbled narrow streets lined with souvenir shops, full of whimsical gifts made from shells.

'Mmmm! What's that smell?' Hassan asked, his stomach rumbling.

'Pasties. The finest in all the land. We're gonna be getting fat here, that's for sure.' Hot meat and finely sliced root vegetables with a sprinkling of sea salt and black pepper, wrapped in shortcrust pastry; a delicacy consumed by tin miners which became Cornwall's legacy.

The flyers were welcome and displayed in windows, others were placed out of sight.

'Why are some people unkind?' Hassan sullen, fanning the wad in his hands.

'Well, that's what makes the world go round, not everyone is nice. People are probably fed up with it being taken over by Emmets. Family businesses have suffered as a result, I expect.'

'Emmets?'

'Yes. Like us. We're Emmets. Occupiers. Colonisers. Because we gotta have nice places for ourselves, and ruin it.' As the slopes began to flatten, they reached the harbour, their mood lifted as they joined the liberal - artists painting portraits and caricatures of willing tourists. They stopped to look in the windows at the canvasses on display. Outcries from the mind's eye, nurtured and visualised from the intoxicating surroundings; a pilgrimage for the creative.

Footfall had increased, visitors eating something or other as they aimlessly strolled looking for the next culinary to try, which made it difficult to thrust the flyers in their hands. An impressive lifeboat station was full of enthusiasts taking shots and posting selfies with the lifeguards.

'Woah! Mum! Look at the boat! And an arcade! Sick! Can we see it?'

'You go. I'll check on Suzie, looks a bit busy. Here,' she handed him some money, 'just the pinball, okay? Nothing else. No gambling machines!' Esme still had that uneasy lump in her throat about coming back, perspiring under the tight material as she received longer stares than anyone else. The belief in her heart was strong however, Esme wanted to follow her faith in her own way not by someone else's constricted idea of it. The decision to marry Musa was one that caused divide with her mother, given an impossible choice to make, her adoration and conviction tore her away from all that was familiar. Esme had been avoiding and hiding ever since. She needed the comfort and shift from not having a father around. Cornwall was the retreat she'd longed for, far away enough from all the drama – a place to start over where no one knew her history. Yet subconsciously she was running back home and into her mother's arms. A place to forget your trivia and fall in love with every part of it. But there was always that lonely feeling, the incompleteness she constantly felt without her. Like a lone boat floating on the ocean, looking for shore. She had made several attempts to find her, but when she got close, she retreated, afraid of the confrontation and being rejected all over again.

The crowd parted to let her through, taking in the pleasant scent she left behind, a smile dressing her beautifully made-up face. Cosmetics from Saudi were the best, and it showed.

Sitting outside the Abadis with Max, she forked the cream cheese frosting on the carrot cake, the best she'd ever tasted. The rebellious decision to skip the gluten free was satisfying enough, zoning out from the sugar rush, people watching, their footwear click-clacking with wafts of Ambre Solaire oil. Esme gouged patterns in the coffee froth, not sure whether she'd missed Musa or not. The toxic bellows in the house, and the hiding of forbidden things from him, which set off fires in her veins, adamant it was causing tumours somewhere.

'Mum! Mum!' Hassan called, pushing through everyone. God, she wished she could escape from being constantly demanded upon, and do everything for Esme for here on in. She refused to have a Nanny, such a detached existence. Spending the day shopping or tanning or something equally irrelevant and self absorbed. But there were times she wished she'd given into it.

'You should see the boat! It's awesome! And I won the pinball! And there's a ride on thing! But can we have a look at the shops now, mum – I'm borrrred!' Hassan whined.

'Harvey, for heaven's sake, let me finish my bloody coffee. Go and see if Suzie needs any help.'

'Seriously, mum?'

'Yes, seriously. You haven't helped with anything since you got here.'

'I made you tea!'

'Whoopty doo, Harvey.'

He stomped off and half-heartedly asked Suzie, with his shoulders slumped.

He returned. 'She doesn't.'

'Fine. But we're just looking, okay? You dare nag me for silly things. I've got enough junk of yours to unpack!'

Hassan picked at his new ornament in his room; an owl made from tiny shells. Well, some of us are suckers for shell things at the seaside. The primitive impulsion to collect comforting trinkets was another side of human he fiercely hung onto. Layla didn't want to talk about stupid shells while she straightened her hair and kept up with social media trends. She was missing her friends and the move was all her father's selfish fault. Layla was tired of running, the fleeing from demons were just his.

Esme's put her new conch light next to the oil diffuser, a mark that she had finally returned to heart, almost. Brushing the dust from the crevices, admiring it as she moved it into various positions. The bulb lit up the inner veins of an abandoned home, the admiration sparking her creativity which had been buried beneath self-doubt. Esme was always a beach person, although she loved nothing more than breathing in the nurturing atmosphere of a forest, she'd spent many a carefree day at the beach as a child. Coming back was completion, even though the feeling of *'too good to be true'* hung around every minute.

Saint Ives had always been a part of her heart, it wasn't touristic like the places in the brochures, there was class and vegan eateries; the elite of the coast. They could afford whatever they wanted and that's all that got them there. Not fate, nor luck – just money and Musa's business acumen. It had been nagging her for a while, an unsettling and awareness of something present, pressing and forcing the issue to move. She would miss the cleaner though and wasn't sure if she even remembered *how* to clean. They would sit and chat for most of the time, it was good therapy, especially from matured and wiser minds. Musa's tiering system never sat right with her.

Rubbing the barrier cream on the dry patches of her elbows, Max stood at her side with bunny in his mouth waiting to be fussed. She patted the bed for him to jump up, it was a bit of a struggle because the bed was quite high, but after a front leg scramble, he made it with a grunt and a huff. Making himself comfortable he lay on his side and pawed her leg. Esme worked her fingers through his golden waves of a fine coat, stroking his face, stopping to feel the velvety fur on his ears. She laughed at his silly expressions and those whiskers on his eyelids that had a comical animation all their own.

'Bunny needs a wash! It stinks!' She picked it up in her fingertips and threw it on the floor. 'Are you happy?' Max pawed her leg harder accompanied with a soft growl, his demand for her not to stop the petting. 'Well, that's ok then. If you're happy, then so am I.' Max became her third child, his grounding presence and solid loyalty a constant counsel. It took a lot of persuasion to convince Musa that having a dog in the house was permissible. He grew fond of him, but constantly washed whenever he was around, cursing him and ousting the hell from him.

She slid into the cool, Egyptian cotton sheets feeling a different tired from the sea air, laying at an angle to compensate for Max. Turning onto her left side, she gazed through the bedroom window at the town lit up in golds, reflecting in the tide. It called to you twenty-four-seven even though you had seen it all, you were certain you had missed something. The smell of the shops was one you wanted to have around permanently; musk, jasmine, and something else that you couldn't decipher. As friendly and welcoming as everyone was, Esme still noticed the stares and whispers from behind the counters.

Almost forgetting the other night time ritual, sliding them towards her, pushing the pills from the blisters, throwing them into the back of her throat and washing them down with a small glass of water. They helped, or perhaps it was the action that did. Her body and mind putting things in straight lines when they dissolved, leaving a bitter reminder on her tongue. Turning off her new light, the reflection from the town danced in her eyes. This would be her new lullaby as they darted about the soft illuminations - smiling contently as they closed, nursed by a hue of lavender vapour and Zispin.

6

Akash

The sea was the brightest aqua and the beautiful day accentuated the idyllic scenery. Relaxed in the lounge window seat, Esme cradled her mug of rooibos tea after placing her belongings just as they were in the old house. Dark blue leathers, tartan throws and plump cushions. A solid walnut coffee table on a rug Musa brought back, her books and Arabian artefacts placed in the alcoves either side of the fireplace. Her favourite possession was the huge Himalayan rock lamp, soaking up the atmosphere and excess moisture. Max thought it passed as a fire, twitching and snoring in front of it with bunny under his front leg. It was strange, the lounge used to be the room where tables were laid out for breakfast, and now it was hers. A permanent holiday, wondering what would winter bring. A dulling of the vibrancy perhaps, with a deeper connection to the elements.

She focussed on the small chapel sat on top of an island at the furthest point near the dogs' beach and art gallery. A dedication to the patron saint of children, Saint Nicholas. Learning it was possibly built in the 1400's for sailors and became a rest point for the missionaries on their way to Rome. But no further evidence to support any of it. Why have another church so far out? Smuggler myths and tales were the backbone of Cornwall's tourist industry however, Esme couldn't help but ponder on the children element. Still trying to fathom why Musa was comfortable to come to a place with so many churches, considering he had such an unhealthy superstition about them.

A wide yawn caused her whole body to spasm, sleep had been disturbed by the settling of old plumbing. The house alive and busy while they slept – righting its old bones. She found it difficult to rest when Musa wasn't around, her protector from the dark. Max was no use in that sense, docile and friendly and always seeing the good in people, just like her.

The kids were on the beach, she could see them from the window albeit in miniature. Another advantage because she wasn't ready to be on display again. Shame of her belief, fuelled by propaganda, had hindered her spirituality and confidence. The effort of just going anywhere these days was traumatic. That was the only beauty about Riyadh. People claimed they knew extremist were no reflection on the majority, but fear was already instilled as well as misinformed judgement. It was just a deviation from white psychopathic rule. Esme was a good ambassador, but it was never about an individual, communities needed to change. Their distortion of the simplest, harmonious way of life had unjustly given it a reputation man had twisted for his conveniences, and fear of women's rights. Women in the town exchanged silent acceptance through their eyes, because it didn't matter what was on the outside, all women reside in the same injustice.

Her mobile pinged a WhatsApp from Musa. A selfie with his associates dining at the Four Seasons. Esme just snorted and gave him a thumbs up emoji with three kisses. She still got a tingle when she saw him dressed like that, her pious rescuer from the sinister control of the world. Esme clung to him, clung to the reassurance she needed to nurse her insecurities. But he had been knocked off the pedestal she put him on, and he felt it, levelling with her. She was over it now, something she told herself of daily, an inevitability of marrying a Saudi and their missions of status. She never knew the other woman, perhaps he was trying to cling onto things too, things he'd lost. Looking for a home from home. He swore, crossed his heart she had gone when he witnessed Esme's reaction. Quiet, collapsing at the sink while the children played in the garden, unravelling the love bound so tightly. She kept it to herself, didn't tell a soul. The pills helped keep the lid on it while she whirled internally like a dervish.

As her mind wandered it always went back to her mother and the heated conversations about her decisions. Then Layla, becoming increasingly distant at sixteen. She longed to have mother-daughter conversations with her, but they always ended up arguing over her clothes and the purposeful rebellion against her father. The battle of wills pulling at her love. Musa didn't help. Esme feared he was covertly arranging a marriage in Riyadh, 'before she dishonours the family' were his words. She wanted to leave so many times, dreaming about the freedom but Esme's devotion and fear of shaking the throne of Allah, kept her where she was; a fabricated warning made by man.

There was another message, *'where are the kids?'*

'On the beach x'

'With you?'

'No. But I can see them from the window x.'

'Are you crazy?!'

'It's fine Moose, I can see them. They are good swimmers. Café needs some attention, and I still can't open that door!'

'Get them! NOW! Never leave them again!'

'Moose, calm down! They are fine. We are not up north anymore.'

'Listen to me, get them habibi. Get them now!'

'Okay. I'll call Layla, she has her phone. I'll text you when they are here.'

There was no response. She rang Layla, trembling.

'What?'

'Your father wants you back home.'

'But we just got here!'

'I know, it's my fault. Just come home, please.'

'*Christ, Mum!*' the line went dead. Esme's stomach burned, ready to strangle her daughter of late. She missed her podgy little hands busy with make believe. Esme brought them up on wooden toys and felts, an ethos from the Montessori school. A place where she and the children flourished, where they were welcomed, accepted and celebrated.

They both came back arguing, Max greeting them with bunny and a silly expression of joy.

'Why did we have to come home? Why didn't you just come down?' Hassan whined.

'I didn't want to leave Max.'

Layla pushed passed. 'That's bullshit,' she mumbled and walked into the kitchen.

'What did you say?!' Esme followed her, rage rising up her neck.

'I said, that's bullshit!' her face red, matching her hair; a vibrant photocopy of her mother. She was involuntary slapped across the face, the noise of skin-on-skin sending shocks through them all. Hassan gasped and stood rigid.

'That's quite enough from you! How dare you! Who the hell do you think you are?!'

Layla stood holding her face. 'I was your daughter, once!' leaving with tears streaming down her face. Esme hung her head and felt like a monster as the adrenaline subsided.

'Layla, I'm sorry!'

'Piss off!'

'Shall I make you a cup of tea, Mum?' Hassan fussed, trying to douse the situation. Esme sat at the kitchen table, tearful and regretful, picking her hands and eating herself alive. What sort of mother was she? Was she going to do anything about what Layla said? Bitterness had been waiting to lash out on the wrong people. Hassan hid his tears; they were having such fun and Baba always managed to ruin it. He made Rooibos, that always relaxed her. Max rested his chin on Hassan's thigh when he sat down.

'Hey Maxey, I'm okay,' patting the dog's head, 'I can swim in the sea Mum! You should see me now!'

'Yeah? Cool. What was Layla doing?'

'Uh, she said I wasn't allowed to tell you.'

'Well, I could see you, so she couldn't have been doing that much.'

He chewed the inside of his mouth, the secret was eating away at him, and he had to spew it.

'You didn't see her when she got us an ice cream from the beach café,' he blurted.

'What do you mean?'

'Surfer boys work there. She was giving them her number and laughing with her hair.' They heard the sudden stomp of feet across the floorboards, one creaked louder than the others, slapping on the tiles and into the kitchen.

'You bloody snitch!' Layla screamed, 'I hate you! I hate all of you! I hope you choke on your gluten-free! I'm going home! I hate this place! I had enough of you freaks!'

'Sounds like you were enjoying it on the beach,' Esme answered.

'Yes. I'm running away with a Surfer! Then I'll be free, free of *you*! And *you*! And dad! I'm going to find love because that's what's missing in this toxic house!' Esme just watched her leave the house with a gaping mouth, jolting as the front door was near enough slammed out of its frame.

'Baba is just a stupid Camel,' Hassan said, his bottom lip quivering.

'Harvey!'

'Well, he is! I'm big now, I can look after myself!'

'Not quite. You still need your big sister.'

'No, I don't! The people are nice, they were looking after me!'

'It's not up to them to look after you! It's…up to me,' her words trailed off into her guilt. If wasn't for that bloody Hijab…

'Just take it off. It doesn't matter, Allah won't mind, I know it. He doesn't want you to feel upset Mum, *please*?'

'I'm not upset, I just want to be accepted! This my choice, no one else's! Why should I hide from their prejudice? They don't think I have a mind of my own and baba made me wear it. But oh, when he flashes the cash around here, it's a different story. I think he should walk into town in his thobe, that'll get 'em whisperin'!'

'So why didn't you come with us? Max will be ok for a little bit.'

'He's not allowed on that beach. I will next time when baba gets back. I promise.' Offering a smile his way as she held his hand. 'I don't know what I'd do without you, sweetheart.'

'Uh, make your own tea?' their chortles broke the strain.

'Oh my God! I forgot to text him back! He'll be having kittens!'

Hassan always giggled at that analogy, imagining them being born from guarded orifices and his father having an additional dicky fit. Not wanting to imagine where *that* analogy came from.

Layla sniffed and snarled as she plodded down the stone steps to the beach, still in a swimsuit with a dark green chiffon over-shirt that just sat on her thighs. She was making her way to the wooden café. There was a queue, but the boy saw her through the other hatch, smirking when he noticed the fire in her eyes. His loose black curls, dark skin and ice-blue eyes were illuminous against his tone, boasting a youthful physique with a tan line just visible above brightly coloured swimming shorts. Different leather bracelets adorned his left wrist and a gold sleeper in one ear. He was the best surfer in the district, well known for his liberty and charm.

'You forgot summat?' he asked, her heart skipping a beat.

'Uh, Coke, please,' taking a twenty from her phone case.

He took a can from the fridge and placed it on the counter, 'this one's on me. If you 'ang on for ten minutes, I'll be finishin.' She agreed, not sure what she was doing now that her rage had cooled. Layla chose the picnic bench on raised decking overlooking the beach, sipping and enjoying the view and regretting her outburst. The surfer boy studied her; the lustrous auburn hair was alight under the sun, but it was the foreign outline that he was incredibly attracted to. Her complexion wasn't that of a red head but that of almond, flawless with eyes like the sea.

'Didn't I give you the sweet one?' he said, making her swing around.

'Sorry?'

'Yer drink. Looks like I gave you the one with no sugar, gowin by yer face.' His accent soft yet brash, rolling his R's.

'Oh, I'm just pissed off with my family.'

'Ah, I see. Fancy a dip?' he beckoned with his head.

'Umm.' Layla pondered, she always flirted but backed off when reality got close.

'C'mon. I don't bite, yet,' he winked. 'Akash,' he said and held out his hand.

'Oh, Layla,' she replied, getting a buzz from the touch. Akash made her feel at ease, the first person not to ask any prying questions.

'Come on then, Layla, *you got me on my knees,*' he sang, 'no strings.' Trotting to the sea, he dove in. Layla followed with her arms folded, hanging back near the thinning waves, flinching at his splashing about. Flicking his head as he broke the surface, she gulped hard at his glistening torso as he moved toward her. Taking her hand, he gently coaxed her in. She gasped when the waves reached her vulva, pulling her up to her middle.

'Have yer seen the town yet?' she shook her head. He dived under again, making her scream when he grabbed her ankles, briefly alerting the yawning lifeguard. He emerged a few inches away from her, his scent causing a sting in her stomach. Dark skin that beaded the sea and a physique that owned it. She held her breath when he tied his hair back, her eyes running along the contours of pecks.

'Nothin like a nice dip when you been stuck in that hut all day. I'll buy y'lunch,' eyeing her up as he strode back to the beach. 'C'mon, maid!' She followed awkwardly, her arms still folded.

Walking to the town, she swallowed nervously feeling uncomfortable with this forward thinker. She didn't give this one her number, because he didn't ask.

'How long you stayin' for then?'

'Oh, um, I live here. Just, up there,' she pointed towards the terrace; certain she could see her mother watching her from the front window.

'Right! We got an Emmet livin' with us then?'

'Emmet?'

'Yeah. That's what we call you lot, coming here stealing our treasures.' Layla gave a sheepish laugh and stroked her hair, wanting to go back and hug her mum and apologise.

'I'm only kiddin' yer,' he said nudging her, 'no need to takes offense. It be yous lot that keeps us earnin' a livin'.' She felt a little more relaxed in his company, his vibe was harmless but there was something she mistrusted and wouldn't be giving herself over just yet. Boys were an annoyance up North, which made Musa paranoid and overprotective, checking her every move until she gave up going out altogether. They left Porthminster and made their way into town; she hadn't gone that far yet. It still felt like she was on holiday.

'Do you surf?' he asked, as they passed the white cottages.

'Uh, no. There were no beaches where we lived.'

'I can teach yer. You gowin' back to school soon?'

'Next month. It's a private school, my last year. My parents don't want us going into mainstream.' She had a heavy heart about going to a new school, making new friends all over again. Perhaps not having any friends was better; no questions, no avoidance or rebelling to fit in. Jealousy was problematic, she was popular because of their financial status, given attention for all the wrong reasons. Envious eyes on her fiery curls that stayed perfect, whatever the conditions.

'Got plenty o'money then, your folks?'

'Something like that,' she flushed red.

'How old are ya? If you don't mind me askin.'

'Sixteen.' The surfer boy smirked, his teeth a little crooked. She kept looking over her shoulder knowing she was pushing her luck, expecting to see Musa at any moment. Although he was thousands of miles away, he had a habit of turning up where she didn't want him to, like a bloody ghost! Her shitty attitude was just bravado, the over protection of her father was comforting even though it stifled her and made her feel left out of life. Her heart thumped because she was actually walking beside a boy, a half naked one, taller than her and 'slit yer wrist' handsome. He felt older, somehow, possibly twenties. They stood out amongst the crowds of tourists, so many people acknowledged Akash; calling out from the whitewashed shops.

'Do you like pizza?'

'Uh, yeah. I do.' All that rage had made her ravenous.

'It's settled then. We're havin' pizza.' They walked down through the warrens then out onto the harbour and into Pizza Express. Akash raised his head to the waiter who acknowledged them with a jerk of his, finding them a good table.

'Alright? What's your order?'

'I'll 'ave me usual and this young lady will have...?'

'Oh, um, just a margherita, please.' Layla answered, the waiter having to lean in to hear her.

'What the lady said and two waters please, sir.'

The restaurant was full of families in swimwear and young locals in unzipped wetsuits. Akash looked around as if looking for someone. She watched his ice-blue eyes search the room, the pupils dilating to let in more light. He blinked as they pulsated, bleeding into the iris, making her feel increasingly uncomfortable in his presence. He was far too confident, incredibly attractive and she was instinctively scared of his testosterone, sitting on her hands so he couldn't see them trembling.

The waiter startled her when he placed down their pizzas. His was obviously the sea-food special, it looked like a whale had thrown up on it.

'Ah! Lovely!' Rubbing his hands together.

'Wow, that's a lot of fish!' Layla said.

'It's good for ya. Keeps you strong and y'mind sharp.' It was a bit disgusting watching him eat the fruits der mer. Layla hated shellfish and felt her appetite waning, just picking and pulling at the stretchy cheese. She sipped her drink as she looked out to the sea front, it was busy this time of year, and difficult to casually walk the streets, so much going on in such a small space. Catching the door, she clocked two girls enter: tight denim shorts and crop tops, with their small handbags hanging on a crooked arm. They came straight over to their table.

'Ello. Who's this then?' one girl asked, glaring at Layla with envious eyes.

'Allo girls. Where you bin 'idin?' Akash asked, focussed on his meal.

'Oh, here and there. We ain't seen you either. This your new fancy, then?'

'This is Layla,' his bent leg began to jiggle.

'You eatin' tha?' the girl asked Layla, and reached over to take a slice of her pizza.

Akash slammed his forearm on the table.

'That's her pizza and she's eating it. You want summat, Tyler?'

'Ooh, we are tetchy today,' she mocked through her nose. 'Come on Brianne, we're not welcome. Let's get some ice cream. See ya, *Layla*!' They left, but not without taking a prawn from Akash's plate.

'Sorry bout that,' he said between huge mouthfuls of food, turning her stomach and giving her a big 'ick.' They didn't really say much while they ate, he was too busy chatting to the others in the restaurant – jeering and shouting over people. She thought he was the rudest boy she'd ever met. But his beauty kept her captivated, such a free spirit with no reservations. There was nothing bothering him, no mental restrictions, must be the enrichment of the coast.

'You finished then? Wanna go out on the boat?'

'Boat? What boat?'

'The big one, there,' he leaned and pointed toward the Lifeboat station.

'*That* one? Oh, I couldn't, I must get back home. Mum will be going mad. That's for rescues only though, isn't it?'

He pushed the chair back. 'It's not what y'know...' he just left, without paying. She panicked as the waiter came to clear the plates, furious that he'd left her to foot the bill.

'I, err, only have this, sorry,' she gave him the twenty from her phone case. The waiter took it, put it in his pocket then handed it back.

'Thank you. Here's your change,' continuing to wipe down the table. She left a little bemused, pulling on the restaurant door and frantically searching the sea of heads for him. Maybe she should just go home, she was beginning to feel afraid and just wanted to retreat to her mother's arms. He was nowhere to be seen, she fought through people feeling inferior and ran back the way they came. Remembering landmarks she'd clocked, feeling safe she was going in the right direction. She quickened her steps looking over her shoulder all the way, Draycott Terrace was welcome. She had tears of regret in her eyes as she ran up the steps, bursting through the grey door. Esme had been cooking, the smell of love wrapped its arms around her, leaning her back against the door to close it.

'Layla? That you? There's pie!' She stayed where she was with a contented grin on her face. Her mother came into the hallway, wiping her hands on a tea towel.

'You alright love? What's happened?' Layla shook her head and rushed at her with open arms,

'I'm sorry mum! I'm sorry I swore! I'm sorry! I don't like it out there!' she sobbed into her mother's shoulder. Esme hesitated, unsure of this love, holding tight and squeezing the tears free.

'It's ok. I'm sorry too, what I did was wrong. It's not your fault.' Max was fussing around them, not wanting to be left out of the hugs. Hassan came down from his room and stopped in surprise when he saw them, his eyes filling with emotion.

'Are you...' he gulped, 'are you friends now?' he asked. Esme beckoned him to join them, her chin over Layla's shoulder. The three of them held on tight to each other, their laughter-filled sobs echoed around the hall. Max barked, wagging his tail and circling them. Esme broke off first, wiping her face with the cloth.

'Come on, let's have a cuppa and some pie.' The three of them sniffed, their hearts full and souls cleansed. 'Go get something warm on sweetheart, you must be freezing.' Layla listened – for the first time in a long time. Esme noticed her features and shape maturing, turning into a beautiful young woman, one she would guard and protect with all she had. There was a special bond between them, even though things had gone a little sour over the years. She breastfed Layla until it was no longer socially acceptable to do so, after trying so long for her. She should've realised then when Musa kept putting off fertility treatment. 'It's in Allah's hands' he said. When she got pregnant with Hassan, she knew her close relationship with Layla would be compromised.

It ended for Layla and her mother's undivided everything, attention seeking and rebelling, playing them against each other. They were all cries for help. Her hate for men exacerbated by her constricted visits to Riyadh, having to fully cover up because Musa didn't want anyone to see her hair. Shopping was the only good thing about Saudi, and appreciation was waning once you knew you could have whatever you wanted. Finding someone to match those standards meant he would have to be an Emirate. A poor man could never look after a woman like a rich one could, her father always said.

The sea air had made Layla blissfully sleepy as she changed out of her swim ware, the *ping* of a message startling her, waiting to be opened. Analysing it as she lay on the bed; no name, no profile and no number. She opened it,

'*Did you get home alright, Maid?*'

7

Encounters

The light burst through the sash windows and bounced off the walls when Esme opened the curtains on a new day, a new love and a new feeling for the house and Saint Ives. Usually, the opening and closing of curtains depicted a dread filled day. But on this morning, it was a brand-new routine and outlook. She also got up for pre-dawn prayers, something she'd neglected for a while after falling out of love with God. Such a cleansing feeling when she did, a binding ritual to start the day off straight.

Her flip flops snapped on the floor as she made her way to the kitchen, calculating how many times we opened and closed curtains throughout our lifetime. Max followed with his feather-duster tail, bunny in his mouth and the lazy tip-tapping of his claws. Stretching near his bowl as a subtle hint, dropping the soft toy by the biscuit cupboard.

She cleared the rough wooden table and began the dishes being careful not to wake anyone. The view from the window was a bit disappointing, facing the neighbour's red brick wall peppered with spleenwort ferns. The house up north had a better view of the garden from the sink, and she missed the contemplative therapy of that; vital preparation for an exhausting day of worry and people pleasing. It was either this or that, you had one thing but not the other in life and there was always a compromise to be had when you followed your dreams.

'Alexa. What's the weather today?' There would be a slight breeze with sunshine and clouds, which meant it was definitely a painting day. Flashes of turquoises and greens washed over her frontal lobe as she daydreamed in the suds' rainbows, she was also in the mood to tidy the back yard.

'*Hello,*' Alexa said, making Esme jump.

'Alexa. Off!'

The light of acknowledgement stayed on.

'*Goodbye.*'

'Jesus, bloody things are taking over,' she muttered, drying her hands as she walked through a Perspex-roofed annex; built for buckets and spades and outside attire. She pulled on the stiff door that shuddered from its warped frame, opening with a laughing creak. Max danced on his front paws anxious to see what was out there, again. He ran out expecting to still have the one hundred-foot-long run, stopped abruptly by a whitewashed wall. A good thirty feet or so, barking at his own echo. It wasn't as bad as she thought, the neighbouring cordylines and phormiums that framed their low wall made up for the lack of lawn and borders. The houses that overlooked them were tasteful, there was nothing 'back yard' about it at all.

'Sshhhh! Max! We'll have none of that! *Whisper* barks only, please.' He gave a little gruff of acknowledgement, but had the last word with one last bark.

Esme swept up dried leaves, stray twigs and sweet wrappers. Weeds pushed through the gaps in the crazy paving which she pulled by hand. The previous owners had left terracotta pots behind with root bound Trachycarpus, crying out for water, noticing the mark of Hamsa on most of the ceramics.

'Oh, you poor things!' The cries and peeps of the seagulls filled her with ease, triggering her childish excitement. They were part of life, a background noise that would be missed if they suddenly stopped. Max settled and sniffed the air not really caring where he was, as long as his people were close by.

'Good mornink,' came a voice over the wall. Max got up and barked in defence, with a hint of fear.

'Oh, good morning – err, Asalaamu alaikum.' She wondered why she didn't receive the same greeting then realised she'd stepped out without her hijab.

'Walaikum asalaam. You Muslim?' the woman asked, dressed in a yellow tunic and jeans, with head scarf to match.

'Um, yes, I am. I just forgot, uh, my scarf,' she answered, nervously pulling her hair through her hands.

'Don't worry sister. No one see you here. I am Raffia.' The woman put her hand over her heart, confirming herself with an accent the same as Musa's.

'I'm Esme. Pleased to meet you. How long have you lived here?' Esme felt even better about her new life, especially now there was a familiarity right next door.

'Not long. You come round, anytime, or you want anything, just you come, okay?'

'Okay, thank you. That's kind. Same goes for you. Well, now you come to mention it, we're looking for a cleaner. Don't suppose you know anyone?'

'I do it. I am cleaner, and dishes. Everythink, I do everythink.'

'Oh, right. Uh, great! When can you start?'

'Just you tell me, okay?' The woman indicated a farewell, anxious to retreat.

'Right, bye then, speak soon!' Max waved her off with a deep growl followed by an anxious bark. 'Max! Stop showing off! That's enough!' He was whining and panting. It was unusual for him to be so defensive, he usually licked people to death.

Esme finished off the sweeping, she found it quite rewarding to have a purpose again. She thought about the dishes, she liked doing the dishes, it was her therapy. Saudi women didn't do the dishes, Musa said. She found that hard to believe. Raffia could do the other stuff she hated, like the bathrooms and fridge, she hated doing the fridge.

The yard looked kempt, and the blank back wall was calling out for a mural. She stood with arms folded, her head cocked as she visualised what she had in mind.

Light on her feet she rifled through the post left on the kitchen table while she bit into the granary bread with organic marmalade, accompanied with her favourite Rooibos tea.

Most were addressed to the previous owners, Doctor Samir and associates. She studied the name, impressed that a bit of breeding had graced the oak floors before she did. The agency didn't have a forwarding address, immediately thinking of Raffia. One other was addressed to her: a thick envelope with no post mark, making a noise of curiosity as she opened it with her forefinger. Her shoulders slumped when it was an invitation to the new Arabic school Musa had arranged. She knew where it was but would have to take a stab at getting there. 'I wished he'd bloody communicate these things to me,' she uttered out of ear shot, sniffing the Hamsa-embossed letterhead, getting a strong hit of Oud.

Making sure Max was settled, she called round to Raffia's. The row of houses were the same, Raffia's a little tidier out front with a mosaic Hamsa next to the front door. Esme admired it while she rang the bell – what luck she was having.

The door opened and the smell of fried fish and more Oud was the first thing that greeted her. Black gold, its intricate extractions fast becoming rare. Arabic music was softly playing, with jingles and drumbeat.

'As salaam alaikum, Raffia - sorry to bother you, but do you know where the previous owners have moved to? I have these letters for them.'

'No bother, is ok sister, come, we speak inside.'

'Oh, no, I've left the children sleeping...'

'They be ok, leave them, don't worry.'

Esme hesitated as she stepped over the threshold, feeling intimidated as Saint Ives seemed oddly left behind once the door was closed; like stepping into Narnia. The house had the same layout as theirs, but the kitchen had been untouched for a few years, the rest mysterious and exotic like a Bedouin tent. The hypnotic atmosphere and pressing negativity reminded her of a recurring dream that had been haunting her. Always waking up when it became lucid.

'Come, come – you like fish?' Raffia asked.

'Oh, err, no thank you, I've not long had something to eat.'

Raffia poured some mint tea, holding a silver teapot from a great height aiming the liquid into a small glass encased in ornate gold.

'I take the letter for you,' she said.

'That's kind, thank you! Do you know where they live then?' She was handed the tea and a small plate of handmade cakes, delicately decorated with pine nuts. 'Sorry, I'm allergic to pine nuts,' she was given a puzzled look. Musa also thought food allergies were strange and completely psychological, blaming the lack of sun and concocted inoculations. 'Um, if you know them, then can you mention the room downstairs please? We still don't have a key and I'm desperate to get inside. I know their belongings are still in there, but…'

'No key, sister.' Raffia answered with a shake of her head, slurping loudly and studying her fried sea bass, before devouring it with her fingers.

'Oh, I see – is it just permanently stuck?' Esme took a sip of the tea that burnt her tongue, feeling suffocated and suddenly suspicious of her neighbour.

'No stuck. The hafiz open it.' The woman licked her fingers and washed down her dish with more tea.

'Hafiz? Uh, memoriser?'

'Naam. Brother Samir.'

'Well, that's who we've been trying to ask. Please mention it, would you?' Raffia just hummed her agreement. 'Right. I'd better be getting back, Raffia. Thank you so much for helping and for the tea. Are you able to clean sometime this week?'

'Inshallah. Just leave door open.'

'Okay. That's settled then. I'll let Musa know first.'

'No Musa, he know,' continuing to fill her face.

'Oh? He didn't mention it. Well, uh, I'll see myself out. Have a good day. Salaam.' She turned awkwardly.

'Wait sister.' Raffia brushed herself down and headed to the hallway, 'I have something for you,' disappearing upstairs. Esme stood awkwardly by the door, looking around and behind, convinced there was something peeking from a doorframe.

Raffia returned, talking to herself. 'This is for you,' giving Esme a leather pouch on a thinner leather string. She regarded it with suspicion.

'Oh, uh, thank you. What is it?'

'Is for you. The Prophet is with you. He sees you. Put rose in garden, okay? He like rose.'

'Well, I, uh. Right, thank you. I will remember that,' taking the gift, her first intention to put it straight in the trash or burn it.

'And this,' handing her a brown paper wrapper, 'you take this. You burn it, in house. Okay?' it was a generous bundle of Oud.

'I couldn't possibly take it, we have plenty. Thank you.'

Raffia shook her head insistently. 'You burn *this* one, today, okay? You have dog, I don't like dog.' Esme agreed and slipped the precious package into her pocket. That old chestnut again with the dogs. The locked room had just become something else, her head filling with accusations, feeling relieved to be going.

'Hey! I'm baaaack!' She called out as she entered the house, glad to be on familiar turf. Max lazily greeting her with bunny. 'Hello!' she called up the stairs. 'Max, where is everyone? And must you bring me that smelly old thing?' Screwing up her nose affectionately at him.

After no response, she strode to the kitchen holding the leather cord out in front of her, pressing the pedal with her foot and dropping it in the bin. Its lid clanging with Max sniffing intently around it.

Layla popped her head over the banister.

'Where were you?'

'Christ! You scared me! I was next door, give her those letters.'

'Harvey's gone to the harbour, looking for you!'

'What?! Why?' Layla just shrugged. 'Oh, for God's sake! I'll go and find him. You'll be all right?'

'Mum, really?'

'Okay, I won't be long. If we miss each other and he comes back, ring me!' Esme ran towards the harbour, having an inkling where he was, but still imagined the worse scenario. She didn't feel as conscious as she hurried through the warrens, no one was staring at her today.

Reaching the bay, her eyes frantically searched amongst the tourists. Pushing through bodies, she looked in the arcade then made her way to the lifeboat station, flashing a quick glance at the Café. She could see the top of Hassan's head milling amongst the enthusiasts.

'Harvey!'

He turned, beckoning her. 'Mum! Come and see!' He was touching the bodywork of the vessel and handling metal attachments.

'Don't touch anything, Harvey!'

'You're allowed. The man said. Where were you, anyway?'

'I was next door for five minutes and you saw your opportunity, young man.'

'Why aren't you wearing your scarf?' Hassan asked.

Esme flinched and touched the top of her head. 'Oh shit!' Hassan sniggered, 'quick, we need to leave, now!'

'But the man said he's going to show me inside.'

'Man? Ok, we're going, come back another day. Let's go.' She panicked inwardly fearing for her fate, feeling stripped of her dignity.

'This your mum then?' Came a strong Cornish accent behind them. A lifeboat volunteer stood with hands on hips, wearing a navy and white checked shirt and denims.

'Yeah, we have to go now though.'

'I see. Don't y'wanna see inside first?'

'Uh, no. No thank you, we must go. Thank you.' Esme snapped.

'Don't be rushin' arf. I'm Peter by the way,' he held out his hand. A tall, stocky man probably in his fifties. Salt and pepper wavy hair and beard, with alluring green eyes. His cheeks and nose were a little weathered but he looked good for his age.

'Oh, um, Esme. Esme Kattan. Pleased to meet you,' they shook hands and she felt invaded, she wasn't supposed to shake hands or touch any other man. What with no scarf as well, she felt unfaithful. Her heart raced, she gulped and perspired.

'That's your café then, I take it? We have you to thank for the donations.'

'It's no trouble. Please drop by any time, it's on the house.'

'Glad I finally got t'see ya. Don't think I've seen thee about.'

'No, I tend to hide most of the time,' a nervous laugh escaped her, feeling child-like in his presence.

'I can see y'have t'be somewhere else. Bring the boy back another day, he can 'elp out if he likes.'

'Can I *please*? Mum? Please?'

'Okay, well, we'll see. Thank you again, err, Peter.' She pulled Hassan out of there. Peter watched her disappear as he wiped his hands on an oily rag. Her hair mesmerising when the sunlight caught it, like strands of fire.

'That's Layla's muther,' Akash said behind him.

'Who's Layla?'

'Her daughter. Bootiful lil' maid she is. Like her muther it seems. They just moved into the Draycott house. It's them alright.'

Peter watched her weave through the holiday makers, her hair like a beacon. 'Shouldn't y'be worken?'

'Nah, I'm stayin' 'ere with you t'day. There's been some activity since they got ere.'

Peter kept his eyes on Esme, until she disappeared.

***

8

MARAZION

In the middle of the sea, Saint Michael's Mount stood proud with a castle and chapel floating above the trees. Two hundred and thirty feet above the harbour, inhabited by a parish and temporary guests separated from society by an ancient causeway, snaking its way to the ancient priory. A place of myths, where pilgrims congregated and offered gifts to bless and protect their onward journey. Secrets lay within its ancient grounds, a romantic sight, mysterious, and sheltering arm against the Gulf stream. There was a sense of rightness, its outline in a well-ordered state and summit to the glory of God, and centre of the villagers' lives.

They arrived amidst dwellings all this way and that, the beach that was once a forest, running the length of the village and coast. Esme parked up, puzzled at the location that was impressively magical, just how she remembered it.

'Why can't we just go to a normal school? It took ages!' Hassan bleated in the back.

'It was six miles away, Harv. You're always exaggerating!'

'Where are we anyway?' He asked. Layla was still finishing her Snapchat streaks, filming their destination with the peace sign and pouts.

'Saint Michael's Mount. I came here as a kid. This can't be it, surely?' she studied the causeway that led to the island. 'Looks like we'll have to be back before the tide comes in.'

'Are there any fit boys?' Layla asked.

'No! There are no boys, *or* girls, understood?!' she looked at them both.

'Yeeessss!' They answered sarcastically.

'Good, just remember, unless you want to get married, any copulating is out of bounds.'

Hassan sniggered in the back, 'I mean it! You two will be the death of me! All this covering up and doing things behind baba's back is wearing me down!'

'Christ mum, chill out. It's not that deep.'

'Uh! It's deep enough! Unless you want to be shipped off to Riyadh, then go ahead. I'm out of it.' Layla just huffed and rolled her eyes, wishing her mum would grow a pair and punch her father all the way out of their lives.

'Is the school over *there*?' Hassan asked in awe, diverting the subject.

'That's what is says here,' Esme checked the embossed letter, twice.

'If the school is in the castle, I'm kissing baba's feet!'

'It's not. And there'll be no kissing of feet, haram.'

'You're always kissing baba's feet,' Layla said into her phone.

Esme shook the letter into shape. 'Says here it's in one of the houses on the harbour. Well, there's only one way to find out, come on. Layla, put that bloody phone away, and stop poking your tongue out like that when you take pictures. It makes me squirm.'

'I'm telling baba,' Hassan said from the back seat.

'Shut up! Snitching freak!'

'Layla! That's enough! Just get out the bloody car, both of you!'

She paid for the parking at the ticket machine, displaying it in the driver's window, trembling from uncertainty and the usual stress of car journeys with those two, tapping her collar bone more than thrice. It would be so nice just to go somewhere without hassle and stupid, pointless bickering. The dream of going anywhere alone was increasing.

They hesitated on the edge of the causeway, aware they were not dressed for the occasion. Esme went first, the children following looking down rather than up, clutching their arms as the wind whipped around them. The waves licked the sides, Hassan studied the seaweed clinging on and dancing with the tide, the smell of it setting off his appetite again.

The uneven surface of original blocked paving gave off its vibe, leading them to the unknown.

'I don't think flip flops were a good idea, looks like we needed hiking boots!' Layla tutted, fretting about her look being spoiled.

'It'll be kinda cool if the school is in here though guys, don't you think?' Esme scrunched the letter in her fist as they walked against the sea wind. 'It's much colder here than back home,' small talk was all she could manage as her nerves got the better of her.

The walk seemed never ending as the mount grew the closer they got. Bracken, heathers and exotic plants clung to the rockface, the trees spilling out from beneath the castle. Seagulls and Terns circled above them as if announcing their arrival, fighting mid-air. Esme got an odd feeling, one of purpose steeped in myth. She'd read about giants protecting the mount from smugglers and Romans. Believing it, imagining it.

'Why is it called Saint Michael's Mount?' Hassan asked.

'Well, duh! Maybe because it belongs to Saint Michael,' Layla mocked with her tongue hanging out.

'Actually, no. Apparently, the arch angel Michael was seen here, protecting the residents and monarchy.'

'Protecting them from what?' Hassan asked.

'Who knows?' Esme shrugged.

Reaching the end of the causeway, they slid their hands along the high wall that led them to the small harbour. A row of cottages greeted them, granite and slate. The master stood up from his seat and morning paper, dressed as a sea captain.

'Mornin' folks. I'm Frank, the harbour master. I'll be taking thee acrossed if tide gets the better of us. You 'ere to see the Castle?' he checked his watch with squinted eyes, 'youm a bit early. It don't open for another hour,' his accent coarse, traditional. He looked like he'd been there since the late nineteen eighties.

'I don't think we're in the right place, Mum.' Hassan said, his eyes running over the castle.

'Oh, we're not here for the castle, we've come to see the private school if there is one here of course. It's quite possible we're in the wrong place,' Esme answered, laughing nervously while tucking her hijab into place.

'What name y'got?'

'Oh, uh...' she clumsily unfolded the letter, her eyes running over the creases, 'Janan and partner.' Frank regarded them, he passed no judgement on anyone, never had, each to their own, but he was slightly confused why a white face would be wearing such foreign attire.

'Ah, I see, beg y'pardon. I can take yer there, no trouble. They be new residents and I'm gettin used to that name. Emmets won't be 'ere yet,' he jeered, moving his cap back to give his head a scratch.

The cottages were greyish, simple, with prepared doorways for when the weather dictated their freedom. Further in there was a café and gift shop that sold the wares and creations of local artists, surrounded by lighter-stoned dwellings. The holiday season was ending, and the visitors would be sparse, the winter long, trapping the residents on the mount most days until the sea gave up its volatile barricade. Their goose bumps began to fade as the houses shielded them from the elements. Frank stopped outside a house with a large, black wooden gate, the private entrance to the castle gardens. Two wide chimney stacks, a bay window on the ground floor and a black front door to compliment the gate.

'I'll leave you 'ere, just give three knocks. I'll be takin' ye back o'er in the amphibious, cuz that tide be comin' in shortly. It won't completely cover the causeway, but ye just be gettin' wet feet.' He tipped his cap and offered a genuine smile that plumped his crimson cheeks. Esme gulped before knocking as instructed, feeling intimidated by the owners of her faith.

'What's an amfibbyass?' Hassan asked with a smirk.

'A boat with wheels, stoopid,' Layla mumbled behind them, stuck to her mobile.

'Huh? Why would it have wheels?!'

Esme's anxiety increased her intolerance to daft questions, 'to drive on the land! Do I have to think for everyone?! Look, never mind about that for now. Let's just wait and see what baba has in store for us, okay? I mean, look at this place, it's beautiful. He wouldn't just send us to any old school, would he?'

Layla rolled her eyes and held on tight to the back of Esme's pink tunic. The wide door opening gracefully.

'Asalaamu alaikum.' A man stood in the doorway dressed in a white thobe with a brown tweed jacket over the top. His face was light, kind and partially covered with a neat grey goatee.

'Welcome. You must be Esmay and Hassan?'

'His name's Harvey,' Layla snarled. Esme closing her eyes to avert the embarrassment.

'Ah, you must be Layla?' The man continued to remain patient with his right hand over his heart. She pushed her hair over her shoulder with a hostile 'flick'.

'Please, come this way.' He let them go first, guiding them with an outstretched arm. The entrance was high with a grand bespoke staircase; thick, balustrades and spindles, with a carved newel post. The floor tiles were flagstone, cool beneath their feet. Two small classrooms off to the left and one large to the right. The howl of the wind and crash of the waves was immediately silenced as they entered a room with a large fireplace and low ceilings. The walls were a deep red with rugs and Hamsas and other odd symbols carved here and there.

'Please, come through and meet my partner.'

At a long, distressed table, a woman sat with great presence. Heavily charcoaled eyes accentuated by a brocade head covering concealing her mouth and half of her face. A black kaftan flowed over her, dressed in vibrant jewellery, accompanied by hedonistic scent that filled the room. The three of them moved awkwardly towards her, exchanging cautious greetings. There was no shaking of hands, just nodding and smiling. They seemed privileged to have Esme and the children.

'Welcome, everyone. I am, Janan.' Her voice direct, muffled from the heavy material with the same Middle Eastern tones as Musa. She stood and seemed larger than when sat down. '...And you have met Doctor Samir?'

Esme gasped. 'Samir? *The* doctor Samir? You're the people that used to live in our house?'

He dipped his head and closed his eyes respectfully. 'Thank you for the letters, sister.'

'You got them already? From Raffia? Gosh, I mean, if I knew, I could've brought them myself, but Musa didn't tell me we were coming here and that you...'

'Forgive us, sister. How are you settling into the house?'

'We love it, thank you. I used to erm, go there as a...anyway, while we're on the subject, I mean, no rush, I know your belongings are still there, they are quite safe I can assure you and I don't want to sound rude, but...'

'We appreciate it, Esmay. Thank you for your patience. Of course, all in good time. If we can just go over the formalities first.'

Esme slumped from relief, that door was unsettling.

While Janan explained policies and procedures she drifted off and started to overthink.

'We only go up to the age of sixteen, so Layla would only be here for a brief time. We supply the books, and she must bring her own hijab for prayer times...' was all she got the tail end of.

Layla shifted in the seat and her fire was rising - she hated it, having been scarred by her father and other schools.

'What made you choose this place?' Esme asked, intrigued. The proprietors glanced at one another, the woman nodding permission for the doctor to continue.

'We are only part time and will be moving to another property once the vacancy of the castle steward has been filled. I have taken up the position for now and will gladly show you around. Would you like to see the classes first?'

She turned to the children. Hassan had tears in his eyes and his bottom lip was threatening a quiver, and Layla looked ready to explode. 'Would you like to look around, guys?'

'Right, well. Lead on!' She followed Samir for the grand tour. He smelt like moth balls but pleasant, a little different from what she was expecting – not like the others at all. Gentle and forgiving with a little humour, portraying the quiet beauty of Islam. Quite handsome, with distinctive large hazel-green eyes he kept wiping with a white cotton handkerchief. Janan was the dominant one, needing her permission to breathe, a complete opposite to the stereo typical expectancy. Esme was a little bewildered by it, what was she doing wrong? Maybe there *was* no middle ground.

The doctor was taken with her, he too carried the fascination of a western woman having the knowledge of his religion with fresh eyes and an unnerving intuition. The religious zeal of converts removing the veils of distortion.

He was looking forward to hearing her speak Arabic with a Caucasian tongue.

Each classroom had the same smell as their house; the heavy scent of Oud. It couldn't be the same as Musa burnt, not at sixty thousand dollars per kilo.

'How many children do you have coming here? I didn't think there would be any to be quite honest with you.'

'We have enough to fill the seats. They come once they know we are here.' His English was particularly good.

'What about the winter?' Esme asked.

'We do not open in winter. The island is inaccessible most of the time.'

Samir seemed shady at times, but Esme was becoming smitten; devoutness and humility all rolled into one beautiful, trapped man – deterred from expressing his emotions for fear of being cast out, which intensified the call for their release. Her resentment began to blur her vision and she had to break eye contact, a rush of guilt following. It was a sharp reminder that her marriage was just physical, a trauma bond briefly satisfied. Holding on tightly to a mistake, because she knew what living a life of broken ties felt like, and she didn't want the children feeling it.

'Would you like to see the gardens and Castle, sister?' He asked and gently moved her forward.

'If we're allowed, I'd love to!' her face glowed and the seed of a new life began to grow, even though it felt a little uncomfortable.

The black gate opened onto the gardens, and with Samir at her side it was like walking through the gates of paradise. Esme had almost forgotten the children as the cobbled path led them through the protection of cedars alongside the tiered rock face crammed with planting. Stones lay at various levels that formed grassed terraces adding interest, the Castle towering above them with jutting turrets.

'Oh, my goodness, it's beautiful! Who looks after them?'

'We have a brother who has a little more knowledge than others. There is skilled work to be done after seasonal closure. Are you a gardener, sister? You are welcome to help. Stay here with the children,' offering a persuasive smile.

'Not exactly. I have a deep appreciation, but that's as far as it goes. I'm an artist.' That last bit slipped out, something she always hid, afraid that being creative was a forbidden and sinful thing to be.

'You paint?' He asked.

'Yes. Oils. I studied for it. Umm, I know it's not allowed...'

'Not allowed? You mean, in Islam?'

'Forgive me. I know what you must think...' Musa's opinions ran over her, like a rusted suit of armour. He said that a creation copied or drawn came with great punishment, and she believed it. Her art was her breath, her therapy and coping mechanism. Dipping her toes into the forbidden when he wasn't looking, maintained the balance as she drifted in and out of repentance.

Samir seemed agitated before his answer. 'Sister, this is a gift, and one that you've been blessed with. Is Allah not an artist himself?' Cool tears stung her eyes, it was like hearing music for the first time, as if God had spoken through him. She looked up, his eyes watering from the wind, a prophetic blessing and release from the cage of opinions. His heart jolting when he saw the plea in her eyes. 'Never feel ashamed of your human outcries, sister. It's what makes us unique. When nothing makes sense, or feels imbalanced, trust it.'

She felt him retreat into fidelity. Damn it, how shameful of her. The inner child latching onto anything that resembled rescue. Esme's soul needed nourishing, and she wasn't finding it in her faith. Samir would take her into the heavenly realms of mercy, but her loyalty and devotion lay with Musa, impossible to leave, surrendering to the familiar rut. Her desires borne amidst the conflict, radiated at anyone or anything that matched her energy. She longed for a father, a leader into the abyss, one to keep her feet on the ground and set her straight. Turning to a higher power seemed to be the right distraction, compensating the loss and her mother's avoidance on the subject. However, the fatherly bond to Musa was overbearing, dominating dreams and interrupting the flow of needs. Musa stayed close, like rain clouds, always knowing where she was and who she had spoken to, like a noose around her neck.

The climb to the castle was a strain on the thighs over the uneven path, sparking excitement in them all, except for Layla.

The excursion was a little overzealous for something she didn't want to be part of.

'Mum! Look at this!' Hassan's voice snapped her out of her self-absorption, she'd been glorifying Allah with every step; it helped take the focus off the anticipation of reaching the top.

Hassan was fiddling with something again. 'Look! An old well!'

'You are right, this is a well, sealed now of course. A well of Himaya.' Samir answered.

'Protection?' Hassan questioned.

'Correct. Your father told me your Arabic knowledge was impeccable, MashAllah.'

'I'm just good at copying. Why is it in the floor and not, like, with a bucket and a handle thing?' Hassan asked inquisitively.

'Because this well is not for water. The pilgrims gave metal to the sea spirits as offerings for their onward journey, and appeasement. Come, there is something else I must show you.' He led them onto the next item of interest: a heart-shaped stone nestled amongst the pathways.

'A heart!' Hassan exclaimed.

'But do you know whose heart?' Hassan shook his head, 'this belonged to the giant, said to protect the Mount until he was killed by a boy from the village.'

'Like David and Goliath?'

'Yes, very similar to that.'

'Cool! I love it here Mum!' She ruffled his black hair then kissed his temple, holding his head in place. Her sentimental spot where she connected and sealed her love, where life itself sat amongst the fragile junctures.

'I'm happy if you're happy.'

'Oh, please! Can we keep going?!' Layla complained, her thighs burning, secretly yearning for Esme to do the same to her. She knew it was her fault for being such an ass, but she had to retain her defence because it was the only way she kept the oppression in check.

'Come and have a look, Layla. Get yourself interested in something other than that damn phone!'

The ascent was steep, their ears numb as the sea wind found them away from the protection of the higher shrubs.

'Can you see home from here?' asked Hassan.

'No sweetheart. We have our backs to it. But you can see Penzance, look,' her arm outstretched to the place she remembered for its sweet Meade and blackberry wine. Where you ate roast chicken from wicker baskets in dim light, and waitresses stomped barefooted on wooden floors.

'Do you miss Saint Ives mister, err...' Hassan turned to Samir.

'Please, call me Samir. But don't tell the other children,' he winked, always with his hand over his heart when he addressed you. 'I miss the seafood in Saint Ives,' a little laughter following.

They continued until they reached the Castle door. The view over the small town was awe inspiring. The wind reshaped their hair and nearly took Esme's hijab clean off. She held it tight under her chin, but it lifted it up at the back, revealing her auburn locks. Samir averted his eyes immediately as a different version of her face entered his mind.

'Please, sister, let's go inside,' he led them through the heavy oak door with cast iron hinge and bracket. A narrow entrance and hallway greeted them with artefacts that adorned the granite walls. Esme stopped to look at an embroidered cloth protected in a glass frame. It was faded but the embroidered Arabic calligraphy was just visible. She ran her hand over it as if it were a mark of territory.

'What's the history behind this one?' she asked, the children went onto other rooms. Samir stood by her side with his hands clasped behind his back.

'This is many years old, sister. It was a gift from the King of Saudi, when the two countries used to trade goods. Tin was in great demand.'

'What century? Surely Asia was closer?'

'Perhaps the quality of tin was not the same,' his expression always pleasant.

Running her fingers over the glass, wanting to touch the calligraphy and get a feel of its origin,

'Oh, look! It says *Al Fatiha*.'

'Yes, well spotted. The opening and guidance from our sponsors. The Emirates and Saudi's have been generous to this community.' Esme felt that he was just pacifying her, 'we must press on before the visitors arrive. After you.' They moved on, but not without her having one last look at the mysterious cloth.

Next room was a cosy sitting room with a fireplace, it looked lived in, occupied.

'Are people living here then?' Esme asked.

'Yes, the owners have their private quarters in the castle.' Continuing into a room with a long table and original chairs, a freeze that ran along the top displaying battle scenes and the culling of rare animals and birds. Layla and Hassan were discussing it, craning their necks to study it in detail.

'Wow, this is some room. What was it used for?' Esme asked.

'Trades, meetings, heavy discussions. We have another guide while I teach, he is deeply knowledgeable, Mash'Allah. He can give you greater detail of this room. We'll move onto the chapel.'

They stooped through ancient doorways, passing pitted leaded windows with dark red cushioned seats so you could gaze out at the gardens below. Very little light entered the rooms from the thick granite that surrounded the frames and arrow slits. Esme felt a little rushed and wanted to study and touch the history for longer.

Reaching the chapel, hosting large stained-glass windows and wooden pews that the children sat in, a little awestruck as they regarded the musty place of worship. Fine moss covered edges of the structure and eroding moulds of Fleur de Lys; Hassan making noises to hear the echo. Esme was interested in the holy figures and villagers in the stained glass, along with a depiction of the Archangel. But there was a particular window she studied a little longer: Hooded figures looking upon child-like skeletal beings. The Hamsa discretely hidden in the art.

'Look here!' Samir deterred, pushing a bookcase away from a small wooden door. They gathered around wide eyed at the reveal of descending spiral steps.

'Wow! A dungeon?!' Hassan asked.

'Yes. A place they put you in if you didn't do your prayers,' Samir quipped.

'Can we go down and see it?!'

'All in good time.'

'What's down there?!'

'A place you don't want to spend a lot of time in. It is said that the archangel came through here to warn seafarers of the dangers of their approaching enemies.'

'Pfft. How can an Angel fit through *that?*' Hassan's eyes were full of wonder and excitement.

'I don't know, but you must be quite special to see an Angel, but who knows. Allah ou alem. This island has many wonders.' Esme suddenly felt uncomfortable, something was waiting for them down there, holding its breath in anticipation.

'Come, we'll go back to the house, have some tea. The visitors will arrive shortly, inshallah.'

After tea and awkward discussion, Esme was beginning to like the idea of her new life especially with Samir in it, a refreshing alternative to what she was used to. They left with mixed feelings and would be starting the school in just over two weeks. Samir took them to Frank who was ready to take them back in the amphibious.

'Cool! We're going in the amfibby-ass!' Hassan jeered.

'Thank you, Samir. We've had a wonderful time.' He bowed his head in return. Hassan felt relaxed about the start, but Layla held on tight to her reservations. She saw the cloaked figures dash passed doorways and scamper up steps, obscuring their faces with the dark purple material.

'Ri. On we go then,' Frank said.

As they left the harbour, Esme remembered something.

'Oh! The door! We didn't talk about the bloody door!' she called out. Samir continued waving and ignored what she said. 'Damn it! That door will be the death of me! I'll just have to call him later, or get a crowbar, one of the two!'

The doctor retreated to the house, entering the hallway where Janan stood with dominance.

'I fear the mother may be our nemesis.' She said, unravelling herself from the veils.

'Time will tell,' he responded nervously.

9

Beaky

Layla stomped into town, feeling liberated as she left the house wearing forbidden clothes. Her hair loose and carefree, red wisps catching on her long, mascaraed lashes.

The cobbled streets were busy, full of fresh faces from off-loaded coaches. It wasn't so bad after all; it might just be the best thing that ever happened. She passed the cinema, a seventies construction listing all the latest blockbusters, a date night was on the cards. The smell of baked pastry and seaweed stirred the peptides as she drew closer to the harbour, a sparkling smile graced her looks from the ambiance of her new home. Warm, quirky and grounding.

Heading to the lifeboat station to find Akash, if he wasn't there, she would try the café at Porthminster. Turning the corner passing the galleries, holistic shops and restaurants, she walked the harbour path on tip toes trying to see over the

Emmets and dodge the slow-moving cars. Her heart raced as she got closer, seeing his beautiful, contoured back. She blushed from the butterflies, but they dropped to her feet when she saw those girls fussing around him. Layla had given up trying to control her jealousy and temper, snorting through her nose and boring holes in them. Tears emerged. Everything changed, the spark dulled, her skin chilled when he turned to face her like he knew she was there. She quickly looked down and hid in the crowd, not knowing which direction to take without looking obvious, bumping into everyone walking past the station in a hurry.

'Layla! Layla! Wait up!' Akash left the girls and pushed through to get to her. He caught up but she didn't acknowledge him. 'Where y'off to, maid?' He asked, 'hey, hey, slow down!' Grabbing her arm, her snatching it out of his hold.

'Let go of me!' she yelled. Akash was slightly amused and a little flattered. He hung back and let her walk on, smirking to himself as he watched her red head bob in a strop through the sea of visitors. She realised she was going the wrong way but had a feeling it would eventually lead her to the back of Porthminster beach. The cottages were different at this end of the town, the ones on the left clinging to the rocks. Layla wanted to check behind her but didn't want to deal with another blow. *'Stupid! Stupid! Stupid!'*

The sound of crashing waves and the screeches of children indicated she was heading in the right direction, the cottages narrowing the way and warming her chilled skin. She took the pathway at the back of the huts to get to the steps to Draycott Terrace, squealing from Akash casually sat halfway up.

'How did you...?!' Holding her heart.

'I knows shortcuts,' he answered and winked, smelling like a dream with an open shirt. Dark with the bluest of eyes.

Her stomach squelched. 'No seriously, that was impossible!'

'Ah, you don't know it 'ere yet. Where were y'rushing of t'anyway? Don't need t'worry 'bout them girls. They just hang around makin' a bloody nuisance o'themselves, wantin' a free ride. Know what I mean?' he stood and brushed off the back of his shorts. 'Fancy a drink from the hut? My treat.' Layla unconsciously nodded and the spark returned.

'Were you comin' t'see me then?' he asked.

She played with her hair and pondered over her answer. 'No, not really. I wanted to check more of the town out.'

Akash smirked and put his arm around her shoulders, she wanted to throw it off but the protection she felt from it was too immense to discard. She stopped at the edge of the sand to remove her trainers, the shaded part cool and smooth beneath her feet, increasing in temperature as they got closer to the café. Akash grabbed two Cokes from the café's fridge, and they sat on the sand looking out to the aqua ocean.

'How did you get to the steps so quickly?' Layla asked, 'I was way ahead of you, in fact, I came the quicker way!'

He liked her accent, with a northern English lilt. 'I like the way yous speak – it's proper. Not like me.'

'So, how did you?' He slurped his drink, scanning the shore from left to right avoiding her question, reaching into his tight pocket to retrieve a gift.

'You'll be alri' wi'me, Layla. Know that. I won't give yer any trouble, kay? Close y'eyes and open y'hands.' She did, with a big smile, wincing from his touch and the clink of beads.

She gawped at the pink pearls in her cupped hands. 'Oh! They're beautiful, thank you.' Moving the odd-shaped precious around her palm. 'My mother has these, but on a necklace. I love them.'

'S'alri. They be real mind you, not from a shop. Don't let your old man see'em though.'

'You know him?!'

'Not as such.'

Layla looked out to sea with him. 'You're right, he'd kill us both.'

Akash didn't respond, regarding her from the corner of his eye - her hair smelling like vanilla as it was teased by the sea breeze.

'I wanted to talk to you about something, actually.'

'I knew y'were comin' t'see me,' he said nudging her gently.

'We went to the school, you know, the one I was talking about. It's in Marazion.' He looked away and studied the coastline. 'Do you know it?'

'Yip. Tis famous place. Me old man works there.'

'I hate it. The people were, well, suspicious. The woman was kinda weird, spooky. I only saw her eyes. Gives me the creeps!

And there were women, I think, in cloaks and hoods! Like monks!'

'She one o'them folks like yer neighbour?'

'Muslim, you mean. Yes, you could say that.'

'And what's the problem with that? You're from the same background, aren't ya? You ain't weird. Although you gotta a funny little turned up nose.'

Layla sniggered and tucked her hair behind her ear.

'How do you know so much about me? I don't class myself as one of those,' she mumbled her last words, drawing circles in the sand. In a line, with a bigger one on top.

'Each to their own, ay? Just let people get on wi'their stuff. Ain't none o'me bizniss.'

'I guess. Um, have you got a crowbar? By any chance?'

'Crowbar? Think there's one at the station. What d'ya want one o'them for?' They were both distracted by people calling out and children screaming with excitement. Akash stood immediately, frantically scanning the shore.

'What's going on?'

He shielded her with his right arm 'wait, just wait,' he said calmly.

Everyone was rushing to the sea taking photos with their phones. Akash leaned into her, pointing amongst the waves, 'do you see 'im?'

She shielded her eyes, 'see what?'

'Beaky. Come on.' He took her hand and led her to the crowds. She pushed the pearls into her shorts pocket holding them there as they trotted through the sand. Excitement filled her stomach as he pulled her towards the tide, pushing to the front. There, in the middle was a lone Dolphin the residents had nick-named 'Beaky'. Esme spoke about the mammal in bedtime stories.

'Oh wow! A Dolphin!'

'Yep. He been coming 'ere few years now. Keeps an eye on us.'

'I've heard of him, but didn't think he was real. My mother told us about it. Why is he by himself?'

'He be the boss.'

She beamed with delight; this place was getting better by the minute. The mammal dived and summersaulted, fearlessly getting closer to the beach. Children had entered the shallows and snatched quick touches of its rubbery skin. A 'rib' came into view, circling then stopping midway.

'Is that a speed boat?' She knew it wasn't, Akash's pheromones were consuming her brain cells. She heard being dull was attractive.

'Not quite, it's a rib and that's me old man.'

The Dolphin circled the rib and popped his head out of the water, squeaking to Peter who stroked its nose.

'Ello old fella.' Beaky bobbed his head, Peter touching the mammal along its side, patting him affectionately. 'Where you bin, ay? Ain't seen you in a while. Got summat to tell us old boy?' The dolphin whistled and clicked, thrashing its tail. There was something in its mouth, something that caught the sun. Peter retrieved it holding it aloft, squinting at the gold inscribed amulet swinging beneath his grip. A stab in the pit of his stomach confirmed the consequences of the Kattans' arrival, had just begun.

10

THE DOOR

Esme had been dreaming about the school most of the night, and Samir. She woke unbalanced and lunged at Max on the bed, kissing his face and absorbing his grounding vibe.

'Come on, babee. Let's get breakfast.'

She got straight into her morning routine of opening the curtains and windows, checking the post forwarded from their old address, receiving all the jarring memories through the manila, wiping away the tears and pushing down the triggers where they belong.

Shaking loose her unhealed traumas, it was time for caffeine and white toast. Getting the normal tea out was her rebellion against the image she had been trying so hard to maintain. Esme was careful what she ate, always thinking twice before she bought anything and checking where it came from and how much of it contained natural or recycled packing.

Ingredients for Hassan's allergens or pork. Anything eaten from outside the house was a potential threat to a life or confrontation from Musa. What a headache that was becoming, in a global market that made trillions on the bandwagon of the conscious.

Sat at the kitchen table, the sun poured through the Velux window blinding her while she tried to text Musa. There was a tap tapping from above; a seagull with its beady eye on her, demanding it be let in for ransack. Its comical feet splayed on the pane and sheer audacity made her laugh. They were a comfort and reassurance her dream was real.

Scrolling through her phone, a little bored, she turned and yelped almost cricking her neck, sure Hassan stood behind her. 'Jesus,' she uttered. It was about time Musa came home, she'd been hearing things during the night. The thud of feet across the floor, doors opening and closing. Unless it *was* Hassan in his restless state. Max disappeared from time to time in the house, putting it down to his need to explore and mark his territory.

Exiting from google, she sent Musa a WhatsApp:

'Salaam. We went to the school! So cool! Hassan seems excited. When are you coming home? We need you here.' With a kissing emoji and three x's. She checked Facebook while she waited for a response. Her neighbour had posted photos of the shop windows in Chester, with their handmade crafts and cakes. There was a ping and drop-down message from Musa.

'Wsalaam habibi. Hamdullah, you like the school. Hassan is a smart boy. What about Layla?'

'She'll get used to it. You didn't answer my question.'

'Ya'rub I can't just leave like that. I have business to sort out. Soon habibi, soon, Okay? Inshallah. I miss you. Maybe couple of days inshallah. Did you check the bank?'

'Yes. All fine. I spoke to Doctor Samir about the room, but we didn't get to finish the conversation about it. I'll text him later, inshallah. Hassan misses you, me too.'

'Don't push doctor about the room. Tell Hassan I miss him too and I have a big present for him. Make sure Layla comes home before dark and no boys! I don't think you are watching her enough. Ok, habibi, I must go. I call you later inshallah. Salaam x'

The bank was always full. At first, buying what ever entered your head was a dopamine hit, which soon became unfulfilling. You never had enough even with an unlimited budget. She threw the phone down, skidding it across the table. Turning her face to the roof window, taking solace from the heat, the seagull still watching. Marazion made her feel insecure, confused and a little overwhelmed. Sitting at the table in silence and alone was her selfcare, dosing as the sun heated her aches and pains.

Finishing breakfast, the rush of caffeine sparked something – it was time to get out a new canvas and paints!

Setting up the easel in front of the lounge window with Max as close to her as he could get, she wanted to paint the bay, build up a collection and buy a gallery in the harbour, one day. It was time to put some of that money to good use instead of Dolce and Gabbana.

Opening the bamboo box that her mother had bought for her, she ran her fingers over the edges and contents, welling up at the smell of turpentine. A smell of individuality, independence and escape. Esme squeezed the oil colours onto her caked pallet, rolling down a couple of the tubes to get the last splodge out. Turquoise, yellow, green, blue and white, with a little purple. She riffled through the brushes in a paint-splashed tumbler. Perhaps she should use the pallet knife today, she pondered over the choice. No, the short hog brush.

She began to sketch the outline, but it wasn't of the bay, it was of Saint Michael's Mount. Agitated as the pencil took over,

'Damn it! That place!' Her stomach fluttered as the vision took hold, her hand on autopilot. She dabbed the brush in the smooth colours, her passion resurfacing. The serotonin flowed, flushing her cheeks. Painting Saint Michael's Mount felt forbidden, but it was compulsive. White peaks of the waves against the causeway, the windswept cedars, castle and visitors with Samir subconsciously among them. She stood back to admire her work, a little editing required in places, and you could tell she hadn't been at the canvas for a while. Esme wanted to sign it just because that mark of ownership, a score on the heart, was too delicious to wait for. She signed it in her birth name: E. Pascoe. It brought such joy and pride, thinking what name she would choose for the gallery. *Pascoe's Paintings.* Far too cringey, she heard Layla say in her head.

'*Hello.*' Alexa announced.

'For goodness' sake. Alexa! Off!' Esme's heart thumped.

'*Sorry, I don't know that one.*'

'Harvey! Stop that!'

'*Watch out.*' It finally said. She was startled and disturbed, then by Max whimpering, not noticing he had gone.

'Max? Max! Where are you babee?' Esme lay down her brush, wiping her hands on her jeans. 'Max!' her mind racing. She followed the bark to the basement. Max was scratching at the door, sniffing the gap, his barking distressed.

'Stop it! Leave it!' Esme ran down the stairs, Max intent on opening the door. Bloodied claw marks and paw prints were on the door and carpet.

'Oh my God! Stop! Stop it! Sit! Leave!' She knelt and held his front legs, the dog panting profusely, his scratches revealing bear wood of the white door. She took off her jersey cardigan and wrapped it around his feet. He held his nose to the gap - the frenzy calming to inquisitive listening.

'There, it's ok. Shhhh.' She stroked his back, then banged on the door with her fists. 'Why don't you open, son of a bitch! Open sesame!' Laughing at herself.

'Mum?' Hassan stood at the top of the stairs, 'what's going on?'

'Nothing. Max is just being silly.'

'Something's in there, that's why.'

'What do you mean?'

'He's always down there, sniffing the door.'

'Since when?'

He shrugged, 'always.'

'It's a mouse I expect. Come on babee, let's sort you out.' She had to pull hard on his collar, then cradled the dog and carried him up the stairs. 'Help me, Harvey!' she strained.

Esme ran her cardigan under the cold tap. Hassan held Max's paws feeling upset as the drips of blood splashed the kitchen floor. Esme gently bathed them, wincing as he yelped and pulled his feet away.

'My silly Max. What were you thinking?' Hassan's little sobs sounding like hiccups. 'Why is there so much blood?'

'Heat and excitement. And stop doing that with thing with Alexa, please! Scares me half to death.'

'I'm not doing anything with Alexa! Walahi!'

'Hmmm, well, I wonder what baba has bought for you. He said he's got a big present.' A smile appeared on her son's tear-streaked face.

'A surfboard?'

'Really, Harvey, from Saudi? I think it's something way better than that.'

'Doubt he's got anything for me. Nice painting, mum. Why that place though?' Layla commented as she entered the kitchen in pyjama shorts and skimpy top, her wild hair resting on her back, 'what's been going on? What's all the fuss?'

'Max was trying to open that door,' Hassan answered.

'Mum, just get a crowbar and prise the bloody thing open. This is our house now, I mean, who the hell do they think they are? It's creepy. Just get their stuff out and give it to the weirdo woman next door.'

'She's not a weirdo! Don't be so judgemental about people! She's a good neighbour, it's the only bit of familiarity we've got here. I did say I would look after it.'

'Yeah, well, there could be drugs in there for all we know.'

'Such drama. I'll wait until baba gets back and watch your language, please.' Layla pulled a mocking face, bearing her front teeth.

'Why have you got to wait for *him?* Can't you make your own decisions anymore?' Esme ignored her, Layla had been speaking far too many truths of late and it was making her feel uncomfortable. She could hide most things when they were little, but not now they had an adult brain, almost, ones she never gave much credit for. She bit her tongue though, keeping her promise to let her children speak out; determined to break the generational curse.

Her daughter had educated herself on what was expected of a man, especially one of faith, what was deemed as baseline. Enforced restrictions on expression and sexuality meant they were becoming a sought-after endeavour. The marriage obligation hung over her head like a loaded gun, watching her father practice with resentment, but he never took the time to be what she needed. His love was tangible and that's all he could manage, all he knew; giving women money kept them quiet, manipulated.

Layla longed to be a daddy's girl, Musa just made her feel like she was a disappointment. Things would be so different if he just took his head out of his arse. He was a bad example which made her jealous of her other friends' 'normal' life, hopping from one friendship group to another, adopting their vibe and often lying about her background. Lack of education made it difficult to be accepted, ditching them when her conscience got the better of her. The threat of hell sending her running back to reconnect with her father's culture.

It was the moments of tenderness that threw a wrench in the works, bringing happiness back momentarily and casting a fairytale comfort, only to be taken abruptly when he lost his temper or told her to change her clothes. Their feeling of safety was waning, his moods were becoming unpredictable, which Esme always overcompensated for. Speaking out would be different now. But there was something else that had changed, his absence was appreciated more than his presence of late. Layla would be looking for a companion with rebellious intentions, and to finally choose herself over everything.

'Let's just bash it down! I hate that door now, it hurt Max!' Hassan hugged Max's neck as he fidgeted from the nursing.

'Max hurt himself from being obsessed again. Keep still! It's probably just a mouse or something, bound to be some in these houses. I don't want to break my promise.'

Layla was concocting a plan as she listened, hoping that whatever was behind that door would put her father behind bars – and those creepy people at the school.

11

EVIL EYE

She stared at her canvas of Saint Michael's Mount that hung above the fireplace, cradling her favourite mug. It was haunting, tormenting, forcing her to think about helping in the beautiful gardens. The thought was growing on her, she was liking the idea of working in such a magical place. Maybe she would, it'll be good for her creativity. The penetrating vibe made her miss her mother even more, she had been thinking about her a lot since she came to Saint Ives. Esme reflected on her childhood, grieving as her eyes walked the canvas. Where was her father, and why couldn't she remember him? Burying the thoughts before she got lost in them entirely – jolting when the phone pinged.

'Salaam habibi. How is my family?'

'Hey, salaam. We're all ok, Hamdullah. What's happening there? How's business?'

'Not much. It's hot, I need cool air and sea! Hamdullah, business is fine. I will be coming back this Friday, inshallah.'

'Ok, good. I've missed you. Can't wait. Love you.'

'Don't speak with Doctor Samir until I come home inshallah. Love you too. Bye x.'

Contented, she gently placed the phone back on the sofa. She couldn't wait to show him around to complete it. It would feel like home again when he was back – although that would come with the usual stresses.

Hassan was in the backyard playing with Max, who was the bad guy glued to the floor with magic seaweed; a way of compromising for Max's bandaged feet. The day's heat had tired them both, Max dosed in the sun, staying consciously alert. Their games an escape and distraction from the anxiety attacks. Hassan was a deep thinker, absorbing everything and everyone around him, feeling things, things he didn't want to tell anyone about. The medication had stopped the visions lately and he missed them, maybe skipping a few doses wouldn't hurt.

Life seemed harsh and completely incredible at the same time and there were days he just wanted to shut it all out and hide in his bedroom – it was the best room in the world, after all. The seagull had been back a few times, tapping on the window in the morning. He named it 'Steve,' it looked like a Steve. It wasn't keen on the soda bread but loved Musa's khubz.

Hassan crouched by the wall, contemplating, running his finger along the lines of mortar between the eroding red bricks, mesmerised and comforted by their repetition. A large cat jumped on the wall from Raffia's side, snapping him out of his trance. Long, tabby fur that was wiry and eyes of unusual colours – one brown, one green. Ears like that of a Maine coon with a human face. It gave a croaky 'meow,' making Max growl and whimper, his tail hesitantly wagging. He didn't mind cats and couldn't really be bothered to get up and struggle with his sore feet, a little wary of the strange feline.

'Oh, hello cat. What's your name?' The cat stared, giving Hassan the shivers on top of his thumping heart. There was an odd smell coming from it, like crude oil. He reached out to touch it or perhaps just prod it, the fur was not what he was expecting, feeling like one of his mother's paint brushes. The animal flinched and fled.

'That was a bit gross,' grimacing and laughing with Max. He knew Max was panting, but he called it his laughing.

'As salaamu alaikum, Harvey.' Raffia said over the wall, giving Hassan another fright.

'Umm, walaikum asalaam. How do you know my name, uh, my other name?'

Raffia smiled. 'What the matter with your dog?'

'Oh, he, uh, hurt his feet scratching the door downstairs. Mum says there's mice in there. I think it's something else.'

'You are handsome boy, like your father, MashAllah.'

'Thanks.' Hassan blushed. It was a bit embarrassing sometimes, especially when the older ladies had to comment and pinch his cheek. It was his maturing pencil-drawn features, his skin a pale olive. Although he still had puppy fat left in his face, Esme saw what a beautiful young man he would become. 'Why are your cat's eyes like that?' he asked.

'She is special, like you. Mint tea?'

'What's her name?'

'Noona. Okay, you come round now, we have some tea together.'

'Oh, no, I'd better not – I'm allergic, to um, things. Mum will be cross.'

'Not problem. You ask your mother, okay? You come, anytime, welcome. I have present for you.' Raffia dipped her head politely and went inside. Hassan watched her inquisitively. Maybe one little tea wouldn't hurt, and how come she knew so much?

He shrugged his shoulders and went back inside, Max scrabbling to follow, limping. Esme was making Quiche, humming to Alexa's chillout choice.

'You're happy.'

'Yes, Baba just text – he's coming back Friday, inshallah.'

'Yay. That lady next door? She knew my name. The Harvey name.'

Esme looked up from the shortcrust pastry with a streak of flour on her cheek, her red hair tied up with a yellow Chrysanthemum. 'Oh? I must have told her when I went round that time,' she pushed the rolling pin, getting into a rhythm that helped her meditate.

'And she knew baba was handsome.' Esme stoic as she turned the pastry, thinking back when she took the letters next door. 'Did you know she's got a creepy cat? Ninnie, no, Noona. It's massive!' Hassan used his hands to illustrate the size, unsure where to stop.

'Oh, you're just exaggerating again. How can a cat be *that* big?!'

'It was! Walahi Mum! Ask Max. With different eyes! And Raffia asked me in for mint tea, told me to ask you. She's up to something.'

'Honestly, you two! Have tea with her and the creepy cat, it's good to spend time with our neighbours, they will remember you for it. Just don't have the cakes.'

Hassan sat at the table and drew patterns in the flour, squishing little bits of discarded pastry into the wood. 'If you think about it, Jinn are the real superheroes, aren't they?'

'Harvey! Bismillah!'

'No, hear me out. We all want to be like them, don't we? I know I do. I'd love to have those powers.'

'Speak for yourself. Don't say that again. Heaven knows what's listening.'

'Hey!' Hassan called out, 'stop eavesdropping, it's haram!' he chuckled. 'And stop living in the plug holes, stupid idiots! Then you won't get hot water on you!'

'Harvey, seriously. You'll have us all cursed. What's that around your neck?' Esme curious at the gold chain.

Hassan touched it, 'baba said I have to wear it.'

'Let me see.' Hassan placed a golden amulet in her palm, triangular, with inscriptions. 'What is it?'

He shrugged, 'he said I must wear it, no questions, and take it off before I go in the toilet.'

'Oh, it's a protection thing. Is it?' She handed it back, 'I've never really understood why they are gold when it's frowned upon.' She heaved a breath and brushed it aside.

'Be kind, ok? Weird or not. Just be kind. And things will have to be a little different when baba returns – no flitting off when you please, he'll be having kittens and I want a stress-free house from now on. That reminds me...' she checked her Apple watch, 'where's Layla got to? She'll have to reign it in, too.'

'I'll go get her!' he stood in excitement, 'I know where she is, please mum?'

'Well, all right. No detours to the Lifeboat station or arcade, okay?' Hassan agreed, grabbing the goggles from the small table and leaving the house in a whirl wind without his shoes, tiptoeing to the beach.

He saw Layla with Akash, sitting on the benches together. Grinning at the prospect of using it against her, he crept up behind them.

'What are you do-ink habibi?!' Deepening his voice. Layla spilling her drink because she turned around so fast.

'You, little!' Her heart thumping slow and hard.

Hassan waved at Akash. 'Hello.'

'Alri'?'

'I'm Harvey Hassan. Layla's annoying brother,' shaking hands with him. Akash studying him intensely.

'I can see. I'm Akash, you can call me Kash.'

'Ha, like money.'

'Yeh. Kind of. Are you a good swimmer?' He stood, taking off his white t-shirt, Hassan gawping at his six pack and pecks.

'Yes. I am. Aren't I Layla?'

'You're a pick me girl, that's what.' She said, closing her right eye from the sun.

'Am not!'

'Are too!'

'I'm telling!'

'Oh, big whoop Harvey. Here, I'll call baba myself, take a selfie with Kash.'

Akash flicked his t-shirt between them. 'Alri' children. C'mon boy. Let's see what yer got.' She poked her tongue out and lifted her red locks over her shoulder, contently watching them walk to the sea. Akash looked over his shoulder, she looked the other way, her facial muscles twitching.

Akash took a run at the waves, diving into the middle and instantly impressing Hassan, trying to look as good to the girls watching in bikinis. Akash broke the surface, without the need to expel water or air.

'Wow! Where did you learn to swim like that?!' Hassan asked, squeezing the water from his nose. Akash grinned, squinting his ice-blues, Hassan noticing he was studying him again feeling conscious about his puppy fat.

'How long can yer 'old y'breath fer?'

'Ages. But don't tell mum, she hates it when I do it,' Hassan answered.

'Yeh? Go on then, let's see it.' Hassan slid the goggles on from his head, held his nose and dipped under, Akash joining him. Counting in his head with his eyes closed, he opened them when he got to forty. Losing concentration when he saw Akash's staring back at him with eyes that had changed, as if compensating for the elements. Alive and chilling. Hassan scream trapped in the bubbles, coming up for air choking and gasping.

'Steady on, steady on.' Akash patted his back, 'thought you said ages.'

Hassan spluttered, retching from the salt. 'C'mon, let's get yer a drink, lad,' Akash deterred, helping him out. Hassan ran on without him, and kept running, all the way home.

12

BABA

Esme prepared the house for Musa's arrival like a headless chicken, anyone would think the king of Saudi was coming for dinner. One of his favourite dishes, Kabsa, steamed up the kitchen; rice with meat and vegetables, served with a yoghurt dressing. She darted around the house burning Oud in a traditional clay bowl, wafting the smoke in corners and praying under her breath. The sweet wood with nuances of leather and spices made her lightheaded.

'Oh, Mum! I hate that smell!' Layla yelled from her room making purposeful retching noises. Her resentment had been building all week. She looked out the window to the bay and daydreamed about her brief, magical moments with Akash, annoyed and a little suspicious that he didn't have a mobile. Maybe it was a good thing. The fact that meeting him again would have to be in secret, intensified the lure. Her phone pinged, it was from messenger. She had been chatting to her friends back home, telling them all about her new interest. She nonchalantly picked up the phone, unlocking the screen.

There was no face on the profile pic, *'someone wants to send you a message.'*

She pressed 'accept' –

'You been thinking about me then?'

'Who is this??'

'You forgot already?'

'I'll report you if you don't leave me alone!! Paedo freak!' She was about to block the messenger.

'Don't do that. Were you looking for me out the window?' her heart raced; her hands shook.

'Kash?'

'Yeah. You, ok?'

'But how did you...?'

'I knows shortcuts.'

'There's no number? Tell me what it is so I can save it.'

'No number, just think of me, I'll be ere.'

'I don't understand. So that was you, the other day?'

'Told ya, u be alright with me. You know what to do now. See ya lata.'

The message disappeared. Layla frantically searched for a number, for anything - there wasn't even a record of the chat. She rushed to the window scanning the beach for him, checking her phone again. A wave of adrenaline ran through her, and she began to giggle uncontrollably from the arrival of love.

Hassan was in his room, feeding Steve and enjoying Max's company for the last time.

'It's your last day up here Maxey. You know that, right?' The dog barked in protest. How was he supposed to keep an eye on his human?

Hassan hadn't said much since the beach, just kept checking his eyes in the mirror, Akash's stuck in his mind's eye. It sparked something, scared the hell out of him, triggered a deep-seated aversion he was determined to investigate.

The three of them eagerly waited in the kitchen, their bellies anxious from the ending of their control-free holiday. Esme turned everything off, it was ready. She walked to the front door and looked up the road. The unmistakable frontage of Musa's white Mercedes was first to be noticed, the neighbours often flashing her a look now and then at the inconvenience of their two large vehicles. He usually drove to the airport in it, but he said he had other means this time. Layla leaned against the kitchen sink, scowling with her arms folded. Although it was a fight to uphold because her new secret was bursting all over her face, and her stomach hadn't stopped squelching since Akash's message.

'He's here!' Hassan shouted, jolting jagged souls. Max barked frantically wagging his tail and bottom. Esme located her son's excited squeal in the lounge, hugging his father.

'But how did you? I was literally by the door.'

'You were making too much noise to hear me, habibi,' he smiled. Wearing jeans and a long-sleeved black jersey, his hair tied back and a goatee so perfect it looked drawn on. Esme couldn't contain herself and she ran to him like a love-sick schoolgirl. Layla rolled her eyes and put two fingers in her mouth. Musa received his wife and pulled her in close, just a little taller than her.

'So good to see you habibi. I forgot how beautiful you are.' His eyes wandered her freckled face, her auburn hair just showing beneath the muslin. It was always like they'd first met. 'It's bladdy cold! Why is everybody wearink summer clothes?! Is there food?'

'Couldn't you smell it? I made your favourite. I missed you.' They almost kissed; the temptation too great. Musa was against showing any affection in front of the children. He gently pushed her away to maintain forthright, Esme helping him with his bags, trying his best to avoid the dog who was desperate for some fuss from the alpha male. Max sniffed his jeans and shoes in detail while he wasn't looking. Checking his bags and suitcase, with a circling tail.

'Layla. Why didn't you hug me like your brother?' She silently answered from her heart; the expletives alone would have gotten her into big trouble. She never looked upon him as a father, more like an irritating older brother – that never seemed to age! They all piled into the kitchen and Musa was happy to be greeted with familiar scents.

'So, how was your flight and everything?'

'Ok, hamduillah. I must eat and then sleep. It looks beautiful in here habibi, I'm proud of you.' He kissed her forehead, she shivered - still madly in love with him. Hassan was telling him all about Raffia and the cat, then the beach and the lifeboat station and the school.

'Okay, okay – that is a lot of information. Let me sit.' He was unusually refreshed for someone who had travelled as far as he had. 'Coffee please, habibi.'

'Coming up. What luck we've had having a familiar neighbour.'

'There is no luck, only fate. Is nice place here, I like it. I can breathe without air-condition! Ya Allah, the heat! Like hell on earth.'

'It's *air conditioning*, Baba.'

'I know, baba is, uh, tired.' He processed his stay and trip in a matter of seconds, ruffling Hassan's hair was what he missed the most, 'so, mummy tells me you like the school.'

'Yeah, it's really cool, and the place is amazing! It's a castle! And there was a giant's heart, in the path!'

'A giant heart? Wow, very good, very good. What about your sister?' Layla opened the fridge for something to drink.

'I am here you know; you can address me directly. I hate it and the people are creepy,' she said as she prised open the can ring, glaring at her father. He stirred his coffee trying to control the fire that was rising. Esme panicked and stepped in immediately.

'You liked the place though, didn't you? The gardens are beautiful Moose, you should see them.'

'AstaghfiruAllah!' Slamming his fist down on the table, 'no daughter of mine speaks to me like that! I expect to come home to a warm welcome, not foul language! And look at the way you are dressed! Get up to your room, go change!'

'I'm not your daughter!' She screamed at the top of her lungs and stormed out. Esme's neck and stomach burned. Hassan picked at the gaps in the pine table trying to control his infamous quivering chin.

'This is your fault!' He shouted at Esme.

'Why is it *my* fault?'

'You feed her too much nonsense! Making her think she can do what she wants! She will be a dishonour if you give her enough...err, how you say?'

'I thought we agreed about this. Just leave her, you're here now. Give the girl a break!' Esme's voice quaked.

'Baba! Stop shouting!' Hassan cried, he hated it.

'Sorry habibi, I'm not shouting at you. We have silly women in this house,' his voice calmed, 'rope!' he finished. Esme went to the annex to hide her emotions, looking to the moss clumps on the corrugated plastic roof, missing her mother even more when she was upset. She couldn't stop the tears that erupted, trying to keep her convulses under wraps. Why was any kind of normality always so short-lived with Musa? Forcing herself back into denial, squeezing her eyes shut and ignoring the overwhelming crush of her love. But a family together was better than a family apart. It even had a feeling to it, one that if it wasn't there would be like hanging over a black hole. Max crept in with a soggy bunny – she stroked his head, wishing she were a dog sometimes. Wiping her nose with a bent wrist, she pulled herself together - inhaling, exhaling. Three times tapping. Putting on a brave face, she went back into the kitchen.

'Right. Food?' She diverted, still sniffing.

'Why are you crying?' Musa asked.

'It's nothing.'

'I know is me who make you cry, habibi. I'm sorry. Just stressed. It's not your fault and you are not silly. I am. AstaghfiruAllah, forgive me. Sometimes my father comes out my mouth.' His apology washed the poison out of her bloodstream, and it was enough. She knew deep down it was just another trigger of her insecurities.

'Right well, I think you should go and apologise to Layla. That's not the way to enter a house and you know it. Heaven knows what it brings in. Oh, and there's been some funny goings on here, too. I swear it's that bloody door!'

Musa slurped his coffee, clearing his throat, 'is not the bladdy door – is your imagination. Because you are alone, your brain think you hear samthing. Don't worry, I am here now. Nothink hurt you inshallah. Just my mouth sometimes, eh?'

'Why do you miss all the bits out, Baba?' Musa shook his head questionably. 'You know, you miss out words like '*it*' a lot.'

'Ah, I see. Because English is my second language, not first. Too many little bits to remember. Your language is complicated. Which reminds me, how is your Arabic?' Hassan froze and looked at Esme.

'Excellent, of course. You wait til Doctor Samir hears it.' Musa bobbed his head with a sarcastic mouth, devouring his food,

'This is good, habibi. You make it just like my family.' Whoever they were, she'd never seen them or met them. Esme's upset quickly vanished and the anticipation to get the kids to bed was growing. Musa wiped his mouth with the cloth he was given, placing it neatly on the table.

'I go for shower now. Sorry Hassan, *I am* going for *a* shower now. That better?' Hassan beamed and jiggled his head, causing a wave in his curls. Having his father back replaced something that wasn't there in his absence, never knowing what it was exactly. A completion, perhaps, because Hassan had to have completion and everything in place.

'Okay. Good. You can teach me, and I teach you. Yes?'

'Ok Baba, deal.'

'No deals needed. Don't ever make deals, with anyone, understand?' Hassan agreed with a slight lump in his throat. It was always a confusing and sometimes contradicting rollercoaster with his father, which often affected his ability to be honest, as well as sleep.

Musa stopped outside Layla's room and put his ear against the door. He could hear murmuring and giggling.

Unable to control himself, he burst through. She gasped and immediately sat up, holding her phone to her chest.

'Baba! Why don't you knock?!'

'Why am I knocking? What you hidink?'

'Nothing! I could have been changing or something!'

'Somethink? What somethink? You speakink with boys?!'

'NO! I'm speaking to my friends back home!'

'Why? What are you sayink? This is your home now. Forget them!' They regarded one another in silence both feeling the lost bond and affection, looking away to avoid confronting it. Musa turned, pulling the door halfway, 'your mother says I have to say sorree. I have present for you,' he said and closed the door, pausing and listening again. He did love her, but not like Hassan. She had changed, become rebellious and he didn't like it. The sweetness and innocence had left, and his love with it. Layla was becoming someone else's daughter, she needed a good Arab husband to set her straight, calm her down and condition her into submission in all sense of things. The tears stung his eyes when he was reminded of the blessings and humility that came with having a daughter, and her little chubby hands he used to playfully bite; his only sentiment of her. They were so hard to tame nowadays, always going against modesty and the expectancies of a good, pious woman.

Turning on the shower, the pipes clunking and banging, his mind was full thinking about Ibrahim and his return to a country that was alien to him. It had its beauty and clean air, streets that were like something out of books he read as a child. He knew the fair maidens would be plenty, instantly attracted to the white Muslim who knew more than he did. His strange little family was all that kept his heart beating. Esme's beauty still rendered him weak, he felt lucky to have her, just regretfully sad he chose this path. Missing the soul of his childhood, the smells and raised female voices that carried over the village. All of that held him together. Home, that's all he wanted.

Holding is hand under the running water, he cursed the inadequacy – the temperature wasn't sure where it should stop. Hot, Cold. Cold, hot.

'I pay all this money and not even the water works! Esmay! Esmay!'

Layla came out of her room, 'She won't hear you! It's not like our old house.'

'Come halp me with this water!'

She reluctantly went to the bathroom. 'What?'

'Is not gettink hot. How you do it?'

'Did you check the pressure in the boiler? Mum says it needs topping up now and then.'

'I cannot stand this inadequacy! You are one of the richest countries in the world and you have rubbish pipes! SubhaanAllah. Ya rub, convince your mother to buy the property this way down.' He pointed to the right indicating the direction of high-end properties.

Layla topped up the water pressure from the cupboard on the stairs. 'There,' she said, pointing out where the needle should be, 'just make sure you don't over fill it. It'll blow up, something like that.' Musa was impressed but didn't show it. A strange thing seeing a woman attend to what he called, immigrant tasks.

'Okay, okay. Who is here for this plummink?'

'Err, I don't know. Ask in the town. Oh! ...' She thought of Akash, a good excuse to see him, 'the lifeboat station, they might know.'

Layla began to feel uncomfortable, awkward to move. Love was there but she didn't know what to do with it. A hug may open the gates to manipulation or worse, submission.

'I have shower, then we see the presents, okay?' She returned to her room. There was the tangible apology. 'And put some lonk clothes on when I am home, okay? All I see is legs. And wear your hijab outside!' He called out. She rolled her eyes, slamming the bedroom door and flipping the birdie behind it. Tears of frustration burst forth, clenching her teeth to suppress them. It was there, just tittering on the surface ready to erupt. Layla was so desperate for male rescue, *any* rescue. Running to him when he came home had bitterly gone, as well as the masculine protection. Huffing, she picked up her phone, her stomach burned when she saw the messenger icon again. Excitement replaced the despair, trembling as she opened the message:

'You alright maid?'

13

SAVAGE BOND

Sat under a parasol propped up in the sand, her hand peaked over her eyes, the soft pink head scarf flapped in the breeze as she watched Hassan swim and dive. She wore her light linens today: tunic, white trousers, and Chanel sandals. The view still took her breath away, the bay protected by the green-covered recess. She watched where people were going, the right side led to another bay away from view and to the train station. But her eyes were fixed on the left at the white hotel built into the rocks, the most expensive with secluded balconies and a 'la carte menu. Perhaps she should nag Musa for a night away in there, Raffia could babysit. The town could just be seen over the obstacles and further out, the chapel on the hill. Overwhelmed with contentment as she studied Musa sat next to her with a coat on, clutching his arms.

'It's freezink!' he shivered.

'Oh stop, it's a beautiful day. Fresh air is good for you. You've been stuck in that merciless heat too long, that's why. Can't be any good for your immune system.'

'*This* is no good for your immune system! I can feel myself gettink ill!'

'Yes! Because you been in that damned heat! Nothing dies there, it just breeds. Here...' Esme handed him a pot of homemade humus and pitta bread, 'there's extra garlic in there to boost you up a bit. Why don't you go in the sea?'

'Are you crazy?! You want to kill me?'

'Oh Moose, you're such a pampered puss. I thought you were a savage. You were last night,' she whispered in his ear and giggled provocatively, picking something out of his goatee.

'Esmay, not outside!'

'Such a fuss pot,' she said, wiping away humus from his moustache. He regarded her with a smouldering smirk, his eyes boring into her soul and sending her defenceless.

'This is good, habibi. Almost as good as Ibrahim's.'

'Oh, how is Ibrahim? Such a humble man. Did you see him while you were there?'

'Yes, he sends his salaams to you.'

'Bless him. He needs a wife. Must be so boring day in day out in that café, knowing you've got no one to go home to.'

'He will be all right, inshallah. No man goes home early when he has a business, wife, or no wife. Café is fine.'

Hassan came running out of the sea, throwing himself down in the sand and dripping on them, sending shocks through Musa.

'Hassan! Blease!'

Esme wrapped him in a fresh towel rubbing him dry all over.

'Why have you got a coat on, Baba?'

'Is cold and you are crazy going in sea!' pushing a folded pitta in his mouth. 'Be careful you don't lose the amulet in sea, understood?'

'Yesssss!' Hassan huffed.

Esme took it in her hand, studying it. 'What does it mean, anyway? I thought they were haram.'

'Protection. Expensive, protection. Are you taking it off before bathroom?'

'Yes, baba! *The* bathroom. Look Mum, I can see our house!'

'I know, we are incredibly lucky. Right, I've got something else for you and don't have anything of baba's, okay? He's had humus,' Esme answered, riffling through the cooler bag.

'Why do you always say lucky? I don't like this word – lucky,' Musa snubbed as he tried to keep his glances away from the half-naked sun worshippers. 'Is not luck. Is fate, hamdullah, is a gift from Allah. I work for this, is no luck, habibi.' Esme turned to look at Draycott Terrace as it looked out to the bay. The sight of it sitting in her chest.

'Our street must be historic. I'll have to look it up.' While the boys ate, Esme breathed in and closed her eyes focussing on the rhythm of retreating and crashing waves, momentarily washing away the darkness. She hadn't been in the sea for a long time, having developed a fear of it from goodness knows when. 'I want to die here, bury me in the sand will you Moose?' She said breathlessly. It was good to see her happy again, memories of the north stifled him. But the dream would be short-lived, they were all unknowingly hanging on by a thread, which he would keep fabricated until it was time.

14

Mint Tea

It was difficult getting the kids up to start the new school. There was shouting and screaming with Musa trying to have a lie in after his late-night prayers. Layla changed her clothes three times, redressed her hair and makeup, which meant they left the house highly strung and ready to kill each other. Esme started yelling as soon as the Range Rover doors were slammed.

'This is *not* how I want to start the day! Why can't you just do as you're bloody told for once? Why has there always got to be this fight? You know what I would do? Just do it, keep the peace whether I hated it or not. Some things in life we must do even if we don't want to. You've had your freedom, now it's back to wearing what is acceptable to baba. You can't have everything your way. I don't, so why should you? Welcome to reality. I'm sorry I chose this path for you. Learning another language is a huge bonus in life. Let's just see how it goes. We don't have to stay,' leaving the terrace at speed, slamming on the brake to avoid a surfer carrying his board. 'If you *want* to work on the checkouts, then tell me now, save me a journey,' there was a pregnant pause, 'Well?!'

'Even if we had top marks, we'd still be working on the checkouts,' mumbled Layla, her face in her phone.

'Not necessarily. A language is a language, it'll get you most places and helps with your math. Because you need help with that, don't you? Anyway, it's also good for creativity and prejudice.' Hassan covered his ears. He hated the high pitch of his mother's voice when she lost it. She wasn't mum when she did, just a deception from his nightmares.

'Why have we got to go?' Layla's temper also escalating.

'It's good for you to be around different cultures.' Esme responded, looking both ways before pulling out.

'Christ. We're up to our bloody necks in culture!' Layla spat, her freckles getting redder.

'Yes, but I'm talking about different ones. From all backgrounds.'

'We'll be the only Brits there, and you know it. Making me feel uncomfortable in my own country, leaving us out of conversations. It's bloody rude, and they're hypocrites!'

'I understand that, Layla. Look it at a different way, this is how I look at everything lately. Nothing lasts. Nothing. Not when your father is involved, anyway. He has these self absorbed ideas to satisfy his own conscience, and we'll just go along with it for now. We can't pass any judgement until we know what's what, and what these people are like.'

Hassan didn't want to take sides, focussing on the passing scenery. He loved his father but not like his mother. But she made him confused from the way she spoke against him, wishing he could run away sometimes and love them from a distance.

'I'm not going to let happen what happened before, okay?' Esme's voice trembled, all of them choking on the statement. She tried her best to deal with the bullying up north. Layla regretted mentioning her religion in school, becoming the subject of a group chat with media influenced slander. She brushed it off, but the cut ran deeper than she dared to admit, and that was where her love for Islam stopped. Assumptions were made to fit into a category that society had fabricated from ignorance. Her individuality bothered them, she owned her decision to remain Muslim and that was unfathomable, fuel for fear and hatred. Hassan was more open and confident about it because it was different for him. It was always, different for him.

'Remember, I'm proud of you, no matter what. I brought you up right, in my eye, anyway. Especially you,' affectionately stroking Layla's hair.

'Why me?'

'You've broken the pattern of generational curses. You're out there, telling it how it is. And as much as that makes me cringe at times, don't ever stop.'

Esme's stomach was doing summersaults when they arrived at Marazion. Her obsession and avoidance had made the place seem surreal.

The day was hazy with a little breeze, and for such a short journey the weather difference was extreme. Stopping at the edge of the causeway the light turning the stones purple, the mount felt magical as the castle windows twinkled, the tops of trees shimmering and beckoning.

'Looks like we're early, can't see anyone else.' Esme looked around and down the long beach. Just a couple of visitors having a stroll and two horse-riders putting their animals through their paces, but no influx of foreign school students.

'Did you get the right day, mum?'

'I think? I read the letter several times, but you know what I'm like. Come on, there's only one way to find out. We'll have a day out here, if not.'

They cautiously followed her along the cobbles, the tide lapping at the seaweed and rocks, calming and clearing their busy heads. Esme's linens flapped around her legs and back as the wind pushed them hard. She held onto her head scarf and squinted at the figure stood at the end of the causeway, Doctor Samir. Her guts squeezed when she recognised him.

'Oh god, it's Barba papa,' Layla scoffed, hugging her waist.

'You're going to hell!' Hassan said to her.

'Oh yeah? See you there, freak!'

Esme stopped in her tracks.

'That's enough! Both of you! I don't want to hear that coming out of your mouth ever again, you hear me?' Pointing at Hassan. He slowly nodded with twitching lips. 'Now,' she pulled on her tunic, 'let's have a bit of respect and keep our minds open. Hmmm?' Esme quickened her step so it wasn't an agonising wait for Samir. She could see a raised smile as they drew closer, his hand over his heart as always.

'Welcome, welcome. Salaams, children, Esmay. You are the first here, I am impressed MashAllah. Perhaps you will be setting a good example?'

'Wsalaam doctor. Is anyone else coming?'

'Inshallah. We go.' He led them to the house, not a soul in sight. 'What do you have on your feet, sister?' He asked Esme.

She looked down, perplexed at his question. 'Oh, err, Crocs. Why?'

'Okay. We would be happy if you could help in the garden today. Can you?' Caught off-guard, she said yes without thinking. Musa wouldn't be happy with her doing such a demeaning, migrant job; they had a status to uphold.

'Excellent. If you go and see the head gardener and I will take the children.' He opened the black gate for her with a persuasive expression. The kids relieved she was staying.

'Okay, erm,' she kissed them, Layla pleading with her eyes. 'You'll be fine, go on. I'll be here anyway.' Samir was keen for her to go, and as soon as she crossed the threshold, he closed the gate behind her.

She picked at her hands as she scanned for someone resembling a gardener, walking on the large green that lay beneath the mount where visitors paused before their grand tour of the castle. The wind hit her in the face as she turned a corner, drying her lips and watering her eyes, stopping to tuck her hijab tighter. Her heart swelled over the unmistakable landscape of Cornwall, the way the houses were lined to meet the sea, perfect and twee with dashes of colour from the window boxes and hanging baskets. There wasn't one inch that spoiled the view or admiration, the unique light enhanced vision and the soul. Continuing, scanning with a nervous stomach, she was pleasantly surprised at the rockeries that led you closer. Bright yellow succulents, aloe vera, yuccas and bursting agapanthus tousled by the gusts. The castle towered above her, perched on the rock face, the path leading her amongst the tiered terraces that were nestled beneath it and gardens which engulfed the rocks. She felt a little out of her depth searching the medieval stone walls for another person, praying they were female or married. Stopping to look at the view of Marazion and ocean, the sun on her face she closed her eyes – life was good today.

'Esme, innit?' A male said behind her. She turned and it took a moment before she realised who the head gardener was; dirty jeans and a checked shirt with the sleeves rolled up to his elbows, the tousled salt and pepper curls and weathered face.

'Peter?'

'Ah, you remembered.'

'Well, yes, you have a distinctive face.'

'I'll take that as a compliment. You 'ere lookin' or 'elpin'?'

'Oh, err, both. But yes, helping, supposedly. I warn you, I'm no expert.'

'S'alri. I'll be showin yer what t'do. I'll give you a little tour if yer like?'

'Well, Samir has already shown me, thanks.'

There was an awkward silence as she followed Peter to the raised areas. They stopped at a long bed full of aesthetically pleasing planting; succulents that were enlarged and bloomed hard from the continental climate. He was heavy on his feet, getting the feeling he wasn't really a people person. Peter was the very essence of Cornwall, portraying the culture in a traditional manner. She felt odd in his presence, as well as protected. Esme touched the stone on the tiered beds, the lichen giving them an established, weathered look - a bit like Peter, full of story and secrets.

'Sun shines right on this side and don't move 'til evenin,' having to raise his voice over the wind. Esme looked around at the ancient walls that separated the terraces, feeling blessed as they stood on a grassed walkways that were a stone's throw away from the Mount's edge. 'There ain't much to do in winter, but you know about that, don't ya?'

Esme used her hand for a brim, because squinting was unattractive. 'I'm guessing it's just closed because of the weather?'

'Aye. Well, best get on wi'it. Ere y'go,' he handed Esme a Dutch hoe. 'D'you know how to use this?'

She blushed, a little bristled by his manner. 'Yes, my mother had one of these. I guess I'm weeding then?'

'Aye, you got it, maid.'

'Are you always this condescending?'

Peter regarded her with amusement. 'You'll get used to it, that's 'ow we speaks around 'ere. No harm meant.'

'Well, it's not nice and quite chauvinistic! You remind me of my uncle Willy. At least he had a bit a charm with it.'

Peter chortled at her. 'How d'ya 'ave yer tea then?'

'What sort of tea?'

'Just tea.'

'Black, no sugar, please.'

'Right. I'll go get us some from the café. Cake?'

'Mmmm, if they have carrot, uh, gluten free please.'

Peter smirked at this fussy, lively woman in her pink and white linen; ones she will be getting covered in dirt. 'I don't know about nuthin fancy like that. But I'll 'ave a look all the same. Will you be 'appy with a normal one?'

'Oh, yes, of course.'

Peter left her, stomping heavily down the steps that led onto the narrow walkway back to the green and harbour. 'Thanks!' she called out. Peter raised his arm without looking back. She was used to being fetched for, but not by a strapping, obstinate man, unsure whose company she preferred, his or Samir's. It should be the latter for pious reasons. She shook it from her head and wondered what Musa was doing, getting that giddy rush every time she did. How *did* she end up with someone so handsome? Last night was the bond she ached for to repair the damage.

He was sorting out his satellite TV today, hoping with all her heart that there wouldn't be a signal, she hated their channels. It was quite stressful to have it on in the house, forcing them to retreat to different rooms. Esme felt guilty for reacting the way she did but couldn't help it, often blaming herself for being prejudice. It was just so awful, bad acting and sexist tropes. Although since the changes, things were evolving in a controversial way.

She worked through the caked soil, taking the weeds from around the plants, realising she was inappropriately dressed. The sun, waves and sea breeze were therapy alone. Esme stopped for a breather and looked out over the ocean, the dimples and imperfections in the blue vastness lightening in colour as it reached the shore, breathing it all in until her lungs were about to burst. Peter's worn boots could be heard scuffing back over the gravel, the arrival of refreshments was welcome.

'Ere we go. One gluten free carrot cake, will that do?'

'Oh yes, perfect, thank you so much. Excuse my manner earlier. I guess you could say it's my defence.'

'Ri, I see. And one black tea, no sugar. I got us some water, cos we'll be needin' it.' Esme took her plastic bottle and placed it in the shade. 'We'll have a sit down then,' tipping his head towards the seating area that was imbedded into the rocks. Esme sat crossed legged, a gap between them.

'Why you so jumpy?' He asked.

'Hmmm?' Esme was beginning to perspire.

'You, you're jumpy. I ain't gonna give you no trouble. Know that. Okay maid?'

'Oh, yes, of course,' nervously tucking strands of hair back into her hijab.

'How long you been wearin that then?'

'About twenty years,' she answered, taking a bite of her cake.

'That long? What made yer do that then? Yer husband?' Esme looked out to sea before she answered that question again, the annoying assumption that everyone came to.

'No. I met some wonderful people at art college and, well, it all went from there really. Call it, the something I was looking for all my life.'

'I see. Scuze me ignorance.'

'That's ok, I'm used to it. Before I decided to enter into it, I was looking for something to fulfil me, for answers. Why we're here and for what purpose. I tried many fads, cultures but nothing ever felt right, or held substance. There was always something unanswered with incoherent threads that just led you to political wars within doctrines. But then I found Islam, and it all made sense. Do you know much about it?'

'Can't says I do. I knows all about the other ones. Like this place, full of wars and disagreements and funny goings orn.'

'Do you have a religion?'

'Not one that you're familiar with,' he looked away, tipping his head back as he drank the last of the hot, sweet liquid. 'Right then. You finished with yer fussiness?'

'Oh,' Esme investigated her paper cup, 'yes, thanks.'

'Youm done a decent job already. I think I'll keep yas,' he smiled broadly at her, accentuating the crow's feet around his green eyes.

Hassan's class were copying from the white board. It was boring considering he was above the assessment. Since reducing the dosage, he noticed he was able to name objects in Arabic, something he hadn't done before; amused and intrigued at this possible new skill. Today's lesson was accent practice on the Arabic letters, forming the phonetics of the word which changed the meaning. His hand was aching as well as his brain. Samir read the Quran at his desk, soaking up the silence and the occasional scribble of a pencil or restrained cough.

'Uh. Please, sir?' Hassan said with a half raised hand.

'Yes, Hassan?'

'Umm, has anyone told you that you look like Mel Gibson?' There were a few sniggers.

'Who?'

'Mel Gibson, he's a film star.'

'Is he handsome?'

'I, I guess?'

'Then, I take your compliment. Thank you,' the laughs were louder from his acceptance, aghast how Hassan got away with it. Two other boys his age sat together on another table turning to look at him, whispering and pointing. He glared back at them, wishing he could shoot lasers from his eyes. Funny how he was the foreigner when it came to Arabic school, but they didn't know what he was capable of when he got mad.

Layla was with one other girl in another room filling out test papers to assess their level of knowledge. Another female teacher sat at the desk in the same silence, adorned in black. Layla coughed indicating she had finished, pushing the paper to the edge of the table. The teacher acknowledged with a single nod. Why was it so strict and regimented? Her heart was burning, she felt home sick, trapped and undermined. Putting her face in her hands she visualised Porthminster and Akash, smiling against her palms. Her phone vibrated in her pocket, reaching in while keeping a close eye on the Gestapo, she glanced at the phone under her desk. There was a message, she beamed as she clicked on the icon,

'You called?'

'Yes, I'm dying here! This school is suffocating me!'

'Lol. So don't go. My old man is working there today.'

'Oh? The gardener?'

'Yea. Do you like the place though?'

'I guess. It's quite unique. I'd better go in case I'm burnt at the stake!'

'Ok. C ya lata.'

'Layla!' the teacher scolded. She put her phone back in her bag, 'no mobiles in class, haram!' Layla rolled her eyes.

'Are we doing *any* work, at all? I might die of boredom! I've aged 2 years, so technically, I shouldn't really be here.' The other girl went red and held in her laugh, a little infatuated with Layla's boldness.

'Sshh! AstaghfiruAllah!'

'No, seriously, why have we got to be so quiet? We're not doing anything!'

The teacher stood and took the paper from Layla's desk, nonchalantly regarding it.

'Your Arabic… is zero.' Confirming it with her forefinger finger and thumb.

'I've had enough of this.' Layla took her bag and left the classroom, the other girl completely gobsmacked, shaking from the ensuing eruption. She got to the front door expecting it to open, but it was locked.

'Can I help you?' Came a woman's voice from the large reception room.

'Open this door! I want to leave!' Janan appeared in the doorway dressed in a heavy green brocade and hijab, the same charcoaled eyes and bulky jewellery.

'Come, we'll sit and talk,' she said from behind the cloth. Layla was still pulling on the door.

'Let me out, now!' The woman walked up to her, or did she glide? Placing her gloved hand on Layla's arm.

'I know how you feel. Please, come sit, join me for tea.'

Layla became confused, the heavy scent of Oud emanated from Janan, her unusual eyes fixed and mesmerising. 'Please,' she repeated softly. She let go of the handle in a confused state, she couldn't help it, Janan made her feel whole, safe. Leading her by the arm, she pushed her gently into a chair.

'Relax. Your Arabic is good. You are special.' Her voice muffled, like her mouth was full of something.

'My Arabic? But she said...'

Janan shook her head and closed her eyes, tutting. 'No, it is good.'

Layla was suspicious of the silver tea pot on a tray, the steam rising from a pinched spout. Small glasses shone with little silver spoons, finishing off the set.

'Don't let anyone tell you anything else. You are highly intelligent, my child.'

'Child? I'm sixteen.'

Janan tilted her head in apology, 'forgive me, an intelligent young woman.'

Layla was sure she smiled behind the material, pouring the tea with a gloved hand.

'Why do you lock the door?'

'Regulations. Do you like cake?' Her voice becoming clearer, like she was speaking in Layla's head.

'Uh...' she warily looked at the neat parcels of pastry and nuts, the ones she was sick of seeing, '...yes please.' A tear was shed as the anger and resentment subsided, leaving behind a feeling of home. She'd missed that, well at least that's how it felt, like the returning of something long lost – maybe it was acceptance.

'I'm sorry, you know, for behaving like that. But I have a lot of things to hate about it.'

Janan sat opposite her, rattling. Layla was fixated on the gold Hamsa pendant that hung around her neck. 'I understand. It is not your language or culture. It must be strange for you.'

'Yes. It won't let me breathe!'

Janan didn't pour herself any tea or eat the cakes. Layla wanted to see her face; it was getting frustrating only communicating with eyes. There was also the urge sit on her lap and snuggle into her bosom. The tea tasted like hot toothpaste and the cakes were divine, not like the dry, bland ones Musa brings home – these were moist from rose water and marzipan. She propped her head up, feeling drowsy.

'Do you know my father?' She slurred, 'he's abhorrent. Do you know that word?' Narrowing her eyes and waggling her forefinger at Janan, the room spinning behind her.

'I'm sure your father is a good man.'

'He's not!' Her torso swayed, 'he's up to something!' Blinking profusely as her vision doubled. 'I want you to kill him, for, my mother. She doesn't know what to do. So, I think that would be best.'

Janan sneered beneath the brocade. 'That comes at a heavy price.'

'Name it.' Layla hiccupped.

Janan leaned in, almost stretching over the table, 'you get me Solomon's skull!' she breathed.

'Wh, what's that?'

'Or fair babies!' Janan hissed.

'Uh, so, to like, adopt? Sorry, I don't understand.'

Janan sat back, 'are you ready to learn now?'

Layla shook her heavy head, 'why do we have to be so quiet? I mean, this is the twenty first century...'

Janan was concealing her agitation, yet allured by the fire residing in Layla. 'I can see why you think that. Perhaps we should ask the other students what they think.'

'Huh! They're too frigging brainwashed to have their own opinion. Sat there, afraid to speak or move. Breathe! Even. Just so their parents can say, oh my child does so and so and this and that. Living their lives through the poor kids, who, who end up marrying someone they hate, obeying misogynistic orders and spending their lives in the kitchen until they bloody *die* there!'

'Would you like to return to class?'

'Do I have a choice?' her eyes almost closed.

'Good. I'll get you some water.'

Esme and Peter made their way back to the harbour, deep in conversation about the gardens. Two women passed them on the green, dressed in hooded purple cloaks. They acknowledged them, Esme looked behind just catching the embossed Hamsas in the weighted material.

'Who are they?' She asked.

'Theym part o'the Castle.'

'Oh. Like a role play?'

'Summat like that.' Peter took her to the house and left her outside the door. 'Well, I'll be seein' ya soon no doubt. 'Ere or back ome.'

'Yes, I'm sure. Thank you, I've had a lovely day. Pop in the café for a tea, on the house.' Peter nodded his appreciation, alarmed at the number of visitors that were milling around stopping to take photos. She knocked the door three times, and waited. It clicked open, Samir brought Hassan out first.

'Mum!' He rushed to her, hugging and squeezing.

'Hey, have you had a good day?'

'Mmmm,' was all she got.

'He did well for his first day, mash'Allah.'

'Good to hear, what about Layla?'

Samir's face changed, his eyes darting nervously. 'One moment, I'll see if she's ready.'

Esme's face dropped as she was brought to the door. 'Hey, mum.'

'Are you okay?!' Samir handed over her bag.

'She is okay. A little bit tired. Her Arabic is exceptional, mash'Allah.'

Esme raised Layla's chin with her crooked forefinger, checking her eyes. 'Did you take something?!'

'No! They gave me tea!' Layla snatched the bottle of water from Esme's hand, fumbling the top and gulping down what was left. Hassan looking on with a gaping mouth.

'Ok, well, maybe you're a little dehydrated. Thank you doctor, we'll see you Thursday. Uh, inshallah.' Samir sheepishly closed the door.

'Layla! What the *hell*?!' Esme scolded.

'They gave me mint tea! I'm fine, stop fussing!'

'You look stoned!' Esme snatched her bag and tipped it out amongst the feet of scuffling tourists.

'It's that bloody Oud stuff they keep burning in there – it makes you high!'

Hassan gasped, 'you said a bad word.'

'Shut up Harvey! Self-righteous snitch.'

Finding nothing and after sniffing the contents, Esme gave Layla the bag and yanked her to the harbour wall to wait for a boat.

'Oww! Mum! Let go, you're hurting me!'

'Of all the embarrassing, cringe worthy…' they all bumped into a dripping wet surfer amongst the chaos.

'Oops, steady now. You okay, Layla?'

'Kash! But how did you…?'

'I knows shortcuts.' They smirked at one another, Akash giving her a heady buzz when he winked.

'Uh, is someone going to tell me what's going on?!'

'Sorry misses. I'm Akash, Peter's, uh, son,' he held out his wet hand. Esme held the tips of his fingers and shook them gingerly.

'Oh, I see. Are you taking us across?'

'Nope. Just came to see if yous was alri' and see me old man.'

'Right…' Esme put her hands on her hips, shaking her head '…forgive me, but I'm a bit confused. How did you know she was here?'

Akash acknowledged Hassan, 'alri' me boy?' Hassan looked away.

'Ok, look. Thank you, uh, Akash, but we've had a bit of a funny day. She's fine. Now if you'll excuse us, we need to get back.' She pushed passed him getting a wet sleeve, pulling them to catch the amphibious. Layla looked over her shoulder at *her* dream boat. He saluted her, his dark skin glowing in the late sun, but not as bright as her auburn locks.

'You're so rude, mum. Jeez!'

'No one tells baba – got it, Harvey?' Esme let them get into the boat first, 'hello Frank,'

The skipper tipped his captain's hat, 'mind how ye go there.' He wanted to help her in, but Esme didn't want to touch another strange man today, she couldn't wait to get home to wash and pray.

Musa admired the satellite installation from across the road. The taupe polar neck, sleeked hair and Raybans prompting second looks. It was the only dish on the terrace because such an eyesore was only permitted out the back. But he didn't care, he needed a piece of home to maintain what little sanity he had left.

'Thank you, how much for this?' He asked the handyman coming down the ladder.

'Oh, fifty will do. Connections were already there.'

Musa leafed through the wad of notes, handing over eighty pounds. 'Take. I am happy with it.'

The handyman dipped his head in appreciation, tucking the folded notes into the breast pocket of his checked shirt. 'You're not from round ere.'

'I don't understand your accent, forgive me. Again.'

'You, err, not from Britain.'

'Ah, no – I am from the middle east, Saudi.' The handyman found it distracting not being able to make eye contact through the dark glasses, just looking at his own reflection.

'Right. I see. You speak good English though, can't say it's English what I's speak. Bet yous finding it a bit cold ere, then. You plan on stayin?'

'We see. Just for one year, somethink like that.'

'Well, I best be gettin orn. I have the boat t'clean. See you in the harbour ma'be.'

'Okay, thank you mister...?'

'Peter, just Peter. Ri'then. See ya lata.' Musa watched Peter leave, heavy on his feet, distracted by Raffia appearing in her doorway, looking a little slimmer and alluring in her dark red kaftan. Musa acknowledged her, checking up the road with excitement running through his veins and loins. Looking both ways again when he reached her top step, she pulled him in by his polar neck, and closed the door.

Esme cautiously drove into the terrace hoping everyone had forgotten about her enraged exit. That behaviour didn't seem to fit into this environment, whereas back up north the majority drove around like it. They stopped at a coffee shop on the way to Saint Ives to get Layla caffeine before they got home, drinking it in the car.

Idling down Draycott, Hassan grimaced at the satellite, noticing Steve was waiting by his bedroom window.

Esme parked against the wall. 'Great. Looks hideous. Just when I thought he'd turned over a new leaf from those channels.'

Hassan clambered out. 'Sorry, gotta go, can't help with anything. Steve's waiting.'

She helped Layla out who was sobering up after the coffee. 'Oh my God! I don't believe it! The door, I forgot to ask about it, *again!* I'll have to ring my therapist. I'm losing it. Harvey!' He turned, just getting to the front door, agreeing when Esme zipped her lips in his direction.

Esme gave a quick check over what Layla was wearing, it was passable, but who knew what mood Musa was in. Max was eagerly waiting by the front door, singing through his nose and tail almost wagging it clean off.

'Hey baybeee! Did you miss mummeee?' Esme dropped her bag and fussed him, almost knocking her over. 'Yes, I know, such a good boy. Okay, okay. Let me get in.' He went to the children in turn, Layla just tapped him on his head feeling slightly hung over. 'Moose! We're back!' They entered the kitchen and dumped their bags on the table. 'Tea anyone? I'm desperate for some rooibos.' She filled the cream-coloured kettle, casually looking up, dropping the kettle in the sink with a yelp, 'Christ!' Noona the cat was perched on Raffia's wall, looking straight at her. She screamed for Harvey, who nearly fell down the stairs running to his mother's aid. 'Is that the cat?!'

'Yep. That's creepy Noona.'

'Frightened the bloody life outta me!'

'She does that. Look at her eyes.'

'I don't want to.' Esme wrapped her knuckles on the window, 'go on! Shoo! Bloody thing!' The cat looked away but stayed where she was, dosing in the orange glow of the sunset.

'You said two bad words, mum.'

'Oh, shut up, gimp! You're actually getting on my nerves! Self-righteous pain in the arse,' Layla slurred.

'Layla! Filters please! And stop saying that word, I don't think you know what that even means.' Layla just shrugged her shoulders at her mother. 'Brrr!' Esme shivered, 'I didn't see that cat when I went in that time. You were right about one thing, look at the size of it! Fancy living with that!' Max picked up his bowl and was pacing the kitchen with it in his mouth, his claws tip tapping.

'Feed Max will you Layla love. Baba obviously hasn't!'

'As salaam alaikum!' Musa called out as he walked through the front door.

'Wsalaam, love, we're in here!'

He ruffled Hassan's hair. 'How was school?'

'Good.'

'Hamduillah. And you, Layla?'

'Fine,' she replied, holding her breath as she spooned Max's food into his bowl.

'Very good, very good. And what about my beautiful wife? Did she have a good day?'

'I did,' he pecked her on the cheek, 'I helped with the garden. You must come Moose, it's so beautiful. Who put the satellite up?'

'A guy – Peter.' Everyone looked at each other.

'Peter? You sure?'

'Yeah. He told me. Messy guy, old shirt. Fifty somethink age.'

'But...what time did he come?'

Musa checked his Hublot, 'I dunno, 'bout half hour ago, somethink.'

'Must be a different Peter. I was helping a Peter in the garden. He's a lifeguard at the harbour.'

'Yeah, thas him. He said come and see a boat with Hassan.' Esme stared at Musa, frowning, going through travel times in her head. They *did* stop for coffee, so.

'Sur-prise,' he held up two white, plastic bags, 'I brought meat, halal.'

'Oh! Great! Where did you get that? I was beginning to get sick of fish.'

'Raffia. She gets the meat.'

'Hamduillah. We are blessed to have such a good neighbour, although her cat is a bit creepy.' Layla slumped down in the kitchen chair, feeling woozy. Musa inspected her clothes and her luscious locks. He wanted to trap her in a box and throw away the key, holding back the stinging emotion that arose in his gut.

'You look tired, binti,' he said to her.

'Yeah, a bit. I had a good day though, from what I remember. Janan looked after me.' Musa agitatedly tapped the table, looking at Hassan stroking Max.

'Why do you love that animal and not your baba?' He asked.

'I do love you. Max is quiet and understands me,' he answered.

'It's a dog habibi, they don't understand. Just food and sleep.'

'Not Max. He protects us.'

Esme tutted loudly, 'can we *not* get onto this conversation please? You know why we have Max,' placing down the tray of tea.

'Allah protects us and heals us. Not a dog.' Musa responded.

'There's a dog in the Quran,' Hassan said.

'Stop splitting hairs, habibi. Is no one mentioning our Prophets name when they are stressed?' Layla moaned and dragged her hands down her face.

'He's trying to protect us from the door,' Hassan continued.

'What door?'

'The one downstairs, the one we can't open.'

Esme scratched her forehead, 'I forgot to ask. Must have been the kerfuffle this morning and the new start got me in a flap. Please, Moose. They are lovely people, but I want that door open. Max hurt himself trying to get behind it.'

Musa slurped the tea loudly and smacked it with his tongue. 'Just a stupid animal. There is nothink behind it and what's to do with you? Is no problem. What you want it for?'

'Storage. I have unopened boxes and I really can't be bothered to go through them right now. I just want them out of the way. We've bought an expensive house and we can't even get into a room, and that's just downright crazy. If it's not open soon, I'm getting Peter to sort it out.' Musa slammed his fist down making the crockery rise and fall, spilling the contents and triggering nervous systems.

'You will not have a man in the house! Leave the bladdy door alone! That is my final word!' He redressed his hair, huffing. 'Blease habibi, just stop making such fuss. Put boxes in the roof. They will tell us when they are ready.' His voice calming.

Esme and the children went quiet. Layla looked at Hassan and they exchanged the same thoughts, although Layla's suspicions against Janan and Samir had cooled somewhat.

'Fine,' Esme surrendered, 'now, let's get this meat sorted and I'll make us something nice.'

'Can we have roast please, Mum?' Hassan asked, 'we haven't had roast for aaaages.'

'There is no roast, you will have Arab tonight.' Musa stood, touching the top of his head, realising he'd left his Raybans at Raffia's.

15

The Alley

Ibrahim closed the café for the evening, checking the door several times, averting his eyes from the Hamsa that had appeared in the wooden frame ever since the lagoon. He was scared, normality had left, constantly looking over his shoulder and catching fleeting shadows from the corner of his eye. Every move was being monitored. There were shapes and symbols that danced around his mind's eye, visible behind his eyelids, accompanied by erratic whispering. His dreams were lucid, some nights he drifted over the city, others he woke up in a sweat fighting for breath. His body felt heavy, an unrested soul and creased brow, praying for the old life knowing darn well that he was at a point of no return. Awake but still living in the nightmares. One thing he had noticed was the improvement of his vision and mobility, putting it down to the adrenaline that filled his veins and denying it could be anything forbidden.

He stopped outside the shisha bar that sold alcohol after hours, catching himself in the window and not recognising himself. His nerves were frayed, and he needed a relaxant. One drink would calm him. What difference would it make? He was already up to his neck in coercion, guilt wearing him down for going against a trusted instruction.

The proprietor was surprised to see the pious customer. Ibrahim gave a covert nod for his order. Shortly after, a tea glass was placed in front of him, the liquid the same colour as mint tea but smelling quite the opposite, potent. He shivered a little, hesitating before taking the glass and knocking it back, instantly regretting his decision, protesting the taste aloud, coughing and gasping.

'Bismillah!' Called out the staff. He'd stepped into the wrong place, the devil had led him here for sure, that's who was in the reflection – his personalised shaitaan waiting for his downfall and surrender. Ibrahim slid off the stool after three more of the burning liquor, staggering towards the door, watched by the tender.

'Leaving so soon?'

Ibrahim stopped, his hand ready to push the door. 'I have made a mistake!' He strained.

'Three times around?' the proprietor jeered.

'You are devils! All of you!' He swung the door open, slamming it shut on mocking laughter. 'AstaghfiruAllah!' Repeating his pleas for forgiveness, feeling vulnerable and desperate as he made his way home. He began to sob from self pity and shame, wasting his unfaltering faith. Ibrahim looked a mess, his tears drenched his face with a gaping, salivating mouth that dripped on the floor. He could take the humiliation no more and fell to his knees, his palms raised to the heavens, pleading from his heart for his decision to be reversed. Erased. Forgotten.

'Brother? Are you okay?' came a sweet voice from a dark alley. Ibrahim immediately stopped snivelling, wiping his face and mouth.

'Who?!' He whispered. A woman came into the light, timid and clutching her scarf. 'Forgive me sister, I am not in a good state from my own doing. I will be all right, inshallah.'

She came closer, her wide brown eyes full of concern, holding the violet chiffon over her nose and mouth. 'Please, let me help you.' She stepped back when she smelt the alcohol on his breath.

'Sister, go home. I need to compose myself, alone.'

The woman stood half in the light and half in the shadows. 'Come! Come!' She insisted, luring him with a beckoning hand, disappearing into the blackness. Ibrahim checked around, surprised how easy it was to get up, his eyes adjusting in the dark alleyway which was filled with the heady scent of Oud. His hands were on either side as he felt his way, tripping over rubbish and discarded bottles, the trill of crickets ringing in his ears.

'This way, brother!' came her gentle whisper. The darkness ebbed and a hue of lavender and golds were drifting from a doorway where the woman stood. Ibrahim halted, confused, afraid to go any further because it felt like another forbidden endeavour.

'Do not be afraid. Come.' She beckoned him, arousing his senses. He cautiously stepped through a doorway, parting a beaded curtain. The strangest music was playing, familiar instruments but distorted and hypnotising. He entered a Bedouin dwelling draped in sequinned muslin and tapestry. Oud was burning in the centre of a round table, the woman resting on a chaise long.

'Are you not pleased?' She provocatively asked. He laughed nervously, rubbing the back of his neck, 'you have been blessed with youth, dearest brother.'

'Sister, I thought...'

'You thought I was going to give you tea and sympathy? That is not what you asked for.'

'Asked for?' Ibrahim's eyes darted as he tried to make sense of what was happening, feeling sure he was dreaming, like the one he had the other night. 'Thank you for trying to help, but this is not halal. Please, excuse me.' He turned to leave.

'But this is what you asked for,' the woman repeated.

'I don't understand.'

'The lagoon,' she said. His mouth dried and his heart thumped, hastily making his way back out – she appeared in front of him in the blink of an eye, causing a sharp draft. Ibrahim stumbled back, caught by a velour sofa.

'Arrrgghh! Aouthou bileh mina shaitaan a'rajeem! Leave me, devil! Leave me!' Shielding his face.

'I am no devil. I am your consequence,' she levitated, pearls dropping from beneath her billowing violet chiffon, scattering the floor.

'My, consequence? Am I dead?' Ibrahim whimpered.

She descended, running her long-nailed hand down his chest. 'Not yet. I am in gratitude to you for my release,' her Arabic a little hard to understand.

'You! The Jann!' A drumbeat began to quicken, he started to hyperventilate, sweat, the dwelling spun as the music increased in speed. She danced above the table wafting the Oud smoke higher into the draping, elaborate cloth – cackling, revealing a mouth of crowded teeth and large hostile eyes.

'Tell me what else you wish for,' swooning in the plumes.

'Undo this! I want you to undo this! Take me back to my old self. I revoke. I revoke!'

The Jann was in his face before a breath left his dropped jaw, 'it is too late!' she retreated to her spot in the Oud smoke. 'Bring me Solomon's skull, and you will get your wish.'

'I, I don't know what that is!'

'Then bring us Musa's daughter!' She delighted at the fear on his face, it was so delicious.

'What? Never! I revoke! Please! I revoke!'

She snarled at him revealing a terrifying mouth, swirling her arms above her head, the dwelling twisting and dispersing.

'Argh! Help me! Please! BismiAllah!' his vision blurring, Ibrahim passed out.

He awoke the next morning in his bed parched with a swollen frontal lobe, checking he was still in one piece.

'Ha! SubhaanAllah! It was another dream!' He swayed to the kitchen, holding his head. Half an hour left before he had to open the Abadis, time enough to sober.

Waiting for the cafetiere he swilled his face in the kitchen sink, the back of his hands catching his eye, puzzled at the disappearance of liver spots, turning them over and back to make sure. He rushed to the only mirror in the house; slapping his face and pulling at the skin that seemed fuller. 'What in the name of Allah is going on?!' Walking back into the kitchen in a daze, the memories of the night before rushing forth, only he remembered it like a dream. How had he got back home?

After a strong, sweet coffee and pitta bread, the bright sun blinded him as he hastily made his way to the café, but not before checking the alleyway first. The shisha bar was closed, regarding it with disdain, tracing his steps Ibrahim stood on the on the walkway searching the street, no alleyway anywhere. An old man sat on the steps of his barber shop, watching Ibrahim in amusement.

'Salaam, dearest brother.' Ibrahim said, approaching cautiously.

'Brother? Where is your respect? Shouldn't you be calling me uncle?'

Ibrahim touched his face again, checking himself in the window. 'Where is the alleyway? There was one here, last night.'

The old man squinted giving a quiet, condescending chuckle. 'Heavy night, was it? How long ago since you came this way?'

'Last night.'

'Then you dreamt it.' The old man pushed himself up on his walking stick, straightening his frail stature. Ibrahim helped to steady the old man. 'What have you got yourself into, eh?'

'I am not sure. Was there an alleyway, before? Or am I going mad?'

'There was never an alleyway, not in this life. I know who you are, your youthful look confused me. I take it you went to the lagoon?' Ibrahim aided the old man to the doorway, 'you can't make good of it. The acceleration has already begun, and you will be fighting to stay looking like that. That's when they ask you for more, what you can't give unless you completely hand yourself over. Don't do it. Grow old my friend, live eternally with Allah, not the devils.'

The Asian boy sat on the step of the Abadis, regarding Ibrahim with a perplexed expression.

'Uncle?'

'Yes, yes. Inside, *quickly*!' he ushered the boy, checking around and locking the door behind him.

'Where's Uncle? Is he sick?'

'I am uncle. Look!' pushing his face towards the boy who studied him with a frown.

'Did you go to the hamem?'

'No! No hamem. Haha! SubhaanAllah!' he pointed to the ceiling. 'I want to ride a bicycle!' grabbing the boy by the arms, 'do you have a bicycle?'

'No, uncle. Have you been taking vitamins?'

'La! I don't need vitamins anymore! Look at me!'

He began to dance around the café making the boy giggle. 'Go get the special meat from the freezer, we open the door with celebration! But ssshhhh!' His finger on his lips, 'don't tell anyone! Tell them, I am uncle's cousin, understand?' the boy agreed. 'Good boy, now go to the cellar for your uncle, bring the salami and black olives, habibi.'

Ibrahim sang at the top of his voice while he prepared tables for breakfast arrivals. The boy was in the tiny kitchen on his tiptoes trying to reach the key for the cellar, his tongue poking out the side of his mouth. The key unhooked and fell into a dusting of reddish sand that sparkled under the light. He touch it, rubbed it between his fingers, smelt it, closing his eyes at the sweet scent of cinnamon. Licking the tips of his fingers, it was definitely sand, but nothing like he'd seen before.

'How is my helper getting on?' Ibrahim called.

'Uh! Yes, Uncle, I'm coming!' With great concentration the boy forced the key to the right, the 'clunk' jolting him and raising a proud grin. Not able to reach the light pull, he made his way down the steps and into the cold store. It was colder than usual on this morning, a new scent stung his nose, catching his hand on splintered wood as he felt around in the dark, his reaction echoing.

'Bismillah!' Ibrahim called down, 'here, let me get it,' Ibrahim took the steps, finding the boy at the foot of them rubbing his hand. 'Prepare the tables instead. I will bring you a Fanta,' the boy agreed, a little spooked, the fragrant sand still on his tongue.

Ibrahim felt for the light pull, tugging the string the light came on with a *'ptong.'* What it lit up froze him to the spot, calling out in shock.

'Do you need help, uncle?' the boy responded.

'No, no! I tripped, that is all. Go back to your job, hamduillah.' Hand over his mouth, unsure if this was a blessing or curse. Wooden crates, one on top of another, branded with a blurred Hamsa. He inquisitively pulled at the straw poking through the gaps. He lifted the crate, struggling, placing it on the concrete, excitement grew in his stomach as well as uncertainty. Ibrahim felt the contents, hoping it wasn't soft and powdery. The crinkle of brown paper packed with hard lumps brought relief, gingerly smelling through the gaps and jolting away in surprise: pure Oud. Kenan. The rarest in the world. Hundreds of packets worth more than gold just in one crate. He ran his eyes over the others, at least twenty, more! His phone vibrated in his pocket scaring him half to death. It was Musa.

'Salaam,' he said breathlessly.

'Did you receive the delivery, brother?'

'Yes, yes.'

'Good. People will come to you now. Charge them what you like. Congratulations habibi, you are free from debt as my debt to you. Salaam.'

'No! Wait! That's it? Just Oud? Is it fake?'

'Brother, it is not fake, walahi.'

'Illegal?'

'Kenan. Not drugs, ya habibi. They come, they buy, and they go.' Ibrahim's stress levels rose, running his hand over his head.

'The Jann. I, I could be dreaming but, is that part of it? And there's something else...'

Musa laughed daringly, *'The jinn are harmless and no different to those that wander the city at night. Perhaps you are a little dizzy from your discovery?'*

'Perhaps, or maybe I'm going crazy. No, but you're not hearing me...'

'You are sweating brother. I can hear it in your voice. Relax. You are the owner of something precious. Just be careful who you speak to, you only sell, and that's it. Run it how you like. Keep the café, use it as your disguise and clean the money. If any big corporations find out, call me first. Don't forget my forty percent.'

'Of course. How will they know?'

'That is not your concern.'

'What about Hakeem, in the arcade? I don't want any trouble.'

'Hakeem sells a compromise. He will send the ones who request the pure.'

'Understood. I will need a new security system,' Ibrahim panted.

'That is not necessary, it is protected.'

He swallowed and gasped for air, 'Inshallah, forgive me, but there's something else. I...'

'Don't say anything. I understand. Stay vigilant. We will speak soon about the next step, inshallah. Salaam.'

The line went dead.

Ibrahim looked around the cold store and daren't question it any further. His old worries had left him, bringing a set of new ones which heated his blood and increased his heart rate. Breaking one of the wooden slats with his fist, he took out a package, gaging its weight. A kilo, maybe less and at least thirty-six thousand dollars worth. He sniffed the package harder; it was different, earthier and from a different continent. Replacing the package carefully, his mind raced as he took the salami and olives from the refrigerator. About to make his way up, his sandal scuffed the concrete floor: red sand that glittered, covering the surface. He checked above and around for any holes, taking a pinch to rub and sniff. It wasn't Saudi sand, but a sand with scent and wonder. Shaking his head and laughing a little hysterically he brushed it off his hands, distracted by the quantity of crates which meant there was at least a million dollars sitting under his nose.

Climbing the steps with ease, he thanked Allah but felt this blessing did not come from the heavens, vowing to do good with his newfound fortune. With the old man's warning ringing in his head.

16

Foreigner

Musa stayed awake after pre-dawn prayers, he couldn't sleep, Ibrahim sounded unstable, and he feared he would not withstand the change of life. An endeavour that wasn't for the faint of heart.

He had the house to himself while he watched the sunrise from the lounge window, slurping his black coffee after inhaling Oud, and wafting it all over him.

It was too quiet, he liked the hustle and bustle of busy streets, a nightlife that entertained you for hours until first light. Saint Ives was void of any life to him. The residents hid in their houses like hermit crabs, but the elite feel of it was something he did like, apart from the bizarre accent. He fancied fish for lunch, it was on tap and a novelty compared to back home. Musa dressed while the house slept, leaving with a heavy coat and no shades.

He walked the empty streets stopping to admire the little white houses, taking joy from the quaintness of it all. The fierce breeze that rushed through the warrens released the Oud from the fibres, giving him another hit. That was the other thing he liked about alien territory, it made the incense behave differently. The seagulls still made his head hurt, coupled with the residents blatantly staring at him; he looked like a film star in his high-end clothing and cleansed appearance. An elderly couple even stopped to take a longer inspection, discussing him openly. Musa swore in Arabic under his breath, if only they knew how much he would be contributing to their backward village. Give him time, and he would buy the whole place, invading and diversifying to attract the elite. There was a run-down hotel on the front he had his eye on, a little bit of renovation and a hefty nightly rate would soon attract the VIPs, setting a tone for the rest.

Opening the door to the Abadis, it welcomed him with the smell of freshly deposited Oud, giving Musa a shiver. As good as the first cup of caffeine. Checking the floor before unlocking the store cupboard, the dusting of red sand confirming its authenticity. Musa tutted at the clumsy delivery, moving the essential items and restacking the crates to his liking. It wouldn't be long before they would arrive from all corners of the globe to buy the Kenan – subconsciously rubbing his hands together. The Summit was just around the corner and a new property in Dubai was on the cards.

The fishing boats were unloading their baskets and boxes. Restauranteurs hung around for their 'catch of the day', filling Musa with wholesome vibes. It was fresher and cleaner than Riyadh, something he felt detoxing his lungs and an air that made him blissfully tired.

'Good mornink. Beautiful day, eh?' he said to them, full of a good mood.

'Mornen. You ain't from round ere,' the fisherman jeered.

'I'm glad you noticed,' containing his rage at the same damn statement that only came from ignorant people with nothing but wet fish in their heads. The restauranteurs were a little more reserved, giving him an apologetic smile. The lady owner of the Rum and Crab shack, couldn't take her eyes off him as she puffed on her cigarette; covertly wandering. Wealth and mystery oozed from Musa when you were in his company, coupled with that drool-inducing face and its permanent enhancement filter.

'How much for the fish?' he took out his money which changed moods, especially the seafood-shack woman.

'You'll get used to our terrible humour. No 'arm meant. What would sir like today?'

'Give me your best.'

'What did y'have in mind?'

'This, here. What name is this?' he pointed at a white container with neatly stacked silver fish.

'That be me best Bass t'day.'

'Fine, give me six. And this, I'll have this,' pointing to the flat fish. The fisher man bagged up his catch, taking Musa's money without counting it – he could feel he'd been overpaid. He touched the end of his cap in gratitude.

'Come again, you be most welcome. I'll be havin' somethin special on Frydee if youm be gettin' 'ere early.'

Musa sneered at the kissing of ass; a superpower he carried around in his pocket.

He politely pushed passed them, waving the cigarette smoke away from his face. The woman doused it with her wedged sandal, following him.

'Uh, scuse me.' Musa looked over his shoulder, 'don't take any notice of Frank, he's a bit like that. Y'know what old folk are like,' she instantly felt nervous when he stopped to listen, her chest and neck flushing in red patches. 'If you're a visitor in these parts, I'd be happy to show you around sometime, make you feel at home.'

'I live here,' he flatly replied and leaned into her, 'and I will neverrr be happy with you showing me around,' looking her up and down before walking off.

'Oh, ok, bye,' taking a puff, 'stuck up basterd,' she uttered, watching him leave, deeply disappointed.

Musa returned home thinking nothing of the conversation, tutting and swearing when he saw seagull poop all over the windscreen and bonnet of the Range Rover, spotting Steve outside Hassan's bedroom window, shaking his fist.

'I kill you!' taking off his shoes by the door, 'bladdy bird. What are they eating?! SubhaanAllah.' Hearing the mocking laugh. Max came to greet him with bunny.

'Stay away from me, animal!' he scolded in Arabic. Max cowered, placing down his toy gently and tasting nervously, his tail tucked under him. Musa walked passed, Max lay on his back exposing his belly.

'I have fish!' he called out from the kitchen. Max followed him and sat by his empty food bowl. 'What? Why don't you leave me, hmm?' the dog didn't falter, letting out a little 'gruff', breaking Musa's titanium boundary, raising a laugh. 'SubhaanAllah. I don't scare you?' the dog's tail began to wag, brushing the tiled floor. 'You have a good spirit. Or are you my devil only to follow me to my grave?'

Musa put the fish in the fridge, keeping some by for Raffia, preparing himself another coffee. 'You can smile at me animal, but I am not touching your disgusting food.' Max licked his lips as the smell of raw fish hit his nose. 'You need bones, kalb, eh?' side eyeing him.

'Oh! Good morning. Did you wet the bed?' Esme came in wearing her pink chemise, putting her arms around his waist, snuggling into his beautiful back.

'AstaghfiruAllah. Why do you speak like that? I bought fish for you, habibi.'

'Oh, from whom?'

'Frank, on the harbour.'

'Frank? What did he look like?'

'Old man, hat.'

'Everybody has the same name around here. What else you been up to?'

'I watch the sunrise.'

'Without me? Why didn't you wake me?'

'I wanted to be alone. To think. Give your animal its food before he makes me sick.'

'You smell amazing,' she breathed in the back of his polo neck, getting a nose-full of musk oil and Oud, 'you're addicted to that stuff. The kids are still asleep,' she provocatively stated. He turned to face her, brushing the fire-red hair away from her face, those light freckles were more visible in the morning and her skin looked refreshed. He could see that Saint Ives had brought back a spark. Musa pulled her in tighter, the chemise rising over her buttocks, lifting her chin to his lips. Max's head tilted from side to side as he watched them, letting out a hungry whimper.

'Back room,' Musa demanded. She led him there by his hand. They did it in a heated mess on the desk amongst Esme's paints and canvasses, getting magenta acrylic all over them. Holding in their ecstasy and nearly bursting from the containment because Hassan would be the one who asked unfiltered questions at the breakfast table. Reaching hedonistic climax together, they were both astonished at the intensity of it, reliving their secret rend de vous from college.

Laying on the floor looking at the ceiling rose, their rib cages heaving, Esme let out a giggle. 'Oh my god, Moose!'

Musa could hardly stand, 'you killed me, habibi.' He kissed her all over her exposed, milky skin and was anxious to shower, holding his trousers up as he opened the door, checking for children – nearly falling over Max who was laying right outside.

Esme stayed, woozy and daydreaming at the patterns on the ceiling. This was their big break. Their surroundings faded and it was just them, here, Saint Ives was a dream, her dream. A compensation. Max came in and licked her face, smelling her body.

'Eck! Max! No, out,' she stood, dizzy, steading herself on the desk noticing the paint on her hands, arms and everywhere else, letting out an almighty shriek when she saw Noona sat on the windowsill, looking in. Esme had her hand over her heart grimacing at the thought that it had been sat there the whole time. The large cat held its piercing gaze, filling the windowpane.

'What is wrong with that cat?! Shoo! Go on! Max, get him!' but the dog just whined, staying back, fearing to go anywhere near the window. She waved her arms around shouting at it, banging on the window, and the cat left.

Feeding Max in a daze, the emotional release had made her hungry and itching to paint the colours from her orgasm on the biggest canvas she could find.

'Hello, sister.'

'Oh! Jesus Christ! Raffia! Sorry, I didn't hear you knock,' reaching for a tea towel to cover her breasts. Raffia clattered and banged about in the under stairs cupboard, Max sniffing her legs and the back of her dress.

'I clean bathroom.'

'Well, Musa is in there, so just do the others and don't wake the kids please.'

'What about back room?'

'Uhhh! No it's fine. I've made a bit of a mess in there with my painting, look at the state of me! I'll do that, it's fine. Thank you.' She caught Raffia looking at the paint all over her, making a strange scowling noise. Max followed her to the stairs, intrigued with her feet.

17

The Chapel

Esme and Layla considered the brightly coloured flyers placed around the town. Saint Ives was hosting an autumn equinox beach party, the town decorated with bunting and string lights, Layla eager to experience the night.

'Can we go mum, please?'

'Not if there's alcohol.'

'We'll sit somewhere else. Come on, please? You can drop a few hints, talk about your art stuff.'

'Hmm, well, I'll have to ask baba.'

Layla huffed, looking out for Akash. He'd been quiet recently, perhaps from Esme's hostility at the school. They window shopped, stopping to take a longer look at the private galleries and their artistic expressions of the bay.

'Mornin ladies.'

'Oh! Peter! You startled me.'

'You comin' t'the beach party then?'

'Well, I'm not sure. You?'

'Yep. I'll be keeping an eye on the midnight swimmers. It be a lovely night, if yer comin. Not much drinkin' goes orn, if that's what's making yer indecisive.'

'Okay, we'll think about it. We're back at the school tomorrow...err, are you going?'

'Aye. Ere, you seen the chapel o'er the other side yet?'

'Not yet. Although I have been admiring it from the window. I mean, I saw it a million times when I was a kid, but I'm a little curious. We were making our way to the Tate, actually.'

Layla did not want to visit the art gallery but being with her mother was all she wanted today, as well as finding Akash. Her fatigued state meant she was unable to 'call' him, the tea from Janan made her permanently lightheaded and she was just drifting through existence, her intuition blocked.

'I'll take yer t'the chapel now if y'like? Cure yer curiosity.'

'That's kind of you Peter, thanks. Layla, you coming?'

'Uh, nah – I'll head back home I think.'

'Ok well, don't get lost, or something.'

Layla regarded Peter and was desperate to ask him where his son was.

'If yer lookin' f'Kash – he be in the lifeboat station,' he smirked. Layla flushed scarlet.

Esme and Peter walked to the chapel in awkward silence. She admired the hanging baskets on the cast iron streetlamps that overflowed with surfinias and lobelia, topped off with small cordylines. Peter stopped at a large sculpture, large enough to look through.

'D'ya know what this is?'

'Barbara Hepworth, isn't it?'

'It be that alright. Youm knows y'onions maid, don't you?'

'Well, I read up on a lot before I came. Didn't want to be seen as the ignorant Emmet. It's changed so much here.'

Peter laughed with delight. 'There's a garden with all her sculptures on display among the herbaceous, if you'd like to go?'

'That sounds wonderful. Are you asking me out, Peter?'

'No, I knows yous got a fella who'll 'ave me guts for garters if I did.'

Esme touched the bronze artwork, biting down on a huge grin. 'So, it was you who came to fix the satellite?'

'Ma'be.'

'My uncle called me maid. Sounds old fashioned now.'

'That's cos I am. Now, come on, cos you'll need your time to get yerself ready for lata.'

'Can we skip the Tate and just go straight to the chapel? I wouldn't want to bore you.'

'It ain't boring, just better to admire nature's artwork outside, thas all.'

They walked single file through the narrow streets with comical names – one called 'Teetotal Street', a sign Esme laughed loudly at. 'Maybe we should have bought a house here!'

'These be two up, two down. No room for no people, just keep y'cat in there, thas all they be good fer. Can't be avin no babies or nuthin,' his voice bouncing off the cottages that were almost meeting in the middle.

'Do you live close, Peter?'

'Aye. I'll show ya one day. But we need to get t'this bloomin chapel before he closes!'

She hurried along in little trots to keep up with Peter's stride, not knowing where to look first. Little painted stable doors and their nautical items that adorned the fronts of the whitewashed granite.

The wind blew the sand in their face when they reached the end of the warrens.

'It be a bit windier up this end!' Peter called out over his shoulder. Back in the light, they had discovered another beach. The atmosphere changed at this end of the town, it seemed a little hostile and barren. Holiday lets and apartments spoilt the look of the place. They reached what looked like a miniature version of the Mount; large expanse of green that covered the rocks which elevated the chapel overlooking the Tate and dog beach. The grey and white construction stuck out like a sore thumb.

'People weren't too happy 'bout it, but it's our legacy. That be the beach you can bring y'dog.' The wind picked up and roared around their ears, Esme quite smug about having hers covered in a floral scarf. She followed him to a narrow, sandy path that seemed never ending.

'He'll love it. Have you met my Max?'

'Aye,' Peter tipped his imaginary hat at one of the station masters as they approached the lookout station.

'Caught you! You did fix the satellite!'

'Not necessarily.'

'You're just playing with me now.' Esme had a good look at all the aerials and masts attached to the small, glassed tower. 'What do they look out for? Boats? People? Both?'

'Mostly. There been quite a few tragedies on them rocks when the wind d'pick up in winter. Your queen pulled the lookouts from her institution, didn't want the blood on er 'ands. Leaving us to keep em gowin us selves. We rely on the locals now, is them that keeps the lookouts gowin now.'

They trod the incline leading them to the chapel, the wind pushing them off balance. It was just a small building with stone benches either side of the door for gazing at the vast blue, the shelter welcome from the bluster.

Dead flowers sat in a clay pot on a dusty granite windowsill with three bibles stacked at its side. There was hardly enough room to swing a cat, let alone congregate.

'What did you say this was used for?' Esme whispered, conscious of the obligatory respect required.

'Depends what era we talkin,' Peter bellowed.

'Well, any era. You couldn't exactly sit in here, you wouldn't fit! I must say, it's smaller than I remember. Guess I was smaller then, I suppose.'

'This is our look out. Call it f'smugglers, lawst boats, lawst swimmers with no bleedin sense.'

Peter studied Esme as she touched the stone fireplace, flinching at the webs.

'Enough touchin. Come see this,' he stepped outside looking out to sea with his hands in his pockets – Esme stood next to him, closing her eyes and inhaling the perfect air through her nose.

'What can y'see?' he asked.

'Beauty,' puffing out the held breath, 'and that sea looks like it would take anything without mercy.'

'Aye, that be true. What else?'

'Well, that way, the surfers and what's left of the tourists.'

'Bloody 'ell. Not that way! This way! Straight out there!'

'Uh, is this a trick question? Something metaphorical?'

'Look,' Peter raised his chin, 'out there.'

Esme squinted, leaning forward. 'Oh, seals! I can see seals! Haha! You have to really look, don't you?'

'Them ain't seals,' Peter said, and walked ahead to lean on the surrounding wall. She strained even harder to see what the dark dots were on the horizon. Peter had gone silent, reflective. She felt his vibe change, uncomfortable in his company.

'Well, look, we'd better be getting back – I appreciate you bringing me, Peter. It was a privilege.' She picked at her hands. Musa wouldn't be pleased with what she'd done.

'I'm sorry maid. Don't take n'notice o'me. Didn't mean to get all uppity at yas. I brought you 'ere cos youm a believer. Ain't many o'them about anymore. I don't wanna be frightnen yous or nuthin, but they ain't seals or dolphins. Maybe you want t'be goin back t'yer books.' He turned to leave, a touch melancholic.

'Peter, wait! What do you mean by that?' Peter carried on, the romance of Saint Ives had momentarily left, and she really didn't like it down this end; it had triggered all she'd buried deep. Tears emerged and she could no longer control it, her anxiety resurfacing, tapping as she tried to keep up.

'Please! Tell me!' Her voice quivered, 'you know what, just take me back.'

Peter turned, 'thas where we's going, don't fret maid. Youm making too much fuss.'

'Don't be such a dinosaur! You're scaring me and are not even appreciating that! How could you? I trusted coming out here with you! You wait until Musa hears about this! I shouldn't have come.'

Peter blocked her way. 'I ain't tryin' t'frighten yer! I was hoping you would know what I's talkin bout! And your fella hasn't got enough meat on im to pick a fight wi'me!' he chuckled at the idle warning. 'You need 'elp with them nerves o'yours. I know just the thing.'

'What?!'

'You ever had Reiki done before?'

Esme tucked the stray strands of hair back in the floral scarf, composing herself as the negative energy of the chapel left. 'No. It's forbidden.'

'You sure bout that? Sounds like you can't do nuthin much. Thas why youm walkin about with a po-face. It's taken y'spirit away.'

There it was, the something she'd lost but couldn't quite put her finger on what.

'Wass a matter? Hit a nerve, 'ave I?'

'Something like that,' she mumbled, looking down at her sand-covered toes. 'Where can I get it done?'

'I'll do it,' he replied.

Esme pulled a face, 'is there anything you don't do?'

'Aye. I don't take maids t'the chapel unless there's good blimmin reason!'

18

Crow Street

Esme had been mulling over Peter's offer of therapy in the washing up. She felt she should go, but the overthinking was stopping her. Anything had to be better than the compressed powder of artificial serotonin.

Raffia was banging and crashing about in the cupboard under the stairs again, causing a headache and testing Esme's tolerance. It was decided, wiping her hands on the waffle tea towel.

'I'm just popping to the shops Raffia. Taking Layla with me. Can you keep an eye on Hassan and Max for me please?'

'Naam. You go, is fine.'

'Shookran, Raffia. I won't be long, inshallah.' She tilted her head towards the front door at Layla, them both sneaking out with Raffia giving them a hard stare.

'What am I going to do?' Layla asked as they walked into town, Esme's nerves burning a hole in her stomach.

'Just sit there, and watch.'

'Err! And what if I don't want to?'

'I'm having Reiki done, not a massage!'

'Yeah, but he still has to, y'know, touch you.'

'We'll see. I feel compelled to go. Just drag me outta there if anything sus happens.'

Number three, Crow Street was a stone's throw away from Tee Total street. The cottages all had stable doors and beautifully adorned window boxes filled with annuals, but not Peter's. His were full of dead things and collected shells, with a Crow skull on the door.

'Eww. That's not creepy at all.' Layla grimaced, as Esme gingerly knocked the top half of the door. It rattled rather than knocked. She straightened herself, the fizzing in her veins pushing her to run. The pulling of a bolt made them both jump and stand rigid as the whole door was opened. The sting of something hitting their noses, Layla unable to hide her disgust.

'Oh, two of yas, is it?'

'Well, uh, no, just me,' Esme answered, her words stuck on a dried tongue.

'Ri. Fine. Come on in then.' Holding the door as they both entered, Layla ducking waiting for something to drop from the ceiling.

It was quite neat and simple inside, surprisingly tidy. Bijou. Smelt like pollock had been boiling on the stove for a month, with undertones of detergent.

'What made yer change yer mind then?' he asked, stuffing little areas of mess into drawers.

'Raffia. Well, not directly, just her clattering about this morning. Must have triggered something. Look, Peter, I'm keeping my clothes on, so...'

He laughed out loud, 'this ain't no parlour I'll have you know. Yous make I laugh, maid. I'll give yer that.'

Esme adjusted herself. 'Right, okay. I'm just making things clear.'

'Aye, you've made yerself quite clear. I could say I'm offended, but then I don't get in a such a way. Right then. Sit 'ere and put yer feet up on this ere footstool.' Pointing to an antique chair which was a little frayed where Peter's hands had settled. Esme sat in the chair, the springs in the seat grinding as her weight squeezed them, wiping her palms on her thighs. 'Relax, maid. I ain't gonna touch yer. Kay?' Esme jiggled her head, a little relieved. 'Ri. Close yer eyes then.'

'Why am I closing my eyes?'

'Yer need t'see inside.' She reluctantly closed them, exhaling, surrendering and trusting the calling. Layla was invested when Peter stood behind the chair, his hands above her mother's head before entering a trance, it wasn't visible what was going on. For what began, began on the inside.

The stresses left her like ashes released in the wind. Esme's face twitched as Peter moved around her, pulling an invisible yarn from her torso and throwing it over his left shoulder. Tingling her feet and hands, her head light and buzzing, all that was buried burst forth. The surroundings became muted and she was floating above the chair, looking down on herself. Flashes of images on Porthminster beach started building into watchable memories. Marmaduke, the small bear she bought from the gift shop, clutched in her hand. She was about four or five, looking up at her guardian; too tall to be her mother. Then the images were shifted to the sea. The moving tide passed her eyes, she was swimming, holding onto her lilo and kicking to push her further out; pearls clutched in her fist. She heard her mother calling, turning her head with a deepened frown, feeling panic and abandonment.

'What's happening?' Layla asked. Peter didn't answer as he continued to 'pull' from her feet. Esme was becoming agitated, her breathing increasing. She flinched when she felt something touch her foot in the water. Letting the lilo go, she watched it float ahead, terrified when she felt nothing beneath her feet. She tried her best to turn and head for the shore, her mother decreasing in size as she waved her arms about, calling her daughter's name. It was a frustrating dream, one she recognised, a recurring one that would upset her for the rest of the day.

It went quiet. Just the lapping of waves around her ears, choking when something large took her waist with vigour, propelling her forward like a torpedo. Her belly was on the sand before she could blink. Emmets gathered around her, their voices muffled and in slow motion, moving aside for a figure that approached, the sun blinding her when she turned to look. Ringing in her ears ensued as she looked through her fingers at the person who carried her. She knew who it was, a fierce love in her gut told her so.

Peter's pager 'buzzed', dropping her down into the seat, Layla's yelp awakening them all.

'Damn thing!' Peter cursed, 'just when we's were getting to the good part.' Esme had landed with a bump, wanting to return to the inner peace. She scanned the room in a daze, Layla regarding her with wide eyes.

'You alri, maid?' Peter asked, clipping the pager back on his jeans belt. 'Saved by the bell, eh? I have t'go, rescue. How you feelin?'

Esme rubbed her face, 'uh, I…' her head span as she rose from her seat. Peter's face with an unassuming expression.

'Steady now, maid. Have a glass o'water before ye go. I best be arf. Make sure you come t'the beach party. Kay? Leave the door open.' He bid a farewell, and fled.

'Why is he like that?' Layla asked, making sure he'd gone.

'Like what?'

'A bloody ironing board!' Esme swayed, holding her head, 'Mum! You okay?'

'I, I think so.' Checking the room, grabbing Layla's arm.

'Do you feel better?'

'I, I guess I do.' Her frown deepened, 'I had the strangest dream...'

'Dream?'

'How long was I under?'

Layla shook her head while she tried to calculate time, 'fifteen, twenty minutes, something like that. It was weird as! I felt like I was sat in a booth watching you! Did you hear the crows?'

Esme snorted a laugh as her conscience began to brighten.

'There are no crows near the sea.'

'Well, there were just now! I heard them on the roof!'

Esme patted Layla's shoulder, a condescending laugh escaping as she reached down for her bag.

'I guess I'll have to pay him later. Whoosh! I feel like I've smoked a joint.'

'Oh my God. I never thought I'd see the day where my self righteous mother was stoned.'

'Uh, excuse me young lady! I'm not stoned! I'm just, well, happy. Free. It'll be short lived once we get back.'

'Christ. Don't let baba hear you say that.'

They left Crow street, giggling, daringly talking about Peter's physique and comparing him to Musa. Their derogatory comments causing them to cackle as they held each other up, staggering over the cobbles from cramped bellies. It had been a bizarre moment, a moment that had unpicked a badly fastened seal.

19

The Portrait

Thursday night and Musa wasn't going to the beach party, but he gave them all permission to go, much to their astonishment.

They arrived at Porthminster, Esme's favourite beach and the main one everyone went to. There was a bonfire set up for nightfall. The café with the balcony would be staying open throughout the night for the adults, and the beach shack was serving soft drinks and party goodies for the children. Hassan spotted a boy the same age and made his way over to hopefully start a new friendship. Layla's stomach churned as she looked for Akash – he wasn't where Peter said he was earlier, and her lovesickness was getting the better of her.

'What's the matter love?'

'Oh, nothing. Just feel a bit off.'

Esme checked her temperature. 'Look, I don't agree with what you're doing. Just forget about this boy, okay? It'll do you no good in the end. He's just stringing you along. You're not much of an excitement anymore now he knows you live here.'

'That's not true. Something's going on, Mum. I don't feel so good after that tea. I feel, well, kinda strange, weird. Witchy weird. What's going on? Tell me.'

'I don't know what you're talking about. Nothing's going on. You've had a bit too much sun.'

Layla wasn't convinced, she knew her mother was completely oblivious. 'I like your new painting by the way, Mum. Bit garish for you.'

Esme blushed and nearly choked, she picked the biggest canvass she could find using up her old purple and gold acrylics, and the squished magenta.

Peter was staffing the lifeguard lookout – raising his hand when he spotted Esme, she waved and nudged Layla.

'I think you'll find Akash is up there.' With that he appeared next to Peter. Layla's heart leapt when he beckoned her to join him, but she didn't go, turning her back and sulking with her bottle of Pepsi.

'That's my girl,' Esme said from the corner of her mouth, clinking their bottles. A rush of joy ran through them at their slither of permissible freedom, they were getting drunk on the very idea of it.

'How come baba let us go?'

'Let's not question it. I hope Max will be okay. He'll be pining for any sort of affection when we get back. Where's Harvey got to?'

'Evenin' ladies.' Akash had made his way down, not to be out done. Still in shorts and open blue shirt, but the scent that came with him immediately softened Layla's sulk. Esme got a flutter from his golden presence and that amazing smell. It wasn't a cologne, more of his own pheromone.

'Hello Akash. Are you helping Peter with the lookout tonight?' Esme asked.

'Yeh. Call me Kash, everyone else does.'

'Oh, I quite like the full version.'

'You alri' then, Layla?' He asked.

'Spose. Where have you been hiding?' he didn't want to answer in front of her mother so tried again to pull her away. Esme knew she would be safe somehow, there was a profound sense of protection that emanated from him, and she had no hesitation in letting her go. Better to be with him than a bad influence. Unless they were vaping behind her back.

Alone with her thoughts and bottle of Purdey's, a couple approached her she recognised from one of her favourite shops.

'Would you like a seat m'love?' they asked her, offering her a fold-up chair.

'Oh, yes, thank you. I didn't think to bring one.'

'Sand gets a bit cold after dark and you'll be wanting a good spot by the fire later.' Their accents weren't as broad as Peter's, they may even have been from a different area.

'Welcome to Saint Ives.' The woman said, happy with her life.

'Thank you.'

'Bill and Margaret,' the woman announced, 'we've been here 20 years and it was the best decision we ever made. Not from here originally, of course.' They all unfolded their chairs and sat facing the shore. 'I can tell you're not a local.'

'No, north England. Chester.'

'Oh, we're from Chester! Fancy that?'

'No way? What made you come here?'

'Well, same reason as you and everyone else. We came here for a holiday and that was that. Chance came up to buy the shop and we ended up staying. It's like our own little secret world, don't you think?'

'Yes, I do. I was hoping to open a gallery as well. I know there are many, but that's my dream.'

'Oh, there's never too many of those. You never know, there's always places to let. Might just be your lucky break coming here. I know a place that's about to become vacant. I'll let you know when.' Only the woman spoke, the husband occasionally mumbled an agreement, supping his organic beer.

'We've had a lovely coffee and cake in your café, too. Didn't we Bill?' him grunting a response.

'Mum! Mum!' Hassan came blundering over with his new friend, a couple of years younger, kicking up sand behind him. 'This is Jack, and he lives here too! And he likes Marvel! We're playing over there, on the decking!'

'Oh, that's great. Hello Jack,' Esme gave the shy boy a little wave. Hassan liked them like that, the mature ones always made fun because he still played with his imagination, feeling there was something underlying with that.

'There's burgers and hot dogs!'

'Well, you know we can't have those. Is there anything vegetarian?'

'I'll go check. Come on Jack!'

'And check for nuts!! Harvey!'

'Kayyy, mum!'

'Aww, does he have allergies?' Margaret asked.

'Yes. The bane of my life! I feel like I'm constantly trying to keep him alive in a mine field!'

'Having kids be like that anyway. That's awful for you, love. How stressful that must be.'

Esme wiped away a tear. 'Yes, it is. We've spent many a night in emergency, trying to fight with the onset of a fatal reaction.'

She hadn't talked about it with anyone, Musa just hid away from it. Layla was still a bit sensitive to dairy, but Hassan's allergies were the serious ones. Saudi trips were highly stressful, checking what was in the food and being on high alert the whole time. She often gave in to not being in control of her son's life, but the instinct wouldn't allow her to surrender.

It was tiring, having perfected blocking the onslaught of anaphylactic shocks by various methods; one was getting him to jump up and down on the spot to create his own adrenaline, while she quietly died inside.

The spray from crashing waves tingled their windswept faces. Esme was looking out and thinking about the chapel and Peter. She was confused what she was supposed to know. There were traditions in Islam she passionately believed in, but Musa would never elaborate or hold conversations about the concealed, even though there were revelations about other life forms. He had instilled a fear of being cursed should she even utter a word about them, curtailing her curiosity in researching it any further. The Jinn. She wasn't even allowed to say it. She often would when he was away, just to get it out of her system. But something had shifted since the Reiki, the crippling and pointless anxiety hadn't paid a visit since. Perhaps it just straightened things out, got rid of some broken toys from the subconscious.

As the sun got swallowed by the sea, everyone took out an extra item of clothing. The music was switched on and the veggie kebabs and barbequed sea bass were coming thick and fast. Others retreated to the restaurant balcony to watch from above, dining on scallops and crisp white wine. Peter came and stood with his back to the shore, his arms aloft to grab their attention.

'Thank y'all for comin! There's plenty o'food for everyone, just 'elp y'selves. May these celebrations continue f'many years to come and may we all b'grateful for the gifts and treasures we're given, and for our protection.'

They all cheered and raised their glasses, some calling out an 'Amen'. Esme raised her Purdey's a little perplexed as to whom or what they were thanking, making up her own mind that it was God, giving her own thanks, 'hamduillah' she mouthed and became teary-eyed from her supplications.

'Kash! Time to light the fire!' he came holding a medieval torch in the air with Layla at his side, lowering it to light the bottom of a large pile of driftwood. Esme regarded the ceremony suspiciously.

'I declare this equinox party – open!'

There were '*ooohs*!' and '*ahhs*' as the whole lot went up in a whooshing blaze. The flames a symbolic beacon that could be seen far out to sea, their faces burning as they became mesmerised by the dance of the orange and yellow spirits.

'I love fires,' Esme said, unable to take her eyes of it.

'Me too,' muttered the woman, 'makes you feel primitive.' Her husband agreeing, the flames reflecting in his bifocals. Peter clapped his hands, snapping the three of them out of their daze.

''Ave you 'ad plenty t'eat you folks?' everyone hummed a yes, nodding sluggishly. 'Esme?'

'Err, sorry to sound rude, but I'm a bit sick of fish and vegetables, thanks. This is fine for now,' holding up her Purdey's.

'More of that then?' pointing at her bottle that was falling from her grip. She studied the contents.

'What's in this stuff?' she strained to read the ingredients, holding it out at different lengths. 'I've had these before. Must have been that wind earlier, I feel so sleepy,' she yawned.

'Party's only just started! Come on. I'll take y'for a walk in the town. Clear y'head.'

'What about the kids?'

'They be alri. We won't be larng.'

'Oh, don't worry, Bill and I will watch out for them. You go. Town is a different place at night.' Margaret offered. Yes, she remembered. The town at night would bring back the memories of illuminated gift buying. Just the best feeling, especially when whimsies were concealed in patterned paper bags.

'Thank you. I have my phone with me, just call.' Esme called out to Hassan and Layla, but they hardly noticed.

They trudged through the sand to the stone steps that brought you out by the hotel Esme had her high hopes about. The lane was full of people going back to their holiday stays or returning to experience the night life; brushed up with glowing faces. There were no all-night brawls or drunken tourists spilling out of bars, but rather civilised gatherings and milling around the bespoke shops and galleries. Black gloss fronted vegetarian delis selling organic skewers and pasti au specialè, but Esme spotted a Turkish kebab house.

'Oh! Is that place halal?' Esme looked for the sticker on the window and stuck her head in the door.

'Asalaamu alaikum!'

The owner and staff delighted to hear it, answering her appropriately.

'Welcome sister, welcome.'

'I'm guessing this is halal?'

'Of course! Come, come. You choose what you like, is free for you tonight.'

'Peter, are you having anything?' he raised his hand in refusal, having his fill of sea bass. Esme left with chicken shish salad wrap, in raptures as she picked out the seared meat from the folded homemade bread.

'Mmmm! This is delicious! You don't know what you're missing, Peter.' Esme ate as they walked. The air, the night, the people, all adding to her culinary experience and filling of an empty stomach. 'I don't remember seeing that place before,' she said through bread and meat.

'It all looks the same when you're an Emmet,' he nudged her. They had to weave through oncoming people traffic, dodging the cars that crawled through the narrow streets. Artists were still painting, selling their complete works of art from the day before. Esme noticed there was a theme running through the galleries tonight – instead of displaying creations of the bay or moored boats, the paintings had changed to mermaids and sea nymphs. Others were quite unorthodox with entwining sea spirits in intricate detail. Purples, lilacs, aqua and emeralds with the white spray of the waves and murky blue of deep water. Peter stood next to her while she got lost in a window, swaying with the brush strokes that spoke to her; she was sure they were moving. Sea chanties were playing everywhere, and Esme was feeling light and contently aroused.

'Like that one then, do ye?'

'Aren't they just *incredible*? Puts me to shame, that's for sure.'

'Have to grab em quick, cos they be gone by tomorra. You got silver in y'purse?'

'Silver? Oh, yes. We call them debit cards, Peter. Honestly, you're such a dinosaur. Can you hold this, while I go in, please?' she handed him her half-eaten kebab.

'After yous, miss.' Peter offered her the open door to the gallery, propped open by an amethyst stone. Some paintings were hung, others drying on easels. The owner briefly looked at Esme and continued with their current project, making her feel comfortable to browse at leisure. Peter hovered by the door, checking over his shoulder now and then. The artist rinsed a brush in the glass jar beside her, wiping it on a grubby cloth, watching Esme swoon over the impressions.

'Can I help you with anything?' she asked.

'Oh, I'm finding it hard to choose. These are absolutely beautiful! They speak!'

'Thank you. I'm guessing you paint?'

'Uh, yes. Just getting back into the swing of it.' Esme's imposter syndrome began to squish her into the floor, who was *she* kidding? Opening a gallery with paintings of her orgasms.

'Forgive me for making an assumption...' the artist turned an easel to face her, '...but is this to your liking?' A portrait of a Marid painted in a rich green, almost black, a muscular male with wavy hair flowing like seaweed, about to break the surface. There was something melancholic about the figure, vulnerable and provocative. So life-like from the fine detail.

'Oh my gosh!' Esme looked at Peter, his face and eyes twinkling, 'yes, I mean, yes! How did you know? It's, oh...!' she held the canvass, and the rest of the paintings were of no further interest.

'Can you keep it for me? We're just having a walk and I don't want to ruin it.'

'Sure, or I can have it delivered.'

'That would be great. Thank you.' Esme was feeling overwhelmed from her gift she was about to buy herself. The artist gave her a piece of paper to write down her address, discretely putting the price on the top left corner. Esme handed her debit card over with no further thought.

'Y'know, you don't have to paint like everyone else. Be unique, your work will be appreciated here.' She gave Esme a written receipt, her motivation renewed.

'Thank you, I appreciate it. I needed to hear that.'

'Sure, so do I sometimes.'

'Well, thanks again. When can I expect it?'

'It will be there when you get back, just don't let it rain.'

'Right. Okay. Bye, see you again, thanks!'

Esme left the shop in a magical mood. Night was drawing close, and the golden lights and purple hues lifted Esme's soul.

'Appy now?'

'Completely. That was just awesome, thank you for bringing me.'

'S'alri' maid. Nice to see you 'appy for a change. 'Ere, finish y'grub.'

'Well, I suppose you're forgiven. Is that what we saw?'

'What d'ya mean?'

'Today, at the chapel when you were horrible to me. The painting. I was *drawn* to it. She *knew* that was for me, how could she? Is this whole night something to do with that?'

'Ma'be.'

'I wish you'd stop saying that and treating me like a child! You hurt me today, I needed that purchase to fizzle out the bad feeling the chapel gave me. I shouldn't even be coming here with you. Do you understand that? Musa will make things difficult for me if he finds out and I don't want to have to deal with him in a bad mood.'

'Everythin is bloody forbidden,' Peter snubbed.

'I want to be clear Peter, there's nothing between us but professional conduct.' There was another awkward silence, wiping her hands and mouth with a serviette.

'Don't flatter y'self, maid. I'm just lookin' out f'yas.'

'But why? Since when has that been your duty?'

'Thas how it tis. Ain't no man in control of n'body. Stupid rules for insecure egos. Tis all.'

'Well, thank you. But there's no need, really,' she looked at her watch to deter the subject, 'gosh! Is that the time? We should be getting back to the bay. Fancy a coffee before we head back?'

Peter tutted and pushed her along by her elbow. Reaching the harbour, the waves lapped the rocks, boats bobbed ringing out their bells in haunting, single chimes. The dark water in the distance shimmered from the moon's reflection, twinkling like diamonds on the surface. There were no limits or barriers, Esme's head was filling with ideas, expanding and flexing after being starved of creativity.

The Abadis was busy, Suzie rushed off her feet. Max surprised them with a bark when he saw them.

'Hey baybee! Why are you here?' he greeted them both with enthusiasm. They sat close to the barrier, a little chilled. Suzie came out with her small writing pad and shrinking pencil, a tad disgruntled.

'Be nice if y'came t'elp this evening!'

'I know, I'm sorry Suze, but Peter kindly invited us to the party. Did the help arrive?'

'Yeah, and thank 'eavens they did! Right, what'll you be 'avin?' she jotted down their order for two cappuccinos, Max glued to Esme.

'I was thinking. Why have late night anything on a Thursday? It's always on a Thursday, did you notice?' Esme stated as she pulled the shredded lettuce from the bread. 'It's weird, don't you think? Late night shopping is a Thursday thing. Marazion means Thursday market, did you know that? You should, being as you're the very bones of it.' There she was, Esme Pascoe. The façade left behind as the atmosphere gently revealed her. Peter couldn't take his eyes off her. The brightly coloured scarf hid a whole new person waiting to be discovered. The external fabrication wasn't her. Money was no match for the magical unveiling of this night. 'I think they are getting us all to gather in one place and things happen on a Thursday. And where does all that water go when the tide is out?' she asked. Peter beamed at her,

'It doesn't go anywhere, y'daft beggar. It's to do with molecules, you should know that. Once one starts movin, they all start. The moon pulls em,'

'Yes, I knew that bit, just wasn't sure where it went. I used to think the sand soaked it up when I was a kid.'

Peter snorted. 'So, how ya feelin now after y'first session?' Esme suddenly felt pressured to get back to the kids, but it was so nice having a break from being mum or wife, something she'd been wanting to do since she arrived. She was here, with Peter and memories, and a dog that offered a pure heart and mind. The town had a medieval vibe to it tonight, even the smells were different to the day. Escaping heat from the granite dispersing a particular scent of sea spray and moss, with an undertone of an unusual perfume. The savoury smells mixed with the sweet, peoples' mumbling and scuffing as they trod the ancient roads that twinkled under the streetlamps.

'*First* session?!' She tucked her hijab into place, picking at her nails. 'It's all changed since I was little. I remember bits of it. Just sections, moments stuck in my mind. We had a beach hut, you know, the white ones that ran the length of Porthminster?'

'Aye, I remember. Beaky was about a lot then.'

'Mmm. We came every year with the neighbours, took us an age to get here. Mum would wake me in the middle of the night, and I slept in the car. I don't know how she managed on her own. We'd book the huts all in a line. Mum would have the stove out, making tea,' she closed her eyes, imagining the smell of dry wood, kitchen things and biscuit tins. A rush of nostalgia and the fulfilment she dearly missed paid a heavy visit, quickly pushing it away before she ugly cried.

'Is that all you remember?' he asked.

Esme hung her head down, exhaling hard through her nose. 'Those public toilets, with my two pence to get in. Don't know why I didn't pee in the sea. We walked around bare footed and fancy free then. Wandering about with no one worrying. What's happened to us all? We'd take a walk to Carbis bay, with fizzy sweets,' laughing fondly, 'I've blocked most of them out. But I'm still home.'

'Youm not home yet. I wuz 'oping I'd unblocked a few things yesterdee.' A pregnant pause forced their heads in different directions. Esme giving her pearls a fiddle. They drank their coffees over small talk and Peter's stories of the town's magic and tragedies.

'Come on, fussy pants. Let's get you back befores youm turn into a pumpkin.'

The walk back to the beach was relaxed and open. Esme did all the talking, carrying her sandals on two hooked fingers. The cool, soft sand relieved her aching feet as they made that difficult walk over damp sand to the simmering celebrations. Max came too, an exception Peter was willing to make for Hassan, who eagerly awaited Esme's return. He liked the change, but strangers scared him, messing with his internal magnets and safety. Peter made sure Esme reached her son before returning to his post, looking through binoculars now and then, keeping a close eye on the young love birds and blackened horizon.

Layla dangled her legs over the lifeguard deck, still drinking cola and finishing off the cold leftovers – she would be hard to keep quiet when they got back home.

Two locals had joined the party, sat close to the fire playing folk songs on a guitar and a frame drum, making Esme want to stay longer and listen to their artistic expressions of sea life and free thinking. She often envied the other lives, living the free and beautiful, while herself and fellow Muslims spent every waking hour prepping for death. She settled near the fire holding her bent legs, swaying with the spiritual melodies. The fire embers racing each other to the moon.

This night set everything down, she had finally come back, and this must be it – all that devotion and patience had paid off, with a heavy sacrifice to dull the perfection. It was better to have a dysfunction amidst the happiness, which made it less questionable.

Musa blew out the candles, taking one last look around the room. There was an inconvenient delivery at the front door, with Esme's name on it.

20

Hostage

It was delivered as promised, wrapped in brown paper with a beautiful, personalised tag. Esme was up before anyone else to hang up her new portrait, putting it in numerous places before she decided on the wall next to the back room. Admiring it while leaning on the sofa with her rooibos, last night's kebab had left her feeling dehydrated and mouth a little dry. Max snored by her feet with bunny after following her all around the house, his furry eyelids blinking and twitching, barking at someone in his dream.

She heard the third stair creak; it was Musa's footsteps. Esme could tell who it was coming down them. With Hassan it was usually two at a time, slipping off the last. Layla's steps used to reflect her persona, but they were lighter of late. Everyone was changing, absorbing Saint Ives positive light and vibe.

'Good mornink, habibi,' he came in with his hair untied and just a pair of grey joggers. Esme amused at this new husband of hers, who usually had to be properly dressed at all times.

'Morning love. Saint Ives got you too, eh?'

He kissed her forehead. 'Did you have a good time?'

Esme was waiting for an outburst, a little wary of his changed behaviour. But he was serious as he brushed her hair from her shoulders, holding it back as he kissed her neck.

'We did. You should've come, they had fish and vegetables and hardly anyone drank,' he wasn't listening, his kisses moving all over her bare shoulders.

'Moose, we have to get ready for school,' they kissed lips, he pulled away tasting with a grimace.

'What have you been eating?!'

'There's a halal kebab place, in the town! It was heaven!'

'Was it clean?'

Esme tutted, 'of course. So nice. Like the night...' she paused, searching Musa's hazel eyes, '...was made just for me.' He huffed through his nose and took her mug, slurping her tea.

'This tea is disgustink, missiz fish and chips. You have light on your face, habibi. I told you this was a good place.'

'No, I told *you*.'

'Okay, okay. I am happy if you are happy. Ya Allah, I am a lucky man. He gave me fair skin and hair like fire, with a soul from pearls.' He placed the tea on the coffee table, looking at her with suggestive eyes. The room filled with an electricity, igniting their loins. Without hesitation they made love on the sofa. It was quiet, not as intense as the other morning, engrossed and unaware of their surroundings. Their mutual pleasure and reciprocated affirmations of forever, brought cool tears to their eyes as they breathed into each other's mouths.

Musa turned to his side and covered them with the throw, pulling Esme in. Laying in silence they gazed out the 'wobbly' windows and just existed together as one at first, then slowly retreated to themselves. She had a fixed smile of contentment thinking about it, while he was thinking about Ibrahim. Max licked Esme's feet, making her yelp.

'How are we going to move now?' he asked.

Esme giggled. 'I think I'll have to stop wearing these chemises, put my old dressing gown on instead.'

'Don't you never!' he tickled her, making her screech and laugh. Max barking and wanting to join in.

'It's ever! Not never! Oww!' she wriggled from his wandering fingers.

'Okay. We can't stay like this. We go together to wash.' That was the broken bond that hurt the most, she'd missed the washing together. It was their thing, a mutual worship and the return of it held her together.

Musa got off the sofa, straddling Esme, quickly pulling up his joggers. 'What the hell is that?!' he yelled, noticing the portrait.

'My present, to me. Do you like it?'

'Are you crazy?! You can't have this here!'

'Why? What's wrong with it?' he tried to take it off the wall, afraid to touch it.

'No, Moose! Please!'

'How much?'

'Does it matter? Okay, three, hundred.'

'You pay three hundred, for *this*?!' he couldn't unhook it, lifting the portrait away from the wall and seeing what was holding it there.

'Please, don't take it down, I love it. Tell me what's so bad about it? Moose? Tell me.'

Musa smoothed his hands over his hair. 'You know is not allowed, faces, haram.'

'Well, it's not really a face. Just the outline of one. There's no features as such. Don't spoil it for me, I had such a beautiful night. I was accepted for once. I fitted in. I felt part of everyone. Do you know what that feels like?' Musa's mood changed, her question resonating with him, something he wanted to experience himself since arriving. There were no tiers of nationality importance here, which he found difficult to adapt to. He wanted to be looked up to by society, but he was just another wealthy foreigner that was a threat to tradition.

'Who make this?'

'A woman, artist, in the town. I was literally drawn in and she had that hidden from anyone else!'

'It have big muscles, MashAllah.' Musa flexed his feeble pecks in gest, making Esme fall in deep. He winked, they hugged, unable to fight after their intense bonding.

'We shower together. Then go wake kids and I make breakfast. Okay?' Esme agreed and followed him, stomping her bare feet on the floorboards, wrapped in the throw.

After Esme and the kids had left, it was just him and Max. The dog curled up by the unlit fire in the lounge, his heart sinking deep from being left with this human who found it easy to ignore his whims.

'You want to go out?' Musa said to him. Max's head lifted quickly, unsure how to react, 'do you? Eh? You want to go outside, dog? We go, okay? Now.' He walked to the hall and took Max's leash off the hook by the front door.

'We go. Look, I put on my shoes just for you, kalb.' Max skidded to get to Musa when he heard the squeaking of the buckle, jumping up and down on his front legs.

'Okay, okay. Be still one sec-cond!' His face full of disgust when Max tried to lick his mouth. 'Aouthou bileh! Walahi you are going to kill me with your diseases.' Musa struggled to attach the hook to his collar as Max couldn't believe his luck and writhed with excitement.

They left the house on a beautiful day. Musa braved it and wore a white t-shirt and black jeans, his hair dressed in the usual manner complete with Raybans. He let Max lead the way, pulling him towards the steps to the beach, passed the back of the wooden café, up the incline to the coastal path that led to another bay over the railway line. Musa was respectfully greeted, the women purposely stopping and asking to pet Max, inflating his ego when they turned for a fourth look.

He rested on a bench at the highest point overlooking Porthminster, sat amongst heathers and gorse. The breeze was harsher up this way, goose bumping his skin. The smell of seaweed and sandalwood relaxed him, wishing he had a cigarette right now; it would go perfectly with the view and aid clearance of this mind. 'AstaghfiruAllah,' he said under his breath, having given up when Esme couldn't conceive. Max sat beside him sniffing the air and passers-by. Jolting when Musa began to stroke him.

'Good boy. I'm sorree I hate you, eh? But you stink! Like drains. Ya'rub.' he laughed to himself and felt a little humbled by the dog's unassuming soul and absolute devotion to humans. Not knowing what to do with his hand after, wiping it on his jeans.

'Okay, we go.' They continued along the sandy path, Musa's head emptying further and discovering another side to himself, Ibrahim still at the forefront. He was different here, he had to be, good job Raffia was next door for a cultural retreat and rant. The path led them to a country road with high hedging either side, secluding the mansions. Musa stopped to peer through the foliage with aspirations of a second home. There was no way he would endure more than one winter here, and Draycott was just an interim arrangement. Max yanked his arm impatient to move on because he could smell something up ahead that he just had to get to.

The road opened and they reached Carbis bay. It was larger than Porthminster, but not as atmospheric. Musa looked for a café, there was one before you got to the beach welcoming train passengers or avoiders of Saint Ives unavailable parking spaces, as rare as sun loungers around the pool.

'We stop here for bad coffee, and you can have water, my friend.' Musa ordered an espresso and bottled water, sitting at a table and chairs that overlooked the beach. It would be the perfect respite if there weren't so many tourists. Musa searched for a container for Max, spotting there was already a dedicated silver bowl in the shade. 'Look at this, SubhaanAllah, they have services for dogs,' he said to himself, 'you know that you are a king here, eh? You get better treatment than me.' He held the leash while Max drank and splashed, nearly choking from his gulping. Musa studied the people from behind the Raybans while he supped, out of place and suffocating. Nobody knew or even cared what his financial status was – they looked, curious as to his nationality, Greek or Spanish. The young women were loitering, but then, what was a man like that doing here with no ring and a dog, staring at the tourists? Which often moved them on, much to his relief.

Subconsciously toying with the snap hook, his eyes wandered the beach and further out, admiring his empire. Soon people would recognise him and praise his generosity, because he knew laying behind the unspoilt was dire need for a cash injection.

Leaning to one side, he fished out a tag from his pocket, looking much like a flat amulet. Prising the ring with his manicured nails, he fed it through Max's collar next to his name tag. 'BismiAllah. You are a good kalb. Look after my family.' Ruffling the dog's head. Max smile-panted at him, feeling protected with a slight sting. This alpha male was confusing, like two people wrapped in one.

Musa was glad to get back to Draycott, rushing to the cloakroom to wash his hands. Max was tied to the front door while Musa dried himself on a sea-themed towel, noticing a fine, red sand on the floor. Testing it with his big toe, another patch lay ahead of it, then another. Footprints, leading to the basement.

'Hassan?! You here?! Hello?!' He looked above him and then at Max, who was rigid by the front door, focussing on him. His stomach dropped but maintained dominance, deciding to follow the sandy footprints. Musa hesitated on the top of the basement stairs, more sand peppering the green carpet. 'Who is here?!' he called out. 'No deposits in houses! You have made a mistake!' he yelled in Arabic. A static silence filled the stairs and chilled his skin.

'BismiAllah! Aouthou bileh minna shaitaan a'rajeem! Your name!' Max began to bark and whimper trying to free himself, distracting Musa and clouding his judgement. He continued down the stairs, stopping at every one to listen. The door was ajar and the red sand entered the room. His heart raced as he pushed the door with the tips of his fingers, almost losing his breath.

'*Touuu-lahhh!*' came a threatening whisper from inside the room, making him jolt and stumble back. He ran back up the stairs on all fours, slipping and falling as he reached the wooden floors, sliding on his knees to get to the front door. Max was frantically trying to release his collar.

'Is okay, is okay. We go, we go,' he grabbed the handle and Max's leash, opening the door enough to get himself and Max through it, but Max broke free from the handle and scarpered towards the basement, skidding and clawing his way to the stairs, barking fiercely as he flew down them.

'NO! Max! *No*! Here! No!' There was a loud rumble and slamming of the door, vibrating the whole house. Musa hastily followed prising his mobile from his back pocket, his hands shaking. Reaching the top of the stairs he tripped over bunny and the barking had stopped.

Musa slumped down on the top step, out of breath, calling Ibrahim.

'*Salaam dear brother!*'

'Wsalaam. Is the delivery safe?'

'*Yes, yes. Of course.*'

'Did you put the amulet in the right place?'

There was an anticipated pause the other end. '*Listen, I fear I have been fooled!*'

'What do you mean, fooled?!' Musa yelled.

'Forgive me brother, I am old, was...old, and easily confused. There was a man...'

'Man? What man? What have you done?!'

'Please, forgive me brother. I am afraid.'

Musa pinched the bridge of his nose, huffing in defeat. 'I was foolish to think my plan would go well. Do not blame yourself, the fault is with me. I should have done it myself. If not the Khararah, then where?'

'Abadis. You see? I thought I had made a mistake.'

'We have both been fooled by an intelligence that wishes to see me avenged.'

Musa felt lightheaded, the flood gates had opened and the inevitable had come much sooner that he had liked.

'Did the other part of my deal work?'

'If you mean my appearance, then yes. When will this stop? I am becoming unrecognisable!'

'No, I didn't mean...wait, did you drink the water?'

'Yes. SubhaanAllah, it was so good! I was thirsty!'

Musa's head hit the wall, his eyes moving back and forth for a solution. 'Do not get addicted to this appearance, they will bribe you for more, and worse.'

'Worse?!'

'Ibrahim has passed away. This is your excuse now. Marid and Sirens are the only ones that can reverse the effects if that's what you want. I can help you with that. Understand?'

'Ha! My chances have just decreased. I am in over my head. I regret agreeing to this, brother.'

'Be patient. I will be seeing you soon, inshallah. I want to put this right.'

'You are coming to Riyadh?'

'No. You are coming here.'

'You got me a ticket to meet my new wife?!'

'And your old self. You won't be needing any ticket. My entrapments have been released. I want you out of Riyadh a little quicker than traditional means. You will enjoy the beauty of the life here, dearest uncle.'

'There was something else. They want Layla, and something, ah, yes! A skull!'

Musa's eyes ran over every imperfection on the wall, 'I will get you through. Do not interact with the Jann, especially the one called Toulah. One of the greatest of shapeshifters. I fear this is who you have been fooled by. Keep your wits about you. They cannot keep any form for long, there will always be something out of place. Is that clear?'

'Yes. I bought a new suit today.'

Musa was forced to smile from humility, 'hamduillah. I am happy for you, dearest brother. I will speak to you soon. Just do as I said, salaam.' He hung up, regarding the basement door whilst trying to muster up a story.

21

THE DUNGEON

Esme and Peter de-weeded the rockeries ready for the influx of admiring eyes. She talked incessantly to hide her nerves, going into detail about the falling out with her mother, which was the most she'd confided to anyone. It was easy to talk to him because he made no judgement, just gave the odd grunt of disapproval or chortle. Peter listened intently while he hand-forked the soil around the base of the Yuccas, keeping a safe distance from impaling leaves. There was an odd familiarity about him that confused her.

Marazion was feeling like a second home, the children were less fussy about going to the school and only ten more children had enrolled with more girls than boys. The mystery still hung around as Esme began to question everything, nothing made sense, especially the school. There were properties in the village that would have been ample; second homes that needed some life.

'You thought more about wha I said at the chapel?' Peter asked.

'Yes. I was deep in thought about it on the beach, and this place,' Esme rested her hand on the top of the rake, 'last night, was magical. I felt accepted for once. I never saw that halal shop before, either.' She squinted and shook her head. Peter pushed himself up on his knee.

'You deserve it,' brushing the dry earth from his rugged hands, 'you put y'picture up yet?'

Esme blushed, 'Yes, what is it?'

'What's what?'

'The painting, what is it of?' peering into his eyes, at his pupils that flexed and expanded. Peter regarded her, his heart skipping a beat, focussing over her head as he held composure.

'Is that what you were thanking? Is it them that protect Saint Ives?'

'I think it's time for a gluten free carrot cake and a funny cup o'tea, and to have a little chat.'

'I can't…' she looked at her watch, 'we've got a parent meeting in ten minutes. Later, perhaps?'

'Ner'mind. I'm going to get meself some tea. I'll see yous later.' He left, stomping ahead like always, his leaning gait pulling at Esme's heart strings. Retreating when they got close to the smoke and mirrors, what *was* going on? She laid down the tools out of harm's way, admiring the castle that towered above her, infallible and dominant, trotting after him feeling a little queasy - her phone ringing on *silent* in the back pocket of her brown linens.

'Khalas. Put your pencils down please.' The boys did as they were told. Samir stood with a smile. 'Do you know what we are going to do now?' the boys lazily shook their heads, hoping it had nothing to do with more writing. 'We are going to see...the dungeon!' there was hushed excitement. 'Hassanan! Let's go!'

The scraping of chairs on the slate floor could be heard in the other class. The boys' feet scuffled as they followed Samir out of the house. There was commotion and talking as he led them to the slope.

'Listen! We will have good behaviour and no touching, unless I tell you. Okay?'

'Yes, Ustaz,' was the toneless answer.

'Good, good.' They liked him, he was kind, fun and easy to get on with. The boys stopped to look at the giant's heart imbedded in the steps. Touching it, trying to pull it out. Samir climbed effortlessly, stopping to check back on them.

'Ustaz, is it a real giant's heart?' they asked.

He chuckled, giving them a condescending glance.

'I think it would be much bigger, don't you? Come now, before the visitors arrive. We don't have much time.' They lingered, discussing how the giant would have been killed and fell in the spot; Hassan acting out the whole scene, making the others laugh. The group trailed off from the drama and ran after Samir in turn. They followed him through the archways and up to the chapel, their excitement echoing. Gathering amongst the pews, they watched him push the bookcase away from the small, gothic door and taking a black key from his tweed jacket pocket. The noise of the lock and key were heavy, clunking into position while they held their breath. The door opened with a creek; cold air rushed at them causing a collective gasp.

'I will go first. Watch your heads! And hold onto the rail! Don't forget to say BismiAllah!' Samir took the steps on his backside, managing to stoop then stand as the steps took him deeper.

They descended the spiral granite steps in the same way, holding onto the eroded handrail. Hassan was fourth in line, stopping at the door, the boy behind eager to push him on.

'What is it, Hassan?'

He gulped, his stomach in knots and coming out in a cold sweat.

'Move! Stupid. Go!' the boy pushed his back harder. Hassan rolled out the way and let the others go first. He could hear the deep echo of Samir's voice and the other boys' whispers. He needed Max. His heartbeat loud and slow, pumping thickened blood around his heavy limbs.

'Hassan?' Samir called up the stairs.

'Uh, yes, uh, I'm coming. Just, uh, tying my trainers!' He looked around the empty chapel, it looked back. The smell of ancient damp agitated his nostrils as he regarded the reassuring essence of light in the stained glassed windows. Samir called again, jolting him.

'O, okaayyy! I'm coming!' He shuffled to the top step, his legs shaking. The magnetic pull of something getting stronger, something threatening. He could hear it calling his name, mocking his weaknesses, sure he was about to faint. He thought of his mother, then his father, trying to fill up his soul with their love and protection. Peter should have come with them, he wasn't scared of *anything*. Then he turned to God, praying, almost begging for whatever it was down there, to leave. Samir saw the fear as Hassan emerged.

'BismiAllah Hassan. You look terrified. Nothing to be afraid of. Look...' they all stood in a circular dungeon; one barred window overlooked the sea, the waves and wind howling round the stone trap. Stepping off the last stair his legs gave way, caught by one of the boys. They all laughed at him.

'Ah! Please, boys! Help him feel comfortable. We are Muslims, we take care of each other. AstaghfiruAllah.' Hassan stood with the aid of two boys, his chest near to collapsing from an unseen pressure. He looked directly into Samir's eyes silently pleading with him to understand, to do something holy. While the boys ran their hands along the damp walls talking morbidly about past prisoners. Samir pulled Hassan close, 'I won't let anything hurt you. Understand? Never,' captivating Hassan and calming his anxiety and sixth sense, which was about to self-combust. As the negativity left, he burst into tears from the rush of piety. He convulsed, feeling foolish and desperately needing his mother. It was always her, the only person that he could turn to, apart from Max.

'Something's happened,' he said through sobs.

'Happened? What?'

'I need to see my mother, please. I need to see her!'

'Okay, okay. We can go now. Boys!' they all groaned and wanted to stay longer.

'Chicken Hassan!' one boy jeered, clucking and flapping his bent arms.

'That is enough! I will be speaking to your parents!' the boy's mood changed instantly, the easy-going teacher was still to be respected.

'Come on. Time for us to go anyway. We will help Hassan find his mother for class points.'

Esme entered the large front room. Janan was at the head of the table, the parents turning to watch her awkwardly sit at the last available chair. Three of them wore the purple cloaks, hoods down.

'As salaam alaikum,' she said sheepishly, avoiding eye contact. They all returned a half-hearted response, huffing at her gate crashing the realms of exclusivity. This was one that had obviously slipped through the net of cultural conditioning.

'Walaikum salaam, Esmay. Welcome,' Janan respectfully said from behind the brocaded material. Esme picked at her hands reading over the sheet of paper in front of her; the agenda written in Arabic. She said nothing at first, already feeling intimidated as they began to discuss the itinerary. She caught snippets of understanding, but the Arabic was unfamiliar to her. Arab speakers had their own dialect, but this one wasn't Saudi - Egyptian perhaps. She began to raise her hand, being ignored as their discussions became heated, with Janan trying to douse the flames.

'Um, excuse, excuse me?' The committee turning their heads in a hostile manner. She was frightened by the deep jade of Janan's eyes, her power filling every corner of the room. She was to be listened to and obeyed, naturally taking the lead and her face covering intensifying the mystery. She bowed her head as a signal for her to speak.

'Uh, I wanted to raise some concerns I have about one of the policies...' her face reddened as they all held their gaze. She swallowed hard, determined to continue, 'it, uh, is in relation to the, uh, safeguarding policy.' Clearing her throat as the pressure held firm, 'I don't understand what you're saying, regarding the locked door,' coughing to loosen her constricting throat. 'I understand that it's for safety, but if there's a fire...uh, also, the staff vetting. Umm, it seems to be missing.' There was whispering among them, in a dialect she didn't understand. She feebly raised her hand again.

'Sorry, uh, could you repeat that please?'

'Forgive us, Esmay. We assumed you would understand. Which dialect do you prefer?' Janan said in a condescending tone.

'Um, Saudi? Or English please, if that's not too much trouble.'

There were huffs and puffs and sniggers from around the long table, mouths turned down.

'You may take the piece of paper with you and present this to Musa. There will be no discussion in English at this time.'

'Oh, right, uh, this, piece of paper?' Janan bowed her head once again. Esme knew it was also a big hint to leave. She stood, clumsily unhooking her Luis Vuitton bag from the chair, close to tears. A pressure against her back pushed her to the front door, her insides on fire. She stopped, looking around at the other classrooms, the rebellion had reached a new level and she wanted her children out of there. Esme couldn't hear their voices, but the cries of babies, staying a little longer to listen.

'Will that be all?' Janan whispered in her ear, scaring her half to death. She opened the door, and fled to the café.

Tourists were arriving in their droves, weaving through them in a panic, the café already with a long queue outside.

'Sorry, sorry, excuse me, I just need to, uh…' she frantically searched the seating for Peter, he saw her, raising his hand. Containing her emotion she pushed passed to reach him. His stature and maturity like a beacon of light amongst her internal hell.

'Tha' wuz a quick meetin.'

She sat, covering her face with her muddied hands, 'was up maid?'

Esme wiped her running nose with her sleeve, relieved she was surrounded by her kin. 'So? Wa'did they say?'

'I just need to get the kids out of there,' she sniffed, her phone digging in her back. 'The purple cloak people were there, and...' she looked at the wall displaying local artists' impressions of the harbour and mount. 'I heard babies.' Making eye contact with him, Peter avoided it. 'Why are they discussing the school and castle in Arabic? Arabic I couldn't understand.' Peter slurped his tea pretending he didn't hear. Her phone was causing discomfort, she retrieved it, burning to the tips of her fingers when she saw ten missed calls from Musa. Esme's face drained of colour, 'oh shit...' she called him back, her hand shaking.

'*Why you don't answer?! I have called you one hundred times!*'

'It was ten. I was in the parents' meeting. Sorry, phone was on silent.'

'*Why?! This is stupid!*'

'I didn't realise, sorry,' she whispered into her cupped hand.

'*You must come home, now!*'

'What? Why? What's happened?' Musa hung up. Esme glared at the screen, her nervous system jarred. There was confrontation in his voice; the tone that everyone was afraid of. Her mind raced, and bowels squeezed, overthinking about what she might had left or forgot to hide from him. Perhaps it was the painting or the canvas from the back room that overstepped the mark. Something haram in the fridge perhaps.

'Wass up now?' Peter asked, eager to get back to work.

'Umm, it was, Musa – he said we have to go home. Sounded urgent.'

'Aye, I heard im from ere.' Peter noticed her vibe had changed, like a doused flame, picking at her fingernails and biting the skin around them.

'Alright then. Do you wanna go on? I'll bring the kiddies back.' Esme had become incoherent, her thoughts preoccupied with made up scenarios, with a pressing need to pee.

'Well, umm, no, that wouldn't be a good idea, not right now. Thanks. Musa would flip his lid.' Peter stood and drained his cup.

'I ain't scared of 'im. He's full o'nonsense. C'mon. Let's get them kiddies.'

22

Trespass

Musa sat at the kitchen table deep in thought waiting for them to arrive. The house solemn and empty, the wind chimes in the back yard disturbing his concentration. The oud was the only thing keeping him grounded, its power overriding his guilt, taking in deep breaths of it. All was well, he was doing the right thing and it would soon ease and settle into its rightful place.

He tapped the ash from the burning wood into clay bowl, like a cigarette. The front door burst open, but it wasn't the usual entrance from his children, Hassan was the first in, sitting at the table without saying a word. Musa raised a wistful smile, his son already spooked, preparing for an uncomfortable moment.

'Hey! We're baaack!' Esme joyfully called out hoping to defuse Musa's anger. 'Maxey! Where's my baybeee?' Musa's stomach churned, cradling his cold coffee. Layla and Esme entered the kitchen, their smiles wiped from their faces as the impending doom hit them.

'Sit down,' his tone sorrowful.

'I have to give you this.' Esme said, placing the creased agenda in front of him. Musa briefly regarded it, the itinery elevating his anxiety.

'What's going on?' Layla asked.

'Blease, habibi, sit.'

Esme's nerves squeezed her gullet and stung her stomach. 'You're scaring me...'

He held her dirtied hands tightly, Layla looking on suspiciously.

'I'm sorree, walahi, I'm sorree. I lost Max.' Layla yelped and burst into tears.

Esme snatched her hands away. 'What have you done?' her mind raced through all the hurtful comments about Max. 'I said, what have you *done*?!' regaining power as she watched him squirm.

'Nothink! Walahi! We were walkink the path to the other beach, he saw somethink and ran away. I couldn't hold the, the, rope! He was too stronk! Nearly pulled me to the ground!' Hassan's burning stare still on him.

'Since when did you take him out?' Esme asked.

'I wanted to. We had good time. Really nice houses habibi, on the path...'

'So where did he run off to? Why didn't you run after him?!'

'I did! But couldn't see where he went. Barkink and noise. He run through big uh, vegetation.'

Waving his arms around, the English making a sharp exit.

'Well, he can't have gone far. I don't know what all the fuss was about. He'll find his way back or someone will bring him back. Was that it?' Musa nodded. 'Did you have to be so aggressive about it? Well, let's go and look for him then! Kids, come on, back out.' Esme walked off towards the front door holding down the vomit that reached her throat.

'I bet he's stuck in that room,' Hassan mumbled. Musa glared at him, his mouth drying.

Esme heard and came back, 'oh don't be silly. We'd hear him barking.'

'No, we wouldn't,' his tone flat, eyes fixed on Musa's twitching face.

'Well, let's look there first then, shall we? Layla, pull yourself together and help us look.'

The kids stood at the top of the stairs with Musa looking down at Esme.

'Max? Maxey? You in here?' squeezing her eyes tight as she listened hard, silently begging to hear a bark or whimper. She turned the handle again, pushing from her shoulder. Standing back, she started kicking it.

'Open! Open! You son of a bitch!' she screamed.

'Habibi! No!' Musa ran down to her, 'I am sorree, ya Allah, forgive me.'

'What the hell is going on here! Where is he? What did you do!' she yelled in his face. Her heart ached as vulnerability and guilt pained his face. He never cried much, nothing seemed to move him to tears. Esme carried his feelings of grief when he was away from home, which always broke down her boundaries.

'It wasn't me, habibi, you must believe me! I wouldn't hurt him! I know I don't like him in the house and maybe this was meant to be.'

'Oh! You would love that, wouldn't you?! Get outta my way.' Esme pushed passed him, calling the children to follow. 'Where's bunny?'

'Is on sofa.'

Esme took the soft toy with her, gripping it tightly, the scent of his dried saliva increasing her determination. Her face distorted from panic and loss.

'Harvey, see if you can find Kash to help. Layla, you come with me, and we'll retrace baba's steps.'

'Let me help, habibi,' Musa pleaded.

'Stay here in case he comes back.' The front door slammed. Her heart was full of hope, but her gut was screaming something else which she chose to ignore, triggering the feeling when love goes missing and life comes to a standstill, which resided in the mouth. Regret consumed her thoughts, the why didn't I and the if only. How was she going to function now and watch the lights of the town and fall into a blissful sleep? He had to be found to function.

Hassan ran the decline to town with vengeful tears. Saint Ives looked different and hostile, sure people were staring at him, feeling shifted to one side with his heart struggling to keep up. He walked past the church and round the corner to the lifeboat station, hearing Akash's voice tightened his throat. It was busy but he barged in, convulsing.

'Wassup dude?' Akash asked. Hassan couldn't speak, blurting out incoherent words.

'Hey, hey, slow down, slow down,' sitting him down on a wooden stool. 'Take a breath and start again lad.' His comforting scent calmed him, his sobs slowed, and gullet loosened.

'Max, is, missing. Help me, please!'

'Okay, okay. We'll find 'im. Alri'?' Hassan cried louder when Peter came to see what all the fuss was about.

'Wass 'appened 'ere now then? Lawst yer muther?' Hassan shook his head vigorously, confused how Peter changed places so quickly.

'They've lost Max.'

'I see. Ran arf, did ee?'

'My dad said he ran off, but I know they took him!'

'Who?'

'Them!' the men regarded one another, 'we need the crowbar! You said you would. We need it to get in that room! That's where he is!'

Esme and Layla were calling for Max along the path Musa took, their hopes high and in denial. Concerned passers-by stopped and asked if they could help, taking his description to gather up a local search team. They reached the end of the path and into Carbis bay, Layla was tearful the whole time, Esme held it together for everyone else.

'Somebody's probably took him in and will see the number on the collar. We're looking for nothing. I just panicked, I guess.' They continued passed the beach café and into unfamiliar territory.

'I think dad let him off on purpose.'

'I thought the same, but now I'm not so sure. He knows how much heartache it would cause, despite what he feels about Max. I don't think he would have it in his heart to do it.' They continued calling for him and Esme noticed Musa was right about the houses up this end, feeling sorry for him stuck at home mulling over what had happened. Her adoration unable to hold any grudge for long.

'Go easy on baba, okay? He must be feeling rotten right now. Imagine how you would feel. I know I'd wanna eat myself.' The memory of her dog consumed her again, calling her loudest almost bursting her vocal cords.

'He's not here, mum. He would've come to us by now.'

'We'll walk a little bit further, you never know. People and dogs have been found in the obvious of places no one thought to look.'

Akash, Peter and Hassan burst through the house, startling Musa. Akash with a crowbar in his grip.

'Get out of my house!' Nervous of Akash's presence as they stormed their way to the basement. Musa charged after them, Peter stuck his leg out to stop him.

'Ah, Ah. No, y'don't. It's about time we got that door open.' Musa stood back, not wanting to touch him.

'Ya'rub, you don't know what you're doink.' Musa shook.

Peter tilted his head, 'oh yeah? Hidin' summat, is it?'

'Look, brother, let me pass!' Musa was visibly shaking, his eyes wide and begging. Peter stood back and let him run to the stairs.

'Boys! No! Don't damage the door!' Panting when he reached the top of the stairs, 'stop!'

'He's in here, isn't he?' Akash said, stood behind Hassan.

'No, no. I swear. He is out there. Think about it, why would he be silent? Where is your intelligence?' Hassan and Akash looked at one another.

'He went in there and ended up somewhere else!' Hassan yelled, pointing at the door.

'Do not raise your voice to me! Listen to yourself! Go and help your mother and stop this stupidity!'

Peter followed, standing with Musa. 'So, get on wi'it then, boys.' he instructed. The boys sneered mischievously at each other.

'No! Don't!' Musa thrusting his hand toward them.

Akash was enjoying watching Musa panic, daringly knocking the door with the crowbar.

'Hello!' They all assumed their positions when they heard Esme's voice. Peter smiling her way as she walked through the lounge. She just about held herself together when she saw him.

'Not found 'im then?' She shook her head a regretful 'no'.

'I'd rather wait here, I feel we're looking in the wrong places or someone may have taken him in.'

'Yeah! He's in this room!' Hassan called up. Akash's skin tightened when he sensed Layla's presence, his pupils dilating.

'Layla! Go to your room! Now!' Musa demanded.

'What's going on here?' Esme asked. A little amused when she saw the boys at the foot of the stairs with mayhem in mind.

'They think the kalb is in the room! Crazy!' Peter's pager bleeped, sending a shock wave through them all.

'Ah, we gotta go son. We's got a rescue. Saved by the bell ay, Musa?' Giving a throaty, condescending laugh. Musa stiffened as Peter brushed passed.

'C'mon lad. Don't worry maid,' affectionately touching her arm, 'he'll turn up. Ain't many folk lawst their dogs f'long. Stay positive. Kash! Let's go!' tipping his imaginary hat to her and Musa.

23

Toulah

Sunset was upon Riyadh, and it was a race against the clock before everywhere closed for prayer. Ibrahim knew exactly where he was going, mistrusting himself, muttering the description of the man he was supposed to see over and over. Musa had left a brief message and one he was compelled to adhere to. He was nervous, adrenaline thumping his heart, unsure he should be meddling with portals. Entering foreign territory and meeting with Musa made him feel acutely vulnerable. There had been a few customers for Kenan, paying off the Asian boy and relieving him of his menial duties. His need to leave the damn place, intensifying.

People were staring as his suspiciously looked around for the Jann to make an appearance at any moment, edging away from alleyways and dark corners. Ibrahim covered his face for protection as he approached the Egyptian restaurant, gingerly entering and checking over the clientele. The proprietor jerked his head, Ibrahim's hand shook as he gave the piece of paper over the counter. The man opened it, folded it back up and beckoned him to the rear of the building, where staff ate plates of fried fish and rice. He was led out to the back, a smartly dressed dwarf boy sat at a white metal table waiting for Ibrahim. No words were exchanged, just nods. The boy beckoned him with short and stubby fingers through more doors, which brought them out into a yard. An Olive tree at its centre obscuring a white-washed dwelling with bars on the windows, and two skinny dogs on guard. Inside, wall to wall seating in green and gold, a large cotton sheet on the floor with bowls and goblets waiting for a serving. The boy didn't speak but offered Ibrahim a place. Shortly after, six men walked in traditionally dressed, pleased to see him, welcoming, touching their hearts following handshakes. One of them, the driver.

'Ah! Salaams, brother, good to see you.' Ibrahim shook his hand.

'I can see you are surprised to see me, brother. Lucky I was there to divert you, eh? Otherwise, you may be sitting here with two heads!' There was a roar of laughter from the others, Ibrahim not seeing the joke. 'I must say, the new look suits you. Calm down, brother. We eat first, eh?'

The boy returned with pomegranate juice, pouring it into each golden goblet. Two of the six men came in carrying a large, silver tray full of rice laden with a carcass of marinated lamb and vegetables. It was a sight to see for a man that had been ravenous his whole life.

'MashAllah, what is the occasion?' Ibrahim asked, his eyes widening at the steaming banquet.

'We eat first, then we talk. You are in safe hands brother!'

Each had their own section to eat from, moulding portions of rice and meat with their right hand and skilfully filling their mouths. Sat with the right leg bent, opening the digestive tract.

'I hardly recognised you,' the driver said. Ibrahim choked a little, blissfully enjoying the feeling of filling his stomach without difficulty or heartburn. The fulfilment flushed heat through his once dehydrated veins, like the first time he fasted as a child and the euphoria of eating at sundown. 'How are you feeling?'

'I feel alive, and scared.'

'This is normal, and you will get used to it.'

'What if I don't want to get used to it?'

'You find yourself a Marid or Siren, that's if they don't kill you first. Half bloods are far more approachable, less of a threat. There are no such species here, they prefer colder waters. Their gifted abilities will give you back what you want.'

Ibrahim swallowed the tender meat, in raptures over its flavour. 'Ah, that is why my brother has arranged this, so I can return to cold waters. Do you go back to how you were?'

'Eventually. That's when you hide.'

'Hide? But, they will be looking for me.'

'Yes, you're dead, remember?' the others sniggered through rice-filled mouths. 'No one cared about you, they won't notice your absence.'

'So, what's your story?' Ibrahim asked, maintaining his guard.

'Why don't you take a look through that door?' the driver said, tilting his golden goblet toward a curtained doorway with a provocative flicker of his eyebrows. Ibrahim regarded it with intrigue, sure he heard female murmurs. He got to his feet, still reeling from the ease of that. Behind material the same as the seating, was a small and sparsely decorated room with different aged girls sat on a large rug. One got up, about six years old, as if it was her cue when she saw him. A crooked smile changed his face.

'Which one do you want?' the driver asked, laughter breaking amongst the others.

'Want?'

'Mmm. Which one do you desire, dearest brother? Take your pick, they are ready.'

Ibrahim looked back at the other girls, scanning their terrified eyes. The six year old already holding his hand. He gently released her grip, and ushered her back.

'These are too young!'

'Marry one! Or two. Make it halal.' The driver filled his face, split with a grin.

'Halal? There is nothing halal about this! I will buy them from you, all of them, but I'll be buying their freedom.' There was loud laughter that rumbled Ibrahim.

'How much are you offering?'

'Fifty kilos of Kenan.' More mocking laughter followed.

'Dearest brother, you insult me. Fifty kilos per head, and you have yourself a deal.'

'I need to discuss this with Musa first.' The mood changed as Ibrahim stood awkwardly in the room, with all eyes on him. 'What exactly is your business?' he asked the driver.

'Me? I look out for brothers like you. I fit in quite well, don't you think? I didn't think I could fool you.'

'Fool me?'

'Mmmm, with my traditional dish and touristic banter.'

'I don't understand.'

The driver's smile turned into a chilling sneer, 'I am Toulah, you old fool. Musa's nemesis and old accomplice, and sister of the one you released from the Abadis,' she bellowed in a female voice.

Ibrahim jolted back, his back slamming against the barred window. 'AstaghfiruAllah! I must not interact with you!'

'Oh please, you offend me. You're stuck with me whether you like it or not. I would use me to your advantage. I could even be you if you needed a day off.'

'Devils, all of you!'

'Come now, you will spoil your appetite. Relax. And it's a little late to be asking to be excused.' Her eyes briefly flashed emerald, revealing the unmistakable set of crowded teeth.

'So, so you tricked me into going to the other lake!'

'Of course. Musa's superior delusion that he was too good to go himself, has backfired. I am grateful to you for releasing my sister and revenge will be sweeter than this marinaded beast,' her menacing smile peppered with meat. 'I have no grievance with you, dear brother. I will be just. You have my word.'

'Your kind are incapable of such a thing! Liars! Cheats!' Toulah morphed into herself, rising from the floor, swirling her arms in rage; the house, other men, food, sofa and girls all dispersing into the whirlwind she'd created. Ibrahim cried out, covering his face and squeezing his eyes shut from sand dust. He could sense his environment change, a strange scent alerted him, one from the cellar.

Opening his eyes, he was confronted with a colossal square sandstone tomb in the middle of an arid place. It still felt like Saudi, only dimensionally different, the realisation of where stung his limbs. Al Ula, one of the world's wonders and ancient dwelling, landing on the frontage to the Qasir Al Farid (the lone castle) and main gateway. Carved into an independent rock with immaculate skill. Ornate ledges with a distinctive abstract roof. Intricate detail and sheer magnitude set in the monumental landscape. Ibrahim became fearful of the decoration and raised symbolic inscriptions all over the weathered fascia, its surroundings desolate and absent of any life, dotted with wind-sculptured rocks and dirt roads. A place rough beneath your feet with intensified heat. Many dare not enter because of the cursed protection that adorned these ancient mysteries. Ibrahim checked himself over, the youth had left. Straining to see, beads of sweat instantly appearing on his furrowed brow, cowering in the shade of rock that cradled the entrance.

'Why have you brought me to Al Ula?!' sliding his aged hand down the jagged surface. 'I am a fool,' he sobbed, 'a fool that followed my desires and have ended up in hell. I feel you are not done with your punishment, ya Allah. Forgive me, forgive my desperation and impatience...'

'Really, such self-pity!' Toulah hissed from the doorway of the tomb. 'You are still on this earth.'

He wiped away his tears with a bony hand. 'What do you want from me?!'

'Come!' She beckoned him into the dark doorway. Ibrahim steadied himself and followed her, reciting, but his words were cut short, snatched from his tongue.

'You cannot utter scriptures when you tread the sacred ground of the Nabateans,' came a deep female voice from further inside.

He squinted at the faint light just visible ahead. 'Bismil...!' unable to finish his words.

'Do you require sustenance?'

Ibrahim's heart beat hard as he stood in the dark in a begging gesture. 'Water!' Kicking over another golden goblet, clumsily grappling for it and sucking out the remains of the spilt water. Looking into the empty vessel, to his astonishment he watched it refill, dropping it in fright, 'Aouthou bileh!'

'Tut, tut. Such superstition,' came the female's mocking voice.

'I refuse water from your magic!'

'Is your creator not a magician? Did he not send magic among you to be admired and practiced?'

'My creator is your creator! It is our test! You are the Jinn, abusers of magic!' Ibrahim spat.

'On the contrary. Ha! The superior species, with your poor eyesight and failing bodies. We are far more superior with our powers!'

Ibrahim's chortle echoed around the chamber, 'the angels were commanded to worship us for good reason. We still thank Him in the face of tyranny or desperation, without seeing or hearing, even though we are plagued by the whispers of Satan. They admire us for that. You may have your magic, but we have intuition and direct connection. Our greatest power is humility and love in great numbers. We are it, and we do not need spells and desecration to get what we want, we have just forgotten how to use our minds.'

'Insolence!' she bellowed, 'you have not forgotten, we have used modern means to erase it! Your fear can be put to beneficial use. Your superstition a contradiction in terms. You are easily led, innocent and too trusting in those above you. You have lost your powers to us, not them. Placing the amulet in the hidden lake awakened our revenge. However...' she lingered on the last syllables in a threatening tone, 'remember who you are dealing with. Do as you are asked, and you will be spared.'

Ibrahim's left palm began to burn and itch.

'Only the akin know the true meaning of our symbol. Let the world think otherwise of its representation. A blind following that keeps us protected in return. You are safe under the all-seeing eye.' Ibrahim searched the dark, his soul in turmoil from crossing the thin line. 'Why does your faith frown upon the greatest power on earth, when it was He who placed it here? He fears the inevitability that more will follow us than the guilt-ridden conscience of sobriety. This is your only price to pay for a life of affluent liberty.'

'*Only* price?! This is the biggest price! I don't want your Oud or your protection, take it! Take it back! Take me out of this! You are shirk!' The shadows moved, agitated whisperings filled his head chilling his skin and erecting the hair on the back of his neck.

'Your loins have led you too far. Make your fortune as you wish. Unless...'

'Unless what?'

'Unless you revoke your declaration of faith.'

'Walahi, never! Never!'

The imposing woman approached. 'Revenge is already set. It is war unless you comply! Idiots! Thinking you can control us with your ranks! You are in the food chain with the rest of the animals! We were first to set foot on this earth and then you came, destroying it, and each other – for money and lewd fulfilment. Fools! Miserable, fools! Revenge is our prerogative until the end of days. Soon, Arabia's depraved lands will flourish when oceans swell and flood, as it is written. And our species will over run.'

'Take your grievances up with Musa, leave me out of it. I will never speak of it. Take the Oud, I don't want it.' Ibrahim breathed, his throat parched. She came close. Large, with brocaded material that adorned her and garish jewellery that jangled; a gold pendant of a Hamsa around her neck. Her eyes captivating and beautifully terrifying.

'Why do you care so much? You have been cheated because of your ethnicity. Take it back, take your fortune. You deserve it.'

Ibrahim was mesmerised by her, wanting to nestle in her bosom. She held the wisdom of the universe within. He was confused, scared yet comforted.

'Did the Jann not satisfy you? Imagine having this for eternity. You do not know what lies beneath the hypocritical white cloth of your brother. I saved you from an unwritten fate. Do you know of his other vocation?'

'It is not my business. I would rather die than be part of your tribe!'

'Be careful what you wish for. You are a distributor now. The scent of Oud is our calling, our invitation to enter the abodes of the pious and continue the corruption of mind and society. Man relies on us to supply, made rare from the desire of opulence. Your status amongst the creations has gone to your heads! You have no more Agar left. Only we can continue the supply,' grinning beneath the cloth.

'What is the price for Oud?' Ibrahim was near to falling asleep in her company and he would have been happy with that. Hypnotised and surrendered.

'Innocents, and their adrenaline. Humans are willing to part with riches and kin to restore their youth, and one we feed on. A mind alteration and sickness we are determined to spread. So easy with such demonic and deluded desires.'

'Never! I will never work for you! I will expose you!'

She raised an eyebrow. 'Those that have worked against us must pay a high price to remain in this temporary life, like the brother you trust. I fear there is a resilience in you.' Janan let out a bone-chilling cackle. 'Do you not see our resentment comes in the form of depopulation? What do you think they do with all those unwanted carcasses? Unknowingly consuming them in your fast foods and medical procedures, sending you all mad.'

Ibrahim squeezed his eyes shut, holding down the bile. 'Please! Enough!'

'Open your mind, Ibrahim,' she calmed.

'Why have you brought me here?'

Janan glided around him, moving close to his ear. 'I see the vengeance you harbour in your heart. Black as a desert night. Upholding your faith by a feeble thread.'

Ibrahim inhaled heavily, her words resonating.

'You serve the very people that took your family. Loyal, for fear of losing credibility with your Lord. It is time to rage a silent war of your own.'

Another doorway appeared, the light blinding Ibrahim. Water entered the tomb, darkening the floor as it expanded, little waves reaching his sandals. His hands and arms were thicker again, feeling his face, the wrinkles had decreased. He had missed this version of himself, aroused from his returned strength. A sharp breeze blew through him as he walked on, drying the sweat, unafraid and drawn in by an alien aroma. Taking off his sandals he walked bare foot onto a beach, the bottom of this thobe getting wet. Ibrahim couldn't take a breath without choking on the clean air. He was on a beach in a colder climate, sure he was dreaming when he saw the Mount.

'SubhaanAllah. Am I dead?'

'Far from it. I shall give you the gift of replenishment in return for your worship. Fill your cups and desires from your own thought. Do you accept?' Janan spoke in his head, tickling and goose bumping.

'I accept,' he answered from a subdued conscious, grunting at the Hamsa imprinted on his left palm.

'Take Musa's daughter to our parallel where you will not age, undetected and free from law. Toulah will call upon you when we are ready for you to receive her. A King has paid us the weight of this Mount in gold, just for her eyes! She will trust you, and her vengeance for her father is great. And if you bring me Solomon's skull, you will benefit from a harem and great powers.' Ibrahim was too dazed to respond, and before a blissful smile graced his lips, he was back in Riyadh, startled by a blaring taxi horn within an inch of his life.

24

Counsel

The journey to the mount was sullen, the kids looked out of the window instead of scrolling social media. Esme was desperate to speak to Samir, he would know what to do.

Make up covered the bruise at the corner of her eye, but not the shame or humiliation. Just when she thought she'd taken back control, she just wanted to leave, doing it several times in her head but other emotions pulled hard, battling with her head and heart all night. Her blame in him triggered Musa, he was beginning to fall apart. Lashing out to silence the noise.

'Did you bring your swimming stuff?' they both hummed a yes. 'I thought it was nice of them to say you could have a swimming break on a Thursday. Told you it wouldn't be as bad as you thought.' The car park was rammed from visitors taking advantage of the last of the pleasant weather.

'Oh shit, it's packed,' no dispute from Hassan this time. 'You'll have to get out, I need to squeeze in that space.' Esme looked exotic with her peach scarf and large sunglasses; she was being watched as she concentrated on getting the Range Rover into a tight spot. Activating the handbrake, a rush of panic came over as she felt it all come apart, carrying her children's emotions, but they were all her own. She didn't want them to have the burden of dysfunctional parents to screw them up for the rest of their lives. There were no options, but an indebted dependency and core values she held onto.

They walked the causeway before anyone else. The mount felt imposing, holding tight to its secret. Reaching the harbour, seeing Samir was all she could stand, pushing her nails into her palms to avert running and crying to him.

'Salaam. My favourite family,' happy to see them, his hand over his heart. Esme's tears rolled out from under her Dior's, leaving streaks in the foundation. 'Come, come. I hear you have had a trial to endure. Please, come.' He led them to the house, Esme's tears were unstoppable as she felt God had greeted her in the form of Samir. She was desperate to speak to him, she needed answers. The children went to their classes and Esme was taken into the long room. Tea and cakes were ready on the table and she felt the warmth and superficial comfort from him. She did love him, she did. Not like that, but like a recognition she longed to see.

'Please, sit, sister.' Samir poured two teas and sat opposite, gasping when Esme removed her glasses. 'AstaghfiruAllah!' he said, prompting a tsunami of tears from her. Samir recited something she didn't understand, shedding a tear himself.

'I have no words of comfort sister, except, whatever the reason, it is not acceptable. You and I know that,' he handed her a cotton handkerchief. She wiped her face, revealing even more of the bruise.

'Brother, I need help. I don't know what help, but I need help. My huz…Musa, there's something taking over. Something bad, I can feel it! We have lost our dog and I know this is haram, but I am desperate to find him. He helps Harv…Hassan, with his anxiety.'

'What is haram? To have a dog? Sister, it is not. A dog is still Allah's creation. A companion, a good companion, mentioned in the Quran itself. I feel your loss. I had a dog when I was young.'

Esme sniffed, her despair lifting. 'You did?'

'Sure. We kept him outside, because he steals the food, y'know?' he chuckled, 'but, he was part of the family. A piece that we all lived by each day. When he died, the whole family grieved for a long while. You see, whatever comes into your life sister, becomes part of you when you give it love. That's all. Don't feel guilty about your grief. Allah loves a compassionate heart. This is our reminders that lives are short and not to get above ourselves. He hears you. But I am not at liberty to say that it will be all right. Ask your heart what it feels.'

'My heart is confused,' she took a sip of mint tea. 'Why is there always tea?'

Samir shrugged, 'I like to be ready for visitors and, well, I like it,' their swallowing the loudest noise in that room. 'The heart is never confused, sister. It is our minds and sabotaging thoughts that confuse us. It always knows what is right and what it wants, listen to it carefully. Give in to it, let it settle. If it doesn't settle, it isn't right for you. The heart is your direct line to Allah. Don't you know it beats out his name just to keep you alive? Grief is our power, sister.' His soft voice held conviction and all she needed to heal. Musa never spoke like that, it was always patriotic rules with a condemning tone. All hell this, and damnation to that.

'I want to leave him. But I feel I need permission to do it. I'm scared I'm going to make the wrong decision again. I always make the wrong decision.' Esme placed down the tea thinking how she was going to approach the issue with the door. She played with the small glass, overthinking it. 'Doctor...I think Max is behind the door.' The vibe in the room became heavy, awkward and she felt foolish for crying in front of him.

He changed leg positions, taking out another handkerchief wiping his watering eyes. Samir stood. 'Please excuse me, I have a class to attend. No need to work for us today. Take a rest, have a look around the town. I pray Allah will bring forth your ease, soon. Salaam.'

She agreed with a smile, her face taut from dried tears. That was it then, no more about the door, analysing Samir's change of moods. Esme wanted to see Peter, he wouldn't be as diplomatic as Samir, and probably make the whole thing worse. Or his practical outlook would allow her to see sense and regain focus. Playing with the tissue, her sniffs echoing in the large room, a walk around the Parish was a logical step and Max was probably being looked after by someone oblivious of their plight.

Straightening herself, setting her hijab right, tapping and trusting, she walked the room. The artefacts catching her eye, wanting to touch things, feeling acutely aware she was probably being watched. The Hamsa was dominant the more she looked; hinted in backgrounds and disguised in the wood fire-surround. There were other carvings, narrowing her eyes to get a closer look. Ancient art or religious symbols, running the tips of her fingers over the raised circles and rectangular significances. Her foot was paused on something covered by a rug. Pushing it aside with the tip of her Crocs, raised in the slate floor was an intricate Hamsa inlayed on a tile of a different mineral. Oud sharply shifted her attention, suddenly filling the room, prompting her to pick up her bag and leave. Head down, she hastily approached the front door.

'As salaam alaikum, Esmay.'

Dropping her bag in fright. 'Oh! Wsalaam, Janan, I didn't see you there. I'm taking the day off, well, Samir suggested I go to err...'

'I wish you luck,' Janan's energy dragged Esme's soul to her feet causing acute nausea, her eyes terrifyingly endless. Certain they were swirling.

'Thank you, um, okay, I'll see you soon, inshallah,' Esme held the crown of her head as she left, desperate to get home and hide under a blanket, her left hand burning and itching.

25

Thursday Market

Beach breaks always prompted mass hysteria among the children. Euphoric in their release as they skipped and ran along the Causeway. Hassan was last, his head hung down from a burst bubble, the cocoon falling apart. He'd lost a friend who held all his weird pieces together, and his father had proved himself to be a hypocrite and fraud. All that kept him hanging on was his mother, the biggest rock in his unstable situation. He kept going over Musa's strike in his head, repeating, replaying, the sound it made and the horrified, defenceless gasp from Esme. That was the worse bit about it, feeling his mother slip away for a moment, carrying all she felt in that split second that changed everything. The 'snap'.

Samir led the boys, passing visitors going in the opposite direction. They followed in an excitable state carrying their rolled-up towels under their arms. Today was an ideal time to get out of school, the stone masons were repairing the wall and drilling was causing disruption, the sound of the sea washing away toxic thoughts.

Checking over his shoulder now and then Samir stood aside to let the boys walk in front.

'Behave yourselves and show the visitors how good we can be. Let's give them a good impression. You are ambassadors of your faith, remember that.'

The boys hurried to the beach, unable to control their eagerness to get into the water as they weaved through the protruding rocks. The mount stood proud in the distance, the haze of the day adding a dreamy look. Samir looked back at it, his heart and conscience heavy.

The girls were the last to leave, only Layla and her classmate Khadijah followed three younger members of the class who giggled and fussed as they trotted behind the assistant; her black covering flapping like warning flags as the wind picked up. Reaching the end of the causeway, they ran on ahead using the rocks as hurdles, balancing and hopping from one to another.

'Girls! Be careful! Don't fall! Your heads! Your heads!' Layla and Khadijah idled behind, a little shy to expose all and enter the sea.

'Are you going in?' Khadijah asked.

'I want to. I haven't been in yet. You?'

'I will if you will. I'm going in my clothes.'

'What? Like that?' Layla looked down at her own jeans, 'I can't go in these. I'll drown for sure.'

'I have spare leggings, if you want?' Khadija offered.

'Oh, err, ok then. Thanks. I guess we're not going back to lesson. What's the occasion anyway?'

Khadija shrugged, 'Samir says it's something they do on a Thursday. No occasion.'

'I thought Friday was the special day?'

'We can't swim on a Friday. It's forbidden. Y'know?'

'No, I don't. Is it something to do with 'being holy'?' she finger quoted.

'I think. But we don't have school on Fridays, so it's probably that. You seem sad today.'

They placed down their towels in a spot away from the boys, Layla could see Hassan on his own, feeling his angst.

'Oh, I'm okay. We've lost our dog. Well, my father lost him. We're all heartbroken.'

'You had a dog?!'

There was the dog thing again, Layla thought. 'Yeah,' picking out the broken shells from the fine shale, 'but now he's gone and I don't like what's going on. Do you find Ustaz Janan a little, strange? I mean, her eyes! They give me the chills!'

'She is to be respected, no one messes with her. She doesn't say much, just floats around the school. Samir fears her.' Khadija said, folding and fussing.

'I don't think they are together, do you?'

'I'm not sure. No one knows her. But something strange happened once.' Khadija whispered.

'Like what?'

'She changes things. The house, it changes sometimes. Like, the doors can be in various places. Or I forgot where they were.'

Layla pulled a faced, 'what is it with doors and this place? The tea she makes, what's in that stuff?'

'She only gives it to the older girls. The younger ones are not allowed it.' Checking around.

'Have you had some?' Layla asked.

'No. I'm not as brave as you. She gives it to the stronger ones. Like you, the other day. Probably testing it on you.'

'Testing it? What do you mean?'

Khadijah took out the black leggings for Layla. 'You must swear to me, swear to Allah, not to tell anyone.'

'I promise, cross my heart,' she made the action, but Khadija was waiting for more, 'okay, okay! Walahi, I swear!'

Khadija got closer, turning her back so they couldn't see her lips move.

'Girls have drowned!' she whispered.

Layla gulped at the possibility, a little smug to have her suspicions confirmed. '*Drowned*?!'

Khadija put her forefinger on her lips, 'Sshh!' staring Layla into silence.

'Sorry. How?'

'No one knows. It's a funny tide here, I guess they got swept out.'

Layla regarded the calm waters, 'swept out? In winter perhaps, but not now. Doesn't make sense. How awful for the parents, though. When was this?'

'Ages ago. School only reopened recently.'

She took a panoramic video of the beach, there was always that release of a gasp when the Mount came into shot. 'Where do you live then?'

'Truro. Not as nice as here. More Muslims there though. This is the only place. Prices are good, and the curriculum.' Khadija felt intimidated by Layla's social status.

'Do your parents know about the...' she checked around, '...drownings?'

'Course not. Do you think they'd send me here otherwise?'

'Hmmm. I daren't tell my mother. Or maybe I should, then I wouldn't have to come here. I just wish we were in mainstream. But my father thinks...' Layla stopped as Samir approached them, Khadija going bright red and nearly peeing.

'Are you going for a swim girls? We have ordered lunch.' Their eyes lit up, anything Samir suggested was always a promising idea and his presence was one you wanted to be around. They trusted him, there was no agenda just a good heart, an exhausted one.

'Put your things with the assistant, she will look after them. Go have fun but be careful out there. Stay where we can see you.'

The girls waded in, flinching at the cool temperature and hopping over the waves. Hassan stood on the shore, scanning the horizon.

'He's quite attractive, don't you think?' Khadija whispered.

'Samir?' Taking another look to decide. 'I guess. I think his outlook is more attractive than his face.' Layla caught Hassan's attention, 'Harvey? You coming in?' she called over the atmosphere of a busy beach. He shook his head, distant and melancholic. The beach was long, open. People were dotted around in their places, some sat on the rocks, some on the causeway. A horse rider completing the scene. The girls shivered the deeper they got.

'It's freezing! The sea is much warmer back home.' Layla said, her teeth chattering.

'I love Saint Ives. Too expensive now. Although we have days out there now and then. You're not from here originally though, are you?' Khadija detecting her slight northern lit, probably inland with Tudor frontages and shops that sold silk scarves and lavender bags.

Layla was becoming conscious of her 'tier' within society. It all seemed normal until she met friends like Khadija, feeling ashamed about her first class lifestyle. 'Uh, no, just north of Wales border, Chester. Do you know it?'

'Yeah, a little. That's posh, too. We're from Bradford, originally.' A heavy populated part of the north, known for its curry and colonist occupation. Layla's nose turned up a little, conscious that she'd done it. 'You'll have a Cornish accent soon enough, Layla. I prefer it here than up there. I don't care that everyone stares at us.'

They stopped when the sea had reached their waists, the waves knocking them off balance. Layla noticing Samir with his hand peaked over his eyes, keeping a close eye. It felt strange and restrictive with clothed legs, but she was comfortable with Khadija, she wouldn't have got away with it up north. Her existence trapped from both sides, trying to fit in and trying to rebel against what caused her to stand out. Her true identity was there somewhere, and Cornwall was beginning to unravel who they were.

Layla dipped herself up to her chin, then back up, back down. Then to her ears, the muffled vibration blocking out the world. Fully submersing herself she felt free of the stress of appearance. She came up for air, pushing her hair away from her face.

'Do you want to borrow my goggles?' Khadija asked with them perched on her head.

'Oh, no, it's okay, you need them.'

'No, it's fine,' she took them off, 'I'm going back, I'm too cold and I need to dry off anyway. My parents are picking me up early today.'

'Okay, thanks. I'll be five minutes. I just need some space to think.'

Khadija agreed and hopped out of the deep, her clothes clinging to her when she reached the shallows. Going in the sea fully clothed seemed, well, absurd!

Clearing the mist from inside the goggles with her thumbs, Layla stretched the rubber strap over the mass of auburn spirals, checking their fit and position before ducking under. The water muting, hearing her own breaths. She grasped the floating debris that passed then checked the seabed for anything worth taking. The sloshing made her forget where she was as she followed a shoal of small fish. Darting, changing direction, picking around her ankles. She bent down to touch them, delighted when they swam through her fingers. What were these unusual fish, with their iridescent scales and neon eyes? This underworld was becoming comfortable, hypnotic and she didn't want to go back to the one above. Entering a water-filled daydream, something caught her eye; a long, dark shape darted in the distance. She tried to follow it, but it disappeared into the depths. Narrowing her eyes, she could just make out its shape, maybe it was Beaky.

Layla came up for air, scanning the beach realising she had ended up further out, but she could still see the boys and Samir. Khadija was sitting on the towels probably freezing to death with wet clothes sticking to her. Beginning to feel the cold herself, she decided to make her way out, pushing herself off the bottom and breast stroking toward the shore. She let out a yelp as something brushed her foot; it was rough, perhaps cloth. She continued to swim with a panic in her belly, telling herself it was probably seaweed or someone's discarded scarf. It happened again, this time across her stomach, feeling larger. The waves pulled her back as she was nearing the shallows, crossing, pushing her sideways. She spotted Hassan, he could see her. Waving her right arm with effort, he waved back.

'Shit. Harvey! Harve...' water entered her mouth, burning her throat. Layla coughed and spluttered, her heart raced, her limbs cramping. Another brush against her legs, she kicked out, screaming. Hassan heard her, calling for Samir. Khadija ran and forgot about their stuff, sprinting along the shore kicking up the wet sand behind her. She always won the races at sports day, wanting to compete and make it a living. But her father said it was a profession for boys and she should start thinking about studying and achieving *his* goals and expectations. The speed liberated her, and she almost forgot what she was running for, wishing she could run forever, away from the constrictions. People looked on but were oblivious. Then, she saw it as she pushed her shins through the water.

Layla felt something soft wrap around her waist, she immediately grabbed it, an arm! She screamed and wriggled. She hadn't prayed in a long time, but this time she meant it, begging for her life. The thrashing blinded her, periodically letting in the noise of the beach. She felt herself being lifted out, taking in a cold, fresh breath. Thrust forward. Relieved, elated, carried effortlessly.

'I got yer, I got yer! Stop yer blimmin wrigglin!' Akash laid her down in the sand, her chest heaving. The sun shone behind him, a silhouetted heroic vision smiling down at her. Confusion, mistrust, adoration and love all at once. Her heart muscles ached as they relaxed and beat from her crush.

'Y'need bliddy swimmin lessuns! Come on maid, let's sit you up.' Samir and the boys came running and crowded around her.

'Layla! Layla! Hamduillah!' Samir's face pale and panicked, 'why did you go out so far?!'

'I'm okay,' she coughed, 'I'm okay,' taking in a shuddering breath.

'Thank you, brother.' Samir said, looking a little sheepish at Akash.

'S'alri. Lucky I wuz 'ere,' he stood and held out his hand. Samir took it, shaking it with vigour, placing his other hand on top. Akash broke off the connection, taking Layla by the arm to lift her. 'C'mon missus. You need summat warm. Where's the boy?' Hassan didn't know how to react and stood awkwardly trying to cover up his puppy fat again, not sure which bits to hide. Akash was larger than life, a real-life superhero. He looked different today, his skin darker and eyes a piercing blue. 'There he is. Yous alri'?' Hassan about to cry. Towels were laid over Layla's shoulders and quivering torso, her innards squirming at what could have happened, and the timely rescue.

'Where's Khadija?' she asked, her teeth like maracas.

'Layla! Did you see it? Did you bloody see it?!' Khadija blurted as she pushed her way through. 'Sorry, Ustaz, but there was something, out there! It went towards the Mount, before he came!' she panted, blushing when she set eyes on Akash.

'Just a shark, or something,' Samir said, with the bottoms of his brown trousers rolled up above his ankles.

'No sharks round ere,' Akash bluntly stated, holding eye contact with him.

'Right, well, hamduillah we are all safe. We're having lunch. Please, join us Akash.'

Hassan lay on his bed, staring through the warped window at the seagulls gliding on the thermals. He hadn't taken the anti depressants in a while and things were coming back, the things his father wanted suppressed. He didn't go to help look for Max because he knew otherwise. Missing his companion so fiercely, hiding in the loft was the only way he could deal with it, that's how he always dealt with it.

Steve tapped the window, slipping on the lead flashing. Displaying his four-foot wingspan when Hassan opened the window. 'You again? Seriously? I'm running out of this bread. Baba will have my guts for garters!' overthinking the idiom.

He broke up the khubz into morsels, the bird stabbing at them. 'Don't know why you don't like mum's bread. We lost Max. He's stuck, in that bloody room. I know it. Don't suppose you can help with your stupid feet.'

Steve grabbed with its yellow beak, marked with a single red dot, its beady eye on Hassan's hands. He stood back in the room, hoping the large gull would follow. 'It's ok, I won't hurt you. Be easier to eat in here instead of that roof.' The rustle of a bag alerted the bird, Hassan producing a fillet of Salmon from it. 'Here, look, I got you this.'

The bird cautiously moved to the window ledge, scanning the room, *'mama ma'* was all it said. Hassan coaxing it in, but Steve had reservations.

'Come on! Salmon! Look!' waving it provocatively. 'Stupid fucking bird!'

'Harvey? You Okay?' his mother called up the stairs.

'Yeah! Fine,' mumbling his last word. Steve took flight without the bait, joining the others in their cries of domination.

Esme lit the log burner for Layla who sat in her father's chair with the throw around her, cradling a mug of hot chocolate. They both stared at the glowing wood, Layla reliving every moment and getting a huge buzz in her belly when she thought of Akash.

'How are you feeling, sweetheart?' Esme crouched beside her, rubbing her hand.

'I'm okay. Just...'

'I know. You've had a bit of a shock. But you're here, that's the main thing. No more swimming on Thursdays.'

'No, it wasn't, I mean, you're all making a fuss. I wasn't that deep. I could've stood up, but I just panicked. Mum...there was something touching me. Something big!'

'Oh, it was probably a fish or seaweed, and your imagination ran away with you again.'

'No, Mum! Khadija saw it.'

'Saw what?'

'Something! She saw what was trying to take me! And, and Kash was *there!* Like, *there!*'

'I think you're in shock love. Just drink up, and you'll see it a bit clearer in the morning. I know what you girls are like.' Esme brushed the hair from her daughter's face, seeing the little girl she'd lost. Layla slapped her hand away.

'Why don't you ever believe me?!' her ocean eyes pleaded with Esme.

'Because, well, it all sounds a little farfetched. Akash was probably, errr…'

'Probably, err, what? Just happened to be there and not working?'

'Well, yes, why not? I mean, who wouldn't notice that red hair?'

'He came from behind me, mum, not from the beach. He was already *in* the water! Don't you get it? And the texts.'

Esme's eyes widened, 'you've been *texting*? Since when?!'

'No, it's not like that. I didn't even give him my number! He just, texts! Usually when I need help. Oh my God, that's it! That's why he came!'

'Hold on just one second here! He's *stalking* you?!'

Layla stood, the blanket falling to the floor, 'Mum! Christ! No! He's, well, different.'

'Sit down! And watch your tongue with me, young lady! They're all different when they're different. Doesn't mean anything. He's playing with you.'

Layla went to look out of the bay window, the panes contorting the town.

'You know that day when we had a fight? I went to the beach to cool down and Kash just, noticed me. Not in that sense, but something else. It was scary, he was so protective, and we'd only just met. It would be creepy in any other circumstance, but not this one. And he's fast, like, fast! He gets places. I stormed off because he was with those awful girls at the station, but he got to the steps here in half the time it took me, from the station! Mum, open your head! Peter, it's the same with Peter! You just don't wanna see it!'

Esme recoiled, taking out her mother's letter from her pocket, affectionately touching the handwriting.

'And where's Baba?'

'The café.'

'Why is he there? He should be here, making sure I'm okay! And that bruise needs looking at!'

'That's why he's at the café.'

26

Revert

Musa thumbed the tafsir beads outside the Abadis, shielding a small glass of burning spirit. The Oud had gone from the stock room, and the pressure was on. The urgency to get Ibrahim out of Riyadh had intensified, but he hadn't been answering his calls. Familiar loyalty had left and it was out of character, but then what did he expect? His percentage was coming in, at least that side of the bargain was kept. Perhaps Ibrahim had no use for him now that he had financial ease, but he needed him to be his confidant and scape goat, and take his daughter to a safe haven. Musa chortled at the thought, tapping the table, the loss of control weighed him down from Esme's surprising change of attitude, she had caught him unawares and he'd been so careful. Paranoia elevated his anxiety as he mulled over the possibility of an unknown impostor or set up, regretting lashing out at her. He felt sick from guilt, ashamed and a dishonour to his family name.

Looking up to watch passing profit, he clocked Akash approaching; his steel-blues fixed on Musa, making him square up and discreetly hide the beads under the table, changing his words of protection.

'Alri'? This seat taken?'

'I don't want your company.' Musa answered, looking out to the harbour.

'That's how y'thank me, is it? You wanna leave that stuff alone.'

'When did that become your business?'

'I see,' Akash turned the chair around and straddled the seat, smelling God-like. 'You need t'pick yer enemies wisely,' he said in a lowered tone.

'Thank you for the advice,' Musa held the shot glass to his lips.

'Youm be steppin' on toes, Emmet. Or should I say, foreigner?'

'Call me what you wish. I take no offence.'

'We ain't havin our reputation ruined cause the upper class got greedy and decided to place his corruption in every port. It ain't appnen ere.'

'This place needs some culture, don't you think?' he sneered and sipped.

Akash glanced up at the café's name, 'we ain't be avin a take-over again. We worked 'ard to protect it. This is our sea and our town! You're attracting the wrong kind and we's have t'keep our women and kids safe.'

'I'm making this town my own, whether you like it or not,' he replied, smirking. Akash's pupils enlarged, his torso jerking, and lips pursed.

'You two 'avin fun?' Peter appeared, diffusing the situation.

'I was just leavink,' Musa stood, knocking back the rest of the glass. 'Sit, you are welcome in my café, have what you want, on the house.' He reached for his phone and wallet, Akash grabbing his forearm with a cold, clammy hand.

'We don't want nuthin from yous,' his grip tightening and eyes changing shape.

'Alri, that's enough Kash, let the man be on his way.' Peter intervened.

Musa snatched his arm back, his heart near thumping out of his chest. 'Your, *son*, needs teaching some mannors. And stay away from my daughter!' speaking his last words in Akash's face through gritted teeth. Side stepping his way out through tables with a light head and hollow legs, maintaining his cool until he turned the corner, leaning against a whitewashed cottage. This territory felt out of his league, Musa was losing Musa, vulnerable and ganged upon. He was alone here, an alien, feeling himself slipping. He pulled and fanned at his clothes to release the Oud still trapped in the fibres, confirming the reason he was here. To supply to the elite and push dwellers out.

The café was just the start, a landmark that would spark the takeover making it impossible for residents to stay.

His forearm stung and throbbed. 'Ya Allah! Not now!' wincing and dragging in air, he telepathically called for her in his mother's tongue. A gentle stroke of his leg affirmed her presence.

'Noona. I need your help,' she purred and blinked, her coat as coarse as wild boar hair, 'the half Siren, it touched me!' checking his worsening forearm from Akash's blistering finger-marks. 'Get the kalb, before they take the whole family and Oud supplies,' he panted, 'I must restore their trust. They are already suspicious.' Noona agreed and morphed back into Raffia, her odd eyes unchanged. Her lips pressed hard on his, the hedonistic fire ignited between them. But Musa's wounds were too great to reciprocate. Leaving a taste in his mouth, like creosote.

'My love, my time and youth will end soon. Give them Layla. I will leave the rest to Allah.'

'We deal with this first,' she said, touching his weeping wounds, 'some infant blood for now, before we have to hide you.'

27

DECOY

Esme wandered the supermarket numb, it still hurt to smile. She was off-balance, sleep deprived and existing on live wires. Her spiritual connection had been severed with Max, like he'd just, disappeared. Intangible hope a torment, honing on the slithers of logic that he must be out there somewhere, crying for her and upsetting herself with that notion. Max was more than a pet, his soul resided within her breaths.

She was thankful for Friday, at least her children were where she could see them. Throwing random grocery items in the cart, avoiding any reflection where should catch herself screaming, 'stupid child'. Staying was a suffocating thought, but not as bad as leaving. The perfume and flowers on the seat of new cars wasn't what kept her, although they were the foundations of thought. It was something invisible, a foot out the door became bombarded with tender moments, acts of service and devotion. Musa would retaliate to her leaving in a way that would cut off all resources, in a world and society that forced impossible dependency upon women. But there was a fire inside, a fire that saw material entrapment for what it was. Esme yearned to lay face down in the dirt, and get the designer labels muddy.

The drive back to Saint Ives was consumed by intrusive thoughts and worry, especially about Hassan; his anxiety had increased and rebellion was resurfacing. She wasn't sure if she wanted that back, preferring him placid and agreeable.

Arriving at Draycott Terrace her breaths juddered as she pulled up outside the house. Esme gazed at the roofs alight from the orange glow of a nearing sunset, a weary smile dropping her shoulders and adding perspective. The silence of the car sang in her ears, warmth emanating from the leather seats made her drowsy. She noticed the sun was getting lower and soon the grey would return. But if the lights still shone at night to send her to sleep, she could pass through the dark and into the brighter days.

Warm tears rolled from her eyes hindering her focus as she took her mother's letter from her bag, the last one she received at least three years ago. The envelope an off-white from a stationery set, holding the perfect package to her nose receiving hints of ink and her mother's faint cologne. Esme's trembling hand clumsily opened it for the millionth time,

'My dearest Esme. This is my last letter and I've not been able to get through to your number. I'm sorry I ever made you choose,

I had no right. I'm a silly old fool and it has cost me dearly. I know you are cross with me. Forgive me, but you have much to endure. Chase your dreams, that's where we'll meet again. I hope you and the children are doing well. Give my love to Harv and Layla and some good old fuss for Maxey boy. Always in my heart, Mum x

'My last letter' always prompted a perplexion from her. Where were all the others? Grief stung her sinuses. She sobbed, choking on regret and an ache that was too great to confront. She had been secretly looking for her mother, a little scared at the women with similar faces, knowing she would've just run the other way if it was her. Practising what she would say to in her in the mirror and the smile she would wear, the thoughts of slapping her and calling her all the names, punching, beating, screaming. Time and prescriptions had erased so much, past holidays in Saint Ives were just flashing images now, ones she clung to.

'Come on Esme, this is no good,' she sniffed, tilting the rear-view mirror to check her face. She was different in her external disguise, an alter-ego in the form of metal and horsepower. The tears had revealed the yellowing bruise, she touched it, igniting a determination. The tantalising tickle of freedom like a dangling carrot, needing a big shift or a bigger threat to move her forward, promising herself that would be her moment. Wasn't it already big enough?

The front door was open as she struggled in with the shopping.

'Hello! Moose! Guys!' Her face creased from the empty house, missing Max going through the bags to see if there was anything for him. 'Hello?! Anyone? Layla! I'm back! Got some stuff!' her heart fluttered from an imagined scenario. 'Perhaps they're having a last swim,' she muttered, not noticing the scatters of red sand on the tiles. Leaving the bags in the hallway, she left the house and made her way to the beach, assuring herself that she was going to see them.

Standing at the edge of the sand between the hut café and finer dining, she peaked both hands over her eyes, frantically searching among the high-pitched screams and racquet games. Tutting loudly when she saw Hassan sat with Raffia on the guest towels. Striding over with tightened lips, the sand turning over her ankles, dousing her stroppy struts, she was ready to tell Raffia how much of a pain in the arse she had become. Invading people's space and privacy, eating all their fish and turning up at the most inconvenient times.

'You could have left a note or called me! I've been worried sick!'

'Is ok, sister, sit. I give you break. Why you don't have rest in house?'

'No, Raffia, it's not ok. You don't just take, okay?'

'Okay, okay, sorree. Sit, we have food and tea.'

Hassan was quiet, head down playing in the sand.

'Hassan is my son, too.' Raffia said, sending a shiver through him.

'Well, that's sweet of you Raffia but with one thing and another, I'm in a fragile state,' Esme knelt in the sand with a *thud*. 'What do you know about Max, Raffia?' Tell me! Has he drowned?!'

Raffia looked out to sea, her gaze steady. 'No sister, no drowned.'

'What then?'

'He come soon. Believe it. He come. The sea takes, and gives.' The looked she gave Esme froze her in time, a hostile stare of deep concentration. She was hard to dislike as she undermined your boundaries, like an annoying aunt that were always sticking their oar in where it wasn't wanted.

'You okay Harv?' Esme asked, noticing he hadn't taken his eyes off the sand he ran through his fingers. He could see the crystal cubes in their thousands and in detail, scared the effect might be from stopping his medication. He didn't know how to replace Max, the PlayStation offered superficial and short-lived fulfilment, the same with social media; doom scrolling for instant dopamine hits. He just didn't have the motivation for imagination, it was like he didn't need that anymore, as if, *he* was his imagination.

'Look, I'm sorry I snapped at you Raffia. I appreciate you looking after Harvey. Would you mind looking out for Layla? I've got frozen stuff melting in the hallway.'

'Is no problem sister. You go, is fine. I look for Layla.'

'Mum! I don't feel well!' Hassan panicked, holding his swelling throat. Esme placed her hand on his forehead.

'Oh my God. What did you eat?' All Hassan could do was point at Raffia's bag. Esme's adrenaline rocketed as she looked through it.

'What did you give him Raffia?!' who just shrugged and acted dumb.

'Come on, let's get you back. It'll be fine, I have some antihistamine. We'll run back, that'll do it.' Hassan was happy to leave, he wasn't doing well in anyone's company, especially Raffia's. She spoke intimately about his father, and knew way too much. She was sus, something he knew from first meeting her. 'Come in for tea, okay Raffia? Layla has...' she checked her watch, 'half an hour, tops. The sun is going down.' Raffia agreed with a nod, her eyes fixed on Layla's bobbing head.

Layla was immersed up to her nose, treading water while watching the beach. She could see her mother waving her arm around, signing she was going back to the house. Layla loved to stay in the sea alone with her thoughts and the reassurance Akash was close-by.

Placing the mask over her eyes, she ducked just below the surface, watching the tide move the sand, plunging her toes along the grooves. The sea was clearer and warmer than Marazion, which was choppy and chilled with a shale beach. Saint Ives having a Mediterranean feel to it in comparison. Layla's amplified movements stopped time as she swam further out, the sloshing clouding perception. Maybe she could swim around to the lifeboat station, it would only take a few minutes. Heading over to the black rocks, older boys were jumping off them, keeping the lifeguard distracted. Her arms ached, but the thought of Akash's protective arms kept her going. The waves pushed her towards them, managing to grab a hold from an overstretch, assessing the situation as the tide pushed and pulled. She clung to the dark mineral, studying the limpets.

'Do y'need a'and up?' asked a girl sat above her. It was one of Akash's fans, Tyler.

'I'm okay thanks. Just going to the next bay.'

'You'll catch yer legs orn these rocks y'know. Trust me, I knows from experience. It's better to walk to it when tide is owt. I'd go back if I were yous. I mean, it's not that bad, but one push from them waves, y'could get some nasty cuts.' The girl pulled the leg of her shorts back, tapping her fore finger on a badly stitched scar, 'see? I did it, ri ere.'

Layla wiped her face feeling a little goofy, all wet and dishevelled.

'Get yourself dry and walk into town 'stead. Don't wanna ruin that perfection o'yours, ay?' She gave Tyler a glare and decided to head back, no further words were exchanged. Flinching when something brushed her leg. It was light, seaweed perhaps, but there wasn't much of that in this bay. The girl watched with a deceitful eye, Layla let out a quiet yelp when something heavier touched her ankle, giggling and dipping her face in expecting to see Akash. Nearing the shore, craving Esme's cooking with thoughts of eating green salad and humus, she was pulled under, like before, only harder.

Her laughter-filled screams were muted as the sea entered her mouth. She came up for air screaming at the top of her lungs alerting the lifeguard. He stood, binoculars out, turning the dial trying to locate the scream.

'Ehcuse me sir,' he looked down from his elevated white chair, 'I loss my dog, please look with your eyes.' He was torn, looking down at Raffia's pout.

'Uh, just one moment, madam,' his search frantic, the screams seemed to have stopped. All he could see were happy tourists, it must be the group of teenagers cavorting and fooling around just about halfway in.

'Please, sir, my dog, you look.'

The lifeguard tutted, scanning the shore one last time. 'What type of dog?' he asked, still peering through the magnified lenses.

'He brown, like gold. Eh, retriever! Yes, gold-den re-tree-ver.' The young man was fighting with his instinct because those screams sounded serious.

'Uh, is that him? Over there? Coming towards us.'

Raffia sneered, the lifeguard not noticing her eyes, 'yes, thank you. Sorree, I just panic. Thank you, sir.' She took Max by his collar; the dog wet and bewildered, frantically looking around for his people. His leash dragging behind.

Layla struggled to penetrate the surface, scrabbling to put her mask on. She was pulled back with force as if attached to a ski rope. Panic-stricken, she tried turning to look at her assailant and the rush of water instantly calmed, it was just her and whatever the dark hand belonged to. It let go, in a flash it was behind her, two rubbery fingers wiped a slimy film over her mouth; she no longer needed to hold her breath. Layla was treading water, the icy depths chilling her limbs and intrigue refocussing the terror. Light from above danced on her feet, her stomach summersaulting from the darkness beneath. The figure emerged in a blur, darting around her, its ambient screeches of intrigue frightening as it lusted over her floating hair.

She felt relaxed in its presence, trusting it, flashes of Akash's features embellished the excitement. Coming closer, the creature mauve in colour, changing, sure it was him finally revealing his identity. Layla forgot she was being pulled through the stuff of her mother's worse nightmares, with nothing but aqua, random vegetation and debris floating passed her. She didn't take her eyes off the being whose hands were large and webbed, a bit like Peter's. There was an innocence about it, a purity yet unspoiled, trusting it as she was pulled over basking sharks. Her mind blown she was happy to stay, her current life non-existent, at one with her surroundings. No one entered her head, life's stresses removed.

The pulling slowed, giving her chance to run her fingers through seaweed and shawls of fish that picked at her flesh, the same fish with neon flashes which shimmered over their scales. The being abruptly left her, buoyant in the deep, her escape visible above, she reached to rise, only to be pulled back down; she had become playful prey.

The water suddenly stilled, and the warmth of infatuation had left. She began to thrash in the deep as her conscience cleared and the aid over her mouth had perished, fearing for her life. Her mother, she wanted her mother - guilt and shame replacing the lust. Trying to release her hand from its grip, they were drawing closer to a rock face with a giant Hamsa clearly visible like a directional sign and mark of territory. Rising towards the surface so fast, she broke the waves with a gasp. Layla took in large gulps of air, straining and coughing, still supported by the creature. Her vision cleared, frantically looking around she knew where she was, which made her panic even more. It wrapped itself around her and within a blink of an eye, they were in the chapel's dungeon. Layla was relieved to be on dry land and wanted to take a closer look at it, but it wasn't the Adonis that took her, the smell was enough to make you sick. She backed away from it, her back against the granite wall. It stooped over, pitiful eyes that portrayed an oppression. She was startled as the iron latch echoed, running up the steps she screamed for help, greeted by Janan.

'Calm now, you are safe. A little wet and ugly, but you have done well.' Janan put a large towel around her when Layla crawled through the door, placing a glass of tea in her trembling hands. Layla succumbed, whimpering in shock. Janan spoke to the Siren in a language Layla didn't recognise, her tone grateful. The creature bowed, then quickly morphed into something without bones, slipping through the barred window.

'What's happening?' Layla sobbed.

'You are my rarest prize, pure human, and greatest revenge. You shall redeem us all.'

28

Sanctuary

Hassan handled the pills he hid in the t-shirt draw, they had been calling him since the nightmares and whisperings. Aware of his identity and lies in the system, perceived as difficult and 'borderline' for questioning narratives. There was a different kind of calling that split him in half, putting Hassan in the corner while Harvey dealt with things. Seeing the metaphor clearly in his mind, the hoard of pills falling from the vertical parting of his personality. He'd started praying again because that made him 'see' even more. Prostration prompted surrendering sobs, the blood rush to the frontal lobe ignited neurotransmitters, taking him to a place he never wanted to leave.

He slammed the draw shut when he heard the bellows of Musa. His father was still in control, the tingle in his hands and stomach told him so. Esme began squealing and yelling for him to come down. He didn't want to go, it had to be more bad news and he wasn't sure what that would do to him.

Someone was coming upstairs, and panting, he heard panting and the distinctive rattle of Max's collar buckle. Pulling the door open, Musa stood there with the biggest grin on his face.

'Sur-prise!'

'Oh my God!! Max! Max!' he crumbled to the floor, Max writhing and licking his mouth, whining through his nose. Hassan sobbed with relief, his voice breaking.

'He's wet. Where did you find him?!'

'He just come from the sea.' Musa said, his forearm burning.

'The *sea*? Err, he stinks! You stink. Yes, yes, you do.' Soul mates reunited with fur legs and arms all a 'jumble.

'Maybe he swam over from Carbis bay.' Esme said behind, her arms folded controlling her little convulses.

'Yes, thas where I loss him. SubhaanAllah, he is clever dog.'

Esme gasped, 'Layla! Harv, Hassan, get your sister. She'll be thrilled to bits!'

'Can I take Max?'

'Definitely not. He needs a bath and I want him where I can see him.'

Max needed the rock lamp, and the same bones he found beyond the door.

Hassan hurried down the stone steps, talking and laughing to himself; his best friend was back and it made everything all right again. Running past the mini golf green, with cordyline and exotic shrubs, passed the huts and the café, reaching the cooling sand that reminded him of the middles of Lindt chocolate. He focussed on the sea, knowing exactly where she was. Standing at the shore, hands on hips, eyes scanning for that familiar head. Cupping his hands over his mouth he called her, grabbing others' attention. Calling again, ignoring the stinging intuition. Walking right then left, perhaps she was with Akash. He headed for the steps leading up to the hotel on the rocks, and his favourite narrow street. There was a small house called 'Crab cottage,' with white walls and a blue stable door. The smell of sea and fried donuts was distinctive of this street.

Reaching the lifeboat station, his expression hopeful when he saw Peter.

'Allo lad. What brings you 'ere?'

'They, we've, he found Max!'

'That's andsome news,' ruffling his hair.

'I'm looking for Layla, she here?'

'I ain't seen her t'day,' Peter's pupils dilated and nostrils flared, detecting something, unnerving Hassan.

'Come w'me. We'll see if we can find Kash.' Peter led him to the pizza place.

'Why did you call him that?' Hassan asked.

'What, Akash?'

'Yeah, and you're, y'know, not foreign.'

'He likes it,' Peter pushed the door open, the smell of garlic and basil stimulating their juices. Those girls were sitting at a table, freezing when they saw Peter.

'Where iz'e?' He asked. They shrugged, gulping down their mouthful.

'Lookin' f'me?' Akash startled them from behind.

'Where you bin?!' Peter scolded.

'About, why?'

'We bin distracted!'

'Was 'appened?'

'We got Max back!' Hassan butted in, smiling nervously as he looked between them.

'Cool, dude!' Peter looked at Hassan, then back at Akash.

'Have you seen Layla, Kash? She was swimmin in Porthminster,' Akash shook his head sternly.

'Son, y'know that boat trip youm always wanted?' asking a bewildered Hassan, 'well, now's yer chance. I hope yous got a strong stomach!'

29

Parallel

Janan took Layla to the school, the table crowded with the members dressed in those purple robes, Oud burning in the centre. Two women stood when they entered.

'Prepare her. He will be arriving soon, and we need to evade the Porthminster Marid.' The women bowed, their faces pale with distant expressions and trippy smiles.

Layla's heartbeat unusually fast, but she trusted what was going on, in a trance. Maybe it was a surprise or school ceremony. Perhaps her Arabic *was* that good after all, and she was going to be the centre of attention, finally.

She was taken to another room at the back of the house, which wasn't there before. Garments and more cloaks hung from gold hangers on stainless steel rails. Make up, hairbrushes and mint tea adorned a long table; it all seemed rather ordinary, like a dress rehearsal. The women never spoke, while they dried and brushed her hair. Layla regarded the tea, turning her attention back to them in the large mirror. Their actions compassionate and gentle, adoring her features while preparing her for something special. Layla's eyes suddenly widened, standing and knocking them aside.

'Am I getting married?!' they stroked her arms, gently pushing her back down into the seat. One offered her the tea, pushing it away and fearing where this was leading, with Khadija's words echoing in her head.

One of them took a long, white satin dress from the rail, reminding her of something Esme wore for bed. They were nodding at her to change into it, shielding her with a heavy sheet of material. The dress clung to every part of her, accentuating her youth. She was beautiful, a broken warrior and victim of her uniqueness.

They led her from the room and showed her to the board. She folded her arms over her breasts as they all made noises of approval in sadistic delight. Janan's emerald eyes glowed and pulsated with excitement.

'Take her! He is close!' Layla looked around for someone, *anyone!* Where was Samir? It was empty, the last boat for the tourists had left over an hour ago and there were barricades on the harbour's properties. The sea breeze goose bumped and mottled her pale skin as they led her to the castle, small stones and protruding rocks piercing her bare feet. The wind lifted the purple cloaks as they reached the terrace, crowding Layla, ushering her inside as they began chanting.

Passing the tourist rooms, they slowed their strides as they entered a cold corridor, a room at the end with a red hue filling the doorway and the unmistakable scent of Oud. The hooded figures entered to the left in single file, the room circular with no windows. Everything and everyone changing in appearance from the primary colour. A large Hamsa was scored into the stone floor, only there were no arabesque formations, but carved serpents congregating around an eye in the centre, yelping when she was shoved onto to it from behind. Her left palm began to burn and itch, rubbing it to try and soothe the irritation. They circled her, their chants becoming erratic and almost choral. Layla trembled, her feet like blocks of ice and a realisation that perhaps this wasn't a celebration she would be pleased to be part of. It was about her, but not one of mutuality. She had become an offering, a sacrificial one – cast out to the devil for doubting and dismissing: a dishonour.

Janan glided in, her eyes large, full of anticipation and a hint of insanity. They bowed at her entrance, the heat intensifying on Layla's palm, forcing her hand to clench.

'You have ALL, exceeded your loyalty and duty to the Nagini!' She bellowed, taking a handful of Layla's hair and admiring it in her strange hands. 'A child born under the regime of the Abadis, will increase worship and fortune and hail justice for ours culled by the hands of hypocrites! Followers of a placebo and false entity. *We* are, the great!' throwing her hands up to the ceiling, accompanied by their voiced appreciation around the room, prompting terrified sobs from Layla. Screaming as the burning intensified on her hand, looking incredulously at the Hamsa branded on her palm. Janan hissed as she circled Layla and the Hamsa, the green brocaded material dragging behind, Layla's eyes fixed on a thick tail that thrashed beneath it. The hooded figures closed in on her, chanting. Layla closed her eyes, waiting for her death. What was her mother going to say? She would surely perish into ash; all she said, all she warned was written on a mental brass plate. Vowing never to swim again, she mouthed verses from the Quran, feeling protected instead of triggered. She was sorry, more than sorry, sobbing as saying *goodbye* felt real enough. Hugging herself, tears of regret splashed onto the Hamsa. There was a low rumble in the room, followed by whispers. The hooded figures parted to make way for something. A bright light began manifesting, increasing in size, fizzing and smoking at its edges. An arched doorway appeared, the bright light doused the red hue and filled the room with love and warmth; was it heaven?

Disembodied drums grew louder, Layla was bemused yet relieved that her fate wasn't drowning, although a direct route to paradise.

'Where are you taking me?!' she turned to run screaming for help, bumping into the women who held onto her tightly. 'Let go of me, you freak!!'

A wind from the door disturbed the room.

'Do not be afraid, child,' Janan soothed.

'Why?' Layla sobbed 'why are you doing this?!'

'You will be safe, treated well. Go with brother Ibrahim, he will ensure you are cared for.'

'But, why… I'm sorry, for everything. I just want to go home, please!'

'It is unfortunate you have bore the brunt of your father's betrayal,' she jerked her head at Ibrahim who extended his arm from the doorway with a sympathetic smile. He had never seen such a vision of beauty, yet his heart ached at the fear that distorted the freshly freckled complexion.

'Sister, we must hurry, walahi I won't hurt you,' that was the word her and Hassan used to prove they were telling the truth, and nothing could break it. She stepped closer to him, not wanting to take his hand. Ibrahim respectfully pushed her shoulder and they walked into the shimmer and into the tomb.

Layla's gasp echoed, swinging around to see the sandstone wall close behind them.

'We must cover you.' He put a white kaftan over her head leaving her to get into it and waited with his back turned, clutching a large, white scarf, 'now this, hide your hair, sister. All of it.'

'But where are we? Are you going to kill me?!'

'No, no sister, I am not. AstaghfiruAllah. You are safe with me. Do not run away, okay? This will be a big mistake. We are surrounded by desert and hungry eyes. These will kill you, not my hands.'

'Where are we?' her tears altering her voice, beads of sweat appearing on her brow. Ibrahim was pained, her innocent fear like that of his daughter when faced with the terror of war.

'Hegra. Al Ula,' he replied solemnly.

'We...we're in *Saudi*?!'

'Yes. It is good to see you again, Layla.'

'You *know* me?!' narrowing her eyes to study his features.

'Come, we must move, quickly.'

'Why?'

'Please sister, we talk later inshallah.'

'But can't we just go back through the door thing?'

'It is not that easy. Just do as I say and don't ask too many questions.'

Ibrahim emerged from the entrance of the tomb he first entered, Qasr Al-Farid, the lone tomb and main gateway. Its unfinished illusion a façade against the changing sky. Shielding their eyes, he took her by the hands as they clambered down the rugged surface, Layla screeching from the light scorpions that scuttled across their path. Her satin dress tearing and lips drying. The sand was gritty and hot, unbearable on her fair feet as they crossed the terrain starved of vegetation, wiping the stinging sweat from her eyes.

Cowbells and the belch of camels penetrated the heavy air of Satan's solarium, with the smell of Oud coating her nostrils and lining her throat, reminding her of Musa; squeezing her lips to control the quivering. The sharp pain that shot through her heart made her feel vulnerable, holding onto the slither of familiarity she was unsure of, remembering Ibrahim being much older. Acutely uncomfortable from holding his hand a little longer than she was willing.

'We must head for the cooler parts, sister. You can rest, get something for your feet and we will decide what we are going to do.' Layla felt his protection was a little weak, not as present as Akash. She did feel his dignity and respect, uncomplicated, who would lead her to the righteous with love and a middle road, bestowing his devotion to her rights.

Ibrahim strode through the grit, enjoying his new body, his face radiant and a vision of piety as his white cottons flapped in the desert wind, euphoric and aroused from its youth and strength. There was also an underlying panic, elated to be holding the hand of the bride he tirelessly prayed for, yet only his creator knew the true intention that lay within his broken heart.

The larger gorges that almost met at their zenith, offered shade and cooler sand. Layla's eyes strained to focus on the vision of camels with blankets over their humps, men dressed like Ibrahim, women with dark and soft coloured coverings-peaches and whites, like Esme. Her mouth watered, she wanted to drink a gallon of that soda Musa always brought back home, which tasted like rotten mangoes.

'I'm so thirsty,' she gasped through tears.

'There will be plenty waiting for us, inshallah. You can have what you desire. Stay close and don't speak if you can help it.

Don't cry sister, I will take care of you, Insha'Allah. Only the almighty is with us now.'

Layla didn't wince at those words for a change, they were a comfort. Ibrahim waved his arm in the air as they approached the incense caravan. The women regarded Layla with large, charcoaled eyes from behind billowing chiffon. She held tight onto Ibrahim's arm as the shadows consumed them, dropping to her knees in relief and gazing in awe at the height of weathered gorges. Bedouins set up camp on higher levels in the rock face, looking over the edge at what was causing a stir. Ibrahim heaved her up, dragging Layla away from the women who began touching, stroking, and reciting. An old woman bared broken, blackened teeth as she cackled putting her smoke-drenched red shawl around Layla's shoulders, brushing the old woman's hand away. Then she felt another hand at the back, then another, pulling at the scarf, lifting it.

'Abadis! Abadis!' they cried. The crowd was gathering and closing in on them; faces, eyes, strangers all speaking at once, bartering with Ibrahim while man-handling Layla. The pushing and shoving suddenly dispersed by a light-coloured camel that waded gracefully through them, forcing them apart. Layla blinked profusely as the animal knelt before them, its blanket a deep purple. She watched it shrink and morph into a woman in veils, her lips protruding from many teeth. Pearls fell from her as she walked towards Layla, the traders scrabbling on the ground and stuffing them into any available pocket.

'You have a prized possession brother, you must take better care of it.'

'You!' Ibrahim gasped, 'from the lagoon!'

'Still naïve for a learned man, thinking you can elude me.'

'I am not used to fraternising with devils!'

'Shame on you for calling me that, for you have become one yourself. I am Jann, I am the desert.' She looked at Layla, her eyes flashing diamonds of light, scaring her half to death with encompassing doom.

'We must keep her in this petrified state to maintain her value.'

'I don't want anyone touching her!'

'That is not for you to decide, you have made your choice. Give her nourishment, then we must move her on. You have done well, human. At least appreciate your gift and freedom.'

She merged with the crowd of marketeers, Ibrahim waited then coaxed Layla towards a seating place carved into the stone, high and big enough to host giants.

'What were you saying?' Layla whispered between convulses.

'Do not speak, not yet. Your voice will cause a greater madness.' She looked up at the precision of the shelter he led her to, not a tool mark in sight. No one noticed her and continued with their tea making and Oud burning. The cool, firm surface was a respite, sending a mild shiver through her, a little hard on the tailbone. She sat with her regrets as heavy as the rock above, her ocean eyes swollen and red.

'Do not cry sister. I have protected you from these eyes. We are in the parallel of the Nabateans, a place I have frequented since receiving my new gift, with all intense purposes to stay and never return to the hell on the other side.'

'Can I speak?' her voice trembled.

'Yes, you can,' he handed her an ornate glass of mango soda, 'is this what you wanted?' she snatched the vessel, gulping down the fizzy contents.

'How is it cold?' sucking the last drops through her teeth, discreetly burping. 'What were you saying?'

Ibrahim distracted, admiring the back of his hands. 'Don't you recognise me?'

She searched his dark blue eyes, flushing from his good looks. 'I remember you in baba's café, but I'm not sure it is you.'

'It is me, only a lot younger,' he looked to the floor, 'I have been foolish and placed my trust in the wrong places. Now there is only one way out.'

'Did my father have something to do with this?' her nerves stung her stomach, the only man she was willing to hand herself over to was Akash, and she missed him badly.

'Indirectly.' Ibrahim answered.

Layla shuffled away from him, the fear in her eyes resembled the fear he once saw in his own daughter's before he left them in the bunker, the one that backfired. Saudi's weapons were the finest, precision made, relentless and gold plated with every woman and child inscribed upon them.

He rested his head on the stone, exhaling heavily.

'I need more, please,' Layla held the glass out for it to be filled again.

'Wait a little, ask again, it will fill,' the mango soda spilling over her hands from her surprise.

'How, how is it doing that?'

'I am doing that. It is my gift from Janan.'

'Will I have a gift?' Ibrahim regarded her, and shook his head. 'Where *are* we?'

'Forgive me, I have wronged you and your father. My revenge was too great, and I made a poor judgement. But I will do my best to make it right.'

'Why am I here?'

'Drink, then we must eat. We have a long night ahead.'

***

30

HASSAN

Hassan's face was alight when they left the harbour in '*Claire's Quest*'. Peter ruffling his hair and chuckling at the boy's excited expressions. Rescue volunteers holding onto anything, not a life jacket or rescue gear between them.

'Is this your first time on a lifeboat Harvey?' asked a man from the information centre.

'Yes! I've been dying for a ride since we got here!'

'Ha, well you got here alive. Glad you could make it aboard and I hear you found our Max? We'll find your sister too, don't worry.'

'Aye, hopefully before yer muther finds owt,' Peter interrupted.

'I know we're not going to find her, you're just looking for sake's purpose.' Hassan commented, leaning back on the controls.

'Oh yeah? What makes yer so sure?'

'I know, y'know,' he leaned into Peter and whispered, 'you don't have to pretend in front of me. I'm not afraid of you.'

'I see. Kash? Harv says he's not afraid,' Akash sneered, redressing his man-bun trying to keep his balance as the rescue vessel bounced on the waves. Hassan gulped at the atmosphere, looking between the two of them. They were a little scary, but he loved them with a strange, rekindled bond which still baffled him. He loved his father, however recent disappointments meant Peter was fast becoming his adopted replacement, a little star struck as he watched him turn the wheel.

'How long have you been a lifeboat volunteer?' Hassan asked him.

'All me life, and my father, and his father, and his father. Where d'ya want me t'stop?'

Hassan studied Peter's profile, fascinated with his bone structure. 'Are we going to Marazion?'

'Not yet. Old on ti',' he laughed, 'we got a choppy ride!'

Akash sat on the floor because his neck was aching.

'I can do the same...with, with my eyes!' Hassan blurted.

Akash casually turned to him, 'like this?' causing the boy to fall back from the heart-stopping gaze of something inhuman, accidently pressing controls.

'Kash, c'mon now, don't scare the boy like that!' Peter said, pushing levers back in their correct positions.

'He said he weren't scared. Anyhow, he's seen em before.'

Hassan licked his drying lips, chest heaving and eyes about to pop out of his head.

'I'm not! I'm not! I can do it!' he composed himself, waiting for the whispers because the whispers helped him. He strained. Akash sniggered. The ringing in his ears prompted the squeezing of his eyes shut and shaking head, snapping them open and making Akash jolt at the piercing colour of Hassan's eyes.

'Aye, he can do it alri.' Hassan began to quiver with concentration. Peter placed his large hand on his back, the other on the wheel.

'Relax son, relax. You don't 'ave t'combust y'self like that. You be half of one, not a full one.'

Hassan fell to his knees, 'half of what?'

'You need a bit o'practice, tis all. It'll come when them pills 'ave left yer system.'

'How do you know about the pills?' Hassan questioned, steadying himself as his vision flashed red.

Akash was still laughing at Hassan's face and bulging eyes, tilting his head to one side from intrigue in the strange boy. Another volunteer swaggered into the cockpit, the woman from the Rum and Crab shack.

'You're trying too hard,' Hassan was confused, 'it comes from in here...' she patted her stomach, 'it'll 'appen one day without you thinking, just watch where you be showin' it off to, ay lad?' He rested his back against the boat, a side smile appeared when he realised he was with kin – isolation leaving through his feet.

'Am I...like you?' he asked Akash who revealed his pointed teeth, still pearly white maintaining his handsome features.

'We ain't the same.' He curtly replied. Hassan touched his own teeth, gnashing them.

Another volunteer held onto the doorway. 'We're approaching Zennor,' Peter acknowledged them with a nod.

'Keep yer wits about ye kinfolk! They have gained strength overnight!' Akash stood, supporting himself, Hassan noticing the blood-thirsty look on his face.

Zennor: the village where medieval carvings of a mermaid adorned the parish. A tale told through children's books and fireside gatherings, said to frequent the church dressed as a wealthy woman, taking children while they slept. Hassan gulped as the atmosphere in the boat grew tense, but this had to be best day ever in his short life. The acceptance alone reignited his sullen heart and love for Cornwall.

The boat gathered momentum then slowed, keeping a safe distance from the rocks. Hassan saw the church surrounded by the grey-stoned village. Peter circled, then stopped the boat.

'Why are we stopping?'

Peter put his forefinger to his lips. 'Kash, keep a look out.'

Hassan followed him. 'Where are you going?'

'T'see where this sister o'yours has gorn,' he ruffled his hair again, then Peter dove off the side with Hassan watching him speed through the water fully clothed. It fell silent while they searched the waves for any movement. Akash leaned on the edge, side eyeing Hassan who was staring at him.

'What are we?' he whispered.

Akash smirked. Handing him something in a small, clear packet. The ones with the seal. He held it up, perplexed at the contents.

'What is it? Drugs?!'

'Yeah, summat like that. Only it be natural. Take one, then you'll see who we are, and get back in there and keep y'ed down. Kay?' Hassan adhered and sat on the floor picking the threads from the hem of his shorts, wary of the dried substance in the little package. He should've been bothered by the fact that Peter just dove off like that, but he wasn't, because he knew all along.

He'd looked at the dried seaweed thing between his fingers a little too long, scared of it. Whispering *BismiAllah*, before throwing it in his mouth and chewing it profusely with his eyes shut, controlling the gagging from the taste of sea and mould. He swallowed it, burping loudly from a protesting stomach. He waited, stretching the strands of cotton between his fingers and mentally unravelling the ball of string that he'd brought from the north. It all made sense why he was so anxious inland – wondering if he could shoot webs from his wrists, covertly trying it.

A squeak from beneath jolted him, standing when it turned into thumps, perhaps Peter was coming back. The boat rocked, holding on as he made his way on deck. Akash thrust a palm through the doorway.

'Stay inside!' there was activity in the water accompanied by strange noises. The volunteers were hitting something off with buoy poles, a greenish hand, gripping the rim of the boat. More of them, Akash hissing and biting anything that came close. The boat tipped and rocked but he wasn't hiding this time; they needed his help. Focussing, he held his breath and strained, waiting for the voices, his eyes burning from the pressure. He felt them change and his whole body convulse from the plant he'd just consumed.

'Wait! I can help! Wait!' his voice deepened, the toxic rush made his head spin, and, in that moment, he was released, grinning so hard. He was exploding into heaven, fractal patterns and vibrancy firing within a great conscience. Everything spoke as he watched his brain activity ignite, and the depth of who he was, who *we* were, came rushing forth in the highest dimensions. We are it, not separate, but part of it all. Letting out a primal scream, Hassan fell backwards, knocking himself out on the controls.

He was woken by gentle rocking and a rhythmic scraping; he was still on the boat but alone. He crawled on all fours and pulled himself up, the Mount filling his view from the window. He waited for his head to stop spinning realising the boat was stuck on the harbour's slope, cautiously walking to the deck and checking both ways.

'Peter? Kash? Hello?!' he heard something in front, then left and to his right; noises he heard before, ones he was afraid of, like something was tormenting him. 'Hello?' he checked his phone – *emergency calls only.* He knew Esme would be going frantic which resurfaced his anxiety, breathing deep in case of a full-blown attack, but there didn't seem to be one materialising.

Searching the long, empty beach he saw Akash dragging something up the causeway rocks, squinting to get a better look. 'What, the, fuh...?'

Was it Layla? His heart leapt then quickly slumped when he realised it wasn't. Whoever or whatever Akash was pulling was not happy about it, making a horrible noise in protest. His instinct was to run back inside, crouching by the wheel.

There was a loud *thud* on deck making him cover his ears. 'No! Please! I'm sorry!'

'Quit yer whining!' Akash said making him jump out of his skin. Hassan immediately held his nose, a stench he recognised from the dungeon, screaming when Akash dragged in the lilac-skinned creature that was gurgling and protesting. 'Stop yer screamin! Stop!' the Siren looked at Hassan and protested even more. Hassan covered his eyes praying and sobbing. Akash began speaking in Kernewek, but nothing he could understand.

'Harvey! Open y'bliddy eyes!' he parted his fingers and regarded the being through them. It scuffled back in fear; naked, muscular with the suggestion of a nose and wide, opaque eyes. Its mouth a little projected housing small, pointed teeth. Hassan noticed the creature's forearms were wounded, blistered. 'There, see? This wretched thing be afraid o'you.'

Hassan frowned, 'of me? Why?' he snivelled.

Akash stood, 'N'er mind that now. We need t'ask this thing who took Layla!' the creature shook its head, features distorted from fear. 'Tell us! Or I'll burn ya again! And it be yer ugly face this time!' the creature raised its arm, the smell increasing making Hassan nauseous; the digested plant about to be projected. It yelled something, choking and spluttering as its body slumped.

'What, what did it say?' Hassan asked with a grimace. Akash rested on his bent leg, he missed Layla just as much as anyone else.

'He be afraid o'you.'

'M, me? Why?'

'How long youm been takin' them pills?'

Hassan searched the floor. 'Uh, uh, since I was seven, I think. I can't remember!' Akash sniffed, giving the creature a pearl, jerking his head towards deck for the creature to leave, watching it scramble over the side in a screeching panic.

'W, what was that?!'

'Siren. Only theym stay in the water.'

'W, why did you let it go?!'

'I's got what I's wanted.' His sudden change in demeanour scared Hassan.

'How do you burn them like that?'

Akash stood, brushing himself down, 'coz we's changes water molecules in the body. Not a burn as such, mores like, a dehydration. Y'see, if ya say summat nice, the water's nice. If yer say summat bad...'

'W, where are the, the others? Where's Peter?' he gulped.

'Them be in the sch, sch, school.'

'Stop making fun of me!'

'You'll have t'buck yer ideas up! Look at yous. This is what we got sent, is it?'

'Sent?'

'Aye, come on,' he held out his hand to help Hassan up. His comforting aroma returned, calming him. 'Don't look so scared, I should be scared o'you.'

39

Limbo

The black sea lapped the shore and the town resumed routine even though the Kattan's life was in turmoil. The small window was open in the bedroom, the echo of Saint Ives a relaxant for their exhausted souls after searching every inch of Saint Ives. Diving teams were scouring the harbour and surrounding coves with the police taking statements. Musa was staying in the café not wanting to go home and face Esme, leaving Raffia in charge.

They lay in Esme's bed with Max in between them, the heaviness of his body a comfort as Hassan played with his ears, his head full of the boat and Esme's vomiting and wailing when she heard the news.

Staring through anything their eyes lay upon, the rhythm of their new home had become bitterly tainted; the conch light adding a soft, agitated glow. Stroking his hair, all the guilt was resurfacing, grief was pushing it out. His curls reminded her of the time she saw him in the clouds from the airplane window. Unhappy with the second pregnancy on her way back from Riyadh, wishing for it to miraculously disappear. She had no more love to give another, having given it all to Layla. She tried for a while for her, did everything by the book. Musa kept regurgitating the same old condescending lines, he wasn't even trying, 'leave it up to Allah' became a cop out. The nestled foetus shaped from cumulus clouds, as big as the sky, carried a profound message, immediately falling in love with the secret she carried in her womb. A love that intensified and continued from the day he was born. A love she always went to, and still did. And Layla felt it.

'Praying didn't work,' Hassan said.

'What do you mean?'

'We prayed and we did everything we were supposed to, and he didn't stop them taking Layla.' Esme's tears filled her mouth.

'And why d...did you give me those p...pills?'

'To help with your stammer and, your anxiety,' she sniffed, 'do you need to up your dose?'

'I haven't been taking them.'

She propped herself up on her elbow. 'Harvey! Why?'

'They weren't for those things,' he turned to her, 'were they?'

'Wuh, well, like what? I don't understand, Harv.'

'Have you been lying to me, too?'

'About what? What's the matter?' she slurred as the Diazepam entered her bloodstream.

'It doesn't matter, just go to sleep Mum. I'll look after you. We don't need Raffia,' he turned his attention to the white ceiling while Esme snuggled into his back.

'Do you remember when I used to eat Max's biscuits with him in the garden?'

Esme snorted, 'yes, I do. Your father never found out. I think he'd self-combust if he did.' They both sniggered hysterically. Loss soon regaining its place and changing the mood.

'Why do you love baba?'

'That's a silly question.'

'No, it's not. Why do you?'

'He's my husband, that's why.'

'That's not what I asked.'

Esme sat up, her vision becoming white, 'too many questions, love. My head is spinning.'

'How can you love him when he does bad things?'

'Harvey! Don't say that!'

He looked away, his eyes filling with angry tears. 'You don't know him like I do.'

'What's that supposed to mean?'

'You wouldn't listen. You *never* listen.'

Esme's stomach squelched. 'I'm listening now. You can tell me.'

'No, I can't. I'll just have to show you. Night, mum. Love you as much as Mr. Big from a big place that went to big university.'

Esme tittered affectionately, 'only that much, eh?'

He turned onto his right-side leaving Esme looking at his back, her mind racing and face ashen. She returned to stroking his hair with a trembling hand, pushing away the worse scenarios her mind concocted, choking on sporadic sobs. She began to hum that strange song when she needed her mother's bosom, making Hassan's eyes heavy. Managing to sing along to the lullaby that brought them back home: *"O'er the horizon...with eyes for thee. Ere I'll be waitin. Remember me. Be treddin the path laden with gorse, there I'll be waitin..."* they couldn't finish it with constricted throats.

'What does it mean?'

'My mother always sang it to me. Just and old seafarers' melody, I guess. It took me back here from the first word.'

It was time to ditch the pills and rely on her intuition which was hanging on by a thread. She had ignored her son's cries for help while she wallowed in her own self-pity, the bond was still strong but only by the tie of familiarity, she was losing him. She missed the little days when their affection was unconditional, days she mourned for in her own company. What went wrong? She felt hopeless, she should be looking for Layla, screaming for her. But this was Layla that was missing, a near woman that would give anyone a run for their money. How could it happen in paradise? Esme closed her eyes, her torso spinning, a numbing washed over her bringing forth reassurance through delirium. She lay on the pillow with a wistful smile, her ears ringing and teeth grinding as the haunting bell of the chapel rang in her head.

32

Revoke

Esme woke suddenly at 3am, bolt upright and gasping for breath. She heard someone calling her through the open window. For a split second everything was all right, in place, then reality hit, and everything compounded. Max grunted as she stirred, looking over his shoulder with dry eyes. Getting out of bed, acutely dysregulated, having to voice its discomfort as she held onto the bed frame. Barefoot, dressed in a long white chemise, she took the stairs and headed for the front door with Max following, squinting from the hall light. Leaving the front door wide open, the waves and voices called her, swaying to the steps and down to the beach - the full moon a spotlight on the glowing satin and loose red locks. Reaching the cold sand, her sobs increased as she stumbled to the shore, pacing and searching blindly.

'Layla? Layla! Is that you?!' She scanned the darkness, pink and purple auroras rippled between the stars. Faint calls of *'help me!'* were heard in the middle, then to the left and back to the centre.

'Okay! I'm coming!' Hesitating when the water chilled her feet. 'Who is it? Layla? Where are you? I'm not angry, it's ok, just, come home, please! I'm sorry! I'll divorce Baba, I promise! I will! Please! Please...' she inched forward, unsure when the lapping waves reached her ankles. She dropped to her knees and raised her face to the night sky.

'Is this my punishment? Did you give me a choice I didn't know about? Or was this all about me loving you instead? Because underneath all the guilt tripping commandments, is just a man-made egotistical god. One who manipulates to be loved like a dependent child. Putting me through hell to make me love you!' More calls came with a delight within the echoes.

She gouged the sand, a frustration in her core like an organism that writhed and begged for release, one she wanted to physically cut free. Max dug next to her making noises of determination and barking into the hole.

'I gave it all! Every piece of me! I lost love for you. Just to scrape through by the skin of my teeth! You're a misogynistic fraud!' she stood, wet sand falling from the creased material.

'You can do what you like to me, I give up. I'm done, done with covering up and shutting up. And give me back my daughter!!' she screamed at the sea, unsympathetically silent in its existence.

'You bloody shit, Layla! Didn't listen, and now look! But oh, you know better because you've lived longer than me! All that effort...all what you put me through!' she ugly-cried to the moon, 'well fuck you, madam!'

Stood at the edge, strange singing rippled the surface, '*Come in! Come! Help me!*' came disembodied female voices louder from all around her. Max barked at them, agitated as he paced.

'*Come in! Help us! Come!*' Accompanied by a tuneful vibration. '*Come in for me!*' The calls were whale-like, then Dolphin and somewhere in between those. There was one close by, Esme edged in, hypnotised. Looking down at her bare feet, the water moved oddly as it reacted to their voices. Her skin goose bumped from a whispered gasp in her ear, a familiar calling, folding her arms as she became acutely undone and vulnerable. Esme inched forward, happy to give in and surrender. Not living was a better option right now. Silencing, finalising.

She drew in breaths, filling her lungs, shaking out the fear through her hands as she waded in.

'Don't do it, maid.'

She swung around, 'Peter! Oh, Peter! Oh God, help us!' Esme pushed the water with her shins to get to him.

'God now, is it? Youm just been cussing y'God,' she knocked him off balance as she threw her arms around his waist, he held her tight transferring his warmth through her cold, wretched body; eyeing the shore, glaring at the shadowed heads retreat beneath.

'I'm so tired of obeying! I can't do it anymore! I feel like I can't even *think* for myself let alone trust my intuition!!'

'And what is your intuition sayin?' he pointed to her heart, 'in there, what's it sayin' in there?'

Esme touched that place, her eyes darted around the night. 'I, I don't know. I can't hear it.'

'You ain't been lisnen to it since y'bloody got ere! I'll agree with one thing, someone did take your spirit away,' he pointed to the stars, 'and it weren't Him.'

As she looked upward, the reveal of her hair was all too familiar to him.

'I don't wanna spoil yer moment, but I think you've already broken free of summat,' her look of despair changed to a provocative one. Peter tried to break loose, wary of her vibe. 'Let's get you back ome, c'mon.'

But a fire was already burning, and he could feel her heart thumping against his checkered shirt.

'Marry me, Peter!'

He released her clasped hands. 'That wouldn't be proper, and I think them drugs be speaking.'

'Bollocks to proper!'

Peter smirked at her flames. 'Aye, I agree, but trust me,' he held her slender hands in front of her, 'it ain't proper.'

She searched his eyes, rejection turning her cold and sick, 'but I love you, God help me, I do.'

'Time has a bad 'abbit of erasin the good things. Givin us memories it chooses, usually the bad. And that uzbund o'yours...'

'What about me?' Musa turning their heads, 'And get your hands off my wife! Esmay! AstaghfiruAllah! Look at you!'

Peter gently pushed her behind him. 'I was bringin her ome.'

'Like hell!'

'I bet. Is there any news?'

'No.'

'Right then. Esme needs 'elp, I'm worried about her.'

'She is not your concern. Dancing out here with the devil!'

'Summat you're familiar with, I'm sure.'

Musa looked drained, his eyes a little sunken and hair out of place. 'Give her to me!'

'I want Peter to take me home!' Esme voiced and shivered. The chilling sea breeze lifting strands of her hair, the light of the moon highlighting her contours.

'You are shaming yourself!' he took off his cashmere coat and clumsily walked through the sand in his Ralph Laurens, the links of his Hublot 'chinking' as he shook the coat into shape. Esme strode passed them making her way to path behind the cafe, screaming for Layla. Peter made a move.

'Don't!' Musa pushed him back, 'I will get her. If you want to halp, stay away from us. I will make it worth your while.'

Peter huffed, 'you wouldn't know 'ow to, Emmet. I ain't stayin away 'til she's found, and you lot are exposed for your crimes!'

Musa pointed at Peter as he stumbled after Esme, 'keep away! For your own good!'

Once he was back on the tarmac, he scuffed his soles to free them of sand. Esme was ahead, unsteady, sobbing and letting out the odd scream with her daughter's name within it. Musa reached out and grabbed her arm, his throat was tight; the perfect white sheet of his existence was soiled and irreparable.

'Woman! Listen! Stop this! Now! Stop!' Esme's heart broke a little when she saw the tears in his eyes, the man that remained on a pedestal all his life was coming undone in an ugly vulnerability that seeped through a well-kept façade. 'Come,' he put the coat around her shoulders, 'I make you somethink, okay? Somethink hot.'

'We've lost our baby, Moose!' tears poured from the blood of her soul, 'please tell me you know where she is so I can at least rest, I'm so tired, please Moose!'

His facial muscles dropped; a permanence paralysed him. 'She is safe, habibi, she is safe. Allah is dealing with it.' She threw the coat off her shoulders.

'Stop telling me that! I can't *breathe* without her!' Haunched, pressing her fingers into her chest, 'she is half of me. I can't let Allah deal with it. I have to deal with it!'

Esme let out a despondent cry, 'have you married her off?!' he looked to the floor, 'Moose?'

'It is not that simple.'

She choked on the flood of salty fluid, her veins dry and head heavy. 'Why, Moose, why?! All this has been leading up to it, hasn't it? Is that why you brought us here? This wasn't to fulfil my dream, but to fulfil yours! She's a *child*, Moose, a child! Out there, scared!'

He stepped towards her, 'blease, habibi...'

'Don't call me that! Don't, touch me! Ever! I'm going to get her back, even if it kills me! And get that creepy woman out of our house! Tonight!'

Peter listened from behind the wooden café, the tips of his fingers petting Max's head, watching her stomp with bleeding feet towards the steps. Musa's untimely arrival may have been just as well because he needed her to keep the fire of resistance, burning.

'Raffia! Raffia!' she called out, upright with clenched fists as she entered the house leaving bloodied footprints on the tiles. 'I want you out, now!' A tall officer appeared from the lounge, hands tucked in his utility vest.

'Oh my God! Have you found her?!'

'Can we just take a statement from you, Mrs Kattan?'

'A statement? I can barely string a sentence together!'

They entered the dim-lit lounge, Max skidded in behind her, his muzzle dusted with sand, making a beeline for the rock lamp. Esme's bones began to thaw as she grabbed the throw from the sofa, wrapping herself in it.

'If you've found her body, spare me the torture and just tell me.'

'No one has been found yet, Mrs Kattan. We just need the series of events from all parties involved.'

'I left her with Raffia because Harvey was having an allergic reaction. That's it. She's sixteen for God's sake, and a good swimmer! Something stinks and I think you're all in on it!'

'I understand how you must be feeling...'

'Do you? Have you got any children?'

'That's not important right now...'

'Yes, it is, if you had kids, you'd know exactly how I felt! Something is not adding up! This is what's important!' The front door clicked shut, Max scrambled to his feet as he let out a solitary, protective bark.

'Do you have any news for us, Sir?' Musa walked in, brushing himself off.

'He knows! Ask him! Have you taken a statement from him?' Esme pointed with a trembling hand.

'We have all we need from your husband, Mrs Kattan.'

'He's not my husband, he's a fraud! He has something to do with this because *he* wanted her out of the way to save his honour!'

'Excuse my wife, Sir, she has taken somethink to calm her nerves, you know?'

'I understand that emotions are running high. Mrs Kattan, when was the last time you saw your daughter, uh, Layla?' Looking at his notes.

Esme demanded Max's company, patting the sofa. He clumsily got up and lay on her bent legs, smacking his chops and groaning as he settled.

'That morning. I went to Falmouth, shopping...' she went through the compromise of her day, stumbling whenever she mentioned Layla. 'We got one baby back and lost another. Don't think I was quite ready for the options I was presented with. Have you spoken to Raffia? Or has she scuttled back home?'

'We have all we need from everyone Mrs Kattan, thank you. We are working around the clock and our teams have gone further afield, so we are not restricting our search in one place.'

'You're looking in the wr, wrong places,' Hassan croaked as he entered the room, his hair flattened on one side and eyes a little puffy.

'We're doing our best in what little light we have,' the officer's lips curled at the edges, shifting in his seat as Hassan made eye contact.

'Duh, don't you have to wri, write things down?' Hassan asked, the officer's vest making noises as he stood.

'Hassan! Your mannors!' Musa warned.

The officer ruffled Hassan's curls. 'I hear you're quite the hero, young man?'

'It was Ka, Kash and Pe, Peter, not me.'

'Ah, but you were brave enough to ride the waves in our own vessel. I'm jealous.

Mister and Mrs Kattan, thank you all for your co-operation. We will be paying daily visits until she's found, and our support staff will also be calling in. Don't forget to call us if you think or hear of anything else. Try not to worry too much.' Esme stared at the glow of the rock lamp, scoffing at the officer's spiel. 'I'll see myself out, take care all.'

The three of them hugged on the sofa, their blinks getting longer and heavier. Musa regarded what was left of his strange little family, a smile from his heart reaching his face.

'Shall I make you somethink, habibi?' Esme shook her head, her love confession to Peter playing over and over. Max was already dreaming, Hassan watched him trying to get a clue as to where he'd been. Sounded like he was barking in his sleep, then his legs went through the motion of running. He placed his hand where he thought his heart would be.

'It's okay boy, you're home now,' his bottom lip quivering.

'You are more concerned about that animal than your sister!' Musa huffed.

'He stops me stuttering.'

'No, you can do this all by yourself walidi, you don't need a kalb to help you. They are too salty.'

'Salty?'

Musa sat, warming his hands towards the burner. 'Yes. When I am near a kalb, I taste salt.' Hassan was amused, and thought it was the strangest analogy he'd heard. He only tasted salt when he was near Akash. He looked over to Esme, her eyeballs moving beneath her eyelids.

'I know you know where she is, Baba. I don't want mum to suffer anymore, just tell us where she is. I won't tell anyone, walahi.'

Musa checked his manicured nails then Esme, 'she is safe. No drowned, no killed. Safe. Okay?' focussing on the dancing flames behind the burner's glass door.

'Are we, like them?'

Musa turned his head to Hassan. 'Who them?'

'Them, like…the, uh,' he could hear the years of his father's lectures and warnings run through his mind like a raging river, diverting him from the truth with superstition and fear, unable to sleep at night sometimes when the shadows took on a living shape in the dark. The pills, the pressure, but most of all, the fear of hell. 'Uh, Peter and Kash.'

'We are Arab! Not western. What are you sayink?'

Hassan's face flushed as panic rose. The unpredictability of his father's moods had taught him how to quickly spin any situation. 'Yes, but mum is Cornish, that's what I mean.'

'Rest, habibi, rest. You are half Cornish, yes, inshallah. You want your favourite drink? I make it for you, eh?' he winked, giving Hassan a wave of lost love and forgiveness.

'Can't we just get her back, together? You and me? Baba and Walidi?'

Musa stood, tucking and righting himself, clearing his throat, 'you forget the times your sister called you names, do you? No discipline, dressing like a woman from the streets.

Huh? Would you prefer a sister who was nice to you? Kind? Made you tea? Prayed?'

'I called her names, too.'

'You were provoked, habibi. SubhaanAllah, I never seen someone so full of hate and attitude.'

'Maybe she was hurt by Islam.'

'Never say this! AstaghfiruAllah! Never! Islam cannot hurt anyone!'

'But Muslims can,' Esme responded with a glazed-over stare.

'Calm down! You are making thinks much worse! AstaghfiruAllah, look at you! She is not dead!'

Esme inhaled to free her jammed ribs, 'how do you know?'

'I think I will buy you a nice gift, eh? Make you feel better.'

She hummed a condescending laugh, 'a gift, yes, why not. That will make everything better, won't it? Musa's way of covering up his shitty behaviour. Being nice, then being shitty, buying affection, and so on. Do you know what this does to a person? Do you?!'

Throwing the blanket off she scrambled to the other stairs.

'No! Esmay!' She flew down them on her stomach, exposing her breasts as the white chemise was torn from her.

'Opennnn!' she screamed, banging her fists on the door in floods of tears. Ramming her shoulder against it and turning the handle.

'Esmay! Esmay!' Musa tripped before he grabbed her, 'stop this, stop!' She was hysterical, her eyes wide. 'Stop it, now!'

'Well, go on! Open it!' she pushed his shoulder back forcing him to sit on the stairs. 'There's something in there that you don't want me to see, isn't there, Moose?' The slap across Esme's face echoed, her head hitting the wall. Shaken out of her hysteria, holding her face.

'*BABA*!!' Hassan screamed and almost ruptured his larynx, pointing a crowbar directly at him.

'I'm sorry habibi, your mother is shouting too much.'

'You get away from her!' he snarled through gritted teeth, Max behind, bearing his and growling.

'It's okay Harvey. It was mummy's fault.'

'It wasn't! It's *his*! All this is his, fault!' stabbing at the words with the crowbar.

'Sweetheart, let's just all calm down, okay?' Esme sat on the last stair; her emotions unable to be seated. She felt lightheaded as her cheek throbbed, feeling for lost teeth with her tongue. Instinct made her touch the corner of her mouth, discretely wiping off the blood in the crease of her knee.

'What the hell are you do-ink with that thing?!' Musa asked, the red mist leaving.

'I'm going to open that flipping door with it and flipping break it!'

'What have I told you about saying that word?!'

'I said flipping, not fucking!' Musa choked on his astonishment, striding up the stairs with no thought except to strike his son. Hassan stood his ground, pushing Musa back with the crowbar, his back slamming into the handrail. Max wagged his tail, not sure what he should be doing.

'We don't need this, do we, Baba?' Esme looked up the stairs, 'tell her, go on! Tell mum who can open the door!'

'Give me that!' Musa snatched the crowbar from Hassan, 'did you know he have this?! And neverrr poosh me again woman, you understand?' he took the crowbar to the Range Rover, swearing in Arabic as he went; metaphorically spitting on everyone. His constitution weak as the wounds weeped and infection took hold.

Esme was too exhausted to react, her silence harboured in a change of sides. It was her children that fulfilled her, empathising with these feelings her mother must carry daily. She was only trying to protect Esme after all, and her mother's love was beginning to shine through Musa's flaws and Peter's eyes.

Hassan rushed to help her, 'come on. Time to leave him, okay? It's fine, you don't have to hang on for us anymore,' his voice trembling and chin quivering. But the love, the times, the other day, the back room, they were real.

'Your father is losing control. Something else is in charge.'

'He hit you, again, mum. Twice. And then it will be again. No more, that's it. I'm fine with you leaving. I'm not fine with you staying.'

'I think my decision has been made, Harvey.'

He helped her back upstairs and to the lounge, sitting her down, covering her, Max licking the crease of her knee and then her fingers.

Hassan took her by the arms, 'Layla is okay. I know it. And when I know it, I know it. We'll get her back. We will. With Peter and Samir.'

33

Basement

She closed one eye and dipped the brush in the acrylics, dabbing the colours repeatedly into the porous surface. Drugged, dishevelled and merely existing wearing Layla's clothes, the scent of her first born comforted her while she frantically painted the back yard wall, sniffing and wiping her nose on the sleeve of the branded hoodie. Hassan had taken Max into town to discuss plans with Peter, and hand out more flyers at the café. The stupor she was in stopped her from ripping her heart out, kneeling and swaying watching a butterfly take nectar from the Valerian growing out of the wall. The seagulls' laughter pierced her head, telling them to shut up, trying to meditate in her creation. Silence fell for a moment, and she heard the front door click shut, turning her head towards to the back door.

'Salaams!' they called.

'Out here!' she barely raised a smile when Samir came with his hand over his heart, dressed in the same clothes, clutching his white handkerchief.

'Dearest sister, I have come to offer my help,' his face pained at her state.

'Thank you, jazak Samir,' she slurred, blinking to release trapped tears.

'What are you painting?'

She looked at the wall because she didn't know herself. 'It's from my dreams.'

He entered the yard, looking over to Raffia's side, 'sister, shall I get your hijab?'

'No.'

He checked Raffia's side again before coming closer, his hands clasped, his mouth turned down when he saw the fresh bruise on her face. 'Where have you seen that?' he nervously asked, grimacing at the intricate symbols and impressions of snakes in an abstract manner. The darkness was feeding off her anarchy and disdain. She didn't reply, concentrating on the brush strokes with a crazed expression. 'Please, sister, I want to help,' checking over his shoulder.

Esme squinted as she looked up at him, 'I beg you Samir, before I disintegrate. My son needs me, but I have nothing left. I might as well be dead. Whatever you say, don't mention Allah, I'm done with that.'

Samir wiped his eyes then crouched; the urge to wrap her arms around him stayed within the control of the suppressant.

He studied the painting and the caked colours on her nails, her hands telling an older tale than the rest of her. The long red hair with rainbow hues from the sunlight and paler green eyes than her daughter, framed a woman stifled in her fabricated prison, a victim through no choice.

'I do not come from Saudi, I am Syrian, and I am not a doctor. It just sounds authoritative and helps to maintain my position in the community.'

'Why are you telling me this now?'

'Because I cannot help you under any deceit.'

'What else?' she asked, he bowed his head and played with the seam of the white cotton handkerchief.

'That is all, for now. Forgive me.'

Esme dipped her head, her heart softening and soul falling.

'Trust Hassan. We shall meet at the mount, soon, inshallah.'

'When?!'

'Soon, sister,' he left, with Esme's mouth gaping. Dropping the brush, she got to her feet and staggered after him.

'Wait! Samir! When?' he closed the front door behind him leaving her stood in the hallway; the hoodie just covering her underwear. The house came to a halt when she heard a noise from the basement. Steading herself on the lounge furniture, she focussed on the stairs, which doubled and eluded her. Holding onto the banister with both hands she took the stairs one at a time, her breathing rapid as she got closer, seeing the door ajar. Pushing it at arms' length, the smell of fousty damp and dry rot flared her nostrils.

'Layla?' she tearfully whispered. The novelty of getting into the room had worn off somewhat. Esme looked up and down the walls and along the ceiling, everything splitting into two. The room was full of sealed cardboard boxes with girls' rucksacks and school bags lined up on top of them. Outdated fads, keyrings of characters long gone from the decade. She prodded them, studying one and pulling at the zip. There was a Nokia, pencil case and tissues along with exercise books, curled at the edges. Esme pulled one out: Arabic exercise books. Her vision and mind sobered, the slate floor freezing her bare feet and soothing the septic cuts. Noticing smaller boxes taped with brown packaging tape, she picked one up and shook it, the contents rattling.

'What the hell *is* this?' Using one of the school pens to pierce the taped seal, pulling at the flaps and bubble wrap, she uncovered Vials. Glass vials, with stoppers about two inches in length. Holding one up to the light, a violet liquid within, perplexing her numbed facial muscles. She pulled at the stopper, it opened with a 'pop', sniffing the contents that had no smell. Esme pondered, squeezing the tip of her tongue into the narrow opening. No taste. Smacking her tongue several times to search for any recognition. Replacing the cap, her eyes then falling on her old white vanity case. Discarding the vial and pushing off the other packages, she released the locks with a 'clunk', the red satin lining raising a nostalgic smile. She didn't remember packing it, or even bringing it. A4 sheets of her old paintings lay face down, creased and brittle.

The first one was an early picture of Saint Ives, signed *Esme Pascoe. Aged 9*. Others of the little streets and cottages, the harbour and the chapel.

A memory came through, not hanging around long enough to grasp. Touching the red satin, a folded piece of paper was in one of the pockets. A child's drawing in green crayon. *Her* drawing. Agitated whisperings began in her head, the paper shook as Esme walked out of the room and back upstairs, holding the drawing next to the portrait of the Marid. They were the same, only hers was of naivety.

She heard the front door.

'Esmay?' Musa, immediately making her stomach twist.

'Here,' she put the drawing in the hoodie pocket and held it there.

'Where is Hassan? And cover your legs!'

'Why, who's coming? He took Max into town and was popping into see you.'

'Sit, sit. I make you tea, okay? It is in Allah's hands now, just pray. You haven't prayed ya habibi, there is power in salat.'

'What good did that ever do?!' she blurted through a salvia-filled mouth.

'AstaghfiruAllah! Stop taking those drugs! You are losing your senses!'

'Yes, they have a nasty habit of doing that, don't they? You didn't mind me taking antidepressants though, did you?'

Musa was static in the doorframe, a little puny. 'Praying nourishes your third eye and is the cure for many thinks.'

'Something you live by on a daily basis, eh Moose?'

Musa leaned into her, he had that look in his eye, the look when he'd been triggered, ready to strike even harder so you questioned yourself and succumbed to a fabricated guilt.

'Do you know, people who don't pray are worse than rapist!'

He retreated to the kitchen, she held reserve, sniffing in her disdain. Hope and breadcrumbs clasped in her hands.

34

Zennor

Peter polished the vessel's under carriage deep in thought, the waiting game was destroying Esme and difficult to watch, glancing at her handing out the flyers at the café to passers-by. She'd lost weight, her face gaunt, fingers bony and dry, looking ten years older than when she arrived. He knew this pain and it was never welcome, the unsettling limbo and inability to function without a numbing aide. He wiped his hands and threw the rag down.

'Is there any coffee orn, Maid?'

'There will always be coffee for you, Peter. You're the only one keeping me sane.'

'Wuss that on yer face!'

Esme touched it, it was a blur now, twinging when she chewed.

He looked down at his weathered hands, 'I'll be around for as long as y'need me t'be.'

'Do you know about the meeting? At the mount?'

'Come t'see ya, did he?'

'So you *do* know?'

'Ma'be.'

'Oh, stop this cloak and dagger shit, Peter! Look at me! I'm living an agonising death, and the only thing that keeps me alive is her...' sobs erupted, dropping the pile of flyers, the sea breeze littering them over the cobbles and under the chairs. Peter picked them up, 'leave them! No one is looking anymore. They don't even care! And what are these damned pathetic excuse for police doing?!'

'C'mon, let's ave you sat down. All this fussin' aint 'elping nuthin.'

'I'm not stupid, Peter. How come Akash appeared everywhere we went, now he's hardly around?'

'He hurts, thas why.'

Esme huffed. 'Maybe he had something to do with it and now he's hiding. Does that mean she's not here?' She checked Layla's location on her phone, 'still nothing, no location. I open this app a thousand times a day hoping I'm going to see that bitmoji of hers, wandering about with headphones on.' She pressed the bridge of her nose to alleviate the sting, 'it's the silence, Peter. I'm trying to listen, so hard! The worse thoughts keep me up at night, the *worse*! And I can't do anything about it.'

'Where's yer scarf?'

'I'm, not wearing it anymore.'

He squeezed her hand. 'Come on, I'll take y'somewhere, 'elp you owt a bit.' She sobbed again, sure she would rupture every organ if it continued.

Peter's old Land Rover rattled all the way to Zennor, there was no conversation but a comfortable silence between them. She was in the safest of hands watching the flat landscape pass, peppered with pink and yellow heathers. The love confession silently thumped around them, but Peter didn't make her feel awkward about it, and she acted like it didn't happen.

Arriving at the small village huddled around the medieval church, Esme screwed her face up at the creepy looking place of worship with leaning headstones that lined the pathway. They parked against the high hedgerows, casually glancing up at the twitching curtains.

'What is this place? Are we asking for a blessing?'

'Overthinkin' again, missus.'

'Well, it's served me well thus far.' The slam of the metal doors reminded her of her grandfather's tin shed where she played with clay pots of dried earth among the webs and wooden benches. It was happening a lot lately, vivid childhood memories and ones she had long forgotten that lay deep in sealed boxes of her conscience. 'What is coming here going to do?'

'Patience.'

'Seriously! You just said that?' he smirked at her, his windswept hair and overbearing maturity was all she could stand in her state. She put her arm through his and never wanted to let go of a limb that felt like it would save the world, discretely smelling his shirt to see if he used fabric conditioner. It was okay now, Peter was here and she could cope with the otherwise hopeless situation. Curtains moved from the twee cottages as he led her up the church steps, the scuffs of their feet evacuating crows that were perched in the tips of the trees, announcing their warning as they took flight. Esme's skin crawled, hugging her arms from the chill of their murder. 'Christ, that's all I need.'

Peter wrapped his knuckles thrice on the weathered chapel door, thumbing the latch.

'Dydh da!' he called out a greeting in his native tongue. A positive response coming from the back. He closed the door, pulling the top bolt across. Pews faced an altar with a mermaid carved into the side panels, holding aloft something circular.

'Fatel os ta?' calling if all was well.

'Da lowr, da lowr.' A woman appeared from behind a red curtain with a reddened face and dishevelled hair.

'Peter! How good to see you again,' they man-hugged and patted each other's back.

'Esme, youm be most welcome m'dear. I made fresh scones if yer care t'have tea and settle?'

'Oh, well, I...' she looked at Peter for reassurance, he dipped his head and shoved her forward. 'I'd love to, thank you.' She felt a little over dressed in front of them, what with Peter and those awful grey corduroys and the woman with khaki trousers and a maroon blouse with a clerical collar. She led them to where she appeared from; a small room with a fireplace and dressed table with a loud mantle clock and whimsical décor.

'Sit y'sel down m'dear. All will be well.'

Esme sat with hands clasped in her lap, holding back continuous tears while looking around at 'home', and the mermaid carvings and gestures on furniture. Peter checked his out-of-date mobile, taking a quick glance at his watch.

'There we are,' she placed down a tray of China teacups and plates to match, and a plate with scones balanced into a pyramid. She disappeared again, swiftly returning with the tea pot, strawberry jam and clotted cream. 'There, get some o'this inside yer. It'll make all them worries go away for a little while. Sugar?'

'Oh, err, yes, please. Two.'

'Blimey! Thas the way,' Peter commented, getting a threatening glare from Esme.

'Now then, I can see your thoughts are wearin' y'down, Esme.'

'My daughter is missing.'

'I know, I know. That's why youm 'ere, put yer mind at rest. I take it Peter has explained?' he shoved half a scone in his mouth, the jam and cream oozing from the sides, shaking his head.

'Explained what? Peter?' Esme asked.

'She wouldn't 'ave bliddy come if I 'ad!' he said through scone and sultanas.

'You paint?' the woman asked.

Esme checked her hands and nails, affirming her identity. 'Uh, yes.'

'Good. Painted anything, unusual lately?'

'Like what?'

'Oh, I dunno, something you ain't done before.'

Esme gulped down the tea, the woman slurping hers with raised eyebrows, 'you mean, what I painted on the back wall?'

'Ma'be.'

Esme's eyes wondered the table and bone China with pink roses, the woman retrieving a notebook from a small bureau. 'Now then, let's see what we got ere.'

Esme looked on with a frown as the woman began to draw, her eyes widening as what she drew was the same she'd painted on the yard wall at Draycott.

'That's it! Oh my god! What are they?'

She then opened an iron box sat on a sturdy, wooden table, revealing a mish mash of amulets, pulling at a golden chain that lifted the tangled mess with it. Freeing itself, the woman held it up to the light.

'It means, we 'ave work to do to get your daughter back. These be wot Beaky retrieves for us, but this one...' the chunky triangular amulet spun on the end of the chain, inscribed with ancient symbols on both sides '...could be the reason why there's bin so much activity in the water, there bin too many of em!'

'Em? Uh, them?'

'The elementals. Marid and Siren, gorn bad. Pillaging our seas, and raping your women to expand and occupy. We are not all like that, are we Pete? Poor creatures are too stupid to know what's right. Theym just following orders from 'umans.'

'Orders? I don't understand.'

'This 'ere be from deserts, placed in these waters to open another port for them to do their dirty work. Tryin' t'get rid of our appointed protectors. Well, we ain't 'avin it in our seas!'

'But isn't the spell broken if you take it out?'

'Not necessarily. It could remain there for years until something attached to it, dies!' she sat back, 'what did you say your name was?'

'Uh, Esme, Kattan.'

'No, no. Your family name me love.'

'Oh, Pascoe.' The woman looked at Peter whilst fiddling with the handle of her teacup. She placed the amulet in front of Esme.

'Recognise the symbols?' Esme studied them, sure she'd seen them in a book or online somewhere.

'I'm not sure. Are they Egyptian?'

The woman shook her head, 'Nabatean. The most advanced civilisation before the Egyptians. These 'ere inscriptions are a hundred thousand years old. A protective guard against their most respected dead. This, this is where your daughter is. Transported through their portals.'

Esme looked up, 'Jordan?'

'Not quite. Al Ula.'

'But that's in Saudi! You mean, my *husband* placed the amulet here?!'

'Well, let's not jump to conclusions me dear, not just yet, anyways,' she rested back undoing her collar and fished out an amulet she kept around her neck, the same circular symbol as the mermaid carvings held.

'This one stays with me. It protects this village and its seas, but I fear that barrier may have been penetrated.' She closed her eyes, jolting Esme out of her seat when she reopened her spherical lenses with dead black pupils, her skin going a shade lighter with hues of green. Esme reached for Peter's hand making him spill his tea.

'Glosbe?' the woman questioned Esme's trembling.

'She's afraid because her faith has forbidden. You carnt blame her for fearing you,' Peter's accent changing a little.

'Humans and Marid that know your scriptures without fault, can help you, Pascoe. Who hold the keys to portals and gateways.'

'I do not dabble in these things, they are forbidden, I...' her lips quivering and bladder about to empty.

'Says you, cursin' at your God the other night,' Peter mumbled.

'That has nothing to do with it!' Esme stood, 'You're an ignoramus as well as a dinosaur! Take me back, now!'

'Just sit down and stop yer bloomin fussin and bloody listen!'

Esme's mouth dropped from Peter's rumbling tone, just as it did at the chapel in Saint Ives. His moods, unpredictable. She gingerly sat, not taking her eyes off him because she didn't want to look at the woman for fear of being eternally cursed.

'Your daughter is alive Esme, but...' she glanced at Peter again who was brushing tea from his arm.

'But what? Please! But what?!' Esme's throat tightened when she had to look at her.

'There is a male, you know him, he has her under his wing, and she is safe.' Esme's tears of relief poured down her contorted face, 'but I feel this man is not strong enough to withstand the journey, as he hath taken the false path of immortality.'

'Not if I got anythin' t'do with it.' Peter commented, licking his fingers.

'Is it Ibrahim? Oh my god, I feel sick,' she clutched her chest.

'Steady now, maid. Overthinking again. 'Ave some tea and be calm.'

'We'll just get on a plane then, go get her. I mean, it will take us a day or two...maximum! We've been wasting time!' Esme began to hyperventilate as hope left her fingers, her palms fixed on the table denying an imminent black out.

'You cannot get to her by modern means. Your daughter is not this side but on the other. The parallel incense routes of the ancients, for now. There is a Jann that guards her, released from its banishment and one who has a vendetta with your husband. Their leader is in the Mount, and prime supply of female innocents.'

'You mean, *Janan*?!'

'That's a pseudonym. She is, Nagini. A powerful entity who supplies the rich with your young and Agarwood.' Acid stung Esme's mouth.

'The new amulets summoned the Nagini, and she has taken ownership of the gates. The myths and legends may bring this land profitable interest, but the eyes of society lay focussed on a superficial world. We remain under the novelty of escapism because exposure of our existence would tip the balance and cause hysteria. Does your scriptures not tell you of this? We have chosen the path of human protection, but fear we are being overrun. Great measures are required to restore safety, but we cannot guarantee all innocents will be saved.'

Esme's stomach squelched as the voice of the woman caused static in the room, the cosy walls closing in on her. Peter was the only thing reinstating normality. She couldn't bare the magnetism that was causing her to fidget, her vision blurred and eyelids became tight, touching them in confusion. Her head spun like she was going under anaesthetic, a high-pitched buzzing ensued and the same erratic whispers chanting. The pastor dropped a small bunch of dried seaweed in front of her, 'consume it, to calm you.'

'No! Stop!' Peter yelled, 'when she is ready. Let me handle it!'

'Da lowr,' the woman agreed, and retreated into her pastoral disguise. Esme slumped in the chair a little dazed. 'You're in good 'ands. My gifts are tied to the village and that's as far as I can go with this. Protect yourself with your scripts, for they are the most effective in this world. Forgive me if I scared you. Peter tells me your intuition is a little, off,' the mantel clock resuming its loud ticking.

'Thank you, really. I have so many questions to ask you!' Esme was in awe of the creature, reinforcing her faith and feeling the overwhelming desire to pray.

'You'll be able to ask me plenty when all the shenanigans are over, we should keep our communication to a minimum for now. You're welcome any time, bring your Layla with you because we're getting her back, okay?'

Esme tears dropped in her lap. 'I will, inshallah, thank you. You've saved my life.'

'Ah, thas what we're' ere for, innit Peter?'

'Aye, c'mon then, maid. We got work to do.'

The door was bolted behind them as their steps crunched on the gravelled path back to the Land Rover. Tin doors slammed, Esme put her seatbelt on, a different person than when she took it off.

'Thank you,' leaning over to peck Peter's cheek.

'S'alri. You got it now?'

'I think? How are we getting Layla?' Peter pulled at the steering, the diesel engine announcing their departure.

'We have t'be careful of what we say now, try talking in code.'

'Code?!'

'We's all under threat now. But I couldn't stand seein' yer like that. We're all hurting, maid. We all want to get her back.'

Esme wasn't listening as her mind emptied from the passing hedgerows. 'Max! He, he, just came back, just like that. Do you think he came through a portal? Why would they take him? In exchange?'

'Someone chose a bloody dawg over their daughter, didn't they?'

'I don't want to believe that. How are we going to just, casually go back to the mount now? You heard her, that, mermaid fish thing.'

'There ain't no such thing as mermaids,' Peter winked.

'Did I imagine it?'

'Imagine what?'

'Peter! Stop that!'

'Your doctor got any pills for fussin? Ay?'

'Ha! You need a pill for, for being bloody obnoxious!'

'Thas no way to speak t'yer elders.'

'Really, Peter. How old are you anyway?' There was a pregnant pause when the indicator blinked loudly, like the mantel clock. 'And what's your surname?' The gears crunched on the vehicle that was confident about its appearance, a strange smell of rubber and seaweed sparked nostalgia in Esme, which would've previously prompted disgust. This would be her go-to transport to get Layla back; transport that would overcome Armageddon.

The pastor finished evening service, bidding farewell to the last of the worshippers, and when the top bolt was secure, it was time for more tea and rune stones. Spreading the stones evenly on a black velour cloth, stirring in the sugar with a silver spoon she pondered at their message. A loud knock on the chapel door jarred her from the seat.

'Just one minute! Is that you Peter? Did you forget something?' huffing as she tugged on the aged bolts, 'service finished half an hour ago and I need my beauty sleep.' The door was opened and there stood an imposing shadow against the night. The pastor gasped and tried slamming the door, but it was near blown off its hinges with the pastor forced back into the pews. She crawled to the back room on all fours with a severely injured back, her skin changing and form morphing letting out an ear-piercing screech of warning. The runes were thrown in the air and table split into two, the trespasser saturating the floor with sea water as they entered the chapel. The pastor opened a trap door in the kitchen and threw in the iron box of amulets before she was pulled back by her ankle and raised in the air.

'What have we here? A traitor!' The pastor hissed and bared short, sharp teeth. 'We need a port in this forsaken place, but you have been getting in the way.'

The pastor tried wriggling out of the grip, 'there are no innocents here for you! Leave us in peace!'

'Because you have been hiding them, hmmm? That was not part of the agreement. They are coming, soon, and we must deliver what they came for. Reopen your gates, or be replaced.'

She was let go by the Marid, landing on her head with a *crack*. The pastor got to her feet with a blood-soaked face, letting out a deafening scream that caused a squall, hurtling the intruder over the pews and smashing into the wooden door frame. The pastor limped after them, dragging her injured leg.

'Leave! You will never have our children. Tell the Nagini she has been met with resistance!' she stressed. The intruder left, the door would have to be fixed in the morning as she checked outside, leaning on the frame, only a few of the villagers' lights were on. Her wounds throbbed and submersion in salt water would be her only cure.

The walk to the cliff's edge was difficult, the coastal wind knocked her back and sideways, the pain in her ankle and head worsening. Clutching her arms, she needed flesh and blood. The thought of the young boy would never leave her soul, all those years ago, enticing him away from the safety of family and love, was the making of her bones. Her ancestors before her whose sole purpose was to lure children and vulnerable males, something she fought against every day. She was better now, had turned herself around and the quiet village.

She stopped by a stream making its way to its ultimate destination through a revene in the landscape, scooping the pure water to bathe her mouth and quench her throat.

Reaching the section on the rocks that had become her aid for the past few hundred years, the descent would be a challenge with her injuries. There was sudden movement behind her in the dark making her lose her footing.

'Dydh da?!' the amphibious membrane cleared the bulbous lenses, heightening her vision. She knelt and began her backward descent, feeling for the first ledge with her foot that were so easy to take on a normal day, but the wounds were making her sick and an already cold blood turning colder. She gripped the grass, squealing when her hands were stepped on from something dripping wet, with the iron box of amulets under their arm. Using all her waning strength, she freed her hands and grabbed their ankles, yanking at them but the tall figure held firm; renewed from the mineral rich elements. Flesh and bone turned to sea water, the pastor gasping at her empty clenched fists, falling backwards and catching a glimpse of the creature that would be taking over Zennor. Flipping onto her front, so she would hit the water in a dive, but her night vision was weak and was caught by protruding rocks, severing her beautiful rainbow torso.

A warning call managed to escape her human lips before the icy black took her, becoming nourishment for delinquent sea and airborne scavengers.

35

Pillage

The cyclist read page four, continued from the front page headline: *'Zennor's Pastor Tragedy,'* biting into the croissant and slurping the flat white.

'Top up?' Suzie asked.

'Nah, thanks. Best be arf once I finished this.'

'Awful what 'appened, innit? What a terrible way t'go. Makes me shiver. Still, at least she was found. Would've been a different story if she'd fell in. Probably got drinkin' and wandered.'

The cyclist folded the paper and left it on the galvanised table, 'they said the same. Police not treating it as suspicious. Carrying out enquiries. Chapel in a state, door was *'blown from its hinges,'* it says. I reckon she was pushed, and they didn't find in her in a good state, either' he fastened his helmet, 'you doing anything later?'

'Who, me? I'm worken.' Suzie answered with a coy smirk.

'Shame. Where's that boss o'yours?'

'Which one?'

'Musa.'

'I dunno. You 'erd what 'appened, didn't yer?'

'Yeah, something funny going on. How can you just disappear in a place like this?' Suzie checked around her, leaning into his ear.

'We think it's them two in the lifeboat station.'

The cyclist huffed through his nose, 'think they need t'look at Marazion before they start casting aspersions.'

'Marazion? Why, you don't think she's...drowned?' she whispered.

'That'd be my first port of call. I ain't been there f'years. I stay away. Kids've gorn missing and no more is said. Once that tide is in, you don't wanna be trapped there, trust me. Have you seen them little fires after dark? We all knows what theym up to. Lighting up the castle some nights in different colours,' he let out a chortle, 'got all the world's elite comin' soon, haven't they?' Suzie shrugged.

'Yeah, well. They ain't coming here to talk about the climate.'

'Police ain't putting any effort in it seems. Poor Esme, she's a wreck bless her 'art. Must be hell.'

'They're in on it. Tell Musa I been looking for 'im.'

'Kay. What's y'name?' Suzie asked.

He straddled the razor blade seat. 'What y'doing tomorrow night?'

'Nuthin.'

'I'll pick y'up when y'finished.'

'I need a name before y'pick me up!' she called out, biting her bottom lip watching him leave. His cycling lycras not leaving much to the imagination.

The external spotlights highlighted the frontage of the café, adding to the cosiness of the town when it began to sleep. People still walked aimlessly to catch the last of the evening vibe before their retreat. Couples leaned on the metal bars and looked over the small harbour, the nightly dog walkers ambling passed, their mutts inspecting the places where Max had sat. Suzie's feet were killing her as she wiped down the last table, she was left alone all day and into the night, no sign of her employers or Hassan. She yawned as she took the tray of coffee cups and cake-smeared plates to the kitchen, tutting when she stepped in water by the stock cupboard.

'This bloody place!' Loading the dishwasher, hanging up her apron, her eye catching more puddles of water. Reaching for her mobile she called Esme, going straight to voicemail, the same with Musa, hesitating over Hassan's number; probably a bit weird calling a kid. Looking around the small galley kitchen she pulled reams of tissue paper from the holder and blotted the puddles, squishing the bundles with her toe. She heard the main door close, giving her stomach a hot rush. 'Thank God! Is that you Esme?'

'Oh, it's you, we're closed. 'Ere, you ain't seen Esme, 'ave you? I wanna sort out this damn water before I shut shop. Unless you know anything about plumbing?'

'I need a drink,' was the late customer's response.

'Please! I'll give you tap water, that's it.' Suzie ran the tap hard. 'Dunno why you couldn't 'ave a bloody drink before you left! Bloody people, I had enough of all o'yers today!'

The customer entered the kitchen and snatched the full glass from her, Suzie watching them gulp, a little fascinated with the blue/green veins that pulsated in their neck.

'Blimey, you been drinking sea water?' they wiped their mouth with the back of their hand, slamming down the glass. 'Steady on! Or you'll be payin for it! Now, off you pop. I'm knackered! And don't think you're having a date until you give me a name,' shooing them out with her hands, them turning and grabbing her wrists.

'Oi! Get yer 'ands off of me!' she wriggled out of the grip a little scared.

'Sshh,' they said forefinger over their lips. Eyes deep green and hypnotic. Suzie relaxed; her shoulders slumped as she slipped into a wooed state. They supported her back when she became limp and surrendered. His scent hedonistic; unusual and indecipherable, with sulphuric undertones.

'I have t'close...' they kissed her parted lips.

'Sshh. Door's already closed,' pinning her against the worktop, they slid her foot sideways with theirs, she protested half-heartedly but the fire in her loins was too great to resist their access and imprint.

The amphibious torso rippled as it reached climax, changing colour and becoming something else with longer nails and a toned physique, entering a psychedelic state from acute bodily spasms. She wanted to scream for help, sure she was in a nightmare, her vocal cords muted and instinct paralysed. It withdrew its abnormality, and she collapsed in a heap, shaking within. She was horrified in her euphoria, glancing up at her assailant with blurred vision, morphing from someone she knew into something she didn't. It breathed victoriously through crowded teeth. 'We will take ownership. Bear the offspring, and continue our reign,' they said, staring at her with eyes that pierced her soul – the room spinning, her head filling with erratic whispers. Her back slid down the cupboard doors, and she drifted into unconsciousness.

36

Rescue

Hassan broke up the bread and balanced it on the rotting window ledge, Steve snatching and chucking it to the back of his throat.

'We're going to get my sister tonight and I don't know how long we're going to be. You'll be alright though, Steve,' he tried to stroke the top of the bird's head, but Steve was still a little unsure.

'Promise you'll be here when I get back?' Steve titled his head to check if he'd left anything behind. 'Mum says we're going to do something brave,' his bottom lip began to quiver. 'I'm scared, Steve,' offering bread from his fingers. Steve grabbed it and took off.

The room's purpose had changed, it had become a space of preparation in the past week. Marvel figures were shoved under the bed, childhood had no place anymore, it just pacified what was really screaming inside. Sensitive, angry Hassan, afraid to let it out for fear of being a disappointment. He stood in front of the long mirror, doing up the buttons on his best shirt. Hoping he looked as good as Akash did. Where *was* he anyway? Some hero he turned out to be. Brushing his hair in place, he blinked, checking his eyes were still working. It still made him jolt, not as much as before, giving him a stinging rush all the same, as if something resided within him surviving on his traumas.

He sat on the bed, Max joining him, the tinkling of the amulet on his collar prompted a closer inspection from Hassan. He rubbed his thumb over the engraved Arabic word encased in other inscriptions. 'The close?' Max smile-panted, 'what are we closing, ay Max?' stroking Max's ears back, leaving him behind was tearing him apart. The dog seemed relaxed and in no need to adhere to the stench of anxiety. The daunting thought of saving his sister was too great without his companion. A soft knock came on the door, which made him check his room before they entered.

'You okay, love?' It was Esme in her grey pyjamas, walking in with her gaze lowered, not ever wanting to walk in on a teenage boy.

'Yeah. Don't tell Baba Max is on the bed.'

She fussed her dog that stood to her attention. 'Have I ever?' she corrected her son's curls that lay on his forehead.

'What's going to happen, y'know, how are we going to get Layla?'

Esme sat on the bed with him. 'Peter is taking us to meet Samir, and we'll just have to trust him.'

'I trust him.'

'Good, so do I. We're leaving, tonight.'

'Does baba know?'

Esme stood, 'no, because I haven't seen him. We'll leave it like that, for now, okay?'

Hassan's unassuming eyes filled with fretful tears. 'Hey, come on, it'll be an adventure. I can't sit around here waiting for that stupid policeman to pull his finger out of his arse!' they both sniggered, a pressure released. 'Okay, it's settled then. We leave soon. Come on Maxey,' she patted her thigh.

'No! Leave him here, please?' Esme agreed, closing the door with a gentle 'click'.

After a power nap dreaming of Layla floating above sands, her hair set free by a warm wind, Hassan staggered to the window that poked out of the roof; the moon in quarters within it. His alien eyes darted over the ocean and horizon. Smiling inwardly at the incredible vision and the detail that flooded his retina, igniting the optic nerve. His brain fizzed, present, aware of his blood rushing through his veins. The sounds of the night, each wave that hit Porthminster beach and dragged back the shells. A louder disturbance drew his eyes to the street, beaming at the green Land Rover that flashed its lights at him. Eager to get to Peter, he straightened himself in front of the mirror, puffing out a chest.

The diesel vehicle echoed through the quiet parish as it pulled up in Marazion's car park, the tide completely covering the causeway. Max agitated to get out, barking for them to take him to the beach.

'Shut up, Max!' Esme whispered sharply.

A rib was waiting for them on the shore, with Frank in his hat.

'Hello again, Frank. It's good to see you.' Esme's eyes filling with more tears she thought had dried up.

He pulled the tip of the captain's hat, 'Good t'see you too, miss.' They climbed in, Peter whistling for Max while he searched the shale for a good pebble. Frank pushed the rib in, Max barely making it as he took a running jump, landing in a clumsy mess as Hassan hoisted him in.

'Luck be with ye.' Frank said, waving his hat at them.

Peter took control of the engine, his heart thumping and stomach burning.

'You alri' maid?' He asked.

'No, I'm not sure why we're here. How are we going to get away with this?' Peter regarded the castle lit up in yellow reflecting in the black sea. He jerked his head towards it.

'Look.'

'What does that mean?'

'Means we'll get away with it.'

'And Janan?'

'She won't be 'ere. That be the residents letting us know.'

Their anxious silence was nursed by the water that parted on the nose of the rib. The mount felt different at night, and the moon's glow was so beautiful behind it. The castle a gothic image so firmly in its foundation, like it had organically emerged. Esme watched her son, his head full of thought as he focussed on the destination, his black curls pushed back like Peter's and profile illuminated.

'You okay, sweetheart?' Hassan just nodded not wanting to look at her. She had put her head scarf back on and he preferred it - the compassionate side, not the crazy lady side. 'Did you take your pills?' she asked. He slowly shook his head, 'good,' she answered, feeling a stability return from not taking hers either. Except the gruelling confrontation of unhealed traumas, emerging like ghouls from their designated corners.

The rib scraped on the harbour's slope. Peter got out first, offering his hand to help them out. Esme took it, squeezing it, pleading with her teary eyes.

'You'll be alri' maid, come on, where's that fire? Ay?' the rib was a little shy of dry land, getting their feet wet as they clumsily got out of the rocking vessel. Max leapt out and barked in excitement at the top of his voice. Esme gasped when she saw Max run to Samir, beckoning them with urgency.

'No time to waste. Follow me. Hurry!' She followed, sniffing and wiping her nose on the sleeve of her cardigan, her teeth chattering. Samir waited for them to join him outside of the school, checking around before they went inside. He closed the door behind them gently, Esme feeling nauseous from the place. There was always the smell of Oud that masked something else, something stagnant, like a stench from the reptilian house at the zoo. She noticed he wasn't wearing his tweed jacket, just the white thobe with a breast pocket for his handkerchief and another object.

'You look terrified sister, please, don't be. We have the greatest challenge ahead, but you will not go alone,' he whispered.

Esme looked between them all, 'you mean?'

Samir dipped his head, 'I am helping you find her.'

She threw her arms around him, 'oh, God! Thank you! Thank you!' He was humbled, awkwardly removing her arms. 'So, you know where she is? You know, what the pastor said?' Esme asked with a spark of hope, searching her mentor's eyes. Samir placed his hand on her shoulder, his expression giving her mixed messages.

'Inshallah. Esmay...'

'Give me your jacket Harv,' Peter said.

'Why?'

'You'll be a bit 'ot with it!'

'Hot? Why?'

'No, no, let him keep it on dear brother, the nights become cold.' There was silence for the moment as they stood in the hallway. Broken by Samir's sharp exhale.

'In the name of the Almighty, the All Seeing...' Esme guarding Hassan and stepping back, '...BismiAllah a 'Rahman a 'Raheem. Take us through under your protection and guidance, and return us with our lives intact so we may continue to serve you in this life and be rewarded in the next. Ameen,' he lowered his head and recited indecipherable chants under his breath. A warm breeze on the side of Esme's face shifted her attention.

'Mum! Look!' the door at the end of the hallway was open. A bright light emanating rays and mesmerising lure of a twinkling smoke screen, distant voices bringing forth a desert wind that made them shield their eyes. Max barked, pulling on his collar Peter had in his grip.

'We must go!' Samir yelled. Esme looked at Peter, his face pained and eyes glistening.

'I love you, Peter whatsit! Take care of Max!' he raised his hand accompanied with a sorrowful nod. Samir coaxed them towards the door, Hassan pushing back. 'No! I'm scared!'

'Say BismiAllah, Hassan!'

'Is it hell?!'

'Dear boy! Trust me!' Hassan squeezed his eyes shut and held his breath, reciting from his chest. Going from the cool stone walls of the house into a suffocating, dusty heat. Esme cried out in sheer panic from the sensation of the transition. She turned to check on Samir, with light on his face and a reassuring smile as the red sandstone closed in behind them, plunging them into darkness. Hassan's release of breath echoed in the tomb, wide-eyed as he checked the adults were still there in the dark.

The door was forced shut by a vacuum back in the house. Silence engulfed Peter and Max as he dropped to his knees, wiping the sparse tears from his eyes.

'I don't believe in ya but whoever's listenin, bring em back to me,' he looked toward the ceiling, 'you carnt keep letting this appen, not anymore! Close these bloody gates when all this is done with. For good!' He bowed his head, exhausted from keeping his demeanour, completely overwhelmed with the task ahead. Max whined and scratched at the door they had gone through, sniffing the wafer thin gap.

'C'mon boy. Leave it. Let's get you ome.'

'Was 'appened to you? Gorn all soft?' Peter jumped out of his skin as Akash emerged from the large room, fresh out of a magazine.

'Where the 'ell 'ave you been?! You could've gorn with em!' Max scrambled to Peter, hiding behind his legs.

'Not without any water, Dad,' he sneered. Peter pushed himself up from his bent knee. 'Ha! Has me old man been cryin'?'

'I ain't your old man.'

Peter headed for the front door. Akash grabbed his forearm, his grip a little lighter than usual.

'You can't keep this façade going f'much longer. You're weak!'

Peter snatched his arm away. 'I got work to do. Someone took the amulets. Know anything about that, ay?' Akash stepped back, his eyes flickering back and forth between a disguise. Peter regarded him with a heightened intuition, the scent coming from him was not quite the same.

'Search me,' Akash shrugged.

'I intend to,' Peter glared.

'What luck Musa brought Esmay back, who knew?' A female voice coming from Akash's mouth confirmed Peter's suspicion. 'Just when you thought you were being clever, erasing her memory and sending her inland. Just remember who you are working for, Peter the holy man.'

Peter opened the door, looking back with eyes that had darkened and altered, 'I quit,' whistling for Max.

He left the door open and walked to the harbour, the rib still in its place with Frank waiting at its side. He put Max in, tying a thin rope to his collar. 'Now. Frank be taking thee back 'ome. Just wait f'me. I'll come an get ya. Don't worry.' Frank was without a hat this time, and his beer belly.

'Take him back to Draycott. I won't be too far behind. Something's 'appened to Kash. So keep yer wits about yers, and tell the others.' Frank acknowledged the command, Max ready for another boat-ride.

Peter watched them leave as he walked down the slope, wading into the icy shallows in his corduroys, tearing away his shirt and casting it aside. Distraught and rebellious, the minerals and immersion soothed his aching heart. He wasn't losing Esme again, or his new family. The depths would erase and rejuvenate him, ready for his next journey. Reaching out he grabbed the Beaky's dorsal fin, the mammal clicked and squeaked, pulling him under, heading for Porthminster.

Akash was on one knee his head lowered, Janan filling the glowing gateway in the house.

'You have done well. A reward awaits you. More will be born unto us, and our army will expand. The believers have entered our realm. Seek out Ibrahim, his conscience has manifested a disobedience. Bring me the skull of Solomon, for I fear Samir has changed sides.' Akash held out his upturned palms, his gaze remaining lowered. Janan dropping small, human bones in them.

'Monitor their movements. Kill them if necessary. We have significant importance arriving, and cannot disappoint. Keep your disguise of the half Siren, they will place trust in you. Don't let Musa's daughter return, she must be delivered.' Akash bowed lower in gratitude. Janan's hand emerged from the brocade; three digits with a thumb either side, black fingernails that twitched over Akash's head, rattling the jewellery, the light breaking through her arms and flooding the hallway in yellow-white glow.

'I endeavour to witness equal loyalty in your sibling.' Toulah stood, reinforcing the image of Akash, the Hamsa glowing on her left hand as she entered the parallel of Al Ula.

37

Musa

He scowled when he heard the front door click shut, sat as close to the burning logs wrapped in the knitted throw. Max rushed to Peter with bunny, relieved to see him.

'Thought I'd find you iding ere.'

'Come to take your Shahadah, have you? You need a declaration of faith to protect you from the darkness that resides within these walls.'

Peter regarded Musa and the walls, undeterred.

'I come to elp. Your family have gone through.'

Musa huffed and shifted his position, 'I don't want your, your, halp! They are in a better place, away from this corrupted society!' his face a little grey.

'And them ands of yours, it would seem!' Peter sat on the sofa, Max nestling between his feet.

'I regret what I have done. I feel like I am eating my shame, cho-king on it!' suggesting a grab to his throat, 'no need for you to push it in further!'

Peter was holding on tight to his reputation, fantasising about snapping Musa's neck. 'I'm getting them back. Layla ain't where y'think she is.'

Musa sat up, revealing his frail body loosely dressed by the taupe polar neck. 'What are you sayink?'

'I'm sayin, she ain't where she's supposed t'be. She be on the other side o'that.'

'Who told you this?!' uncrossing his legs.

'The pastor. Y'know, the one who been murdered?' Peter said in an accusing tone.

Musa tightened his grip on the throw. 'We cannot get her from the parallel, she's gone,' he resided.

'Not necessarily. Samir's gorn with em.'

Musa threw off the woollen pacifier. Peter a little shocked at what he saw.

'Wass 'appened to ya?!'

'Your son did this to me! I was not ready. I needed my strength to save her!'

'He ain't my son!' Peter stood to affirm his words. Walking to the window, he scanned his territory. 'He's half Siren. I took him in.' Peter picked at his hands, 'another rape and murder orphan from those disgusting creatures out there!' pointing to Porthminster's shore. 'We've worked bloody 'ard to keep em out! And then you came, and messed it all up! Yer bloody deserve it!' Musa turned away, pinching his bottom lip.

'Where were you, anyways?'

'Hidink. Look at me!'

'Yeah, well. How old are you? Or should I say, were you?'

Musa pushed himself up from the armchair; his jeans dropping a couple of inches from his waist.

'That is not important. Is she with Ibrahim?'

'Aye.'

'Hamduillah, this is positive.' Musa ran his eyes over the crumbling mortar between the fireplace tiles, 'what did I expect? Eh? Thinkink I could deceive the Nagini.'

'So, you knew about the doors?'

'What can you do to halp?'

'I wuz 'oping you were gonna suggest summat. I wanna know everything. Why you came, what your plans were, before I put my trust in you.'

'Do you drink coffee?' Musa asked, his demeanour changed.

'No. Tea, and water, please.' Peter answered, returning to the sofa.

Musa shuffled to the kitchen to swallow his pride; handfuls of his hair falling out and resting on his back.

Peter comforted Max, ignoring the whisperings in the walls from a species chanting a prophecy. The dog quivered and panted. 'S'alri' boy, Pete's 'ere. I ain't let nuthin urt ye.'

'Halp yourself to whatever you need,' Musa said, returning with a tray laden with refreshments. Peter turning his nose up at the gold plate of dates.

'Ain't y'got any scones?'

'Pfft! Sand cakes with sultanas, you mean. No. Dates have everything you need, but check the middles first.' It was ending for Musa, here, now. A bad choice or a fateful decision, his soul grappling at what he'd lost and was losing. He took a brown package from atop the fireplace, his trembling fingers fishing inside for one shard. Lighting its end in the log burner and wafting the sacred smoke over him, coughing up his lungs. Peter waved his hand to redirect the silver trails. 'Don't you like it?' Musa asked.

'I'm not partial to it, no.'

Frowning at Peter, watching him gulp down the glass of water, 'have you been drinking the sea, brother?' Peter just passed a look toward him. 'This is Kenan. The rarest in the world, and no other scent like it. Kept in the safes of perfumeries and prestigious museums,' he held the shard up in worship that had travelled continents in the blink of an eye. 'Man cannot obtain such treasures anymore, they are hidden from our eyes and transported through ancient routes. We have used up all our resources, and made it extinct! All we have is cultivated sticks. Too impatient to wait, having to graft anything to get close!' Incense routes had been shut down by war, the parallels of Al Ula was rife with the rarest, without the need to cross bordered continents. In a world void of any Agar trees, wood of the Gods, the supplies used as bribes and currency. The only tree left in Asia remains heavily protected and worshipped by monks. The Arab world living to experience just an atom's weight of its scent.

'What's the connection?' Peter questioned, throwing a date in his mouth, stone and all. The crunch sending shocks through Musa's brittle bones.

'The selling of souls. My soul. Back home, you cannot make a livink from a café, not anymore. I just use them for storage. That's why I can live comfortably as a Café owner.' Slurping his coffee. 'I am entrustink you with my family. I don't know how much longer I have left. Hassan needs a father and guidance. All I could do was suppress his, breeding, until this moment.'

'You made im afraid of it,' Peter spooned the fourth sugar into his tea.

'What else could I do? What would a kid do with that kind of, of, power?!'

'You never gave him chance to find owt.' Peter sucked in his tea. 'What else? Why did ya come ere?'

Musa's guard was already down, huffing in defeat and slumping back into the armchair, running his hand through his thinning black locks and regarding the freed strands in his fist. He wiped his face and goatee, licking his teeth, 'to supply the Summit with Oud, and my daughter.'

It went quiet, Peter's face burned, looking to the wooden floor. 'How did you get yourself into this?'

'I reverse the effects of black magic. Leading black magic stings in Saudi, and parts of the middle east. They are real enough. Good money if you have the stomach. Toulah was my accomplice, she would help locate spells, going against her own at times. You see, you have spells in the earth, water and air – leaving it to the elementals of those planes to safeguard it and carry out its intention. Humans are more disgustink than any devil. Willing to defile themselves for revenge.' Never in his life had he seen such desecration, and animals he never knew existed. Mutants of familiarity that were usually pets of the Jinn. Worshippers found in caves or abandonment, sitting in their own faeces for days on end just for a spell to make someone love them, or never love again. For riches or revenge. Sometimes he didn't know what he was seeing, just desperate, needy souls that had completely lost their way. The most forbidden practice in Islam, yet the most common.

'We are the owners of it, the best you can get when it comes to casting spells. No other script or book has the same effect. It must be the denouncing of the Quran, or nothing will work.' He got up again, restless as he confessed. Limping over to the window, his pain burning. It all looked golden as it started to fade. So many years it seemed, yet the quickest were the years he watched his daughter growing up, passing like hours.

'I was in great demand here and back home. A powerful shapeshifter, Toulah's sister, was asking for impossible conditions resulting in suicide, and the trade of children. I made her go against her own kin, so we could execute it, burn her with our scripts. Another trapped in water. Ibrahim was fooled into releasing them,' he gulped down his coffee. 'Toulah served me for many years, and I had to betray her. There is no match for a vengeful Jinn.'

Musa held onto the chair as he eased himself back into it with despondency, 'I was to be trialled for murder by Janan's committee, unless I became a supplier of human cargo. I agreed, just to stay alive. Running and hidink ever since. I didn't come here to fulfil Esmay's dream, but to fulfil my con-dishon. What goes around…eh? The leader of your country is greenwashing you all into thinkink the summit is for the environment,' he huffed, 'same goes for all the others. Making their mark, like pissing dogs.'

Peter toyed with Max's ears as he listened.

'I married Esmay to fulfil the request of hair of fire and eyes of oceans. A king has been waiting for my daughter. He must have the patience of a saint, SubhaanAllah. I hope his loins are dried and beyond saving.' His words trembled, swallowing down the tsunami of grief and guilt.

'It was me who cast the spell on Esmay, and summoned the threat in these waters. I needed her away from you,' sneering at Peter's gaze was a form of defence, the darkness still resided even though the size of a mosquito. 'She was about to marry a good man, the spell not so easy on him, he was pious. Toulah found her for me,' he scoffed, 'her scent was easy to follow from this location. It was in Allah's hands whether she gave birth to a child like her. I prayed she would take after my ethnicity, no one wants an Arab. Do they, eh? So, I persuaded poor brother Ibrahim to help me undo it. And I would have succeeded if I wasn't so bladdy deluded!' He had been a difficult man so that letting her go wouldn't be so painful. But his fabricated family were his very existence, battling with shame while trying to uphold reputation and honour. 'You should be humbled I brought Esmay back.'

'What about the other stuff?'

'Abadis? A gift of youth given in return for worship of the Nagini. Only this youth is not in the form of a lagoon, but the adrenaline of scared children. Adren-o-chrome. Something I have become dependant upon,' raising his chin to the ceiling. 'There are laboratories in Europe extracting the compound, although infant blood can be taken directly, but it's not quite the same. Keep an eye on the countries being protected and heavily funded by western corruption; that is where the labs are.'

Peter huffed through his nose 'yous sound like a load o'bloody vampires!' releasing what sounded like a growl from his gullet.

Musa's reaction obstinate, 'Marazion has been the connecting incense port to Al Ula for many years. Guarded by Janan and her followers. She is the owner of all routes and suppliers of untouched children and adolescents. How do you think I maintain my looks and third eye insight?' They regarded one another, a resistance and respectful distance on both sides.

Peter was seething beneath his checked shirt, 'I's got seaweed that'll do the same thing.'

Musa blurted a laugh, 'I doubt that will get me seventy seven thousand dollars a barrel, my friend.'

Peter's body stiffened, fighting with an overpowering killer instinct he'd trained hard to keep below the surface. 'And the other amulets?'

'Shields, markings for the deposits. The Summit will change the heart of this small town. The price to live here will be out of reach. Driving out tradition. An elite market.' He chuckled at his analogy.

'You ruined their lives with y'doctrines! Keeping them in a bliddy cage!'

'No! I saved them! I pray one day you will see it. But don't look in my direction, we have tarnished the most beautiful way of life with our hypocrisy and need to compete. I represent the worst of all examples in this world.' They had ruined everything, caused hate and divide, a contradiction in their worship. The world's cabal needed to eradicate the likes of Ibrahim and Samir, the light they carried, a little heavy from resistance against the western world. Simplicity gracing their hearts, and ability to live from the land without usury.

Musa sniffed from a cold nose, returning his hands to the dying flames that had reddened Peter's face. 'It was Esmay's dream to come back home,' his voice calmed, 'she talked about it all the time. Something that never left her, like a piece of her heart. Masir. Fate. The beginning of the end.' He looked

Peter in the eye, a man that scared him to death, 'you sent her away into the fire, dearest brother. I knew this place would be my final destination, a moment I have been waiting for to escape this hell. What better way than to use it to bring her back home. She deserves it.' He swilled the gritty dregs around in the Ikea cup, biting back the tears.

'So that was the plan, for Samir to take em through?' Peter asked, Max flinching from his erratic petting to suppress instinct.

'No, my plan was for Ibrahim to marry her. That way they could not touch her, she would be imprinted and impure. I did not want to be your enemy, brother. I wanted your halp. Inshallah, Ibrahim will do what is right. I trust his heart. Janan will have coerced any of them for the skull of Solomon. You've heard about this, I take it?'

'Ma'be.'

'I see. Well, Janan will offer whatever your subconscious tells her, in return. A priceless artefact attached with great powers. It is said you can access any portal with it. I wonder if it can get you into Jannah, eh?' Laughing at his own joke. 'This means heaven to you, my friend. It's not easy to attain. If only there was a bone that could do that, we would all be killing each other for it.'

'Is Samir worken f'the Hamsa?'

'Ah, the door opener, and in high demand. Only those that have memorised the Quran, the Hafiz, can access the doors. Or you can be like me, praising my creator with crossed fingers behind my back. Bah! Do you know why the world wants to eradicate us? Casting spells through media to make the west believe we are all terrorists?!'

Peter shook his head, unaware of most things as he didn't have a television, or access to social media come to that. He lived freely and off the vibrations of the elements.

'We hold the secret to life's purpose and its end!' Musa proclaimed.

Peter's eyes met with Max's, smiling at the dog to ease his quivering. 'What's been the constant problem with the door? And that strange bloody cat, stealin Frank's catch!'

Musa squinted, his vision blurring. 'Come, you can see for yourself.' Peter followed an aging Musa, his looks still visible and hostility humbled.

'There is a big distraction comink, more will be taken. Your work will be cut out for you.'

'Where have they taken Kash?'

'I fear he is restrained, you may have lost him, for good.'

'I ain't lawst him! I knew it weren't 'im. He wuz…different.'

'Sounds like Toulah my friend. The finest shapeshifter there is, but she has a weakness: vanity.'

'Best Kash is ere, out the way. He wouldn't survive if he went through.'

Musa winced at each stair, 'the authorities will be displaying it openly, playing with minds. Conditionink them to turn a blind eye. Using big corporations and pop stars to blind intuition and steal energy.' Musa held onto the handrail.

Max tip-tapped behind them stopping at the top, sitting and throwing his head back in protest. Musa reached the bottom of the stairs and turned the brass handle of the door, which opened like any other. The smell that escaped made Peter cough, cautiously reaching the bottom looking into the small room where the piles of rucksacks still lay and filled his vision, unable to cross the threshold, noticing the raised Hamsa on the flagstone floor.

'Here is, your, evi-dence,' Musa panted, throwing his hand up towards the boxes and ruck sacks with Noona sat on top of them. 'The missink children of Marazion, and my accomplice, Noona.' She arched her back and hissed at Peter, the boxes concaving from her weight.

'How come you opened the door?'

Musa tapped his nose, 'privileges dear friend, privileges.'

'Yous can open the door at the mount then.'

Musa waggled his forefinger, 'not so easy,'

'Why?'

'Janan watches me closely. Your myths and legends are about her. She is far more intelligent than to be deceived.' Musa laughed loudly. 'It's like a dream, no? Everybaddy excited to see this place, Ooo! Look, how beautiful, how mysterious,' he took a breath, 'Janan must be executed and all involved, and that includes me in this cocktail of haram. We break this chain, we break all others. Esmay will also be free of my spell.'

'How do we do it?'

'Break the gates. All of them. Then it will all…collapse. The Arab world would have to go back to basics if the routes are shut down. War on neighbourink resources will increase and, dar-dee-dar…' circling his right hand, 'you get the picture. The prophecies are gathering momentum. They will have to find ways to dehumanise and distract. Saudi will be competetink with the US for this accolade. We strive for perfection in everything, except our hearts.' Musa's aging had accelerated, breathless. 'Why don't you come in? Look at what we've been hidink behind the infamous door.'

Peter ran his eyes over the doorframe, 'I don't like spiders, or altars.'

'Noona eats the spiders. And this, 'altarr' may get you through, insha'Allah.'

'I thought only Samir can do that.'

'I understand your trust in me is fragile, brother. But what have I got to lose? Eh? Look at me, I am a dying man before your eyes. At least this way I can perform an undoink without consequence and insha'Allah, receive forgiveness.' He took in a sharp breath as the wounds on his forearm throbbed and burned, gingerly holding them for any ease.

'Your orphan has great powers, my friend. It must have been difficult to keep him on the straight path. I commend this. You should put a high price on his head.'

'Shouldn't we get those looked at?' Peter pointing at Musa's deep wounds in the shape of Akash's fingers.

'It is too late! Death is my only cure, brother, and the end of all of this. Unless you have some Adrenochrome lying around?' he jeered. Peter was unresponsive and repulsed. Musa cleared his throat, hating himself all over again. 'Janan will have my replacement ready. You will see my photocopy after I have passed, hmm? But with somethink missing.'

Peter regarded the melted wax on the silken cover; amulets draped over the tiers beneath, a dark basket with small parcels of lint, casting a furrowed brow on it all.

'What do I have t'do?'

'Nothink. I will do it for you. Inshallah I will open the portal here once Raffia has placed the spell with the earth Jinn to protect the process, and get you the other side safely. We don't want you ending up in oblivion. If not, we must go to Marazion, take our chances.' Musa looked Peter up and down, if he entered another realm they would make him King of it. 'We must give you somethink so you can last without sea.'

'I can last. I don't need no spell.'

'I am cas-tink you into a climate the same as hell! Trust me, you will need one.' Musa rummaged through an odd basket, looking like something from a museum, choosing a parcel then changing his mind, mumbling. He held up the tight parcels in turn, clutching one and smiling, 'Ah! This one!' Holding it out for Peter to take, 'put it around your neck.'

Peter took the leather lace and held it at arm's length, 'wass this fer?'

'To keep you alive.'

Peter gingerly placed it over his head, regarding the triangular pendant bound in black leather.

'We call this a Taweez. It is specific and only for you. Your personalised Jinn trapped inside the script!' Musa chortled, with Peter's trust fading, taking another look at it. 'Don't open it yet. You will know when.'

'When do I go through?'

'When Raffia has placed the spell in Al Ula,' forcing a smile Peter's way.

Max's frustrated bark made them both jump out of their skin, 'be quiet, kalb! You'll wake the dead with that noise. You also need a change of clothes, brother.'

'Ain't nuthin wrong with me clothes!'

'Are you always this stubborn?'

'Ma'be. What appens when I get through?'

'You are on your own. I have somethink that will fit you, Insha'Allah. You also need to learn basic Arabic. Ya Allah, my hope is tired but what else do we have?' Musa became unsteady, falling onto the altar and knocking everything off. Peter automatically rushing to help, stepping on the Hamsa. His left palm began to burn.

'No!' stumbling back out of the room, 'what have you done?!'

'It was the only way to get you through!' Musa strained.

'I ain't becoming one of you!'

'You will not survive without it!'

'I shoudda known you'd trick me into summat!'

'I have not tricked you, dear brother. I have given you protection for this journey. You cannot pass through otherwise. You will not be harmed and inshallah it will get you what you want. Use it how you see fit to get my family back, and Ibrahim if he so wishes. I am not a fool, I know your orphan had his protective eyes on my daughter. I'm sorry I mistrusted him.'

Peter breathed heavily as he watched the symbol materialise on his palm; like a regretful tattoo.

'Now, go back to your home. Walahi it will be within forty-eight hours, no later, insha'Allah. If you haven't been summoned by this time, you must return here. I cannot guarantee we have not been heard.'

'And how do I get back?'

'I pray you find Samir.'

'Meaning, I might not come back?'

'Nothink is guaranteed, only the way in. Unless you get your hands on the skull, which is doubtful. Now, go! I am tired. I ask you this one favour, take the kalb home with you, the animal is unrested here. Leave him with Suzie if we are successful.' Peter dipped his head, clenching his left hand. He climbed the stairs and clicked his fingers to beckon Max, the anxious golden retriever grabbing bunny and eagerly following Peter out.

Musa sat on the floor, Noona jumped off the boxes becoming Raffia as her large paws hit the flagstone. She knelt by his side, stroking his face.

'You have been my most treasured protection,' Musa breathed, relieved to be speaking in his mother's tongue. 'Intelligent and wise deceiver. Go live your life after your last duty. Find what makes you happy, with fish.' They laughed together, a solitary tear rolling down her face, not quite free of the wiry fur.

'I shall never love any other. You are my only and last love. I am happy here, with your permission to stay.' Her soft purring words gently arousing him, giving her a solemn nod of approval.

'Take the spell, for Peter, near the tombs. Please, he has good intention. Make sure he passes through with ease.' She agreed, kissing his hand. 'My loins are aged, precious Noona. Janan took all the supplies for the guests. I need, more adrenochrome, so we may part with lasting memory and heal my wounds.' She agreed and kissed his thinning lips, her cat teeth catching on the delicate skin, sending pleasurable shocks through him. 'You understand why I had to do this now?' She lay her head upon his chest. They caressed in silence and stared at the ceiling rose with shared thoughts. So many years together, finding Musa when Toulah had left him. Arriving at his door, begging for food and joining him on the prayer mat as she placed her trust in him. His prayer cleansed her turmoiled soul; playing with his hair when he prostrated. Noona became Toulah's replacement. Loyal and less of a threat. She reminded him of the women he admired in his life, watching them all leave before him, a consequence he bore for the path he chose. The novelty of youth and power played no part in that moment. He loved two different females, with equal intensity. Both the make up of him. Noona adhered to his request to be ordinary and serve Esme, yet her jealousy burned. She was still a Jinn whose scorn was no match for any woman.

Peter and Max idled through the dimly lit town. It didn't offer the usual comfort, it felt hostile and a darkness had descended. A line of string lights above them paved the way and shadowed the whitewashed bricks. Everyone was inside when they were usually sitting on steps greeting you as you passed, offering a drink or light conversation. Weaving through the warrens to his two-up two-down in Crow Street, pushing the stable door which was always open. The smell of damp and stale milk stung Max's nose but it was better than staying with Musa and that damn cat that hissed and forced him into corners. He sniffed the stone floor, his tail circling, but he was happy, getting himself comfortable on a straw mat by the unlit fire. Peter caressed the back of the chair that Esme last sat in, his gullet making an odd noise as he held in an emotion he was sick of feeling.

Max had already settled, just biding his time until he was needed.

'You 'ungry, ay? I got fish, y'like fish?'

38

Qasir Al Farid

They organically joined the tourists as Samir helped them down the rocks outside the main gateway and tourist attraction in the present day. The coarse sand entered their footwear, making the trudge difficult through the guides and camels that were just for stereotypical expectations. The breeze a recycled heat, carrying nuances of tradition and something Esme recognised, stopping her dead.

'Wait! I, I can smell her! She passed here!' The fresh scent of Layla's hair an osmosis through her, setting off hysteria and burning tears, pulling at Samir's heart.

'MashAllah you have good senses, but there are scents from the restaurants. Please, try to relax. Okay?' She agreed, sniffing and wiping her face.

Hassan was silent, agog, acute anxiety thumping his heart. Good memories flooded back along with the bad. The restrictions on his mother and sister, the televised executions, the control and frustrated shouting which only ever instilled fear of his father, everyone pussy footing around for the holiday. There was never any family to visit, just Ibrahim and a few other guys that would have covert discussions with Musa, while Hassan supped on smoothies like a gooseberry at the Al Masaa. His heart was a lonely place; too many emotions and conflicts to absorb and deal with whilst maintaining the toxic masculinity he was expected to uphold. Dealing with it by shutting off, retreating. Still unsure of himself, his identity, who was he really?

Seeing Esme wear her scarf again brought comfort in a familiar, but he was missing Max, aching for him to be by his side but he would surely fry in the heat with all that fur. More squared tombs anonymously appeared in the sandstone, identical frontage and architect that could not be compared to any. Each having carvings of lions, eagles and an effigy of cattle, all provocatively lit up by candles, lighting the way for an arrival. Most could only be reached by helicopter. Hassan gawped at the place where Samir was heading, the place where Ibrahim and Layla took shelter, only there were no incense routes, but high-end alfresco dining and a mirrored conference building that reflected the rugged terrain and its visitors. Becoming an inanimate, flawless mirage.

Spherical boulders painted in assorted colours were dotted around the reddish landscape, looking like giant gumballs. Trampolines imbedded into the sand with led lights that reacted to your jumps. Organised exhibitions for the travelled and University breaks, groups of keepers of Al Ula and campaigners made the attraction one to remember, adding intrigue to the unexplained.

They stopped at a diplomatic velvet rope to the entrance of black and maroon fine dining, nestled in a chasm. 'We rest here, have something to drink and reserve our places for tonight.'

Next in line, greeted by a well-presented waiter in a black satin suit dressed with a red cravat, not even a bead of sweat beneath the heavy damask pattern. His arm leading the way to their table set upon the sand. It was impressive how they managed to make you think you were inside because of the quality of the fittings; you almost forgot you were amongst wind-sculptured gorges.

'Asalaam alaikum. Welcome. Welcome. Please, sit.' They sat amongst those that had paid the earth to visit, flying or travelling for hours. A place on their bucket list. The rocks towered above them creating a secluded respite. Esme and Hassan unable to take their eyes off their surroundings, feeling subdued by the effects of the trauma and sophisticated lighting.

Their waiter handed them long glossy menus, Samir thanked them, placing his face down on the table. 'Choose whatever you want if you still have an appetite. However, may I suggest you drink and take the juices they have on offer, before filling your stomachs with meat.'

'Strawberries, I need strawberries,' Hassan panted.

Samir amused by his childish mannerisms. 'I am sure they will meet your needs. And you, Sister?' Esme was still reading the English beneath the Arabic, the sweat running down her spine and soaking into her underwear. She was home just minutes ago, now she was choosing from a menu in a sought-after destination. Perhaps it was an illusion and really, they had all passed out in Marazion, hoping she would be patted on the face by Peter at any minute.

'Umm, the uh, tropical smoothie, I guess, please.'

Samir agreed and politely beckoned the waiter, ordering with a litre of mineral water.

Red and green lasers suddenly raised heads, dancing around the rockfaces with music to accompany their rhythm.

'We will wait until the festivities get underway, and inshallah I will find who we are looking for.'

'Why can't you just, open another door?' Esme asked.

'I reside under the watchful eye of Janan,' Samir opened his left palm revealing a faded Hamsa, quickly hiding it.

Esme gasped, 'how come I didn't notice that before?!'

'It is my pass, but no longer my following.' Hassan checked his left palm followed by Esme, Samir snorting a quiet laugh.

'So, you know, about the rucksacks?' Esme pushed.

'Ah, here come your refreshments,' Samir leaning back in his chair to give the server room.

'Where have you come from?' the waiter asked.

'Marazi...' Hassan didn't finish after Esme elbowed him in the ribs.

'United Kingdom,' Samir answered.

'SubhaanAllah! You have travelled far! Welcome to Al Ula. Stay the night, you will be most welcome. I will bring you something special.' He made eye contact with Samir, who gave a nod for that something.

Esme drew on the metal straw, the thick medley of blended sunshine coating her inflamed gullet, while her eyes wandered around the other tables at black-haired women, head to toe in top brands and subtle decorations of gold.

'Mmm! This is amazing!' Hassan said between straw sucks.

'Hamduillah. Sister, have you relaxed a little?'

Esme wiped the condensation over her face from the glass. 'A little, yes. Thank you. I still don't know how...'

'I know you are feeling doubtful but look at what we've achieved. Should that not put your mind at ease? We crossed over with the guidance of Allah.'

'What if, I, I just can't comprehend she is on the other side of this!' she whispered across the table.

'I understand. Would it help if I told you...' he checked around, continuing from behind his hand, '...people access it daily. Does this ease your doubt?'

'I guess? But, how?'

'Baba knows,' Hassan piped up before sucking up the last of the smoothie, loudly.

Esme choked, wiping away the spittle from her lips.

'Did you see the room?' she asked,

Hassan shrugged. 'Max went in there and ended up here.'

Samir blurting a nervous chortle, 'MashAllah, I knew you were my best student for a reason,' dabbing his watery eyes with a brand-new cotton handkerchief.

'I am?'

'Most definitely. Now, you must eat. I recommend the T-bone steak.'

Esme was still finding it hard to believe that anything that happened was done by the permission of piety. 'So, this is a trafficking gateway?'

Samir cleared his throat and pulled the tablecloth straight, cocking his head. 'Relax, sister. Trust in Allah, and enjoy your adventure!

'We've just walked through a portal, Samir!' she whispered, 'you knew where Max was all along, didn't you?' He beckoned the waiter once again, Esme regarding his beautiful eyes and face. The light that emanated from him made you watch your p's and q's. She did trust him, more than she would dare to admit however, there was something underlying and there would be no greater trust than what she had in Peter. Her heartbeat for him, his grounding presence and brash outlook would probably be out of place, but she couldn't continue without it. He was her 'go-to.' Each thought, incident, he always crossed her mind.

Lasers and artificial hues illuminated Elephant rock, a formation that lived up to its name. But there were no drive-ins to watch from the rockface tonight. When the air cooled, the starry sky expanded her conscience, complimented by fire pits amidst the protection of the backbones. Bedouin shelters circled the entertainment with lanterns and decorative lights, low tables adorned with silver trays and dishes filled with Medjools and candied fruits. The hypnotic beat of darbukas filled the night and ignited their sense of self. Hassan jiggled his hips amongst the musicians and a smile had returned, one that came from his boots. He was confident in what he felt and trusted it because his gut had never been wrong. 'Doombek, da doombek', pulling at the burdens and releasing them. Samir clapped with reserve as he sat beneath the red and gold damask, patiently waiting for the 'something special'.

Esme looked on from sunken luxury seating, absorbing the vibrant company. She still felt out of place, even though she fitted in perfectly. Returning to Saudi, ignited the trauma that lay oppressed in her fibres. Doing her best to dump them back where they belong. She daydreamed at her surroundings, her rose lips twitching when she thought of their way in. It was like walking through a short kaleidoscope, heavy with unseen guardians and the end of life. Her eyes wandered, lost in the opulence of the log fire in a reflective bowl, the light wind pushing the flames this way and that. Places were of five star and above, just like Riyadh. She missed the culture, the emotion stinging her sinuses and reaching her eyes. It would be hard to leave it behind when it had become such a big part of her for seventeen years. Such an important cultural enrichment for the children. The tearing apart of the family unit would be by her own hands, a tormenting guilt that stopped her moving on more than Musa ever could.

Scanning the merrymakers, she noticed a man had joined Samir, chatting with mint tea and blanched almonds. Esme's attention shifted as she tried to read them. Delight struck her face when she was beckoned by Samir, her stomach filling with butterflies as she entered and took a seat on the low bench.

'Salaam Alaikum.'

'Wsalaam, sister,' the stranger reciprocated, 'how are you feeling?'

'Anxious, dizzy, terrified.'

'Of course. Inshallah you will be with your daughter soon.'

Her eyes instantly filling with tears. 'Are you the man who can help us?'

'Inshallah. How is your head for heights?'

'Heights?!' the stranger laughed mockingly, placing a muslin bag on the pressed material. More magic, Esme thought, her heart rate reacting.

'Why must it be connected to the forbidden?'

'This is an entry ticket not a spell, dearest sister.'

'Same thing. Ticket spell.'

Samir shifted forward. 'Where must we take it?'

'Old town. Daylight,' he took a small hand-drawn map from his shirt pocket, unfolding it and flattening the creases, 'it is not too far in. Just here…' tapping the spot on the drawing of squares and rectangles, depicting the ancient village in the oasis of palms. 'There will be an inscription, like a sitting dog, but with the nose of cattle.'

'What is the connection with cattle?'

'The Nabateans were the first to farm such animals and offer them for sacrifice.'

'Sacrifice?!'

The stranger loudly amused, 'don't worry, sister. Did you leave your bones?'

'My, my bones?!'

Samir sheepishly took a full napkin from his breast pocket, revealing steak bones.

'Ah, excellent,' handing Samir the small bag pulled with string, 'Allah be with you.'

'That's it? Bones and a bag of haram will get my daughter back?'

'We hope for the best, in all things. I pray for your ease. Salaam,' he stooped his way out, taking Esme's hopes with him.

'Bones?! Samir, this is voodoo shit! Seriously!' the longest passage of her holy book came to mind, a warning and example of such practices. 'It won't end well,' discretely wiping the sweat from her top lip.

Samir read her thoughts, 'we cannot open doors with piety and script, sister. We are merely offering the animal, not worshipping it,' tucking the bag and napkin back in his pocket.

'To whom? Or What?' The angel she imagined hanging over him fell abruptly; God's presence a farce. Same old story and disappointment striking fear into her.

She snatched the nearest glass of tea, raising it towards Samir, 'fine. See you in hell.'

39

Peter's lot

Faded photographs and half drunk tea lay discarded on the worktop of the two-up, two-down; Peter had left in a hurry. Twenty-four hours and he wasn't prepared to wait any longer, already on his way to Draycott with Max at his side. Maybe he would find Musa dead. The wait had been an agonising one, Saint Ives had gone suspiciously quiet, and he should probably take a walk up to the lookout and chapel. The absence of Akash and the Pastor left him desolate, Max was all he hung onto and vice versa. He passed the Abadis, giving it the side eye then a double take as the door lay open with a bicycle on its side and discarded helmet. He stopped, waited, Max walked in with a wagging tail in the hope his person would be inside.

'Max! Get 'ere! Stay!' tutting when the dog completely ignored his commands, 'dammit dawg!' Peter followed, moving the bike from the doorway and leaning it against the building.

'Ello! Suzie? You alri? Ello!' his skin prickled and pupils enlarged. 'Max! Ere boy!' patting his thigh and grabbing his collar, pulling him out. The leash Esme tied him to was still on the picket fence, clipping him in under protest. Max barked and pulled, 'no! Youm bliddy stay there! Y'here me?! Else there's no fish lata.' He rolled down his sleeves, doing up the cuff buttons as he walked back in.

'Suzie? You 'ere? Someone is, I can smell ya!' he called out, standing in the doorway with feet slightly apart. The cyclist appeared from the kitchen; Peter squared up.

'You'd better come see this.' Peter followed to find Raffia face down over the threshold of the stock room.

'You called anyone?' the cyclist shook his head, 'go outside an' watch Max,' Peter instructed, crouching down and checking for life. 'Christ,' he mumbled, looking back into the stock room wide eyed at the branded wooden crates that radiated the smell he hated. She was clutching something, he prised open her left hand, she was holding a vial of lilac liquid in the hand where the Hamsa matched his, still feeling tainted by the other night. He took out his mobile and called Musa.

'*I said forty-eight hours!*' Musa answered.

'Yeah, I know. It's been cut short. Raffia, is dead.'

There was a static silence.

'*Where?*'

'Café.'

'*You can see her?*'

'Yup. She's right in front o'me. And she got summat in 'er and.'

'*Bring it, and get out! Get out, now! Go! Come to the house, now!*' Peter backed away, pushing the vial in his back pocket, turning over the 'closed' sign before pulling the main door shut.

'Who is she?'

'Friend of a friend.'

'And you're just leaving her there?!'

'It's complicated.'

'Is it summat to do with Marazion?'

Peter regarded the cyclist with a squint, 'why didn't you call the police?'

'Gut feelin.'

'You doin' anything right now?'

'Uh...no, no.'

'Good. You're comin wi'me. You can get t'see the man 'imself. And where's Suzie?'

'Dunno, that's who I came to see, she stood me up. Thought it was her at first.'

Max had to be dragged up the steps when they got to Draycott. Peter knocked a few times, trying the handle.

'Patience!' yelled Musa from the hallway, fumbling at the chain on the door, his eyes reddened and face sullen.

'What is he doink here?' pointing to the cyclist.

'He came t'see ya.'

The cyclist gawped at Musa.

'Yes, yes, it is me brother,' he laughed and coughed, 'you might as well come in now you're here.' Musa turned, his back slightly haunched, wiping away tears. Peter entered with a reluctant Max, jerking his head for the cyclist to follow. 'How is the kalb since leaving hell's gate?'

'He's appy.'

Musa returned to the chair in front of the burner, waving his hand towards the sofa for them to sit.

'This is the uh, thing I found in er and.' The vial lay in Peter's palm, Musa snatched it and clutched it in his fist.

'What does nosey parker want? Come for your package, eh?'

The cyclist gulped, 'I err, I'm not sure why I'm here but I've been tryin' to see you for a while.'

'What for? Kenan? Magic? This is what magic does to you dear friend. Stay away from it.'

'No, none of those. I came to tell you I've been getting an army together...'

'Pfft! This is not the Aven-gerrs, dear friend.'

'Hear me out. We don't want our country taken over and made inaccessible, and we don't want this summit ere, either. People are losing their omes. We know what has been going on in Marazion, and we wanna put a stop to it...'

'Have you any idea what you are dealink with?'

'We dunnit before, in the past, we can do it again.' Musa and Peter regarded one another, Musa blurting a condescending laugh.

'Why not? What have we got to lose, eh? Gather your people, but we must get Peter through first,' he pushed himself up with a wince and groan, 'timink is everythink. What do you intend to do with your...*group*?'

'We storm the mount and kill the woman, with the help of the rowers.'

'Ha! I think you have been watching too many moovies dear friend. Janan cannot be overruled, by anythink or anyone.'

'That's the name this time, is it? Or do they go by another name?' Musa and Peter exchanged silent information.

'She is Nagini. And what do you think you have to defeat this powerful entity?'

'Numbers and noise, the rest is up to the boy.'

'My son?' Musa gazed into the fire, the dancing flames flickering their message, 'very well. Peter, brother, are you ready?'

Peter stood and pulled his shirt straight. 'As I'll ever be I'spose.'

'We must change your attire brother, you cannot enter like this.'

'I ain't changing into nuthin else. I'll go as I am. Take it or leave it.'

'Then we take it. When you are through, inshallah, you make your way to the restaurant that sits in the chasm. Inshallah you will reach them in time. No conversations, except to ask if they were seen. Don't think it is over once you find them. Bring them back through the door at the mount and it must be closed off. How long can you manage on dry land?'

Peter stiffened. 'What makes y'think I can't manage?'

'Oh, just a, how you say? Hunch,' he smirked and reached for the small, brown package of Kenan on the mantel piece, throwing it in Peter's direction. 'Your pass, should the Hamsa not suffice. Offer one piece if you find yourself stuck. We cannot be sure Raffia took the protection through, so I must open the gate for you. It is too risky to go the Mount.' Musa coughed and retched as he led them to the stairs. Peter's heart was about to make an appearance in his throat, holding fast to his image, fearing he would never return or ever see his home again. He was bound and wouldn't have it any other way. Maybe it won't work because of his obligation, half hoping it wouldn't and trust Samir a little more than he did.

Musa missed the younger version of himself that knelt at the altar without any cracking of knees, expressing his effort loudly as he went down with the help of Peter.

'Bah! The Kenan!'

'Here, have a piece o'mine,' Peter handed him a medium sized shard from the package.

'Jazak, brother. You are a good man, err, well, whatever.'

'Where am I going through?'

'The lone castle, inshallah. Qasir Al Farid. The main gateway. I pray we do not have to take a trip to Mara-zi-on.'

The cyclist stood in the doorway eyeing up the rucksacks.

'Good God alive. Are they what I think they are?'

Musa turned to look at them, as if he needed reminding, but made no comment.

'I need to concentrate. Think good thoughts and if you know how to, pray! I must summon something undesirable in Raffia's absence.' The sting of grief splintering his bones.

The whisperings began in their heads, Max whimpered for Peter at the top of the stairs. Musa lit the shard and waved it around him in a ritualistic manner, reciting as he did. The candles were next; red for fire element and protection. Then the black Babylon, the ultimate colour and recognition to the practice, and magic aide of teleportation.

'I cannot guarantee that what comes through will be holy. Just keep praying.' The cyclist only knew the Lord's prayer, Peter just held firm to his ancestry.

'Err, what's happening?!' the cyclist asked, holding up his arm watching the hairs stand on end. Peter put his finger to his lips and shook his head feeling a magnetic shift, different to the feeling at the school. Like a compromise was about to be had. There was a blood curdling screech and something appeared at the top of the stairs, prompting a yelp from the cyclist, moving Max aside. It crawled on its belly to the bottom, primitive and hostile. Its skin an insipid grey with eyes that reflected the dim light from the swinging lightbulb. The stench of dank, dark places stung their nostrils as it entered the room at speed, slamming the door shut. 'No!' Peter shouted, trying the handle, turning it back and forth, pushing the door with his shoulder.

'Musa? Musa!' using all his strength.

'Look!' the cyclist pointed to the foot of the door.

A thin strip of yellow light made Peter release the handle and stand back, Max ran down the stairs and began to scratch the door, barking and crying.

'Leave it dawg! Leave it!' pulling him back by his collar. The door clicked, Max's head tilted. The door opened and blinded them, a warm wind rushing forth moving their hair and clothes, and Max's fur. The dog yanked forward, Peter held him tight, the cyclist trying to catch his breath as he gasped in awe.

'Oh. My. God!!' he yelled over the howl. Peter swallowed hard and inched forward, shielding his eyes. The whispering had been replaced by low rumbles and distance female voices, the light alive! 'GO!'

'Take the dog!' Peter demanded. The cyclist reached down to take Max's collar, but he released himself from Peter's grasp, and entered the light.

40

Reunion

Motionless clouds glowed orange from the rising sun, offering little relief from the heat Esme hadn't missed, which near burnt your skin clean off the bone. She could feel the sin on her tongue like a jagged pebble, blocking the flow of sincerity. Guilt had no place, she did her best at her own compromise. With nothing but herself, no rosary, no script, she carried out her remembrance on her fingers, odd numbers of worship to repent for what she was about to do. She began to rock as her devotion intensified, mouthing her begging. Maybe God was also in on it after her outburst on the beach, sending her mind off at a tangent.

Esme's sleep had been erratic, dream-filled with Layla and on high alert while Hassan snored, and Samir slept like a sleeping thing. Studying him in detail there was still something angelic about him, the way he functioned, a little envious of what it must feel like not having to survive on live wires. She felt a change since being pushed through the portal, it seemed to have a detoxing effect; dare she think it, a rejuvenation. Her thoughts were clear, she hadn't felt this well in a long time. Coming off the pills was daunting, but she wanted to find Esme Pascoe buried beneath Kattan, and the synthetic emotions. She felt a liberation in Al Ula, self-aware, free from judgemental eyes. Running away as always, which became her captivity, plunged into facing herself. Having Hassan by her side, her safety net and daily crutch, holding her hand in secret and telling her he loved her at random moments, made Esme feel purposeful. She envied the mothers who had dependant sons, wondering if they knew how blessed they were.

Continuing her worship, she was distracted, something was circling the luxury pod. Scratching and sniffing. A low growl, turning her head to locate the sound, crouched and ready to run. Samir warned there would be Leopards on the prowl. She shook him gently, '*Samir*! *Samir*!' whispering urgently. '*Samir! Listen*!' he sat up in a daze, holding his finger up to silence her.

'We do not have what you want. In the name of Allah, leave!' His command waking Hassan.

'Max?' Hassan slurred, the animal's nose pushed through the opening of the pod, Esme shrieked but Samir was unreactive.

'Oh my God! Max! How did you get here?!' her eyes darting as Max wriggled with excitement amid their fussing.

'I knew it! I knew you'd come!' Hassan laughed, screwing up his face as Max licked him in a frenzy. 'You knew how to get through, didn't you boy?' Max repeatedly barked a signal.

'So, this where youm be 'idin.'

'*Peter*!' Esme unable to hide her delight, as he poked his head inside. Samir doing his best not to show his true feelings.

'MashAllah brother, how did you make it?'

'Musa,' Peter answered, kneeling. Wiping the sweat from his brow with his sleeve.

Esme's face was alight, 'you alri' maid?'

'I am now. But how did he do it?'

'That don't matter.' The Kenan was useful as promised, the waiter only too pleased to tell him where they were, for just one shard. 'So, what's 'appening from ere?'

Samir stood, taking dates from the golden servers. 'We eat then we go to the ancient village. It is a tourist attraction now, so we will not be out of place. That's where we place the offering and inshallah, we go through. Keep a close eye on Max, and do not let him wander. However, you cannot go through dressed like this brother. They will see you are from this side, and we do not want to attract unwanted attention.'

'Fine! Sounds simple enough.' Peter huffed, 'and then?'

'Then, we find Layla, inshallah. But it is not over when we do.'

Esme snapped her head around, 'what do you mean?'

'We cannot get back through the way we came. You remember when our aid asked you if you had a head for heights? Well, we have a greater journey to fulfil in order to return.'

***

Esme had fallen deeper when she saw Peter in white jodhpurs and tunic, it suited him. He caught her staring at him, increasing perspiration, unsure how long he would last in the heat. A red Discovery was waiting for them after a light breakfast. They piled into the cooled vehicle, Max's presence regarded as a strange companion on this journey. The dog was on pins, quivering every which way he looked. The vehicle rocked Esme as she let the landscape pass through her mind. How bizarre this was, the wonderment, lifting depression as purpose and perspective were seated. Acutely aware she was existing for destination and temperance in all the chaos.

Hassan lay his hand on Max's back, beginning to enjoy the experience and take in the opposite side to his mother. He felt like he was on planet Mars, all that was missing was his sister, subconsciously pointing out something to her.

The short trip was made in silence, the guide having occasional trivial discussions with Samir.

Arriving with other luxury transport and tourists, the entrance to the old town was adorned with traditional earthenware and more coloured boulders and pompoms. Makeshift stalls and shops displayed historic paraphernalia, tourists milled around with groups taking selfies and making videos for back home. Samir tipped the driver with 'something special' and beckoned them all with the tilt of his head. They followed him in hurried footsteps, Peter with his wide strides and clumsy feet. Samir couldn't find any sandals to fit him, so his toes were protruding a little.

'This bloody heat and sand be summat else!' he moaned.

'I know right? The floor is *literally* lava!' Hassan jeered, skipping to keep up with him. Max was picking up familiar scents, searching, circling.

'Max!' Peter called, the dog immediately running after them and walking beside Hassan. Esme was behind, absorbing, distracted by opulence. Unimaginable luxuries at every turn, Saudi's most guarded secret was fast becoming known to the world, and its archaeologists heavily protected.

Samir checked around before he turned sharply into the oasis of palms and nepeta. The roofless village a maze, Hassan eyes everywhere as he felt the residue of long-gone occupants. It reminded Esme of something from Raiders of the Lost Ark, in fact it was all turning out like a movie. Samir made it difficult to keep up, turning this way and that then down walkways then right, sharp left. He stopped, checking the walls, brushing dust from crevices.

'Look for a cow, or something that resembles one. Hurry!' They dashed through corridors and investigated rooms once occupied. Dried palm leaves hung through rafters supported by mud bricks; it was like the occupants had left in a hurry all those centuries ago.

'What about a dog?' Hassan said, touching a placard next to the doorway of a derelict abode. Samir pushed his hand away to inspect it.

'Yes, yes, this is it! Well done!' Patting Hassan's back.

'But you said cow.' Peter questioned.

'This is a cow.' Samir ran his finger around the outline, blowing the dust away.

'Don't look like a cow t'me.'

'I can see your point brother. They are sat like this, perceived in a regal position,' touching and admiring the impression. 'Incredible.' He whispered, taking a closer look. 'The Nabateans were an advanced civilisation, they even had women's rights and the kings served the guests. Then, they disappeared, just like that. We can only assume the Romans took over or the sacrifices were their demise.'

Hassan yawned at the brief history lesson, Esme and Peter swallowed their gathering saliva as they listened intently. An anxious pause among them all, still tripping on the fact they were there. He knelt beneath the placard and dug with his hand, retrieving the bones from the serviette and small parcel from the aide.

'What the 'ell are you doin'?' Peter asked. Samir didn't answer as he placed the items in the hole, covering them over with his foot. The whispering began in Peter's head. Max looked up at him and whimpered, 's'alri' boy. Yous be calm now.'

Esme held onto him and Hassan as they watched Samir close his eyes and recite, certain it was in Latin, hearing a faint 'Ameen' at the end. They all investigated the space beyond the doorway, Samir wiping his eyes with the serviette.

The ground beneath them rumbled, unsteadying. Max got to his feet and barked. They stood apart watching the sand vibrate, handcrafted plates fell to the floor and the smashing of clay pots could be heard all around them.

'Samir?!' Esme called out in panic.

A white light manifested in the room, the sand swirling into a small vortex, darting in the space.

'BismiAllah! Go! Now!' Samir yelled.

'You first!' Peter insisted. Pushing past him, Samir entered, his arm outstretched behind him for all to take and make a chain.

'Don't let go of each other! Send in Max!' They inched forward with eyes squeezed and mouths buttoned. The ringing in their ears intensified as the panic rose from the pressure on their torso. Hassan could smell Oud and burnt sugar as the density of the portal began to thin. The faint belches of camels, ringing of cowbells and voices reassured him of the short transition, and the fact he was still alive.

Samir was first, then Peter, Hassan and Esme still holding hands as they merged with village life. Esme immediately covering the bottom half of her face, holding the peach chiffon in place. They were pushed and shoved by women with eyes heavy with kohl, carrying baskets and armfuls of material, calling out in an Arabic dialect no one understood. Samir continued to pull them through the warrens. Max chased strange, skinny cats and stole food from clay plates on doorways. Esme wide eyed at every dwelling they passed hoping to catch a glimpse of Layla. Material adorned the women wrapped around in layers with gold stitching, multiple bracelets and hands covered in henna. It would be difficult to find anyone. The four of them stuck out, but no one really took second glances, they were used to it. Nearing the exit, passing through nepeta laden paths with young Palms, they were back where they started without the gum balls and mirrored structure. Samir halted them, Hassan stuck to Peter from the sudden hostility and bizarre sensation, the stench of dung triggering fight or flight.

'Are we in the past?' Esme whispered in a high pitched panic.

'No. We are in a parallel. We did not time travel, sister. Listen…' they circled him, 'there are no smoothies or pampering here, be vigilant, stay with me. We head to the tombs and find shelter in the rocks where we will sit and wait.'

'For Ibrahim?'

'Inshallah.' Esme's stomach buzzed with hope, 'however, if we get separated, you cannot go back the way we came. My access is limited. Instead, you uh…' he looked to Hassan, '…you are a man here not a boy, be brave, we are depending on you.

Okay?' Hassan let out short breaths, confused and too scared to answer.

'But you'll be with us, right? We'll be with you, Samir, won't we?' Esme asked anxiously, her mouth dried from the heat and Samir's sudden drifting.

Esme suddenly broke up the huddle as she yelped from being touched by an old woman who stank of fires, her smile blackened and crooked, speaking in an unfamiliar tongue. She looked to Samir for help, the woman stroking her arm, lifting her hijab to see what was underneath. Esme pulled away 'La!' she scolded. The old woman inspected the others with wandering hands, making noises of approval until she got to Peter, gasping and uttering words of protection exposing a cracked tongue coated in gooey spittle.

Samir said something, distracting her, she turned and studied him up close. He repeated it. She cackled, holding out her weathered hand. Samir gave her three gold coins and a T-bone. She laughed and licked her lips, clutching them to her chest, beckoning them with a crooked finger. Esme linked arms with Peter, he winced and clasped her hand.

'Did y'understand what 'ee said?'

'No. But I'm confident she knows something, I refuse to let anything negative get into my head, there's no room! So, was it easy getting through? I mean, how did Moose do it?'

'Can't say I liked it much. I felt meself crystalising, thought I'd lawst Max f'good. But he were waitin f'me on the other side.' Esme related to the sensation Peter described, like a mini death. 'Your fella did it from that room you carnt get in, with some creature I t'aint never seen afores. Bloomin terrible it were.' She could tell he was nervous, speaking like the BFG. 'Y'know about Akash, do ya?'

Esme shook her head. 'He's 'ere somewhere, but it aint 'im, and it's my fault Layla's gorn. I took me eyes orf the ball.'

'No, it's mine, Peter. For marrying that shit head. And he isn't my fella.'

Max writhed in Hassan's grip, trying to jump out of it, 'stop it!' he commanded through gritted teeth. 'Peter! Help me!'

'Let him go, son. Trust im.'

'No! He'll get lost! I, I can't!'

'He found you, didn't 'e?' Hassan took in Peter's words, Max looked up at him with that smile and for the first time, a plea. Hassan closed his eyes and let go.

49

Miracles

Layla was fed up with dates and dry bread washed down with camel milk. Ibrahim said it was all they needed, just like breast milk. She craved something fresh, meaty, even disgusting fish would be nice, and the constant fantasising about coca cola was beginning to drive her mad. Just like fasting: the mental torment and constant battle with your cravings that were your daily emotional crutch. She was losing hope of ever being found, tired of being consumed by herself and paranoia, convinced it was a set up for her asshole behaviour. She would do anything to be back in Saint Ives watching Kash eat those gross pizzas, and she never thought she'd miss the sound of her mum yelling at her. She said sorry with each step they took, pushing passed odd strangers, Ibrahim making her anxious about her hair.

They joined a group of seated men who spoke in broken English, and seemed out of place like them. Withdrawn girls were glued to the men, clutching head coverings and picking at the food they were given. She tried smiling but they looked away, in fear of terrifying eyes that were everywhere. A couple were of foreign origin, but the rest similar to her complexion and bright eyes. People moved around them, stuck in the middle of a route, but it was the only place in the shade. The ambiance reminded her of numerous holidays, with poor souls trying to sell their wares. Only they weren't selling hats or caramel covered almonds, they were selling humans and Kenan.

Another man and scared girl joined the circle, they welcomed him as they both sat. The girl's head scarf pulled back a little as she knelt, Layla gasped and stood up.

'*Khadija*?!' she looked up at Layla, joyful tears glazed her fearful brown eyes. They met in the middle of the circle and threw their arms around each other, sobbing and laughing. The men in protest demanding their silence and to sit down.

'Shut up! All of you!' Layla screamed, the other girls hiding their delight behind striped material. 'Don't you know who my father is?!' her voice broke, and she collapsed in the sand.

The girls hugged and dried each other's tears, 'this is a miracle!' Khadija said, 'now I know Allah is with us!'

'He's in on it,' Layla murmured.

Khadija wiped the strands of hair away from Layla's damp face. 'No. No, sister, don't say this. He's our only hope.'

'Yeah, what luck.' There was that hope shit again, the placebo we're made to swallow just to coat over our intuition. The men returned to their places, mocking the girls and teasing one another on who would reap the highest price. The other girls regarded their surroundings and new arrivals closely, a rebellion rose in their guts making a collective telepathic decision that Layla was now their saviour. But the smaller girls were near to heart failure; plucked from a dysfunction or compromise for felonies within memberships, offering the promise of a better tomorrow until they got pregnant, and so the cycle repeated itself. With an endless supply for sordid gratification, the 'special' were reserved for summits, success gloating and sacrificial obligations.

Ibrahim guarded the girls from the others and gave them something from under a cloth.

'Drink,' it was cola and Layla couldn't contain her ecstasy.

'What about the others, uncle?'

'We need to keep my gift to ourselves. Sshh! We cannot save them all, sister,' flashing a quick smile at Khadija.

'What are we waiting for?' Layla asked.

'One of them will come and choose who they take first. Inshallah not you, but I must show willing. Although I do not have any intention in letting you go, either of you. If they decide to take you, I will do my best to negotiate a delay. Your fear may be subsiding, which is a bonus.'

'So, that's it? The more afraid will go first?'

'Mostly. If it wasn't for your hair and eyes, you'll get sold.'

'*Sold?* Where?'

'Slavery. Prostitution, even sacrifice.' The girls looked at each other and around the circle.

'You actually just said that in front of us.' Layla grimaced.

'Forgive me. AstaghfiruAllah. You need to know. Inshallah this will increase the fire in your desire to survive.'

'What's prost, prosti, prostitu…'

'It's not good,' Layla cutting Khadija short.

The cola went straight to their heads, at least, that's what it tasted like, setting off giggles and crying all in the same breath. Layla held in a burp, running her tongue over her furry teeth.

'So, how come it's cold?' she asked, the burp finally released.

'Drink quicker!' Khadija was a little drunk on corn syrup, caffeine and Ibrahim, swooning over his dark blue eyes.

'What about some for the others?' Layla whispered. Ibrahim lowered his gaze and shook his head. 'Why? Please, uncle!'

Their circle was disrupted by a striding light-coloured camel, accompanied by veiled beings without feet. The anticipation of the 'take' causing hyperventilation among them all. Silk hung from the animal; deep purple embossed with Hamsa. Morphing into a tall, voluptuous woman, her skin pale and lips violet, she glided towards Layla who stood in defiance, her heart beating in her ears. The Jann from the lagoon had returned to fulfil orders. Long fingers freed a strand of Layla's hair from the hijab, rubbing it between them and grinning. Chanting whispers began in Layla's head, trapped in a chilling stare. Soulless, with magnetic malice, the iris changing colour with vertical black pupils, flexing and pulsating. Layla was paralysed, transfixed, her fear dousing the rebellion only just present.

'Enough!' Ibrahim shouted. Layla fell to the floor. The Jann cackled and looked around the other girls who were just as terrified. The men prostrating as they waited for her selection.

'It seems the late arrival of our client has let you off this day, one more day won't hurt after sixteen years of waiting. Lay-lah!' she hissed. Ibrahim closed his eyes and slumped his shoulders in relief. 'I shall return for you and live my life in the generous bosom of my leader, eternally free of your father. I dare say you shall also share my amusement in this knowledge.'

A much younger girl levitated involuntarily, then one other, setting off screams from those left behind. They struggled mid air as their feet left the ground, pleading with heart wrenching cries as they drifted towards the Jann.

'No! Leave them!' Layla screamed.

The Jann revelled in the travesty, her head enlarging and legs elongating as she morphed back into a camel. The girls absorbing into the torso, becoming part of the manifestation. Fading cries for help prompted a primal weep from Ibrahim, curling both hands into fists as he fought with triggered grief. Celebratory laughter from the men increasing Ibrahim's disgust as they tossed pearls and small bones in their palms.

'May Allah cast you into the deepest pits of *hell*!' he said to them through rebellious sobs. Khadija placed her hand on his chest, falling to her knees with him. Holding his face, she wiped the tears with her thumbs.

'There will be mercy amongst the tragedies, uncle.' Ibrahim sobbed louder, wanting to rip out his heart, wanting to be an old man again and sip strong coffee in his kitchen where the end was closer. Khadija's affection paining him.

'We will return, tonight, to free you and the others,' gulping on his tears.

42

The Shiqq

The fire crackled and spat, lighting up their faces as they meditated in the flames. Crickets sang their nocturnal rituals and thin lizards hunted in scurries. Layla leaned back on her hands and gazed at the billion stars among the vivid nebulas, flinching when she felt something touch her fingers.

'Wow. There are *so many!* Is it real?' She was looking for a twinkling star, so she could relay a message, in awe of the pink clouds which bustled in groups against the indigo night. Stretching, rushing through clusters of stars. It was like an observatory without the tech. Her thoughts on perhaps our eyes were limited on the other side, and once we saw through the fabrication of reality, we could see more than we ever did.

'We are in the same place, sister. It is difficult to explain. But I find reassurance in this. I prefer it this side.'

'Do they have the same things like, governments?'

'Yes, and just as corrupt, but not human.' Ibrahim poked the fire with a withered stick, setting off sparks that fought one another. 'Janan governs them all.'

'How come you didn't age?' Layla asked, drawing circles in the sand.

'I did. I am seventy five. My hair as grey as silver linings,' he looked at her, imagining Musa and Esme's turmoil, knowing only too well how it felt. The torment of not knowing, and no longer feeling the connection to your child. 'Then, I took revenge, and paid for it with fake fulfilment. Inshallah we will free the others soon.'

Layla studied him, reflection freeing her mind. 'I think we go grey because all the unconditional love leaves us, like your children. I see it now, especially with my mother. I noticed, like, bits of her hair changing.'

Ibrahim was humbly impressed, 'MashAllah, sister. It seems a detox from the evil screen has been beneficial for you,' toying with little stones, his mood changed swiftly. 'We must head for the Mustatil, before first light.'

'What's that?' Layla asked, drawing the outline of a skull in the grit.

'It's sacrificial ground. It means rectangle, its shape and curse. Everything is cursed here. We need bones from sacrifice to get you back home. I am not educated enough to get you through without them. Holding faith in your heart is not always a big enough key. We have a risky path ahead of us. I will do my best to get you back. We should be safe, no one goes there because of the...'

'Because of the what?'

'Just remember, we are not on the same side of normal. There are things here that can no longer be seen elsewhere. Muslims are forbidden to enter the Mustatil and tombs, but it will be the only way to save ourselves.'

Layla returned to the drawing, it was good therapy, 'what's a Solomon's skull?' she asked, causing Ibrahim to choke a little.

'How do you know about that?'

'Janan asked me to get it for her...' she picked the sand from her fingernails, 'in exchange for my father's death,' tossing a small stick into the fire, 'so, it's not just you who hates him.'

'I do not hate your father, sister. He has been good to me, and if I had followed his instruction, we wouldn't be in this position. I was entrusted to get you to safety, but I lost my mind to revenge. Hamduillah I came to my senses, you should do the same.'

'When are we going?'

'When I am happy those disgusting humans are asleep.'

'You were willing to be a disgusting human.' They exchanged an awkward glance across the flames. Ibrahim patted his breast pocket with the last bone and shard of Kenan in it.

'I have one bone left. The girls will be bound to their traffickers, but not with rope, with a spell. We must find a Bedouin caravan to sell our souls to release them, I cannot perform anything myself. I am under scrutiny with a big condition over my head. I do not want to open a door for what I must bring back in return: a bribe and violation of my morals.'

Layla studied him piling more sticks on the fire; the glow illuminating his unusual eyes. He had done nothing but protect her, his words of Islam gentle, middle ground, and a revelation. When she felt acutely vulnerable, he calmed her with his stories of fate and humility. That's all it took, a kindness and appreciation of her given rights as a woman - swallowing his own pride and masculinity to honour female. She had spent many hours making excuses for her father, that's all he was doing too, protecting. But in his own sordid, conditioned way. The time spent without her phone decluttered her subconscious, thinking about her mother constantly and regretting being such a bitch to her beautiful brother. Shedding tears when images of his hurt face and those cute, squidgy eyes came to mind. But it was Akash that ran through her like liquid gold, coating her veins and loins. She knew that he was something out of the ordinary, with a presence dancing inside her like fireflies; her ultimate beacon of rescue.

'Like, I mean, what's the point? Running from death, worrying about it, trying to save everyone from it. It's gonna happen one way or another. So sad, really, being happy knowing it gets taken one day. Y'know?'

Ibrahim's dark blues filled with resonance, 'yes, I know. That's what makes it so beautiful.'

He let Layla sleep while he watched over her, using the flames to inspire his new mind that had been picking stuff out long forgotten. Memories that were pleasing to be in the company of. His wife and daughter were so clear when he thought of them, the grief intensified from it but he still felt blessed to have them close in his mind's eye. Rubbing the back of his hands, free of liver spots and dehydrated veins, his heart heavy with regret. He quietened the ache by pleading for forgiveness on his fingers, each section of digit a worship. The hand of a Marid or Siren would return him to his old self, Musa said. Huffing to himself at the slim chance of that ever happening on arid land. Earth jinn were tricksters, he'd seen several in their dark veils floating over the sand, menacingly sitting in the canopies of Palms.

How *did* he get here? Moved with momentum before he had chance to rectify. He fitted in quite well, without prejudice. There were no segregations, no wars, just the fight for survival and primitive existence we'd had long grown out of - oppressed by greed and reliance on external sources. He liked living this way, a detoxification for his soul and return to earth.

Reaching into the breast pocket of his thobe, he took out the shard of Kenan, but burning it may bring back crushing flashbacks, all he wanted was to go back 'home'. Just a feeling now. He held a small portion of the shard in the flames, making a figure of eight with the smoking ember, mesmerised by the glowing tip. Wafting it towards his face and over him, its particles grounding, briefly glancing at Layla he caught a pair of eyes fixed on him through the fire. Jumping to his feet, choking on his scream so's not to wake her.

'Leave! Jinn!' he whispered. The creature remained in a stooped position. Ancient, its nose as though it had been dragged down its face with two fingers. Darkish skin pulled tight over protruding bones: Reptilia with human detail. Holding a shield that seemed part of it, wary of Ibrahim with a primitive vibe. They circled the fire analysing each other, the creature settling back into a crouch. The type of Jinn that was grounded, unable to shapeshift, serving the Nabateans for centuries before their mysterious demise, left to obey those that crossed the parallel route with supplies of the rare.

'Are you, Jinn?' Ibrahim gulped, his throat half closing and his blood running cold over and over. It didn't answer, its tight mouth moving oddly. Ibrahim looked at the shard in his hand, then at the creature. The exchange between them telepathic.

'We do not speak then, Jinn?'

'Are you foe?' came a voice in his head.

Ibrahim checked behind him, terrified. 'No. Friend, I am, friend,' he panted.

'What service are you summoning?' the voice in his head said again.

'Uh, service?' he looked back to the flames, 'service' he muttered. 'Rescue and transition,' he replied authoritatively. 'A bond needs to be broken. An Abadis bond.'

'You tread a treacherous path.'

He looked at the Hamsa on his left palm, the creature saw it and made a strange noise, edging backwards. 'Naam. A path I want to undo.' Ibrahim relayed the location of the girls, but having to look at it, twisted his soul.

'Did I prise you from a safe place, Jinn?'

'I do not reside in the realm of dreams. Our existence is present. We are Shiqq.'

Ibrahim's skin goose bumped at that name, accounting for the creature's appearance. There were copious names for creatures of the unseen, but they were increasingly becoming 'seen' nearing the end of days, drip feeding disbelievers before the evident return and battle. Ibrahim had avoided such dealings and never spoke of them in a house or gathering, their existence undenied and forewarned. Uttering protective scriptures was a way of life for a Muslim, and here he was face to face with the worse one he'd seen.

Layla stirred, moaning as she sat up rubbing her eyes and yawning. They both looked at her, Ibrahim anticipating her reaction. 'Sister, we have a guest. Do not scream.'

Layla set eyes on it, the Shiqq giving her a blank stare. 'What is it?!'

'It is here to help get us and the girls back.'

The creature moved in a state of anxiety, *'you carry cargo of Nagini!'*

'She is also cargo of Kattan,' that was all Ibrahim could think of, it was worth a shot. 'We must get to the Mustatil. I would be honoured to have you with us.'

'Your humility is endearing. I shall honour your request,' and it bowed.

They followed the Shiqq single file like two meerkats. Camels were resting beside dying fires and sleeping caravans, one belched making them jump out of their skin.

'Jee-sus! I *hate* those things!' Layla whispered.

Ibrahim spoke over his shoulder. 'Hold your tongue, sister. Not all are just Camels.'

She gulped and kept a close eye on them. Nerves rose as they drew closer to the recess, the guardians' sleeping noises echoing around the cooled walls. The creature held up its scrawny arm to halt them. Layla screwed up her face, bumping into the back of Ibrahim.

'Eww. What's that *smell?*.'

'Urine. They are bound by a powerful spell so they cannot escape.' Layla held her nose and the tears back, placing her hand on her stomach in a protective manner. She waved at Khadija, who waved back with a pleading face, streaked with dried tears. Their faces dirty, huddled in drab, grey blankets. The creature hobbled close making the girls flinch and whimper. He paused, looked back and held out his hand for the bone. Ibrahim dropped it in the strange hand, the creature consumed it within its organic shield and began the recital. Its lips barely moving, raising hands above his head as if he were about to part the red sea. One girl stood free, then another and Khadija, excitement swept them. Ibrahim hushing them all as the men stirred, holding their breaths until they returned to slumber. He urged them to tiptoe over the men, and they could hardly contain their relief, letting out little yelps as he lifted them down to safety.

'There's one left, she's…she can't move.' Khadija sobbed, her convulses echoing.

Ibrahim trembled as he looked for her, choking when a child lay on her side, about eight years old, barely covered by the grey blanket. The tears flooded his throat from the familiar expression of a dead child; like they were sleeping, the hate of the world having left.

'I see her.' He choked. She looked so much like his daughter, the grief that revisiting with great intensity. The girls gasped as he clambered into the carved rock, not seeing a much younger girl left behind. Her matted blonde hair just visible beneath the covering, with piercing blue eyes and a thousand-yard stare. Ibrahim's heart twisted as he took her plump hand, brushing the dust from her petite face.

'Come, but you must be quiet, like a mouse! Okay?'

'Wo ist Mama?' she asked.

'Oh, she's German!' Layla said.

The girl pulled at the head covering with her dumpling fingers, smelling the worse. 'No, no. Uh, stay, keep,' Ibrahim pressed, tucking in her golden locks. She held up her short arms, her gum-drop chin quivering. He closed his eyes while he decided, his heart louder than his disgust, he picked her up with his head to one side, lowering her into Layla's arms.

'Uncle! What are you doo-ing?!'

'Im getting the other one. We can't leave her here!' Stepping over the traffickers with inches between them, the dead girl lay at the back, luckily a couple of feet away from them. He knelt, lifting the blanket to check how her fate had been bestowed, holding his fist to his lips at the bullet wound in her chest. 'No, this can't be.' He whispered to his lord. Wrapping her tighter in the blanket, carrying her back through the sleeping devils, nearly falling as he slipped on the soiled floor.

'Okay, go!' he strained, 'walk slowly pass the camels!' The girls held onto one another as they crept through the small gap in the rocks. Ibrahim trotting behind, the little girl falling asleep on Layla's shoulder as her head bounced. There were human outcries from them as they made it out into the open. The dark blue night and moon casting their shadows onto the sand. 'Wait! Girls! Stop!' He stood there, with the dead girl in his arms. 'Shiqq, can you help?' Ibrahim checked behind for the Shiqq, but it had gone.

'Why am I still trusting these Jinn?' he muttered. He looked around at the impenetrable, wishing he had a different kind of gift. 'We must bury her, sisters.'

'What happened to her?' Layla asked. The other girls, three of them high school age and desensitised to the horrors of life and male urges.

'She got shot.' The American one answered, matter of fact. 'Ambush crossfire.'

Ibrahim looked down at her angelic features, his tears soaking the fine, red dusting on his face. 'I did not think my heart was capable of aching ever again. But on this night, O'Allah, you have put life back into it so I may grieve. Hamduillah.' He felt real, sympathetic, having lost certain emotions from the magic. He placed her down to ease the weight from his arms, kneeling with her.

'Oh Jinn, I ask you to help us, for we are without aid to bury this child. I only have my bare hands to dig this solid ground.' The girls looked on, huddled together.

'*Shiqq,*' came the voice, jolting Ibrahim at his side.

'Forgive me.' The creature looked upon Ibrahim with eyes of a Geko. It's skin like stained cloth with faded blue tattoos of a tribe. There were ancient catholic vibes coming from this being, battles periodically crossing Ibrahim's mind. He squeezed his eyes shut trying to deal with the imbalance. Maybe it was the clash of different energies, or the creature was drawing from him; acutely aware he was a mere meat carcass protecting a complex mass.

'Please, can you help?'

'*Take her to the tombs. Do not set her in the earth.*'

'They are cursed, I cannot. I want her to have peace.' The girls were frozen by the Shiqq's presence, except Layla, who was studying it in great detail, her arm numb from the sleeping girl.

'Alone in the earth, she will be robbed of her bones. Which sits better with your conscience?'

Ibrahim picked her up, holding her closer. 'Then we go to the tombs.'

The Mustatil was not far, Ibrahim grateful for his borrowed strength, for an old man would not make the trek over the foreboding terrain and an extra burden.

43

Naga

Hassan drew circles in the sand with a charred stick, sheltered beneath an outcrop. The old woman led them to an unsafe, congested area. Max was difficult to convince to move on, frantically searching among the routes and stalls, sneezing from the residues of incense. Samir got nervous and they left.

'Maybe we're in the same place and it's all an illusion, on both sides,' Hassan mumbled.

Esme hummed in agreement, looking up at the captivating sky, her hands and legs numb she'd been looking so long. 'I really thought that old hag was leading us somewhere. What did you say to her, Samir?' He had become shifty ever since.

'She said she had seen Layla, maybe it was just for the bone. But claimed she touched and saw her hair and tried to barter with brother Ibrahim.'

'Wait, *barter?!*'

'Do not worry sister. I know the brother would not have let her go, if his reputation surpasses him. They may have a spell attached to them which makes them unseen. The Jann would not want any vagabonds taking her, she is too precious with a high price. I think we were close, which is positive, inshallah. Stay positive, sister. It's a powerful tool. Use the stars as your guide.'

'Like Bethlehem,' Hassan mocked.

Esme looked back to the night sky, crammed with more stars than she'd ever seen her entire life. It was better that brooding and going insane at Draycott, and at least she was doing something with her favourite army, revelling in the absence of Musa.

'I didn't want to look up at these in case one twinkled, I know that would be her. Have you seen those little balls of light travelling at sonic speed, Harv? We must be somewhere else, right?' Hassan chuckled to himself, to think, all the imaginative play between him and Jack, what would he think now?

'We're running out of dates n'milk,' Peter said, petting Max.

'I'm sick of dates and milk. How do they even *live* here? I need a smoothie!' Hassan whinged, his gullet like a sand pipe.

'This is only a stop gap, like a motorway service.' Samir answered.

'At least they have burgers and chips there, and toilets!'

'The weight loss will do you good, Hassan,' Samir winked and chuckled.

'This heat is eating my weight!' he retorted. 'And why have we got a fire, anyway?'

'It keeps the predators at bay,' Samir stood, straightening his clothes, 'unfortunately, there are no bones to be picked or strawberries to suck. We must leave, before first light. We cannot spend a minute longer on this side, or we may never return.'

'We passed a caravan on the way. I could see if they got summat.' Peter offered.

'No, Peter, I don't want anyone going off. I'm on pins!' Esme protested.

'I'm just goin' there, with them Camels. They must have sustenance I can pinch,' he pointed in the distance to the gathering, peppered with dying fires.

'Let him go, sister,' Samir dipped his head at Peter.

'Keep hold o'Max and no one comes folluz me. Got it?' Esme jiggled her head and watched him leave, 'and no bloody lookin' either, maid!' she huffed and went back to the fire, picking her hands.

'Get me a smoothie!' Hassan whispered loudly. Peter saluted mid air, without looking back.

He strolled into the resting caravan, the camels watching him approach. One lurched forward ready to stand, Peter gave it the side eye and the animal sat back down. Erected tents housed Bedouins sleeping on their right sides, drunk on fermented dates and Oud, the outsides abundant for the taking. Peter could pass for an Arab with his aging curls and nonchalant attitude to the surroundings. Searching among strewn crockery he found fruit for Hassan; smelling it to decipher. A mango perhaps, or similarly exotic. His eyes focussed on the darker corners, the fake Akash was close, catching his scent on pockets of warm air. He noticed one particular camel hadn't taken its eyes off him, slightly different to the others. He patted his chest checking the Taweez was still there and the Hamsa on his left hand; unsure how to use either. Peter searched among the clay pots and bowls, taking one of dates, milk and a type of soft bread. It looked better than what they had eaten earlier.

'Abaaaadiiisss, impossstaaaaaa!' something hissed. Peter continued searching the vessels and would deal with whatever it was when he was happy he'd had enough.

Arms full, he turned, bumping into a camel. They regarded one another in silence.

'Move! Yer stupid lump!' Peter's heart large and fearless.

The camel's eye changed to that of a serpent. 'What species are you?'

'Let me pass. I have, children of…uh, Kattan, to feed. Have to keep em alive,' he winked and swallowed down his words.

The camel's eye scanned him, 'what regime?'

'Porthminster.'

The camel's eye now fixed on his, 'you have Kenan.'

'Aye. Wanna piece?'

'You speak in what tongue?'

'Kernewek,' holding up his left palm. The camel flinched, moved back and bowed, Peter looked on, perplexed. Side stepping, he walked on, checking the animal was still bowing. Quickening his step, focussing on the outcrop, he looked over his shoulder again and the camel was following. 'Bugger!' he cursed, breaking into a jog, but the camel's feet could be heard pounding after him.

Facing the animal in a confronting stance, he felt alien, completely out of his depth, searching his mind of what to say. The bluff seemed to work earlier or was this camel thing more astute than he thought? He missed home, the fresh breeze and the perpetual crashing of waves. It stopped, expressionless, just like a camel.

'So, you have brought a friend?' Samir said behind him.

'It followed me!' Peter whispered from the corner of his mouth, holding one of the bowls under his chin.

'Welcome, Naga. We are honoured to be in your presence.' Samir announced and offered a slight bow.

'You have a bone finder,' the camel said, straightening its neck with a fixed squint on Samir.

'What have we done to owe this pleasure?'

'I serve the regime of Porthminster now,' the creature said. Samir bit into his grin, meeting eyes with Peter as he passed.

'We are eternally grateful,' hand over his heart with another bow, the camel mirroring it. 'We have thirsty guests with specific needs to help with our journey to the Mustatil.'

'What business do you have with the Mustatil?' it asked.

'Err, to fulfil a superior request,' his smile quivering. Samir led it to the outcrop, it regarded them all with critical glances, jolting when Max barked, retaliating with a loud belch. Esme screamed and guarded Hassan.

'Everyone, we have been honoured by the presence of the great Naga. Offering replenishments and guidance.' There were faint, nervous hellos and a deep growl from Max.

'Which cargo do you carry?' It said, with Esme and Hassan gawping.

'Cargo of the Zion,' Peter answered, handing out the crockery. The creature knelt then sat, chewing imaginary cud. Max strained to take a better sniff, curling his lip and exposing his teeth. Esme let him loose, he ran then skidded not wanting to touch it. Studying the creature's legs and the weaved blanket that lay over its hump, gingerly sniffing its back end.

'I should eat you kalb, if you were not the finder of bones.' It said.

Hassan's skin crawled from its voice; in your head but disembodied, squeezing your soul. How did it speak so well, for something so gross? He watched Max sniff every inch of fibre on the blanket, flinching at prickly stitching. It wasn't fur on its body, but a leathery skin that resembled it. There was a rancid smell coming from it and Hassan's grimace widened as he gorged on unknown fruit.

'Do I repulse you, apprentice?' it said.

Hassan looked behind him, then back at Naga, prodding his chest. 'Uh, uh, me? Me?' Naga released a low belch from within, and returned to chewing.

All with satisfied bellies and throats, eyes on the strange camel, Samir clapped his hands to get their attention.

'Are we ready, partisans?' Peter kicked sand on the fire and Max bounced on his front legs. Esme exhaled and tapped her collar bone three times.

'Ready as we'll ever be.'

Ascent

The shelter of the tomb was cooling, their breaths and movement echoed. Covered in tactile forebodes, smaller versions of the Al Qasir Farid in a haphazard line nestled into rocks, with identical frontages. The girl was respectfully placed in a recess the length of an adult, and away from the floor. They tied the blanket around her and lay her on her right side. Ibrahim tucked in exposed corners and affectionately patted where her head would be.

'Bismillah. Fly little bird, you are free from the monsters.' His belief a consolation that they became birds of paradise, under the watchful eye of the prophet with the same name as his; a guardian until they are reunited with their mothers on their passing.

Ibrahim gently rocked himself with eyes closed, finding comfort in the mumbles of the girls' chatter. Their hearts were lighter from the sweet liquid he had given them, a deep coloured refreshment he remembered from a west African acquaintance, bestowing great benefits and instant well being. His improved memory had made him dizzy, trying hard to shut it down before anything else materialised.

'Are you okay, uncle?' Layla asked.

'Hamduillah, binti. But my heart is sick.'

He looked at the American, then back at Layla. 'I know why they kept her and brought her through. But I cannot discuss this with you, it is too horrific sister.'

'To harvest her skin and organs. They are worth more than us.' The American's voice nonchalantly echoing in the tomb.

Layla took in a sharp breath, needing home.

Ibrahim held onto his bent legs. 'I saw them do it to my own people. We fought to get to the rubble before anyone else. They left those trapped underneath it, but stole the ones intact.' The American began to shake, she was missing a hit.

'I never gave my girls a funeral. I am not sure which was worse, that or not saying any last words to them. We are advised to settle for the less of two evils. I am still trying to settle, hamduillah.'

Layla patted his knee, deterred when she heard movement and voices approaching the tomb.

'Uncle!' she whispered. He called for the Shiqq from his diaphragm.

'*They cannot see you.*' Came the reassurance from the Shiqq.

The girls huddled, covering their eyes while Ibrahim hid with his back to the stone. He heard the stride of a camel accompanied by heavier feet with a lighter animal that lingered outside. It could be anything, a monstrosity disguised in another skin. He held his breath, kicking sand towards the opening to warn whatever it was intent on staying, the girls letting out little whimpers of fright. The intruders moved on, everyone letting out heavy breaths of relief, holding their thumping chests. Ibrahim took a quick look at Layla comforting the girls, which prompted regretful tears. He bared no ill will with Musa, it was his own foolish fault it had come to this. Perhaps both were to blame, and turning back the clock was a gift out of reach.

'We must leave, before first light.'

The trek to the Mustatil came cloaked in anxiety, Ibrahim's soul was jarred from other children being brought through neighbouring tombs before dawn broke, wanting to save them all. An unstoppable conveyor taking them from coercive care, silent and defeated, the trafficking a compromise from a living torment, and their new destination coated with false promise.

Tired and wretched, the girls' fear had subsided, needing their familiarity however traumatic. Layla and Khadija held onto one another as their feet burned.

'We must be in the same place, right?' Layla said, 'I mean, it's the same sun and same heat. I'm confused.'

'We are behind a curtain, that's how I see it. A transparent one. Same place, just concealed.' Khadija assured.

'Makes perfect sense.' Layla huffed, dehydrating quickly.

'What do you think would've happened to us, if Ibrahim changed his mind?' Khadija asked, her head down.

'Let's not dwell on that, ever.'

'Do you think we'll get back?'

'I'm sure of it, I feel it. Mum says, if you believe something with all your heart, it will happen. We underestimate ourselves because we've been brainwashed into believing something else is in charge of our thoughts and powers. Hasn't let me down yet.' She missed her mother and mobile, thinking there must be a thousand messages from Akash, because that's all she'd done was think about him. She was calling to him through the stars, convinced he would grab her by the waist at any moment, tensing from the anticipation. Absence did make the heart grow fonder, her mother said it was because we left a part of ourselves in the other person.

Ibrahim pushed passed them and regarded the climb ahead.

'Are we in the right place, Shiqq?' he looked around, the creature often disappearing then materialising out of nowhere, giving him a rush of burning adrenaline.

'Begin the ascent with caution. I am at your side.'

'Oh my God. There must be a thousand steps!' Layla complained, the climb by means of carved steps into the side of the rock mountain, the Mustatil at its zenith.

Ibrahim wetted his parched throat with a deep swallow. 'Little one,' he tapped the German girl sleeping on his shoulder, 'wake up, time to walk, habibi.' The child rubbed her eyes and snivelled, her cries getting louder as he placed her gently down.

'Shhhh! don't cry, you will wake up the Angels!' She didn't understand but his compassionate expression soothed her overexerted heart.

'Come,' Layla held out her hand, humbled as the girl took it with little convulses.

'She must be terrified,' Khadija said, disguised in a smile.

'We all are. We've just been taught to hide it, like everything else.'

Ibrahim stood at the foot of steps, a staff from the Shiqq in his right hand. He looked up; the steps a representation of the many trials he had endured in his life – the end eluding yet leading with hope. The trafficked girls followed him. Layla and Kadijah the last with the little one. The shift of gravel beneath their feet shot panic through them as they watched the debris plummet. The steps no more than two feet wide and a foot deep but steep in depth, toes hitting and scraping as co-ordination was hindered. The little one climbed them on her hand and knees, uttering words of make believe, talking to imaginary company, which comforted the others.

Ibrahim stopped to check on them.

'Keep your breathing steady!'

'Are we, nearly, there, yet?' Layla said at the back, raising a smile from Ibrahim.

'Not yet. Do not think about it. You will go mad. Just worship with every step. We will be at the top before you know it, inshallah. If you make it, there will be your favourite drink waiting for you. Hold onto one another. Come!'

45

Mustatil

They moved towards the inaccessible. Superheroes from all corners of life, each one with self and the bare minimum to survive. Sunrise expanded their fibres and quenched their arid hearts. Paired off, love and hope moved one foot in front of the other. Their vulnerability enhanced this moment, reliant on a monumental landscape that held no mercy, a power in contrast to the oceans.

Naga strode with Samir by its side. Esme's heart vibrated her whole body, trying her best with the therapy exercises. She was close to slipping into a fake scenario coma, death laying at the end of her nose.

'Youm be gettin yerself all worked up again. Breathe, maid, breathe! You passin' out ain't gonna 'elp nobody.'

'I just want to get her and go home, or I *am* going to give up.'

'No one's givin' up. Remember when I took ya to see the pastor?' Esme nodded a yes, 'well, you were about to give up before I took ya, so, just keep that in mind. Innit?'

'Yes, and if you weren't there, well, I would've...'

'Well, yer didn't and I'm 'ere now. Kay?' she linked her arm in his. She was right, it *was* the arm that would save the world, Musa at the forefront of her mind. He was haunting her, watching, making sure she was still his.

Resting under the shade of another outcrop, near to finishing the supplies between them. The milk had refilled itself more than the dates by the grace of Naga. Hassan always smelt it before he drank, hoping it wasn't Naga's milk. Silent in their feast and quest, each of them carrying a life invisible to the naked eye but tangible when they were forced to face it. Esme's throat tightened as she processed the journey while studying her hands. They didn't look so 'picked' anymore. The sun had turned her milky skin to almond, conditioned without pretence. Touching her face, she could feel her lips were fuller and skin smoother and her nails had grown into organic French manicures. She hadn't noticed Peter's smug glance at the change in her eye colour, but she did feel Musa was there again, certain she caught him in the peripheral. He knew, he always knew, even in her dreams, forcing her to retreat into the familiar dysfunction. The thought made her look at Peter. His strength unaltered but he was quiet, not really eating whilst observing, a little nervous of Naga.

'I got summat to tell yer,' he said. Esme squeezed his arm tighter, 'Y'don't know what's bin gowin orn, do ye?'

'In what respect? Musa and his fakeness?'

He patted her hand affectionately.

'The stuff he's into,' Hassan piped up behind them.

'Well, I got something to tell you, too. I got into the room after Samir left, and found...' Esme said.

'I know, I saw thems too, when I had t'come through.'

'I'm not talking about the rucksacks and bags, and I saw the altar if that's what you mean. Albeit in my stupor. But I also found something else. Vials, loads of them, full of like, a purplish liquid. Do you know what they are?' Peter looked ahead, his squint a little exaggerated.

'But that's not all. There was a picture, one I drew when I was little. It was the same as the portrait I bought,' Esme looked up at him, his gaze still ahead.

'Fancy tha?' Peter laughed and deterred.

'Look at me.' She demanded. He turned to her, 'it was the same, picture, Peter. Is it them?'

'Ma'be.' he turned back to the landscape that was beginning to weaken him.

'The town, that night. There's something you're not telling me.'

Peter's heart thumped, jerking his chin upwards to avert the subject, her heat and vibe penetrating his thick walls.

'What will you be happy to get home for Peter?' Hassan deviated.

'The sea, and...' he stood, flicking a date stone in Naga's direction, 'me boat.'

Back on their journey, Max knew where he was going, Naga followed confidently.

'Do not cast your eye in the darker corners, keep your glances ahead,' Naga said to them.

A warm wind blew grains into their faces. Sand devils danced around them, dispersing and reforming. Max was tracking, veering off, and circling in one spot beneath the steps.

'The bone finder speaks! We climb the steps to the Mustatil!'

Max dug, then moved on, then dug again.

'Opener of doors?' Naga called.

Samir appeared like a servant, 'yes, Naga.'

'I cannot climb in my modified state. You will go with the kalb.'

Samir considered the hike up the highly degraded steps leading to the symbolic structures and ticket home. 'SubhaanAllah. It is the same as the other side. I thought it would be intact,' he murmured.

'Have they not travelled through the lands and seen the end of those before them?' Naga quoted, 'the others will wait in shelter until our return.'

'What?! No! There must be another way!' Esme panicked.

'Does the she-human not know the great?'

Samir glanced at Esme, widening his eyes to silence her.

'The human does not need to see your greatness. I am sure she is already impressed.'

Esme folded her arms and pursed her lips, her intolerance for inflated egos increasing. 'We're all going, that's final!' Esme said, affirming her words with the stamp of her right foot.

The camel shook off the blankets and dust, letting out an almighty belch, forcing everyone back. Naga began to elongate and thicken, the legs folding under it, turning copper and black, growing in length, the ears disappearing and the leathery skin becoming scaly, reflective shields. Samir closed his eyes and prayed like he'd never prayed before, protecting himself over and over, repenting, begging and perspiring.

Naga whipped its head round at them, Esme slapping her hand over her mouth to stop her screams. Peter stood in front of her, guarding with both arms, his left palm burning.

'Do they not see how great I am?!' it bellowed. Samir terrified by the enormous Cobra, with his eyes squeezed shut. The pursuit of Solomon's skull eluded him, the stench of Naga affirming a greater power, the murder of one of the most powerful of Jinn would cost him an agonising sentence.

'I hate snakes.' Hassan mumbled, his heart large from the expanding aorta, knowing there was something not quite right about it all along.

'Come! Opener of doors. Bring your apprentice and strange species!'

Max waited for Hassan, they stood at the foot of the incline as Samir briefed him.

'We are looking for, uh, cattle bones or similar. My abilities are limited on this side. When Max finds the bones, show them to me first. Not all will be the right ones.' He pulled at his collar. Samir had changed, as if coming undone from a guilty conscience. 'Do not interact with anything other than myself. Understood?' Hassan let go of Max's collar, the dog running on ahead, slipping on the loose chippings. He had been living on milk and bread for longer than he cared to, getting to the bones was all he thought about.

They had to make the rest of the way using all their limbs to reach the highest point where the constructions were. Naga slithered up the steps with ease and Max ahead, Hassan having palpitations when he kept losing them. 'Why did it have to be a flippin snake?!'

Esme took the steps with her back to the rock, her head looking at Peter's back, the drop turning her stomach. Hassan praised his creator with each step; his father taught him that. Peter led them behind Samir, striding effortlessly ahead. Esme was trying so hard not to hyperventilate, but the further they climbed, the more the desert wind blew. The view over the rocks and tombs with strange happenings and species below them, would remain in her conscience. She was slowing, her eyes closed, praying through sporadic yelps. Her hands flat against the rock and her ears her guides.

'Mum, I'm here, just open your eyes.'

Esme shook her head vigorously, 'I can't, I can't!'

Peter stopped when he heard her distress.

'Open yer bleddy eyes, maid! Ere...' he took her hand, making her jump and scream. 'Now, one foot in front o' the other. Bit by bit. Ain't no rush. Ol' big head and Samir will have to wait. We's more important.'

'I can't do it, Peter! I can't!' Her stomach ceased when she blinked, catching a glimpse of how high they'd climbed. 'Oh my God.'

'Go up on her 'ands and knees and just look at the steps, not down there!'

She opened her eyes, her gaze fixed on Peter's face. The scorching wind moving his hair, tightening the burnt skin that made his green eyes look like jade stones. 'C'mon, m'love.' He uttered, 'if y'fall, I'll just fall with yas. Kay?' She took Peter's hand and concentrated on the steps and his sandaled feet. His large and rough grip was the grounding soothe she had been missing all her life.

'How abouts we sing a song? Ay? Take yer mind orf it.'

They moved forward, and she could only think of one song:

"*O'er the horizon...with, eyes for thee. Ere I'll be waitin. Remember me. Be treddin the path, laden with gorse, there, I'll be waitin. Remember meeee!*" she screamed as her foot slipped off the edge. Breaking loose a stone, grazing her leg as her foot travelled through mid air - pulling Peter with her. Esme was going over, not wanting to believe it, glancing at her son's terrified face. Her whole body jolted when Peter seized her forearm.

'I got yer! I got yer!' The sun shone behind him, silhouetting his physique - bringing stabbing flashbacks from crow street's Reiki session. Hassan grabbed her other arm, both trying to pull her up. Her feet scrabbling over the jagged ledges, trying to get a foot hold. Their voices muted and movement in slow motion, all she could hear was her own breathing. Regrets, unfulfilled wishes, flashed before her. She thought of who she was leaving behind, and the two people that would have to hear of the news before they ever got to see her again. Air was squeezed from her lungs when something constricted her waist, lifting her up; Naga's tail unfurling as it gently placed her back onto the steps.

'The disadvantage of legssss!' Naga mocked, and continued the lead.

Esme lay in a heap, breaking into hysterical whimpers. 'Thank you!' she called. Hassan's chest heaving as he rested against the sandstone mountain. Peter stood, a chortle breaking his face.

'What's so funny?!' Esme snapped.

'You don't do things by halves, do ye maid?' She gave him a harsh glance, holding out her arm. He took it and heaved her up.

'Ri. Take it bloody steady, now!'

'Mum...' Hassan panted, 'I think I hate you right now.' Leaning on his knees, dragging in hot air.

'Thanks for the love, Harv.' She jeered, her vision doubling.

Brushing himself off, his limbs shaking, he gave her a forgiving smile, and they moved on.

When they finally reached the flat, Max headed to the circular structures that housed sacrificial offerings, sniffing erratically around the sides of the slate pits.

'Oh my god. My mural!' Esme scrambled to Max, 'these are from the mural! You saw me paint them, Samir!' She touched the enigmatic structures in awe, strategically placed and in perfect symmetry. Circles in a straight line with a larger one at their end. Many others, only seen from above, a long triangle with the same circular ending; the one the mermaid was holding. 'What are they?!'

'The main ritual gateways, the anchors of the parallel. The deposits of favours, and re-entry into our side. Maps and codes to the skies. Only Allah really knows.'

'You expect me to believe that *you* don't really know, when these structures were practically carved in your face every day, Samir?' she clambered into the first circle, landing on ash, the haphazard slate reaching her middle. Crouching, she sifted through it, uncovering charcoaled bones.

'So, these are our ticket home?' she stood with a bone between her forefinger and thumb, studying it, dissipating into ash from the slightest touch.

'Sister, it's better if I look. This parallel is not safe...'

'Why are they burning the bones here?' She questioned, eyeing him.

Samir's gulp was audible.

'To stop them opening portals? Maybe?' Hassan answered.

They were distracted by Max's incessant barks. Naga was a Camel once more, stood chewing by the only large rock that offered some shade and a cavern.

'We cannot last without shelter, sister.' Esme missed her Dior's, the permanent squint was giving her a headache, and if she heard Hassan mention he was melting one more time...

'Fine. You dig, we'll rest.' Samir happy with her surrender.

Max relaxed with Esme, his panting erratic. Since reaching the Mustatil the ache of loss had faded as her eyes wandered the tones and textures of the landscape. The absence of greenery starving the soul. A merciless existence, yet the most resilient. The endurance of human tested, unfaltering. She surprised herself, not quite believing she had made it alive, her petty comforts having been passed through a Mangle. Over analysing her mother's letter, wondering when 'the dream' would be materialising.

'I hate this heat,' she said, the sweat making everything stick to her skin. So many regrets, but each one had led her here, alone with her dysfunctions and enrichments from the lessons. Every sense had been accentuated since she came through, the brain fog had lifted and she felt aware of movements and contrasts in the place she never quite fitted into.

A different scent suddenly invaded the ones that would be a trigger for the rest of her life: the sweet and heavy aroma of vanilla.

46

Redemption

After hearing voices, Ibrahim emerged from the sheltered dwelling a safe distance from the circles and Mustatil. He peaked his hand just in front of his eyes, the rising sun pressing the urgency. Layla watched him closely, perplexed when he suddenly ducked.

'What is it?'

'Are we to trust this, Shiqq?' Ibrahim looked either side of him for the creature.

'*Proceed. Be cautious of the Ungulate and what guards the bones. The zenith approaches.*'

'I shall remember you in my prayers.'

Layla strained to make out what was ahead, her swollen cerebrum throbbing.

'What the hell is that?' It looked like an animal with unusually long legs sniffing the ground. She straightened, the heat shimmer falling beneath her vision, she let go of the little girl's hand, hoisting the hem of her grubby dress and striding to Ibrahim. She shielded her eyes, involuntarily widening from realisation.

'It can't be. Oh my God! Oh my *God*!' she screamed, 'it is! It's Max! It's Max!' she ran, her feet pounding the terrain, sending shocks through her bones, feeling like she was running in a dream. 'Max! Max!' she yelled, breaking her voice. How, how did he get here? The question running over in her head.

Samir heard, and called to Esme. 'Wait sister. Don't cross yet! It is not safe! It may be a trick!'

Esme spotted her, blood draining into her core. Her nervous system released and adrenaline dilating her veins, she instinctively ran calling her daughter's name, running into a light as though running into heaven. It was just her, acutely aware of the ground squeezing her calves. Her skin sparkled, shedding an invisible carcass, present, alone, barely reaching what she would die for. The ache to return to unconditional love was too great to bear, the run seemed never ending, a green mile and rite of passage. Allah would probably take her now, right before she got to smell her daughter's hair again. She promised all there was to promise even ones she could not keep, offering her soul just to reach her, just to be forgiven and fill the vastness of maternal loss. Panic rose as she mistrusted the vision, calling her name repeatedly to be sure she wasn't delusional.

'Show me it's you!' Layla took the scarf from her head, holding it aloft. Reaching her first born in a co-dependent state, they fell onto each other in a heap of joyful sobbing, panting with dry mouths and fulfilled souls. Everyone reaching them with Hassan and Max joining the emotional reunion.

'I thought you'd never come. I thought you'd never *come!*' Layla bawled.

'Always, through hell if I must. We're here now, we're here. Sshhhh, it's okay now,' rocking her daughter in her arms, the world could fall around their ears. The expelling of her agonising wait shot through her mind. The drag through despair lifted. It was at the point before her knees hit the ground when mercy arrived.

'Alhamduillah!' Samir exclaimed with Ibrahim seconding the praise.

'Thanks to you, Ibrahim,' Esme's tears sitting in the corners of her smile to him.

'It was my given duty,' he bowed.

'The girls!' Layla jumped to her feet. Figures emerged on the brow of the Mustatil in a shimmering heat; Peter behind them, carrying the smallest. Unable to contain the relief that escaped their throats.

'Ello, little maid,' Peter said, kissing the top of Layla's head.

'Where's Kash?' Layla sniffed, looking up at him with eyes full of anticipation.

'Ain't you fed up wi'askin that? He's home, somewhere, we hope.'

'Brothers and sisters, we are in a vulnerable state,' Ibrahim looked behind and beyond, expectant. 'We must move to the shade, dear brother. I ask you in the name of the almighty that you lead this family and girls back to safety.'

Samir succumbed, 'yes, of course. Please, we rest in the shelter, hurry!'

Esme and Layla gazed at one another, neither of them believing it. Hassan pleased with himself, because he knew it, like he always knew it.

'Naga, with your mercy, the extra cargo needs water and fresh clothing.' Samir asked.

There was a sudden gush of water from the rock, everyone watching in awe as it miraculously poured and flowed. The girls squealed between ravenous bites of dates and gulps of milk from clay vessels that surrounded Naga.

'We are forever in your debt, Naga the great,' Samir bowed, maintaining the ass-kissing. The camel opened its eye, sending chills through him.

'My accolades were in need of replenishing. It is I honoured in your presence, opener of doors.'

Esme requested the men turn theirs backs as she helped the girls take off the grubby grey coverings, revealing scars on their wrists and hearts. The stench of stale urine from the little one was the worse, washing her first. Esme contained her pity behind a smile as the child convulsed, reaching out and crying for Samir. Max offering giggles as he licked dried tears from her face.

'She prefers male comfort?' Esme asked.

'I like him, he's kind.' the American girl answered; the spokesperson for the other two. Esme noticing an Australian lilt from one, but the other didn't speak much, a girl of dark skin and tied back hair.

'How long were you here for?'

'Days, maybe. I don't know.'

'Did they hurt you?'

The girl shook her head. 'No. Just pushed us around and yelled in our faces. Touching. Y'know?' She hugged herself, raising her shoulders.

'Where were they taking you?'

The girl shrugged, 'they just kept us until that, *woman*, came,' she wiped away a solitary tear, tucking her hand back in her armpit.

'Woman?'

The girl nodded erratically, 'like that thing,' glaring towards Naga, 'only she smelt better.'

'And then?'

'No one knew. More men would come at night with a different girl.'

'Do you know where they came from?'

'The tombs, there's hundreds. Then, wherever the camel-woman decided to sell us.'

The water kept coming, the little one quivering with fear as Esme respectfully cleansed. Her small hands with troubled finger movements.

'I won't hurt you, darling.' She soothed, sharp saliva gathered in her mouth as she envisaged the child's ordeal. Her little convulses and trembling limbs was all she could stand, empathy a great weight on dexterity. 'We're opening an orphanage when we get back. Not a damn school!'

'They used the smaller ones for their blood.' The American said, hiding her forearms as she washed, 'posting her on social media.'

'Her *blood*?!'

'Yeah. They think it makes them younger, ignites the third eye. They made her scared first, for the adrenochrome. Hollywood fulfilments. Because most of the surgeons are dead, y'know? There were others, doctors, lawyers. Taking the blood and selling it to elites that were losing their looks.'

'Andreno – what?'

'Adrenochrome. It's like, a compound from adrenaline. Like this, purplish liquid.' Her syllables with song and pitch.

Esme felt nauseous, tasting the horror on her tongue. 'Oh my God,' catching her breath and holding down her stomach. 'How old are you?'

'Sixteen.'

'Did they do the same to you?'

'No. I'm too old. I was an escort, sometimes they would sell me for the night to the rich. It gave me a clean bed, I guess. Their beds were disgusting.'

'How did you end up here?'

The American wiped the palm of her hands, studying the Hamsa there. It was like a ticket, a brand. An elite barcode, she liked it. 'There were, arguments? Like, shouting and the leader was stressed. It got heated, pistols in each others faces, y'know?'

Esme didn't know, and had difficulty in believing any child could survive such conditions with mind intact.

'So, one night, things had settled down, I guess. They were drinkin whiskey and grabbing the girls, makin fun. Then, outta nowhere, the men that brought us here? Came through the freakin walls!! Like, I swear miss. I was clean. Ambush was a mess. They all got shot in the head. I was kinda happy. Freakin pigs. Most girls got caught in the crossfire. I guess they were the lucky ones.'

Esme was paused in the ablutions. 'No! *You* are the lucky ones! They died without feeling freedom, or what real love was, or, or the warmth of a loving home or mother.'

The girl folded the old garments, 'are you my mother now?'

Esme offered and empathetic smile, gently cupping her face, 'I'll be whatever you need me to be.'

The girl continued folding the soiled material, 'and that guy. Is he head of the operation?' jerking her chin toward Samir.

'Samir? Good heavens, no. He helped us.' Esme laughed nervously.

'But he was the first one through the walls. He seemed to be the one controlling the shining door.'

Esme's blood left her limbs, acidic vomit reaching her mouth. 'No, you must be mistaken. I mean, are you sure?'

The girl jiggled her head, 'uh, huh. Real sure. He didn't do the assassination. He just kinda got us away from the bullets. I thought I wuz trippin, it was the prettiest thing I ever saw. He's wunna the good guys. Told us things would be better and we were going on to serve Kings and Princes. Sounded like the best news to me. I like fruit and nice food, clean sheets.'

Esme's bottom lip trembled, a grey mass of doom expanded in her ribcage. The scenario of never finding Layla almost stopping her heart, her brow deeply creased from the thought of it and the cuts on the little one's wrists and syringe points in other places. 'We all have the ability to change if we listen to our conscience.' Esme said.

The girl huffed a laugh, 'like Pinocchio, huh?'

Sitting back-to-back with Layla, Hassan shook his head at the incredulous moment, sipping strawberry smoothies from golden goblets; courtesy of Ibrahim. 'Steve says hi. I wonder how he's doing?'

Layla snorted, 'shitting on baba's poncey car with a bit of luck!' they both laughed hysterically, startling the adults.

Tears appeared when they thought of home and the chance of getting back moving further away.

'I still hate you though,' they linked pinkies.

'Me too,' Hassan said.

Layla craned her neck to get a better look at her brother, 'you've changed.'

'Have I?'

'Yeah, and your voice has gone deeper. Ma bro, turning into a dude,' she held out her fist to be bumped. 'I'm sorry, Harv.'

'For what?'

'Being an ass. I was just...' she turned her attention to her mother, tending to the others, '...jealous of you. Baba poured all he had into you and made me feel like a disappointment. I didn't matter to him, because I wasn't meeting his expectations of a little missy dressed in a hijab,' she wobbled her head, tucking her hands under her chin, 'he cut me off and made me feel inadequate. I know he had something to do with this. If *he* doesn't rot in hell, I want my money back.'

'It wasn't because of that,' Hassan murmured into the smoothie. 'Don't you see it now?'

'See what?'

'He was trying to protect you.'

Layla swivelled round to face him, 'he sold me! And practically married me off!'

'He had no choice!'

Ibrahim shifted, disturbing Khadija who was sleeping at his side, 'it was not your father, sister. It was I who turned against your family.'

'I hardly recognised you, Ibrahim. What made you come here?' Esme asked, wrapping the little one in light garments.

'I followed my instinct and I wanted to redeem this tragedy and get her back to you.' A silence fell among them, alive in their guts, eating bowls of food that were of unusual taste and texture, supping their favourite beverage. Khadija leaned against Ibrahim as he told them everything, blaming himself but Musa.

'He trusted you'd do the right thing. He knew your 'art would make the ri' decision.' Peter said, tearing away strange flesh from sharp bones. Ibrahim placed is right hand over his heart and dipped his head, full, forgiven and in turmoil.

'Well,' Esme spoke through tears, 'don't blame yourself, we've all had to part to play in it, one way or another. What about you, Samir?' she asked, a sharpness within his name, all eyes turning to him.

'I am the opener of doors until my last breath, server of the symbol. I was waiting for you,' he gave a forced smile her way. 'Janan runs through us all.'

'Why were you waiting for us?' Hassan asked.

'You're my saviours. My, avengers,' he smirked. Peter looked between them, releasing a contented laugh.

'We don't have much time. Please hurry, Esme.' Samir pressed and stood, beckoning Max.

'Uh, a little help perhaps then? Layla? Khadija? Get off your butts, wallowing is not helping me!'

Max dug each circle he was inertly placed in by Samir, sniffing up the ash and sneezing it back out. Charcoaled bones disintegrated between his paws and dusted the little bits of fur in between. Samir check over his shoulder and the landscape ahead, the beads of sweat falling from his face and dripping on his garments. The openers of doors were forbidden to procreate, the gift dying with them. He thanked his father daily and prayed for his mercy, holding on tight to the reassurance that it was his ticket to eternal bliss. Yet the fear of death gripped him, meeting his creator in the current state would not turn out too well. He closed his eyes as he faced the sun, begging for its intensity to turn *him* to ash. Asking for forgiveness and guidance on the less of two evils, and battle with the love he harboured for Peter.

'Why aren't we digging for the bones? I feel useless sat here,' Hassan said and yawned as they all watched from the shade of the sandstone, the girls curled up amongst them making up for their sleep deprivation. 'Thought he said we had to hurry, had to get here on first light, or something.'

'The kalb has lighter and even weight. And you have time when you are with the Great,' Naga responded, Peter resting against its belly and blanket with his arms folded.

'Yeah, why did we have to get here for first light, Uncle?' Layla asked.

'He procrastinates,' the Shiqq spoke in Ibrahim's mind, appearing behind them. Ibrahim remained silent as he watched the creature move without anyone noticing. His heart constricted as he set eyes on it, though used to its presence. He froze, his gut squirming with doubt as he watched the Shiqq creep to a particular spot. Esme noticed Ibrahim's eyes look beyond her, turning around to check.

'What are you looking at?'

Ibrahim gave her a vacant glare, dismissing her question. 'I think you are sitting on something,' he replied, giving her a shiver.

Esme lifted her buttock and looked. 'What do you mean?' she regarded him, moving onto her knees making the others shift. She brushed the surface, shrieking as the loosened sand uncovered an angle of bone. She pulled at it, only it wasn't a T-bone, but a femur.

'Everyone, up!' They followed her instruction, Ibrahim catching the Shiqq disappearing into the rock formation. Esme's eyes scanned the area where they were sat, a pressure in her stomach confirming the worse. 'Layla, take the girls away from here. Quickly!'

A sudden wind blew over the surface, the grains rattling over more bones. Protruding rib cages, skulls and perfectly placed limbs in the direction of the circles. Esme hopped over the small skeletons, her steps as if on hot coals. Moving into the sun, they searched the ground frantically, Hassan fixated on a steady movement breaking the compacted surface.

'Something's beneath us!' The ground rumbled, erupting mounds appearing everywhere.

'Naga the great! You came to aide us with your greatness!' Esme yelled. The camel got to its feet and shook itself, hissing back at her and immediately changing into the Cobra, smashing the rock formation with its snout.

'Ya Allah!' Ibrahim cried. Peter stood back and watched Naga effortlessly punch holes in the sandstone. Flipping its head round with the Shiqq in its mouth, and throwing it to the ground. Ibrahim squeezed his head as the screams from the creature near split his skull.

'Slay your spy!' Naga spat.

Ibrahim looked down on the pitiful thing, a faint plea crossing its soulless eyes.

'Stop! Stop!' Samir intervened out of breath, returning with Max. 'I have what we need,' looking away from Esme's glare. 'For one last time, please, I request the protection of the Great,' bowing his head.

'And what will the Great, receeeeive?'

Samir took a breath, 'the finest accolade you will own.'

The cobra drew close, Samir turning his head with eyes shut. The Cobra's tongue brushed his cheek. 'How sssso?' a rumble brewing in its throat. There were gasps when Samir held up a human skull with gold caps on its molars, the precious metal also filling the gaps of cranial sutures.

Naga drew back with an aggressive hiss, 'this is not possible!' Circling him, eyeing up the skull as Samir's heart almost stopped. Ibrahim was drawn in by its lure, Layla too. The sun glinting the gold, the skull taking on a godly presence.

The Cobra snatched it, throwing it up high and receiving it with a hungry mouth, grinning as it swallowed. Ibrahim and Layla rushed forward, their hands grabbing.

'No! Forget it!' Samir scolded.

'But that was our way back home!' Layla screamed back.

Movement began to increase beneath them, mounds formed before their eyes, slow and steady like something was being awakened.

'Fool! You have brought the cargo to their demise!'

They all looked to their feet; noses with little horns were just breaking through the mounds.

'Mustatil Vipers!' Ibrahim yelled, 'back to the shade!'

Max barked at the emerging threat, digging into them to pull out whatever was in there.

Naga sneered, stretching its constricted skin, 'did you belieeeve that the bones of cattle would save your soul? There are a million beneath your feet!' Peter looked over to the girls, then to an outcrop about fifty yards ahead. 'Are you dying yet, Marid?' Naga hissed at Peter.

'Marid?! Ya Allah! A miracle!' Ibrahim cried.

'He dunno what he's sayin,' Peter responded curtly.

'Please. Marid, touch my arm! Take me out of this misery!' Ibrahim took Peter's large hand and fought to place it on his forearm, Peter resisting but Ibrahim held firm. The burn of his touch made Ibrahim cry out as his molecular structures altered and near crystalised. Peter searched Ibrahim's conscience for his worse memories, both reliving them through his eyes. He found the one he was looking for, bringing on a flood of tears, Ibrahim's heart skipping a beat when he saw his wife and daughter, love visiting then swiftly leaving.

'Gimme the spell!' Peter demanded.

Ibrahim let go of the hypothetical opaque ball that had been sitting in his chest, watching it leave him like a droplet of water. He felt his flesh shrink around his bones and the drawing down of his facial muscles. 'SubhaanAllah! I was heard! I am forgiven! You are not the Great, oh Jinn of serpents!' Ibrahim exclaimed to Naga, watching the transformation of himself take place.

Samir pressed everyone to run back to the outcrop with chaos ensuing, but there were two missing: Where were Esme and Hassan?

47

Messiah

Akash covered their mouths as he watched from a distance.

'No screamin' or yellin.' Kay?' they both gave restrained nods. Akash removed his hands, finger by finger. They had missed that face and smell, if a little tainted; he was home wrapped in skin.

'What now? Going to kill us?' Esme asked, her torso shaking.

Akash sniggered, 'Why would I do that? I came here t'save ya!'

'That's not what we heard,' Hassan said, amazed he could almost see through Akash's skin. It wasn't him, that he was certain.

'Aww, that aint nice. I miss Saint Ives and, you need me when we get back.'

'In what sense?' Esme said, her rage rising, fingers twitching ready to claw at his face. But the heat weakened her, she just wanted to lie down and sleep for a decade.

'Getting back is a piece of cake. But I don't think youm prepared for what's on the other side.'

They both watched Akash 'glitch' before their eyes, standing back, unsure what he was.

'We needs that skull, t'get back!' he strained, doubled over and on his knees.

'The one Naga just swallowed?'

He laughed, continuing with a whisper, 'bones are currency 'ere, but yer don't need em to open doors, unless...'

'Unless what?'

'Unless it's sacrificial bones.'

'But I saw Samir open them with steak bones!'

Akash smirked then hung his head. 'He wuz bluffin. You need kids to get back through.'

'Alive, right? You mean, alive kids?' Esme pressed.

'Y'need to listen. We 'ave t'be quick and get fru them doors, cos I'm running out o'time and so is Pete. Hassan don't need no bones, thas why he's 'ere.'

'We're not leaving without the girls! I am not going through that again, because I'm sorry to say, I've lost all trust in you! You let me down, Kash.'

His bottom lip rippled, and eyes morphed through their disguises. Hassan wanted to help but Esme stopped him. 'What's wrong? Are you dying?'

'No!' he strained, heaving his tight chest, 'I have t'get back t'the sea!' fighting to keep form.

'Ah, so it's for your benefit?' she leaned into him, 'I should leave you here to dry up and rot! You deserve it! Traitor! Killing for that, that *woman* for your own gains!'

'I ain't killed no one!'

'I don't believe you! You look different.'

'I'll proof it t'ya!' he spluttered.

'We're not leaving without the girls! Understand?!'

'Okay!' he coughed and retched 'Okay! Please, I need water, *please*!' Akash cradled his stomach and looked up at Hassan. 'And what you waitin' for? Ay? You haven't done anything, and youm the one they need!'

Esme let out a yelp when Hassan's eyes changed to a deep amber, the pupil dense and endless. 'There he is,' Akash laughed through his cough, hunched over in agony.

She didn't know her son in that moment when their life ran through her mind. A messiah stood before her, one she feared.

'Don't be scared, mum.'

'Are you like your father, Harvey?' Esme was in awe of the eyes that set off his skin and dark hair. Unsure was he was about to do with his hands,

'I will never be him.' The floor beneath them shook, more vipers pushed their devilled noses through the coarse sand. Esme screamed, suddenly feeling cool air behind her. A bright doorway shimmered, whispering.

'Go get help, mum. Meet us at the Mount.' She looked between them and before she could speak, Hassan pushed her through it.

48

The Mount

Esme landed in the basement at Draycott.

'No! Harvey! No!' she snivelled and sobbed in confused panic. Tapping her collar bone until she almost snapped it. Wheezing from hyperventilation, trying to focus and quit surmising.

'Why did he do it, why did he do it?' Sifting haphazardly through the tipped altar, rifling through the amulets and Taweez. The rucksacks, grabbing them and hefting them up the stairs. Her stomach burning when she remembered Musa.

'Moose?' her voice dry and trembling. Poking her head around the doorframe of the lounge, just a strange smell greeted her and a dying fire. She dumped the bags on the kitchen table, feeling for her phone in the sand-filled pockets. She never took it.

'Alexa! Call Musa!'

Alexa buzzed a malfunction. *'Sorry. I don't know that one.'*

Esme eyes searched the floor, 'the café!'

Saint Ives bit her as she left the house, stopping outside Raffia's and knocking the door, stepping back checking upper windows.

'Raffia! Raffia! Hello?' it seemed lifeless. She hurried down the steps, running into town, the tears blurring and drowning. Alone was a desire once upon a time, now it pushed her to the precipice. It was evident she couldn't function without her kids, her heart didn't quite beat fully without them, plunged into vulnerability to realise. There were still people, albeit flimsy and insubstantial, repeating it to herself as she burst through Margaret and Bill's gift shop.

'Ello Esme. Have you got any news?'

'Please…' dishevelled and out of breath, 'have you seen, Musa?' Esme's clothes creased and dirty.

'Wass appened my lovely?' puzzled at Esme's change of eye colour and complexion that was like porcelain.

'Margaret, have you seen Musa?! I need to get back, I need…' she collapsed, Margaret catching her.

'Bill! Bill! Get me a cuppa tea! Pronto!' the cosy shop with lit conch lamps, and the smell of sandalwood prompted an eruption of emotion from Esme. 'Look at the state of you m'luv. What's appened?' handing Esme a whimsical mug of sweet tea. She cradled it, controlling the tremors.

'Margaret, you wouldn't believe me if I told you. We found Layla but…'

'Oh! That's wonderful news! Bill! You hear that? They found our Layla!' Bill emerged making noises of approval. 'So, what's all the upset for then, ay? Overwhelming, I bet. Good cuppa will sort that out.'

'No! I mean, sorry,' she huffed, 'she's not here exactly and, everyone else is with her. I just need Musa. Have you seen him at all?' Margaret put it down to hysteria and her tea always put things right.

'Youm not making much sense darlin. Drink up and we'll call the constable, hmmm?' Esme gave the empty mug back, high on refined sugar and caffeine. It was sorely missed.

'I appreciate this wonderful tea, Margaret. I feel much better. I'm sorry for bursting in like that. We just have another urgency, and I must find my huz, uh, Musa.'

'Don't be daft. Thas what we're 'ere for, innit Bill? Look, if yer can't find him, just come back and we'll get some help t'gether. Alright?' Esme didn't know what it was, but Margaret sparked fight or flight.

'I certainly will, I promise. Excuse my bad manners and thank you for that tea.' She fled with paranoia. People stared as she speed walked through the town, with head down. The kebab shop dark and hollow, most of the galleries were closed, and it was eerily empty and grey.

Reaching the harbour, the wind blew the sand dust from her clothes and dilated her parched veins. Holding onto her scarf trying hard to keep it together, no one was sat outside the Abadis, the chairs and tables in place. Esme anxious as she approached the door, pushing it and slapping it when it didn't open. Peering through the pane of glass. 'Shit, my phone is in there!'

'Hello, Esme,' the kind voice of the Lifeboat attendant startling her.

'Oh! Thank God! You haven't seen Musa, have you? Please, I need help!'

They shook their head, 'sorry, no. Does that mean you've got some news?'

'Not exactly. How about Suzie?'

'Haven't you heard?'

'N, no? Heard what?'

'She got fed up wi'waiting f'you. And where's everybody else?'

'Um, at the uh, place. With Layla. Look, I need your help, I'm desperate. I need to get to the Mount!'

'Aye, I guessed that when Peter didn't show. Yous best come wi'me.'

He led her to the chapel, the walk a pleasure in the cool breeze, taking in home as her head span. All she thought about was Layla and the girls, the transition too surreal to accept as she convinced herself she was dreaming from a blackout. Passing the lookout, the volunteer gave a convert nod to the occupants, giving her a smile with light amber eyes. She gasped, trotting after him as his stride widened. Suzie was with the cyclist, leaning on the wall looking out to the same place Peter got agitated.

'Blimey! We thought you were never coming back.' Suzie said.

'So did I! We just, hit a problem, with, uh,' she looked between them.

'Who got you back through?' the cyclist asked.

'Harvey.' The three of them exchanged mutual glances, 'wh, what is it?'

'Time to get to Marazion,' he said.

'Listen, you needn't keep anything from me. I won't be surprised, especially where I've just come from. You know where they are, don't you? And what I saw. What are you?' she asked the volunteer, 'Marid?'

'I'm assuming that's the Arabic translation. Then, yes.'

'You?' she asked the cyclist, who blurted at the accusation. 'So, what are we doing here?' the cyclist jerked his chin out to sea. Esme's mind acutely open than the last time. She could see them, their heads just above water as if waiting for an intrusion or instruction. Heads that morphed, making you strain your eyes to make them out.

'I see them,' she whispered. 'Are they foe?'

'They are.' Suzie commented.

'Listen, I didn't know you were, y'know. I would've given you more help. I'm so sorry, I feel awful.'

Suzie faced her, caressing her bump. 'I'm scared what it'll turn out t'be,' her eyes searching Esme's for answers.

'Oh, as long as it's a healthy one, that's all that matters,' feeling she had missed the point.

Suzie turned away and looked out with the men.

'No need t'be scared Suze, we all turned out alri. As long as we've got Pete,' the volunteer reassured, his hand placed on her shoulder.

'What's the plan?' Esme asked with urgency.

'Have you got a strong grip?' There were sniggers through noses.

'I've been hanging on by my fingernails recently, so we're good to go.'

Volunteers kitted up, the large orange rib gracefully left Saint Ives harbour with Suzie waving them off, staying behind to watch the café. Esme quickly checked her phone, a flurry of supportive messages from friends brought on tears, with the absence of anything from Musa.

Into full throttle as they left the harbour, the nose bounced on the waves with faces screwed up from the icy spray. Esme hugged her legs filling her pining heart with prayer, surrounded by two formidable species, and one divine intervention. She could see the landscape pass through the gaps between them, staring a little longer at one of the volunteers. You really couldn't tell the difference, there were no obvious signs except for the eyes with a pupil that bled into the iris, triggered by high emotion. A thousand questions crossed her mind, her son one of them, changing their relationship from the lifted veil.

Reaching Marazion chilled and bewildered, Saint Michael's mount loomed out of the grey. Turning into the bay, a humbling vision greeted them: Pilot Gigs with oars held vertical, at least twenty of them. Sailing boats prepped and pushed offshore. There were battle cries and chants as they surrounded three white luxury yachts with blacked-out windows and empty decks, weaving through the perimeter of the flotilla. Esme could just make out '*not our land! Not our children!*' from most, goose bumping her skin. Yellow smoke bombs billowed their defiance from the gigs supported by Seagulls and Terns circling above the immanent battle. The cyclist gave Esme a side glance with a huge grin as her face beamed with pride and humility. They weaved in and out of them, the six plus crew and coxswains dipping their heads in acknowledgement. She recognised some from the town and sure a few had visited the café.

Reaching the slope of the mount's harbour, one of the volunteers signalled with two closed fingers for Esme to get out, the cyclist helping her, having to shout over the din. 'We wait!' he yelled in her ear, 'I'll stay with you!' She was pleased, her stomach buzzing and hair completely on end at the solidarity of a community suppressed by fear and political injustice.

'Who's in the yachts?!' she asked.

'Elites!' The cyclist replied, 'ere for the summit, and our kids!'

In the turret, the hooded followers were lined up with babies cradled in purple swaddling. The leader duly dressed in red, and one from the parents' meeting. He dipped his thumb in a golden bowl, anointing the infants' foreheads with blood. The door burst open, dousing the candles and interrupting the ritual, causing the babies to gasp and flinch. Janan hovered in the doorway, adorned in green brocade, her eyes alight.

'Toulah will be entering with the cargo. Kill them. We have a resistance to face. Is the half Siren and Musa contained?'

'Yes, your highness.'

'Good. Naga has the skull. We are close to claiming back the silk road.' Eurasian routes spanning over six thousand kilometres, playing a central role in facilitating the East and West, Janan would reopen it as a parallel and transportation of children and adrenochrome, invisible to the human eye.

She glided in, swooning over the bare, wriggling babies, becoming agitated from her presence. The red light made it easier for them to see her, causing their plump limbs to tense, crying when she removed her face covering.

'Yes, be afraid, you will be worth more. I may just have one of you for myself.' She cooed, making her way around to terrify and choose the fairest.

49

Taweez

Space was running out between their feet as the giant vipers emerged from their slumber.

'Retreat to the shade!' Samir called out. The girls screaming as they hopped over the attack. The line of shade shrunk beneath the outcrop as the sun rose, all of them inching further against the rock, the depth of the shadows decreasing to the size of the largest foot. They all watched in horror, near to standing on tip toes. The Mustatil serpents were almost out of their burrows, Max barking and snapping his jaws. The little one screamed as one rose in front of her, as tall as she. The child would be easy to swallow, and the precious bones would lay dormant in its belly until the call of the Nagini. Samir moved in increments to his breast pocket, pulling out a pocketknife. Peter gathered the girls behind him protecting them with the span of his arms, glancing at Samir with deep green eyes, the heat weakening him and tearing down his walls.

'Don't forget your Taweez, brother,' Samir whispered to him.

The snap of the blade distracted the viper away form the little one. It drew back, ready to strike Samir, releasing a guttural hiss as it lunged forward, setting off more screams. Samir thrust the knife up into its lower jaw, the girls squirming and covering their eyes. Withdrawing it, his hands covered in black blood, impaling the serpent's torso, pulling the blade and splitting it open. There was retching and voiced disgust as white, gelatinous infant bones spilled out of it. The viper slumped and twitched through its end as it fell onto them. Slipping the knife back in his breast pocket, one killing wasn't enough as more emerged with increased determination to destroy. Peter touched the Taweez, Musa's words echoing in his mind, *'your very own Jinn, wrapped in the script...'* he clutched the pouch and snapped the leather string, wasting no time in picking at the bound package attached to it. Samir watched in anticipation, mistrusting what would manifest. A strip of leather was freed, the rest unravelling in momentum, leaving Peter's hands. A swirling wind, increasing in size, formed before them.

'SubhaanAllah! Jinn of air!' Samir cried. Everyone shielded their eyes as the wind expanded into a protective wall, pushing the vipers back into their burrows.

Peter kicked away the dead viper and watched the ground consume it. 'I bleddy 'ates this place. I needs me sea!'

'I'm right with you, brother.'

The wind stayed over the burrows, a flash of tormented faces appearing within the wall of sand with melancholic wails coming from stretched mouths.

Naga slithered through it with a wild grimace, moving closer to pin them in place.

'I have an offer if you let us go!' Samir pleaded, not sure where to set his eyes on the cobra.

'Offer?' Naga hissed.

'The boy!'

Peter protested, giving Samir a hard stare.

'Ah, the apprentice,' Naga sneered, looking at Layla. 'We have waited a century for Solomon's skull, I am not about to give it up for an apprenntiissss.'

'Then take me! Let them go!'

Naga eyed Samir, mulling over the decision. 'I have all I want, I no longer need your accolade.'

Peter hollered over the wind, 'I wanna go 'ome. Now!' holding tight to Max's collar.

Samir looked beyond Naga, his mind sharpened by adrenaline,

'You are free! Jinn of Air! We no longer require your enslavement!' There were instant cries of relief from the wind, forming into recognisable limbs. 'Go! In the name of the Almighty, go! We are in deepest gratitude for your sacrifice.'

The sculptured sand left in an upward motion, bending and swirling, dispersing. The impression of a woman's face etched in the particles, euphoric in her release, prompting tears from the older girls. Layla wishing her mother had seen it.

The ground became active from the silence, two vipers emerged either side of Naga's belly and buried their fangs into its armour. The cobra let out deafening screeches, the fire in its veins shrinking it back into a camel.

'Now, Shiqq!' Ibrahim called. The creature appearing with its organic shield, casting it over the camel like a leathery tarp, hardening to that of stone and trapping Naga beneath it.

'Good! You are the great Shiqq, I shall remember you as my greatest revenge!' Ibrahim danced.

'I cannot hold the Cobra for long.'

They all heard running towards them with intention, raising a smile when they saw Hassan, with Akash behind him, churning up dust as they pounded. Layla choked on her delight when he glanced her way, raising her hand to him. Her stomach dropping when he hardly acknowledged she was there.

'Wakanda forever!' Hassan opened a shimmering door that split the mounds. Then another opposite it, creating a howling wind casting sand into their eyes, the vipers retreating.

'Where's mum?' Layla called over the howl.

'Safe! Go! Uncle! Go home!' Hassan yelled to Ibrahim, but Khadija pulled him back.

'I want to stay with you!'

Ibrahim stroked the grains of sand from her face, 'I do not know how long I will stay young! I will be an old man again and you will grow to repulse me!'

She shook her head with tear-filled eyes, 'I can't go back, I don't want to. *Please*?! Come with me!' She knelt, clutching his white thobe.

'Do not beg me, sister. This is not the right place to stay. Your parents will have died a little from your absence, and I do not want to be responsible for their grief. I have caused enough.'

She sobbed into the cloth, the scent of Oud and fires the essence of him.

'You have fallen in love with acceptance, not me. Please, up, get up.'

Khadija pulled herself up by the material, he caressed her face with an all too familiar ache in his heart. 'I will die a happy man, habibi. You have showed me the love I was searching for, if only fleeting. Go, live your life how you wanted. Things have changed now; your father has mended his ways. Trust me. Run, run for your life. Show the world how free you really are, they are waiting for you,' he kissed her forehead, and pushed her through the opposite doorway.

'Go! *Go!*' Hassan yelled at Layla. Her face shone with pride at her brother, and deep embarrassment from Akash. She held her breath and entered with the girls. The faint cries for Ibrahim from Khadija twisting his heart.

Toulah was pressed Layla had gone through, envisaging the wrath from Janan. But Naga had the skull, and she wanted it. Peter's was squint was studying her. 'Alri, old man?'

'I think we should leave you ere to rot, Toulah!'

'Aww, that ain't no way t'speak t'your son.' Peter held his stare with intentions of snapping the shapeshifter in half. He circled her, eyeing her up and down, in awe of the perfected imitation. 'And don't even think about it.' She said to him, exposing a row of gruesome teeth his way.

They were all relieved to enter the warmth of the sun, fear had chilled their bones. The remaining door was a mirage that shimmered and fizzed. The voices beyond it louder and light brighter.

'I can't hold this door open for much longer, uncle!' Hassan struggled, his hands outstretched.

'MashAllah. Look at you. If only we knew, all those years ago. I have seen all there is to see. My bed is calling me. My grave. I forgot how stressful it was to be young.'

'I am returning you to Yemen, uncle.'

All Ibrahim could do was smile through tears that fell into it. He showed them the shard of Kenan from his top pocket. 'I have all I need. Shiqq? Will you accompany me to my resting place?' The creature released Naga from the trap, wrapping its shield around Ibrahim, 'farewell. I am forever in your debt, dearest Hassan. Do wonderful things. Tell your father, I am sorry, but exposure is immanent. Inshallah the world will take notice.'

The Shiqq's shield increased in size, flapping from the door's draft, and gradually engulfing him. Ibrahim began to age before their eyes, 'Thank you, Peter the Marid! Allah be with you! Thank you! Shiqq? Take me to rest beneath the Dragon trees!' and then, they were gone. The Hamsa disappearing from his left palm.

There was no time to reflect or grieve, 'Ustaz! We need to go, and we need you!' Samir checked behind him. Naga coming round, rolling its eyes.

'This ain't Akash!' Peter said, pointing in Toulah's direction.

'There is no time! We'll go on three!' Hassan held onto Peter's arm as they posed in the starting position.

'One…two…three!!' Hassan, Akash then Samir, Peter last with Max.

Naga a cobra once more, awake, nose-diving after them.

50

AVENGERS

They entered through the doorway of the school, Naga smashing the doorframe behind them and continuing out the front door. Their bodies were strewn over the cobbles with granite and mortar exploding onto them. Max scrabbled to retaliate, barking ferociously at the Cobra. Naga snatched Max and tossed him aside, then Samir, hurtling him into the garden wall, expelling a scream from his cracking bones on impact.

The commotion alerted the Coxswains, instructing the crews through megaphones who lowered the oars into frenzied and hostile waters. The rebellious Marid and Siren gripped the sides of the Pilot Gigs trying to tip them over, getting bludgeoned by the 32-foot-long Cornish Elm oars.

Hassan ran to Max. Blood pooling from the dog's ribs, his mouth frothing and eyes distant.

'No, Max! I'm sorry! I'm sorry!' Hassan sobbed, trying to stop the bleeding with his trembling hands. Max looked at him, his duty done, it was okay to leave now. He didn't know the fear of death, just an acceptance when it arrived. No emotions of last, of never, of eternity. It was their retirement of devotion and time to live beyond with a memory and serving of a different kind. 'No. No. Max, no! I can't, just, stay, a little longer, please! We didn't finish our game…'

'Oh my God! Harvey? *Harvey*?!' Esme screamed, running and throwing herself on them squeezing and kissing Hassan all over his wet face. The horror increasing as her third baby didn't respond in the usual way, not even a wag of his tail. 'Come on, let's get him in the water, help me!' They dragged Max to the edge of the slope, the gentle waves lapping over his legs. Max was running in his head, running with purpose as his eyes drooped and drifted.

'Such a good, brave boy. Try and hang on. It'll be all right babee, okay?' Esme sniffed, the sea salt adding a glimmer of hope as the dog winced from the sting.

'He needs more than sea,' the cyclist said, 'any takers?' he said to them; their faces perplexed. Wrapping his jacket around Max's middle, he lifted him, 'I'll take him to the parish. He's pretty messed up.' Esme trusted him, stroking his wet and bloodied fur, kissing his muzzle.

'Don't you leave me, Maxey. You hear?' her voice broke, convulsing at loss that surrounded them, waiting for God to take his pick. 'Thank you, for everything.'

'No, thank *you*,' the cyclist acknowledged, while fate danced above their heads. He carried Max across the causeway, ignoring the hissing and gurgling from the rebellious occupants of the sea.

Hassan composed himself, with a positive worm in his belly as he watched the cyclist struggle with his best friend. 'I have to save Peter and Samir.'

'Where are the girls?'

'Safe. Which is gonna piss some people off.'

'Go, and be careful!' Hassan gave her a condescending smirk, his eyes a waning amber and an unusual, thicker frame, hardly recognising her son.

Hassan strode back to the house, faced with Peter confronting Naga.

'You're on my turf now and you ain't welcome!'

Hassan held his breath when Akash appeared behind Peter restraining his arms in place, sending shocks through him as Naga took its first strike at Peter's chest, buckling his knees.

'*NO!*' Another, fangs piercing and tearing. Akash throwing him aside and grinning when Peter squirmed in his own blood.

Hassan thrust his hands forward, they must do something. Another door appeared from his spiralling emotion. He charged towards Akash, 'arrgghh!' pushing him back through to Al Ula, nearly breaking his forearms. The door closed in on itself and it was just Hassan and Naga. But he knew he wasn't anything from a Marvel movie, in fact, he wasn't sure what else he was capable of, other than knowing stuff before anyone else and opening portals.

'Why did you turn against us?!'

There was a grunt from Samir. 'In the name...of the...Fattah,' he strained, clutching his broken ribs. Naga flipped its head toward him and hissed, bearing translucent fangs and flaring its neck 'I condemn thee...' Samir continued.

A thundering roar shook the ground, loosening guttering from the cottages. Naga morphed back into a Camel, bowing its head with nose to the ground, the skull emerging from its mouth coated in saliva. Hassan gagged and thought they had won, until another tremor unbalanced him. The trees shook around the castle, swaying from the unstable foundations. Windows cracked, some shattered. The frenzy in the water had ceased as the rebellious retreated to the causeway's edge, clinging to the rocks to prevent anyone crossing. The hooded figures emerged from the garden gates carrying the crying babies. Hassan choked, looking at Samir who averted his eyes in shame, crying out as his left hand burned. Peter also gurgling from his torture.

'Remember...' Samir choked, 'David and Goliath...' What was he supposed to do? He just opened doors and got angry. 'Take the skull. Close the Mustatil gates! Go back! Only you...can, do iiittt!'

'Go back? No!'

Esme watched the hooded figures walk the causeway in a ritualistic manner, her heart wrenching from the desperate cries of infants. Infants from dishonour, addiction and coerce. Something big had entered the bay, moving the flotilla aside like leaves and away from the yachts. The frenzy had erupted again. Gun fire and elevated emotion over low a murmur that penetrated the ground, causing waves that crashed the shore and capsized the lighter sail boats. Esme turned her attention to Peter; his light a little faded. Blood drenched the white tunic, his wounds visible through the frayed tears. His left hand contorted from the burning Hamsa, certain his skin was sizzling. She caressed his face, wiping away debris from his beard, noticing Crows gathering in the trees around the castle, cawing a warning, increasing in numbers and fighting for branch space.

'Don't you die on me, Peter whatsit.' His eyes flickered open, they felt awkward in the moment. Esme breaking it when she squeezed his hand, bringing it to her lips with a grounding love, less forbidden.

'Harvey...has t'go back through!' Peter coughed.

'No way! No one's going back there!'

'He must...break the gates, maid. Take the...skull...back. Please. Get me to the water...' his head hit the slope, a breath leaving his lungs like it was his last.

Fishing in the pocket of his dirtied thobe, Samir pulled out a bone, holding it out for Hassan to take. No words were spoken as they kept their eyes on Naga.

'Pray, before you open it...break the Mustatil circles. Break the gate, and get the skull back to Al Ula!'

'But, how? You can't even move the stones! And the snakes! How many do I break?!' Hassan's breathing became erratic, looking at the odd bone between his fingers.

'Go to the old town, the way we went in. Get to the first circle and remember your amulet.' Hassan touched the chain; he'd forgotten it all this time, now it had become a conscious thing.

'Now, throw it!' Samir whispered, 'throw it at Naga!' the camel opened one eye, 'now!' Hassan did it, the bone landing on the knee of the animal.

'In the name of the almighty!...' Naga quickly morphed back into the Cobra, ready to take a final, fatal strike, '...we shall re-enter in your name! Return us, so we may continue to worship you in this life!' a door opened behind the cobra. Hassan took a run for it, grabbing the skull and diving into the blinding shimmer, with Naga following.

51

DAVID

Back in the Qasr, he had no time to think, scrabbling from his all fours and heading for the opening. Scarpering out not knowing which parallel he had entered. Naga wasn't far behind, smashing through the ancient structure and nearly collapsing it. Hassan fell from the cobra's force, grazing his hand, the heat as though plunged into an oven. Naga close behind, running, falling he panted in panic, tears filled his amber eyes. He didn't want to be back here with no idea what he was supposed to do. Remembering their steps, sweat stinging his eyes, the cobra on his tail hissing and voicing its greatness and threat of death.

He was on the side of now, heading towards the mirrored events building. Naga's belly scraped along the dirt road, tourists and guides ushered inside, closing the door and making Hassan feel acutely alone.

Naga halted, seeing itself in the mirrored structure, delaying the chase.

'There is no other greater than Naga the great!' The cobra paced, eyeing itself in the pristine venue, confused as it reflected the contrasting terrain and bright blue sky. Everyone safe inside the optical illusion, its purpose fulfilled: to deter the prophetic battles of human and primitive alien. Hassan continued to the old town, looking over his shoulder now and then. Reaching the oasis of palms, confused at the water up to his ankles. He paused to look up at the umbrellaed palms, taking a breath and absorbing the refreshing water that escaped the porous rocks. Fastening the skull in his shirt, he shrieked when his ankles were pulled, falling flat on his face, then flipped over with aggression.

'Threw me back in, ay?!' Akash yelled in his face, pinning him down by his wrists.

'Get off me!' Hassan struggled, 'let me go! It's not you!'

'Give me the skull, and I will. Yer snivellin' little rat! Ha-ha!' Curious as Hassan looked over his head, grunting as he was snatched, swinging from Naga's mouth. Hassan got to his feet and ran towards the roofless warrens, his feet sloshing, and haste hindered. He had tunnel vision and finding his way around was easy, hurried as Naga smashed through the mud walls. Finding the room he waited, the cobra destroying the ancient dwellings with fire in its black veins.

'In the name of the almighty...' the sand devil appeared holding a golden light within, Hassan waited, Naga almost touching him, he entered the shimmering door, Naga following. Running through the warrens the other side, dispersing the occupants as they screamed and fled. Hassan ploughed on protecting his eyes, not wanting to look back at the crashing and smashing. Bumping into the incense caravans and traders, pushing them aside. His mind raced through his next steps, there was no way he could run all the way to the Mustatil. Hassan stopped and turned to face Naga who relentlessly charged. 'Stop!' holding the skull above his head. Naga slowed to a slither, grinning as it came close.

'I know where the impostor is.'

'You! Are the impostor!'

'No, I'm not. I am the opener of doors. You only got through because of me.' Naga's scales twitched on its head, deep in thought, circling Hassan.

'Give me, the skull! I have no use for you!'

'I will if you take me to the Mustatil. I know where the impostor is. It's hiding there. In the sculptures.'

'They are not sculpturessss, they are gates! Liness of energy! A signal to the ones that spy from above!'

'Whatever they are, the impostor is there, taking your glory!'

Naga snarled in defeat, 'ride the one and only great, and show me, opener of doors.' Morphing back into the camel. Hassan threw the skull in the air, caught by and swallowed by Naga, gingerly mounting the saddle made from a strange, stitched skin. The scratchy under blanket irritating his calves. He held on tight when Naga got up, throwing him forward then back as the camel stood.

Proceeding to the Mustatil, Hassan felt like Lawrence of Arabia only it wasn't as romantic in real life, with no head covering or sunglasses.

'Please, hurry. I'm dying in this heat.'

'That is the whole purpose, opener of doors.'

'You can kill me later. First, we must find the impostor and salvage the bones.'

'Which Marid tribe do you belong?'

'Porthminster.'

'Hmmm. Cargo thieves. Then you shall be killed.'

'The sun will kill me before you do if we don't hurry.'

A door materialised, Hassan slumped forward when they arrived at the Mustatil through it, barely hanging onto life. Having no recollection of the transition. He had not been eaten, but with blurred vision and a throbbing brain, the plan and his life eluded him. He licked his lips with a sticky tongue, swallowing razors as he tried to muster up some saliva.

'You are nearly dead, half Marid. I shall end it quickly for you.'

'Please...water. Please.'

The camel knelt on all fours; Hassan slid off the saddle landing face first on the burning ground. Water suddenly splashed on his face, licking it from his lips then dragging it into his mouth with his hands as it poured freely. His gullet burned, crying out from the bittersweet relief. He was being drenched, nearly drowned. Naga released a guttural laugh.

'Pleasure can also kill you, half Marid!' Hassan stood, wiping the water over his face and clearing his eyes.

'Thank you, Naga the great. This will carry great rewards for you.'

It became cobra once more, 'from whom? Nothing is above me! I am my creator!' it bellowed.

'You cannot create yourself. Even Nagini, your own mother, is above you.' Naga flared its nostrils, inhaled and hissed in Hassan's face. 'Maybe the impostor created you.'

'Then I must destroy it!' Hassan made his way to the circles with Naga following violently, dodging the rising mounds of the vipers detecting the return of the skull.

'Wait here. I know where it's hiding. You can surprise it with your greatness.' Hassan climbed into the first circle, the bulky slate reaching his middle. He brushed away the sand to uncover the charred bones, containing his horror when newly laid bones broke the surface. Naga became impatient and searched further afield.

Remembering the amulet, he took it off, holding it up in the sunlight, the glint blinding him. Damn thing has been the bane of this life.

'Hassan?' jolting at his father's voice. Searching with his hand peaked over his eyes, there he stood.

'Baba?' Musa was a vision of youth again. His white thobe and perfectly dressed Shemagh made Hassan's heart sing. He'd forgotten about him in it all, but not the things that happened before. 'Is it really you or just another trick?'

'No trick, habibi.'

'Prove it.'

Musa got closer; it was him, or a clever version. Hassan bit into his quivering lip, he wanted to forgive, he wanted his father back ruffling his hair.

'MashAllah, you look handsome. I'm not so sure about your Marid eyes.'

'I like them. I'm proud to be Marid,' there would normally be an eruption, but there wasn't, just a sympathetic smile.

'What are you doing here? It's dangerous, habibi.'

'I'm breaking these flippin things! To stop them taking the kids, and return the skull. Peter and Max are dying...' holding in the emotion he was afraid to show.

'How is your mother?'

'Holding it all together, like always.'

Naga returned, cursing and quoting its greatness. 'Who crosses the path of the Mustatil?!'

'The impostor.' Hassan climbed out of the circle, watching Naga getting ready to strike. Musa turned to run, Hassan leading. Naga smashed the circles frustrated at its miss, splitting its snout as the jagged slate pierced the copper and black scales.

'I am the only great Naga! You must die!' Musa tripped and fell managing to get to his feet. Hassan cried out as he focussed on the last circle, the largest. The smashing and crumbling of slate carried on behind him, contorting his face to keep the momentum. They all reached the last circle. Hassan shocked at Musa's condition; gaunt and bony.

'What happened to you?!'

'I am soree, ya habibi. Forgive me. The doors have the most incredible powers, but it was not to be for me. I have reached my end. You must return Layla, they will not stop. Your mother will be next.'

'They ain't having her! Or anyone!'

'Take my hand, walidi. I don't want to leave without remembering you.' Musa held out his hand, Naga grinned and swayed behind him, looking forward to its meal. Hassan looked at his father's hand, something was different. He edged backwards into the last circle and held the amulet above his head, shifting Naga's attention.

'You are both created by the same power, the same energy. You cannot rule in this life or the next. What will you say when you are questioned about your disgusting work?!' Naga curled its lip, drew back and struck Hassan, knocking itself out on the invisible dome protecting him. Hassan let out an inconspicuous laugh, backing further into the circle. Musa morphed into Toulah, crouched and baring her teeth.

'I knew it was you! Stupid fucking Jinn! You will never be human because you don't have our unique superiority. Even the Nagini serves humans!'

'Who gave you the amulet of the Mustatiiillll?!' she hissed.

'A friend. Someone who loves me, not like you. No one loves you.'

'Does the kalb still crave the bones of infants? Does it plead in agony from its new addiction?' Hassan felt bilious, not his Max, he would never. 'Did the kalb not lead you to the Mustatil? The finder of bones. Your father gave him to us so that he would lead you to your deaths.' She touched the shield, her long, light fingers manipulating the invisible force.

'You lie!'

'Yes, I'm quite good at it. Even your dumb Marid of Porthminster fell for my, dis-guises!' she jeered. 'Solomon's skull is the only opener of doors, you will never match its power.' A condescending cackle escaped her. 'The Nabateans were one of the greatest of civilisations, disappearing without trace. Persecuted for their intelligence. Al Ula will preserve its legend and continue serving the Nagini.'

'Where is my father?!'

'Oh, such futile emotion, yer snivellin little rat!' She grinned, the most bone-chilling grin. Her eyes bore through him, eyes that were gruelling, seductive. Running her hand along the shield as she began circling it. His heartbeat hard from a mind in turmoil and confusion.

'Bet you can't turn into me,' he said, his voice quaking.

'Oh? Is that a challenge?'

Hassan nodded nervously. He turned his body to follow her, his feet catching on small rocks and bones he didn't want to study. Toulah mirrored what he wore, the veil morphing into black curls. He gulped as he looked at himself on the other side of the dome. She stopped and stood rigid, just like him. Hassan was captivated, each expression, movement, was the same, only, there would always be something different, something, not quite right. He'd heard about the Jinn that lived parallel to us, the Qareen. Our personalised photocopy that existed alongside us.

Something heavy was shifting, the head of Naga. The large, flickering serpent eyes opening just enough to see its target. Raising its weary head high, mouth widening, bearing down on Toulah and swallowing her whole, its head still spinning. It came crashing down, breaking the last ring of slate and Hassan's shield. There was a pause before Naga began to convulse and roar in agony as its belly expanded, stretching to its limit and splitting open, oozing out a wet and sticky she-camel. Morphing back into herself, Toulah took the skull from Naga's stomach contents. Hassan's mouth gaped as the cobra's nerves kept it alive enough to speak.

'There is only, one, Naga the great,' whipping the tip of its tail round and decapitating her.

Vulnerable and nauseous, Hassan watched two heads roll while reciting, hoping the breakage in the circle was enough to complete the closure. The Mustatil serpents emerged, swarming Solomon's skull and taking it beneath. The vipers left behind devouring and tearing at Naga and Toulah.

A door appeared to Hassan's right. 'Take me home,' he said and walked through, clutching the amulet.

52

SERVANT

Re-entering the school, slipping on splintered wood, Samir was lying next to Peter with Esme on the slope, bathing their wounds in the sea.

'Mum!' Hassan ran to her, Esme hollering when she saw him covered in red dust and splatters of dark liquid.

'Thank God! How come you were so quick?!'

'Quick? I was there for ages!' He heaved and couldn't hold it in, turning to the side and spewing.

'Hamduillah!' Samir strained, 'that means it is done! Is it done?' Hassan confirmed with one nod, wiping his mouth.

'Naga is dead, and Toulah. They killed each other. You should've seen it Ustaz! Naga exploded!'

Samir closed his eyes and laughed with approval, his tears falling into the sea. 'And the skull?'

'The vipers took it back, and ate them.' Hassan always had a morbid curiosity, satisfied and shaking from adrenaline.

Samir winced at his pain, 'O' Allah! We are at your mercy. Bestow your forgiveness upon us as we lie here holding on with but an atoms weight of hope.' He shivered, his teeth chattering as he looked at Peter. The first time he had seen him so quiet, lifeless and fading before them. His strength and demeanour no longer in the vessel that held a grounded soul. Esme returned to the fussing, cupping sea and pouring it over Peter's wounds.

'Peter? Peter! No! You can't leave us. Please! Look, look...' she continued cupping, pouring, cupping and pouring. The lacerations on his chest protruding, his skin pallid and goose bumped.

Hassan looked over to the white yacht and pilot gigs. Things had gone quiet. 'Where are the purple people?'

'In the yachts.'

'What are we going to do now, Ustaz?'

The floor beneath them shook, a rumble rippled the surface of the tide. Hassan turned to see the trees move once more, disturbing the crows. The breaking of windows as the rumble grew into a quake. His mouth dropped when Janan emerged from gardens, a giant woman. Her brocades missing, revealing a face that reflected her surroundings, her eyes of swirling seas and galaxies. Lurching over the lynch gate and straight to the harbour wall and entering the sea, causing a swell. The rebellious gathered around her in worship. She peered into the yacht, scaring those on-board half to death. They had never seen her like this, only in her familiar form, their adoration and worship increasing. There was rage and discontent in the way she moved, her garment organic, becoming her environment in a hostile manner. With one brush off her hand, the pilot gigs and sail boats were capsized, elm oars slapping the surface. Nagini was all encompassing, carrying conflict, holy wars and evil. The things of beauty attached to her began to darken, the stench of Oud and new blood burnt the nostrils of all who inhaled it.

The negative was building, intensifying. Confusing onlookers as they were halted, held captive in awe of what rapidly changed into images of greed and divide. Crews draped themselves over hulls, saturated in defeat.

'Go! Ya Allah, go!' Samir coughed. 'You have to finish it!'

'But she looks pissed off!' He clutched the amulet. 'Where's Akash when you need him?'

'In the dungeon,' Samir murmured.

'What?!'

'The dungeon! Go!'

The Nagini fizzed into the sea, prompting a mass, panicked exodus.

Hassan peered around the chapel door, shards of light penetrated the holes in the stained-glass windows projecting onto the pews and red carpet, the remnants of incense smoke dancing in their light, shrouding piety.

'Akash?' he gulped. The vibe full of static.

'Is that you dude?' came the faint reply. Hassan followed his ears to the small door behind the bookcase, pushing it aside and lifting the iron latch. He jumped when Akash was eagerly waiting at the top of the stone steps. 'Boy, are you a sight f'sore eyes!' Hassan regarded him with wariness.

'Listen. I don't trust who you are, even though I've just seen Toulah lose her head. So, no funny stuff, okay?'

'Bloody 'ell. Was 'appened t'you?!'

'I bucked my ideas up, like you said.'

'C'mon, we ain't got time for no explanations.' Akash squeezed himself out of the door, pushing passed Hassan, brushing himself off and clicking his neck.

'How long have you been in there?'

'When you went through the first time. Janan put me in 'ere. Said there were pearls down 'ere f'me. Bleddy lyin' freak. You know what she be, don't thee?'

'But you were there, in Al Ula. You got my half side going.'

'It weren't me! Okay? I can't go through. This is me destiny t'stay 'ere.'

'No offense, but I don't believe you. Like, at all, ever.'

'Suit yerself. Where's Layla?' Akash asked, redressing his hair.

'Safe, and on a need-to-know basis.'

'Ah, c'mon! That ain't fair!'

'I trusted you to take care of her! And I'm just...' he screwed up his eyes, throwing his hands down, 'I'm confused, okay? I saw you multiple times. You didn't protect Layla, and you held Peter for Naga.'

'What you blimmin talkin' about?!'

'Where's my father?'

Akash shrugged, 'Dead or drinkin some poor blighter's blood...'

'What!?'

'Yeah. Well, not *exactly* dead, per se.'

'I think Peter's dying.'

Akash looked down, touching his human nails. 'We needs to call the dolphins.' Hassan squinted at him, his eyes turning a deep amber. Akash caught them, stepping back with a bow.

'Forgive me.'

'Wha...what are you doing?'

Akash's head remained lowered, 'I's got no respect. I shoudda known when we went to Zennor, in the boat. But I didn't trust it. Just tell me what I have t'do.'

Hassan walked passed him with a smug grin.

'We're gonna finish this shit.'

If they could walk back to the harbour in slow motion, that would've been the icing on the cake for Hassan. Especially when Esme's eyes and face lit up when she saw him, accepting who he was with her fondness and pride about to burst. Whose child *was* this? It was a struggle getting Peter and Samir out of the swell, Esme near giving up as Peter remained unresponsive.

'You'd better be you Akash, or I'll kill you myself!' instead of a cocky answer, she got a bowed head, perplexing her radiance. 'Please, Peter needs help. I don't know what else to do!'

'We needs Beaky, ma'am.'

'*Ma'am*? Is this a joke?'

Samir raised his head, 'believe him,' wincing at the burning in his chest. 'Siren, serve, the...'

'The?' Esme pressed.

'Marid,' Samir heaved out a rattling breath.

'But I'm not a Marid,' she looked at Hassan, then Peter, Akash still annoyingly bowing. 'Akash! Stop that!'

'Yes ma'am,' raising his head, his eyes endless and the iciest blue.

'So why have you been an asshole?'

'It weren't him, mum.'

'So, who got Suzie pregnant?' There was an awkward silence.

Akash jerked his chin out to sea, 'them, out there. Your huzbund broke the protection line with his fancy necklaces.'

'Stop this blimmin fussin,' Peter mumbled.

'Peter! Akash, do something!'

He gladly obliged, his skin changing sumptuously dark as he entered the water. His full-body wave motion propelling him forward, clawing the rebellious that had created a protective barrier against the Dolphins. Muffled squeals and screams as eyes were gouged and sternums punched. Akash released his alarm, penetrating the deep causing nearby dogs to bark. The sound waves pushing aside Janan's henchmen.

53

Draycott

Layla was frying eggs for the girls at Draycott Terrace, while Khadija sobbed at the kitchen table. Both their minds on the mauled seagull on the steps.

'I hope that wasn't Steve.'

'Who cares about a bloody Seagull?!' Khadija spat.

'He did you a favour, y'know. Imagine waking up one morning and seeing your grandfather lying next to you. Eww,' she shivered.

'He was the only man I ever loved. The kindest, sweetest man.'

'*Ever* loved? You're bloody sixteen! You've got your whole life ahead of you. There are plenty of kindest and sweetest. F.Y.I. Samir is free now.'

'Ugh! Samir will control me like my father. No running, no breathing.'

'Meh, I think you'll be surprised. Unless he's gay,' making Khadija choke on her stale bread.

'AstaghfiruAllah! How could you say that?'

'Oh, please!' flipping the greasy egg onto the fifth plate, 'I think he was just hiding behind Janan, afraid he'll be stoned to death, or worse. That was his contract.' Turning off the gas, she called out to the others who were adorning the sofas under Esme's throws. The little blonde girl was having a wander around the house, touching expensive things, and revelling in the feel of the pristine cotton sheets on the cleanest beds she'd seen.

'What we gonna do with the little one?' the American asked, 'what are *we* gonna do? Here we are in a stranger's house, waiting for fried eggs.'

'At least we are eating fried eggs in someone's nice house and not waiting for that camel and those, men!' The girl from Australia said and broke into an ugly cry. They all surrounded her, consoling each other. Layla stood at the door with the tray of congealing eggs.

'Guys, no, come on,' placing down the tray and joining in the hug. Khadija soothing with a wobbling chin. 'We'll get you back home, okay?' wiping their eyes and sniffing in tandem.

'How?' they all asked,

'The way you came in. Welcome home, habibi.' Musa stood there, the little one in his arms.

'*Baba*?! But, I heard you were...'

'Dyink? I know, right?' the taupe polar neck sleeves to his wrists, looking freshly groomed and smelling of Oud.

'How do I know it's you?' she said.

Placing the little one down, he held out his arms with that smile she'd missed, the smile that said all was forgiven. 'Hamduillah you are back safe,' his hazel eyes filled with gratitude, hugging her, stifling his tears of relief. 'I'm sorree. Okay? I know how much you have been through. But you are back, and safe and walahi I won't let anythink happen to you again,' the girls watched in awe, a little envious Layla had such a fit father.

'But where were you? All this time? We nearly...'

'I know, I know. I had to let Allah do the rest for me. I was up to my neck and any attempt would have failed. I am proud of you, habibi. You are amazink.'

She gulped down her emotion that constricted her throat. The room was silent as they all watched the touching reunion, Khadija hoping hers would be the same.

'How are we getting back home, sir?' the American asked.

'I will help you. I am Musa, not sir. Eat and drink whatever you want, and I will help, inshallah.' Layla made them jolt as her tsunami of suppressed resentment erupted in a primal scream, contorting and falling to her knees. Musa swallowed hard, looking around the room at the judgemental glances.

'You were ashamed of me!' she yelled, dribbling onto the Persian rug.

'No, no, habibi, I wasn't. I was afraid, walahi. Afraid.'

'Do you know what they do?!' she screamed, her eyes filling with vengeful tears.

'Ya Allah, forgive me, my daughter, blease,' he knelt with empty hands.

'Is that what you've done? Did you do those things?!'

'No! Walahi. I had to hide. I did not do anythink like them.'

'But you supply them!' the girls watched the conversation like a tennis match, the little one holding tight to Khadija in front of the rock lamp, which began to fill the lounge with its warming glow as the light faded, its orange stars on fire in their eyes.

'Yes, I am a fool and hypocrite. There, I admit it to you. I am not above you, in this moment I am not even worthy to be beneath your shoe. I was afraid, and pooshed into the corner. I knew this was a risk, but you didn't disappoint me. Marry who you want, but marry who you love, and find it in your heart to forgive this foolish man.' His palms upturned and brow furrowed, flinching at her convulses.

'I'm sorry, but I can't forgive you just like that and don't guilt trip me into it either,' slowly composing herself, feeling cleansed and decluttered. Being brow-beaten into forgiving those that did you wrong or face the side eye from God, was a toxic and false preach. She would forgive when she felt the organic shift and not before. And that was okay.

'You deserve everything that's coming to you, and that won't be from me. But if you go back to how you were, I'm leaving. I won't be destroyed all over again. I've been to hell and back and I'm sorry, too. That's what you get when Allah lifts the veils on oppression. Yet you still did it.' She stood, wiping her nose and face on the dirtied robe Ibrahim had given her, reliving the ordeal from the cloth between her fingers.

'Ibrahim didn't deserve it, but he did it for you and it set him free. All I can say is that you chose the right person to take care of me. I just wish he was my father instead of you.'

An audible gasp from Khadija snapped all heads round. Musa looked to the floor, his thumb nails having a fight. Any punishment from his maker would be no match to that of his own daughter's. 'Hitting my mother, you disgusting excuse for a man!' she yelled into the top of his head, the American restraining her.

'Okay, okay. Layla, let it go, let it go. It's done. Sir? Please, we wanna to go home.'

Layla snatched herself out of the grip. Musa veins void of testosterone and ego. He too was faced with self, one he did not care to confront. Standing, unable to look Layla in the eye, pushing his hand into the pocket of his jeans checking the vial of adrenochrome was still intact. His returned youth a temporary one, so that he could perform an undoing all of his own.

'Okay. Everybaddy, I'm soree but you cannot go back.' There were cries of disdain and disappointment. 'You,' looking at the American girl, 'where did you come from? A home? A family?' she shook her head. 'Then what am I taking you back to?'

She shrugged, 'just home, I guess. I wanna start over. Get my life back together.'

'Stay here, there will be a home, for you all. When you get everthink together, the world is your oyster. Inshallah. Getting you back through is a significant risk.'

'What about her?' pointing to the little one, her plump hands clasped from the tension.

Musa's heart ached, about to throw up, fanning his polar neck and breathing in.

'You are her family now.'

'But she keeps asking for her mother!' they cried.

'She was asking for love, protection. No person. She does not have one. All of you...' he looked at them in turn, 'this is what you are looking for, not a someone, but a feeling only Allah can give through mercy, and what any good person can give you. Come!'

He led them to the basement. The altar had been reconstructed, the rucksacks gone.

'Blease, first one,' he asked. The American girl stepped forward, her limbs trembling.

He gave them each a Taweez, like Peter's, instructing them to stand on the Hamsa as he did.

The anticipation in their bellies stung as well as uncertainty. Once finished, Musa began preparation at the altar to open the largest door he had ever opened, all eyes looking on with intrigue.

He absorbed the anguish and trauma from all of them.

'I am sorree,' regarding Layla with pride. 'When the light appears, stand back, okay? Immediately.'

The girls jiggled her head, taking a sharp intake of breath from the burning on their left hand. 'You cannot be touched now. Any of you. I have protected your souls.'

'What are you doing?' Layla asked.

'I am getting help. We go to the mount, get our family. It is all I can think about in this moment, it's worth a shot. We are facing a great enemy,' setting his eyes on the little one. 'Ya Allah. What have we done?' She was smitten with Musa, wanting to touch his goatee and study his eyes. Placing trust in his good looks alone.

'She doesn't speak English. They can't get away with it anymore. The authorities need to know, baba!'

'Is that what you think? No, they will silence us and use the routes for themselves. Don't be fooled by the illusion, habibi. I will go, and inshallah return. I am needed at Marazion, to finish it.'

The light appeared, the little one reaching out, 'Mama?'

Musa crouched to her level. 'Ja, deine Mutter ist hier.' Layla was gobsmacked at her father, so much so, a deliverance manifested. 'Stay here. Inshallah my Lord gives me permission to return.'

'How long will you be?'

'If I am not back in half hour, go save your mother. And get the meat from fridge. Now!'

'Meat?'

'Go!'

Musa walked into the pulsating portal casually, the little one clapping her hands and squealing. All had been forgotten in the safety net of number 3 Draycott Terrace, the present was to be lived. But the collective nightmares and trauma would remain forever, for all.

Layla led the girls to her room to choose whatever they wanted from her crammed wardrobe. Khadija abstained, getting the bag of meat instead.

54

EFREET

The girls sat on the floor outside the basement door in a change of clothes, waiting for Musa with the bag of meat. They were starting to receive love, not the love they were told they needed which involved sick gratifications. It was hard to accept, mistrusting the fuzzies they were feeling.

The American caressed the needle wounds on her arm beneath the Balenciaga sweater, her mind harbouring a darkness that had reached its peak, allowing the light to penetrate. They got her addicted, kept her in an accepting state. She had literally been around the houses: Elite parties, business meetings and royal rituals. It was hard to detach from it because she'd convinced herself a million times over that it was okay to be under the suffocating weight of a sweating man; the only mindset which saved her soul from splitting in two. Just closing her eyes knowing it was always over quickly, wishing she were the little ones who didn't know any different, and who thought it *was* love.

Twenty minutes had passed and suddenly their chit chat and reminisce was halted by the floor shaking. They stood, holding onto each other, edging backwards into the adjacent wall.

'What if...' Khadija gulped, 'Janan comes for us...'

'She won't. It's baba, I know it.'

The house shook at Draycott Terrace, something it had gotten used to. Doing all it could to keep the occupants safe as the mortar loosened between the granite. Loud banging on the floorboards prompted screams. Doors rattled and wood split.

'BismiAllah!' Khadija sobbed, squeezing her eyes shut into Layla's arm. The light reappeared in the room.

'See, what did I tell you?' the door growing in the centre, swirling and hissing.

'Stand back!' Yelled Musa, distant from within it. The girls sheltering amongst the coats hanging on the wall. A large hand reached forward, Khadija feeling the blood leave her head. Then a knee, thigh, torso and head! Efreet. The largest of the devils. Gold bangles stacked on either arm. Capable of destruction, unsurpassed malice and possession. The girls voiced their relief as Musa entered, heaving the Efreet out of his way.

'Is that, is that...' Khadija asked.

'Yes.'

It crouched in the room, having to sit due its size and heavy, twisted horns with the mannerisms of a Gorilla and hell's torment. The powerful owners of magic and greedy souls, dragged from the underworld to serve another foolish carcass. The girls pinched their noses at the acrid smell of sulphur and soiled cloth. Hundreds of thin, sharp yellowing teeth glistened behind a wide mouth that had crunched on bones and bottles of liquor.

Musa held out his hand for the girls to stay put.

'Aouthou bileh minna shaitaan a'rajeem,' Musa nonchalantly recited, making the Efreet snarl.

'I shall reward you greatly.' The devil shifted arrogantly, snorting through its large nostrils. Khadija studied it in awe, only ever reading about their antics and passages of protection. It was nothing like she imagined, or anyone portrayed: reddish skin and black eyes that seared your soul. Tucking her hijab tighter around her head and covering her crown with her palm, because that's where they entered. The large bag of cattle meat and offal slid across the floor by itself and stopped at its feet.

'Will you help us?' Musa asked. The Efreet regarded its nails, picking meat out of its teeth. The smell was unbearable, making them nauseous. Musa could barely tolerate its murderous glances, buckling from the pressure of the entity's stare. 'I have Kenan. Here, and in Riyadh. Take it, take it all.' The amulet around Musa's neck was all that kept the devil from pulverising him. It lewdly curled its lip at the girls.

'Girls, left hand!' they showed the Hamsa on their left palms, making it huff in defeat. It flicked the first two fingers of its clawed hand, opening another door. The girls gasping when they could see the Mount and the chaos beyond.

'We all go! Now!'

55

Elemental

Marazion's beach was littered with drenched warriors as the girls and Musa joined them, only one noticing their magical entrance. The Efreet did not wish to be seen and hung around behind Musa, for its calling and condition would remain with him for the time being. Although the temptation to break so many bones was a great distraction as its black eyes wandered the vulnerable. Janan sensed their arrival, tipping the yacht like a toy boat as she moved, unsteadying the elites carrying out their rituals inside. With one hand gesture, she instructed her elemental army into battle.

Musa gave her a chilling sneer, his vengeance and redemption, his own. Regarding the giant mass of his persecutor with a healthy fear in his heart.

'Go to your mother, habibi. Now! And remember your Taweez! Use it!' They each clutched the bound Jinn around their necks as they hurried to the causeway, their steps quickening when they heard the screeches of the Marid.

The girls hugged their waists as they crossed the ancient stones, Layla carrying the little one. The rebellious hissed at them from the increasing tide, crawling out onto the rocks. A north wind began to blow, agitating the waves, the sky blackened and a faint rumble of thunder muted the atmosphere.

'Something's coming,' Khadija said, inhaling in the sea air and cooling her arid lungs. 'It's so nice to breathe clean air again.'

'Guys...now's the time to use the Taweez.' Layla said.

'But what's in them?' the American asked.

'There's only one way to find out.'

'You go first then.' The Australian said to Layla.

Layla gave the little one to Khadija, taking the Taweez over her head, continuing their strides as the Marid closed in on them.

She found an end to the bound, picking at it, unravelling in one go and it falling at her feet. They stopped to look at it, waiting.

'Nothing's happening,' said the American, as they all looked down on the saturated bundle.

'Wait. Was I supposed to recite anything?'

'Peter didn't.'

'Maybe we all have to open them, together.' The dark girl, who never spoke, suggested.

'I think she's right.' Layla said, offering a smile of elation towards her. 'Quickly, open them! Keep walking!'

The girls unravelled their packages, anticipation in their bellies as they watched the binds fall onto the causeway and into the gaps between the cobbles. There was sudden thunder above and beneath. The loudest clap caused them to duck and scream. The waves either side began to rise, forming walls of sea. Ten feet, fifteen, twenty!

'Run to the harbour!'

Their soggy sandals began to perish as they ran for their lives, the Marid pushing their faces through the wall trying to grab them, catching their hair with claws. The wall's girth increased, pushing the Marid onto the rocks, piercing their rubbery skin.

Esme saw it, 'oh my God! The girls!'

'Allah be praised for the Elementals!' Samir cried.

'Mumm! Mum!' Layla called over the roar, overstretching a full arm-wave. Esme left Peter and Samir, running to them and calling out their names. She accepted this would be it now, losing and running as her daughter found her wings to fly, embracing acceptance and surrender. Layla was wearing her hijab with the peonies, Esme ran her fingers over the folds to check their correctness, their eyes exchanging mutual expression.

'Asalaam alaikum, missus Kattan,' Khadija shivered.

'Wsalaam, dearest Khadija. Your parents must be frantic. Is everyone okay?' Their answers were vague, overwhelmed.

'Hello sweet darling,' Esme said to the little one, stroking her white-blonde hair into place, the approaching wind changing it again. She held out her arms to be carried by her, the love of women nourishing and nurturing the void.

Generations walked the causeway, survivors of patriarchal curses and ambassadors of rights.

'How are they?' Layla asked, looking ahead.

'Not good. Come on, they'll be pleased to see you all.'

Peter barely hung onto life. His skin pale and lips mauve. Samir had managed to sit up, despite his broken ribs.

'Ya Allah!' he sobbed, 'how great is your mercy! Hamduillah,' a smile breaking his tears as he laid down, his little laughs of joy healing in the pain.

'I think I've ruptured something pulling these two out of the water.'

'What the hell happened?!'

'Naga. And, well, a shapeshifter, Toulah. It wasn't Akash. Hassan killed her and Naga, it's all been quiet eventful.' The little one's arms outstretched towards Peter, grunting for his attention, opening and clenching her fleshy digits. Esme set her down, toddling up to him she knelt beside him, missing his protective masculinity. She gently picked pieces of shell from his face and beard, showing one to him, 'mus-chel,' she pronounced, throwing them into sea to watch them get snatched.

The swell of his heart closed his eyes, 'thank you, tiny...maid,' he wheezed. The wind howled and waves crashed against sides and up the slope, the sky getting greyer like a winter storm in November. The girls huddled together, their eyes upon the broken heroes and the yachts that triggered past trauma. The memories of the fear they felt when older men greeted them with raised Champagne flutes and that nauseating look in their eye.

'Where's Max?' Layla asked, just noticing his absence.

'The cyclist took him to the parish. He got caught in the crossfire, he'll be fine. They're just checking over him,' giving her a reassuring touch of the arm, desperately holding in her tears.

'Harvey?'

'Top castle terrace. On the lookout for something, he said.'

'Akash?'

'Ain't you fed up wi'askin that?' Peter strained, blood splattering his lips as he coughed. 'Good t'see you, little...maid.'

'That's enough Peter, you need to rest! Dolphins are on their way.'

'No...maid...youm ain't...lisnen!' No one heard him, their attention averted.

'Dad's here,' Layla announced.

Esme squinted towards the beach. 'Thought he was dead,' she muttered. No such luck, that's how it always was, wishing for something so hard it tantalised itself out of your reach. Bang, bang, bang, was the only relief.

Layla looked in the same direction, 'me too. He helped us all, and said sorry. A proper sorry. And I told him what despicable person he is. Bringing back an Efreet in the process. Not sure what he has up his sleeve for that.'

Esme had outgrown her rescuer, the grief of that pulling her in different directions. Flashes of their embraces stung her, the years spent all leading up to this moment. Preferring the new place she was in now.

'Get the girls to safety!' Samir stressed and began reciting. Every vein and fibre in his body burned from his betrayal, the weighty and threatening presence of a crescendo was too much to bear in his fragility.

Esme knelt beside Peter, stroking his hair and face. 'I'm going to see Musa,' she whispered to his cheek, leaving a trembling kiss on his forehead.

'It's always the good people that endure the most,' Layla commented, watching Samir writhe in agony. 'God, I feel helpless. We need reinforcements.'

Her blood thickened and vision danced when Akash emerged from hostile waters like an Adonis, his eyes illuminous blue against the fading of his dark pigments. His teeth shone at her, long curls lazily here and there. Perfection tainted, but Esme said that was usually a good sign.

'Alri' maid?' slapping his face when he got close. He smirked, rubbing the stinging mark. 'I deserve that, I guess?' Layla affirmed with one nod through a hot rush of lust.

'Akash, take the girls to a resident please.' Esme asked.

He dipped his head, 'yes ma'am.'

Esme stood at the edge of the causeway, this path had changed so much since her right foot had graced it. Becoming her cathartic guide.

'Esme!' Samir called, 'wait! Do not, cross it!'

56

Saint Michael

The wind whistled down the cannons. Hassan felt as though he was on the outside looking in up there, he was the guardian of all things as he looked down upon a sea alive with battle, fixated on the agitation tarnishing the heart of Marazion. All the teachings and research that had remained in his numbed conscience had spilled out in an ugly mess.

Rain splattered his face, but he did not flinch, it was welcome. The cooling drops soaking into his skin that was near burnt from its bones, raising his face and arms out to the side twirling while he rejoiced. A sharp glint caught his eye, the dark grey cumulus parted, and the sun broke through, illuminating the turmoil. Something came with it and overshadowed the bay, billowing into its shape.

Hassan gawked as it passed over the Mount. 'It's here,' he uttered in awe. 'It's here!' he yelled, frantically waving his arms but couldn't be seen. Seagulls gathered around the forming of wings which gracefully enlarged and dominated the sky.

'It's Mika'il! Mum! Muuum! It's Michael!' transfixed, he watched the shape of the angel building with cool tears in his eyes; the giver and protector. Trapped residents emerged from their barricades, the crews and lifeboat volunteers knelt in prayer and humility on the beach.

Sun rays turned the rockpools into mirrors and the causeway granite glistened in golds and mauves, and evil had no hold. Janan's barriers had fled to sheltering rocks beneath allowing Beaky and his army to storm the bay in synchronised diving. Ploughing through and ramming the bellies of Janan's henchmen, clapping their jaws in threat. The whistles and clicks celebrating the victory. Hassan saw something bigger enter with them, a shadow at a slow and steady pace, breaking the surface and releasing a ton of air through its blowhole. The mammal that had briefly visited once before, to test the bay's depth.

'Whale! A whale!' he yelled to no one, feeling alone in his experiences.

Barnacles lined the scored nose that emptied gallons of water before thrashing its tail down onto the yachts in turn, splitting them in two. The freed babies spilling out and bobbing like corks. There were gasps and cries of contempt from the crews recognising the floundering elites, their purple gowns dragging them under. Janan was fraught with the arrival of the deity and nature's defences, darkest thoughts and desires with the world's worst screaming within her manipulation.

Esme had reached Musa on his knees, his palms raised to the heavens in praise and plea. She tripped and stumbled as she watched the divine dominate the sky, glorification broke through humbled tears, pulling her scarf tighter and checking she was presentable.

'Look Moose! SubhaanAllah!' Musa was reciting, his eyes closed. Esme quickly held her nose as the invisible presence of the Efreet's sharp scent caught her unawares.

'My love! Take me to the mount. I want to see my son. I have reached my end. Forgive me for my disrespect to your honour and for leading you into my mistakes. Pray for me, inshallah. Although I do not expect you to. You had the strength, I did not.'

'You're bleeding, Moose' she said, wiping it away from the corner of his mouth, the invisible bond rushing through her fingers. 'Why can't I let you go? What is it that holds me?' Musa smeared the remnants from his lips with the back of his hand.

'I will break the spell for you, habibi. You deserve your freedom. But that means I go with it.'

She joined him with palms upturned, their path and intuition confirmed. The clouds began to dance, moving around the Arc Angel in devotion. The rain fell harder on Janan, the wind blowing her off balance. Everyone was sombre, united, differences aside they all had the same heartbeat on the shale.

'Peter is dying, Musa, and Samir isn't looking too good.' The mere mention of his official name affirmed her change; the 'new' wife.

'We go.'

An embrace hung between them, but Esme was not ready to fall again. She enjoyed residing within her guard she had been constructing, albeit bitter and void of forgiving. Often referring to her marriage like a fine China teacup, with a slight chip on the rim.

'I don't think you're ready to see the consequences of your actions.' She led the way back, every step an empowerment and worship. 'Peter needs help!' she called over her shoulder. Her feet freed as the designer shoes fell away, emotions running high passing floating, content babies in the rockpools. Musa didn't hear as he checked the waters, feeling vulnerable on the causeway, its length daunting and end eluding, trembling at the presence of Mika'il.

They reached the harbour wall, greeted by Akash with Peter in his arms.

'Please, Akash, save the babies in the pools!'

'Ain't no need, ma'am. They be alri. We's got t'get Pete to Porthminster, aysap.' Esme fussed with Peter's tunic that clung to jutting bones. He too was half of himself and unconscious.

'Asalaam alaikum,' Musa said sheepishly, nodding in Akash's direction, 'thank you.' Akash reciprocated the forgiveness.

'Will he be, okay? They'll fix him, right?' Esme asked. Akash thinned his lips into a maybe. The lifeboat volunteer arrived in the rib, checking over Peter, giving Akash permission to enter the sea.

'Look, look, Peter whatsit, listen. You hear me? Listen! You're not leaving us! Okay?!' Esme's voice faltered as she ran alongside. Musa hung back, accepting his new position in her life.

Peter's head turned to her, 'Pas. Pascoe.' He breathed.

'What did he say? What did you say? Peter?' Esme's hands were still clutching his arm as Akash approached the greying blue.

'Ma'am, we got t'go.' The splash of dolphins hurried them, led by the clicks of Beaky. Akash walked the slope and continued to his middle, loosening his hold on Peter for the mammals to take, supporting Peter under his arms with their beaks and respectfully pushing him out of the harbour. Esme held her breath when they submerged him, dorsal fins and tails thrashed the surface, and they were gone.

Layla and Khadija cried as they watched.

'Why didn't you two go with the others? It's too dangerous!' Esme scorned.

'We didn't want to watch from the window. We're in this now, to the end,' flashing a slight smile to her father.

Michael spread its wings over the Mount, keeping the sun on the beach and rain over Janan.

'Doctor Samir, I have immense gratitude to offer you,' Musa said with a slight bow and hand over his heart. Samir just glared, nodding once. 'Where is my son?'

'Castle. Terrace. Walk, up this way, brother,' Samir wheezed, pointing to the path.

'Dearest brother,' Musa crouching to Samir's level. 'I will finish this today. My fate calls me. You know what to do.' They both laid their hands upon each other's shoulders, an ending between them. The men's interaction gave Esme enough time for her and the girls to save the babies. Reaching the rockpools below the causeway, the infants were floating on their backs startled by the sudden splashes from rising waves.

'Oh, you poor loves.' Esme clambered over the rocks, tearing her linens. Lifting the babies one by one and handing them to Layla and Khadija, checking their left palms.

'At least they're branded. No one can touch them now.' Layla said, the dripping wet wrigglers cold and disgruntled. Overwhelming love filled them as they walked back to Samir, cooing and squeezing.

There was a blood-curdling scream from Janan when she saw Layla, feeling the theft of her cargo. Raising her arms she crashed the waves against the causeway, shaking under their feet. Breaking, crumbling.

'Run! Go!' Esme yelled.

Khadija's foot caught, falling with a *slam*. The babies still in her arms, a pause among them before they screamed from the impact. Layla and Esme still running over the upturned cobbles. The rebellious saw their opportunity, scrabbling to get to the babies with drooling mouths. Khadija cried out, the other two well ahead. She gasped as she watched the causeway ripple and bend, the babies crying themselves blue. Her ankle throbbing, this must be a sign she thought, a sign from Allah that she wasn't meant to run ever again. Her father was right, running was not for girls, because they *did* fall at the first hurdle. She squeezed her eyes shut, gripping the babies tighter as the approaching stench of sulphur announced death and defeat.

'*Come in! Come!*' came female voices, dissipating her fear and opening her eyes to see what was beckoning.

'*Jump in! Save us! We need you!*'

'But, but I can't!' she called, searching the rocks.

'*Help us!*'

'Where are you?'

'*Here! Jump in!*' sweet, melancholic singing began, raising a blissful smile from her.

'Okay,' she slurred, 'just give me a second, the babies, I...'

'*Give us the babies!*'

Sudden hissing and the cracking of bones snapped her out of it, catching a blurred image of Akash.

'C'mon, quick!' hoisting her up, her vision clearing and focussing on his dispersing dark blemishes. Taking a quick glance over her shoulder at the seagulls descending on severed and decapitated Marid. They ran, *she* ran, even with a throbbing ankle.

Esme kept her steps firm while the rain began to beat her face. Janan's rage overtook her, striding ahead to get to the harbour before them, climbing over the wall and shrinking to her familiar size. The sea closed in behind them, Layla just making it with Akash and Khadija close as the last piece of causeway was swallowed up by rough waves. The temperature dropped and a storm erupted, turning the sea into a hostile grey with foaming white peaks. The three of them shivered with their babies, frightful of Janan's presence as she stood in Frank's spot, and began removing her green brocade.

57

Letters

Esme's gaze wandered over the serpent half of Janan as the brocade fell, mimicking the surroundings like a chameleon. A shimmer ran over the scales of a rising torso, keeping Esme hypnotised. Hands shaped like Hamsas which Janan thrust back with her head, crying out in dominance. An iridescent body with prominent bosoms, and head of a wild woman. Her hair alive, writhing, a strange vocal clicking began forming in her throat as the screams died down, about to regurgitate something. Esme's muscles were paralysed, the babies wriggling and almost falling from her arms. Edging backwards took great effort, a strained scream escaping her drying mouth when Akash tried pulling her away by the waist.

'*Take the babies, and girls! Go!*' she whispered. Akash averting his eyes from Janan's as he rescued the babies from Esme's limp limbs. Khadija and Layla followed him into one of the foster houses, the traumatic cries of infants arousing Janan, grasping Layla's waist with her tail, hurling her in the air making conscience-altering noises from a voluminous gullet. Layla frantically pushed down on the constriction. Akash ushered the other girls into the head gardener's cottage, slamming the door behind him.

Esme's eyes were fixed on the swelling in Janan's throat that moved toward its mouth and her daughter fighting for breath, the scales fizzing as the rain hit harder.

'Our father, who art in heaven. Hallowed be thy name...' spontaneously escaped her. Grimacing as a strange clicking turned into retching, the mouth widening to let the mass escape. Her mind couldn't fathom the emerging regurgitation, a grimace was the only reaction.

Settling, sprawling, expanding, it became clearer what was amongst the tainted mucus: little shoes, skulls and hearts that still beat amongst her mother's letters. The letters of warning, of protection and confession, spilled onto the harbour floor in front of her. All Esme could do was voice her horror in a stifled yelp.

Janan grew larger from human pity and disgust. Freeing Esme from the hypnosis, she crawled and sifted through the sticky mess, her mother's writing in blurred blue ink, forgetting Layla. The Nagini voiced her power and headed to the turret with her most desired cargo gripped in her tail.

Samir had managed to drag himself to the garden gate, just making it inside. Pulling himself up on the stone wall, his cries muted by the storm. Staggering along the path, holding his ribs, each step excruciating. The wind whipped through the sheltering trunks, reaching the door to the castle drenched and breathless. The stone had cooled, chilling his skin through the light cotton, desperate for his tweed jacket. The place was deserted, with a strange smell hanging in the air.

Making it to the turret, the circular room lit in red, he searched for the marking on the floorboards. The inscription of a Mermaid, barely visible on an aged plank, Samir yelled as he kneeled; sure he was about to die. Lifting the plank with his fingernails, his hollers of agony echoed when he heaved at the iron box out of the hole, hurling it beside him, certain he'd broken another rib. Standing with legs apart, he tried lifting the box. 'Ya Allah! Help me!' Salivating from the pain and sobbing a little as he made his way out, only to be thrown backwards by Janan as she entered with Layla. Ducking through the arched doorway, the Nagini slithered to the stone font, producing a sacrificial knife and holding it aloft.

'If I cannot reap from your high price, I shall reign from the rebellion that runs through your blood!'

58

Offering

The harpoon travelled across the turret, perfectly straight and beautifully aimed, penetrating Janan's back. She dropped Layla and the blade, clutching the protrusion between her breasts. Akash stood in the arched doorway, Samir laughing with elation; his teeth smeared with blood.

'Help me with the box, Siren!' but Akash rushed to Layla first. He lifted her off the cold floor and dived into her eyes, unworthy, a mere vagabond in comparison. She wrapped her arms around him with relieved sobs, pressing the side of her face into his chest.

'What y'got this on for? Ay?' he said, pulling at the peony silken scarf.

'No!' she held it, but the auburn curls burst out of the material like milkweed seeds.

Janan reached forward in a crazed manner, the red hue dulling the vibrancy of Layla's locks. Black blood poured from the wound and pooled on the floor, touching the holes from the rain on the scales. She carried the disdain of injustice as the control began to leave, needing young blood to replenish. A sudden stench of sulphur halted the room, something shook the turret. A black vapour entered and circled it, Janan became agitated as it hovered above her. She took in a breath, and the Efreet entered through her back, pushing the harpoon out.

'You must go! Now!' Samir cried. Akash took the iron box under his arm and tried lifting Samir, but his injuries were too great. 'Leave me! Take, the box, to the well – ask, Mika'il, to open it. *Go!*' Akash and Layla ran out of the turret, leaving Samir watching Janan cradle her head, screaming, shaking it, trying to expel Efreet that was splitting her insides. Samir lay on his side and could feel himself fading away, not wanting to die in that damned place. His fear of Janan instilled as she thrashed about like a grieving mother. Janan's roars paused life, his heart almost ceasing when he felt her intention and control that resided within him. A noise that played over in his head when he slept, waiting for her next destructive demand.

He pulled himself along toward the door.

'Help me, Samir! Or I will revoke your gift!'

He turned, his face creased from an anger and disgust long overdue, 'fuck, you!' finding the strength to heave himself up.

'You will no longer be the opener of doors! I will expose you! Feed you to the Saudis and have you brutally executed!'

she bellowed in a deep voice, the Efreet taking over her body, turning her male.

'That was never up to you,' he coughed, limping out.

Layla and Akash battled against the storm, pushing them two steps back as they staggered down the pilgrims' slope and steps to the well, holding onto one another. Reaching it, they knelt at the sealed opening.

'What do we do?!' Layla shouted through the rain, the heavy drops falling from Akash's long eyelashes, his eyes pulling her into them, endless, eternal and hers. She looked upon his mouth, wanting him to speak so she could watch his lips move over his teeth. He seemed to be turning before her, a savage Pisces laying beneath her blind adoration. He moved closer, so many things wrong about it. Akash tried his hardest to retain the image she fell for, but the agitation of battle was much stronger. His skin blushed in deep mauves, she gasped at the movement of something else alive within him.

'It's okay! I don't care! I love you!' She yelled.

Akash revealed his sharp teeth in a smile. Nothing about him was gross, just a beautiful wonder who burped fruits de mer. She was careful, their lips swimming in the rain. A bond made with a forever, until death would truly part and maim. She became a little afraid of the intensity and sudden bites and squeezes from him as he wandered down her neck and onto her shoulders. Layla surrendered herself into the rescue. Akash snarled, pulling her in tighter, squeezing the air out of her lungs.

'No!' she protested. He let go, kneeling with his hands placed on his lap. 'Not yet, we have to marry, or something.'

'Youm nobody else's. You's mine, and I yours, til death. I bear witness, and believe in your God! The only God!' he confessed over the down pour. His skin lightened, and eyes resumed their blue. Their embrace softer, love conquering. Samir approached with humbled expression, a little envious of something he may never feel.

'O Mika'il! Please, open the well!' Samir called with upturned palms. The concrete splitting, sealed for centuries and touched by millions, cracked and fell into the cavernous drop and waves below.

'Throw it in! Throw, it in!' Samir shouted to Akash, his self-pity replaced with hatred and determination, letting out a submissive cry when he saw the shadow of Michael loom over them. Akash heaved the box of amulets to the edge, the waves below rushing up the well and spraying his face.

'How's am I gettin this square box in this round 'ole?!'

With that, the circumference widened. Without hesitation, Akash pushed the iron box and they all watched it disappear. Swallowed up by the Mount and guarded within its belly.

Janan screamed as she slithered towards them, feeling the amulets leave her. The arms buckled and contorted as the demonic fight from within continued. The Efreet uncomfortable in its vessel, unable to fit or possess it like that of a human. Akash pulled Samir into the well's sheltering wall, waiting for Janan to pass, unaware of them in her turmoil.

Layla covered her ears and hid her face from the screaming. A scream that triggered the buried and forgotten, burning in their chests. Janan heading to the castle's terrace.

59

Retribution

Musa reached Hassan before her, in a confronting stance with deep amber eyes.

'My son. SubhaanAllah, I am proud of you. But those eyes will always trouble me.'

Hassan opened a circle of fire to his left, 'go! And never come back!'

'I must finish it! I want your mother to be free, habibi. She will never be free while I'm alive.'

'Please, Baba! Then you can come back, when it's all over!'

'It will never be over while I'm alive, habibi. Close it, my son.'

Hassan was pained, running and throwing his arms around his father, then pushing him away. 'You never came for us!' his bottom lip quivering.

'I had no strength. I am soree, for everythink. I have been a bad example for you. Do not take my behaviour as a guide. You have a good heart, a strong one mash'Allah. Like Ibrahim.'

'The Shiqq took him back home, to the Dragon trees,' Hassan said solemnly.

'Hamduillah. This is good news.' A solitary tear rolled down Musa's face and into his goatee. 'I will leave you with good people. You don't need me.'

'I know why you did it. I know why you gave me the pills. I know! And, and, why you pushed me to learn!' Hassan's emotions erupted, 'I don't want you to go. I killed Toulah, and Naga exploded! You should've seen it!'

Musa laughed adoringly and would miss those stories. 'MashAllah, that is very sick indeed, bro.'

They continued with their hugging, Hassan struggling with the rush of letting go as the embrace felt empty.

'I can't let go! It will be okay now.'

Musa shook his head, 'no, habibi. It won't. As long as I am here, nothing will be okay. We will be constantly fighting and movink. I cannot put my family through it anymore. Be brave, walidi. Allah's plans are the greatest, you will see.'

Hassan shrieked as Janan loomed from behind Musa, taking him by the scruff of his best shirt, stained and dirtied.

'Let me go!' he wriggled.

'No! Put him down! Not him!' Musa yelled, striding after her as she took Hassan to the cannons and raised him to the dark skies in revolt.

'I am not of your creation! Your prisons cannot hold me, or scriptures burn me! We die and we shall reincarnate! I will avenge you and reside within the fires where I shall be content! Taking your worshippers with me!' Michael sent the rain harder, the Efreet leaving from the top of her head. 'I am greater than you, Efreet!' The large devil roared from its freedom, the want of return to desolation too great to stay. But its only way back was through blood and filth, scouring the rocks and shore for the escaped elites: black magic packages in the form of flesh and bone. Its eyes locked on an iconic leader, one with the darkest secrets. Baring its teeth into a grin as it read their insidious, detached mind. An icon, and greatest advocate of depopulation. A man who had out-lived many from their endless supply of Adrenochrome and false worship. It twisted into the blackest vapour, and entered the vertex of its chosen vessel to rage terror on humanity.

Seeing Hassan looking so small in Janan's grip was a painful perspective for Musa. Hassan's cries broke over the wind, calling for his mother.

'My eyes are not working!' he bawled.

'It was never your eyes, Harvey!' Musa called. 'The amulet! The well wants it!'

Struggling and convulsing, he pulled the chain over his head.

'I'll drop it!' he threatened, making Janan hiss. She let him go, the fall twisting his ankle.

Every moment came to this moment in his head. The fixing, the full stop.

'Do you want this?!' he chastised, 'then come and get it!' He ran, Janan's lip curling, taking Musa by the waist with the tip of her tail.

Hassan hyperventilated as the decline nearly made him trip, ignoring the fire in his ankle. He reached the well, everyone happy to see him.

'Hassan! Hamduillah! Remember, we still have Goliath!' Samir's chest laboured with erratic breathing. Layla moved closer to Samir, clutching his arm. Akash stood in front of her, his purple veins visible on the surface of his skin. Hassan held up the amulet within the invisible shield. The torturous bellows of Janan could be heard as she appeared through the storm, with Musa gripped tightly.

'Release my father!'

Her deformed hand hit the invisible barrier, Hassan swinging the amulet of the Mustatil mockingly, his eyes harbouring movement within.

'I killed your son, and your filthy side kick!'

Janan released Musa and whipped the barrier with her tail, hissing and baring fangs. 'You will never escape the serpent, half blood! Your torture and inner fight will be eternal against the symbol!'

'It's over!' Samir yelled. 'Your evil…is over!' She was faltering from the rain searing her armour. The cold blood even colder and blackened heart vengeful and merciless. All endings were temporary, and she would return from the strength of her followers. She felt no loss, but an imminent hibernation until warmth and worship returned her. The deceit of her symbol worn by many, and serpents that would deceitfully represent honour and integrity.

Taking back Musa, she squeezed him, feeling his spine crack, his cries of agony penetrating the storm. He surrendered himself, listless in the grip of Hamsa, returning to old age as the effects of the adrenochrome evaporated.

'The well, habibi, drop it in!' Hassan gripped the amulet he was reluctant to let go of. 'You don't need it anymore! Walahi. Throw it in!' Musa strained through his pain. Hassan held it above the opening, telling the amulet it would be missed, bestowing gratitude for its aid. He let go, whispering *'bismillah'* as he did, taking away another lifeline from Janan as it was swallowed, the well taking on a living presence that seemed hungry for more.

'There is one left!' Musa strained. Janan squeezed tighter, Hassan's hope faltering as he witnessed his father's fragility.

60

THE CLOSE

The sea began to part from the causeway, making way for the divine support. The half bloods of the parish healed him enough to run, injecting life. Barking his loudest as he ran, unphased and impatient. Parts of his fur stained with a green substance.

Khadija was comforting Esme knelt amongst the horror Janan had left, when they heard him.

'Oh my God, it's Max! Maxey boy! Come on boy!' slapping her thighs. The girls saw from the gardener's house, banging on the windows and chanting his name, the little one wanting to be set free to pet him. Reaching them, he briefly sniffed at the regurgitation but there was no time, barking in a frenzy for them to follow.

Up the agonising pilgrim hill, announcing *'I'm here! I'm here!'* Esme and Khadija followed him to the well, their calves burning. Max smile-panted from the scent of his family, tainted with the stench of corruption. He barked and barked, he was on his way, they had to wait, stay alive.

They all heard, standing to greet him.

'Yes! Come on Kalb! Yes, bring it! Clever kalb!' Musa cheered. 'Habibi, take his collar!' he instructed Hassan, his bones being crushed further. The last of the amulets tinkled and shone from around Max's neck, his tail wagging when he saw them, skidding from fear and the threat of the monstrosity. Hassan quickly unclipped the collar, 'the close' catching their eye.

'Harvey! *Harvey!*' Esme screamed, running up the hill with stiffened muscles and a sticky envelope in her grasp.

'Mum, go back!'

'You can't have my daughter!'

Janan hissed, but it wasn't Layla she wanted, revenge lay with Hassan. 'Your daughter has an imprint! Your son will replace my door opener.'

'Not on your bloody nelly.' Esme said. Her eyes glowed green making everyone gasp, raising a smirk from Hassan. She stomped the cobbles, thrusting the gelatinous letter towards Musa, her face flushed with anger. His reaction shameful and defeated. Snatching Max's collar, she threw it in the well, more scales fell from Janan's lower half, lunging forward to grab Hassan. Akash stood in the way, her claws just catching his blemished chest.

Esme was halted by Musa's pitiful eyes, a gut-wrenching parting ensued as reality hit, one that was agonisingly overdue. She thought she was ready, wanting him dead so many times, but she knew that wasn't physically – Esme longed for the death of exhausting pretence.

Hassan watched in horror as Janan's jaw began to dislocate and stretch. Musa gave that smile, the one that said he was proud of him, one that had succumbed. His heart bitter-sweet and torn, the love of his son keeping it beating.

'Be brave, habibi,' he whispered through his torture, before Janan pushed him into her enlarged mouth. Hassan hurling Akash aside, managing to grab his father's trouser leg. He cried after his baba, fighting off his mother wanting to dive in after him, just managing to keep her son away. Musa's feet the last to be seen, the gullet consuming, crushing.

'Nooo!! Baba!'

'The heart!' Samir yelled, 'take the heart!' Max licking the rain from Samir's face.

Akash ran to the back of Janan in a flash, restraining her arms behind her, his bare torso breaking out in maroon bleeds. Hassan saw the blackened wound from the harpoon, disgust turning his guts. Samir reached into his pocket, throwing the flick-knife in Hassan's direction. Catching it mid-air he took pleasure in the release of the erected blade, but he wasn't using it. Running, rage turning him primitive, his eyes glowing amber as he plunged his hand into Janan's chest. Passing the squelch of moist and oozing tissue, he grabbed something pulsating and large. It was cold, and hard to pull. Janan thrashed, Musa still passing through her. Hassan grunted in frustration as he twisted something dead yet alive. Pulling, yanking, Janan gurgling. Akash restrained harder, almost snapping her in half. Hassan now standing on the stomach, still pulling, the heart grasped in both hands outside of the body, black arteries and tendons hanging onto it. Esme grabbed the knife, charging with a battle cry, severing them with one swipe sending Hassan hurtling backwards with the heart gripped in both hands. Black blood projected over the cobbles and Janan's slumping body. She reached out to the heavens and Mika'il, her green serpent eyes dying and fading with a grotesque gaping mouth. Esme sunk the knife in the snake half of her, splitting it, Musa and more skeletal goo being born from her. A faint scream leaving Janan in a last breath.

The well reopened. Hassan held onto the pulsating organ turning an insipid grey, letting it fall from his hand and into the hollow. The well increased in size once more, with purpose.

Rushing to Musa, Esme wiped away the cloudy slime from his face. She wasn't sure if he was. Looking at his chest for movement, his body still as if embalmed. Eye sockets sunken, like he had passed with everything else attached to Janan. Musa looked blissful like he did after night prayers. Pity and guilt twisted her innards, because somewhere in Musa was a smaller version of herself.

'Baba! Baba!' Hassan shook him, checking over his body. 'Kash! Do something! Please!'

Akash knelt with him, breathless, the blemishes fading.

'Let him go, Harv. He's gawn.' Resting a comforting hand on his shoulder.

Hassan pushing it off.

'No! What do you *mean?*'

'Harvey, you knew this was the end. It had to be.' Esme curtly stated.

'Well you're just glad of that, aren't you? So you can have Peter!' He pounded Esme's collar bones with his fists. She let him rage until it sobered, sobbing in her lap. His voice breaking when he repeatedly called out for his father. She rocked him, stroking his hair and reconnecting with his temples, her fingertips burning from absorbing his grief.

Janan's limp body began to slide headfirst towards the well. Layla watching in disgust, her stomach in knots, unsure if she would ever get over the vision that would be hard to unsee. She was torn about her feelings, but her father's empty, greyish expression will be tattooed forever. Khadija covered her mouth when Janan's fluids splashed upwards as the snake end poured in and slapped the sides of the well like a large hose. Musa also began to shift, but Esme held tight.

'No! Help me Harv! Hold him down!' the pull was strong, the Mount wanted everything consumed. A scandal and secret it would bury deep.

'Let him go, turn him on his right side. Make du'a.' Hassan surrendered. Akash was the only one who had the strength to turn him, less grossed out by the mess. Musa was drawn towards the well with dignity, allowing them to say their goodbyes and pleas of mercy.

Forgiveness and an uncomfortable ache settled in Esme, touching Musa affectionately as he slid away. Layla covered her eyes when he entered the well, the circumference shrinking. He slipped in gracefully, closing behind him and resealing. Max titled his head from side to side as he watched, hearing what the others couldn't.

Clouds dispersed, sun rays flooded the Mount and bay leaving the sky brushed with peaches and blues, the seagulls scanning the carnage from way above.

'You are my best, student, Harvey,' Samir gasped. Max licked his tears, forcing giggles that hurt. 'Good dog, good dog. We did it, eh? You are my second best student.'

He sat, panting fiercely, content and pleased with his work. But the run along the causeway was the best run he ever had and often dreamt of.

'Go on, read it to them.' Khadija said to Esme.

Esme gulped, her throat sharp and dry as she unfolded the sticky letter in front of them, glancing at her children, the others, the mess and Akash with an expectant smile.

'Um, this is a letter from my mother, one I never received,' she cleared her throat, holding the saturated parchment between her fingers. Restricted gullet and chest tight, breathing through the palpitations, Khadija urged and reassured her, because she wanted to hear it again.

69

PASCOE

Esme locked the door to Pascoe's Paintings, a parting gift from Musa left on the kitchen table in a white envelope, marked with three kisses. There was cosmetic work to do and the bare walls were waiting to be filled with her experiences. The painting of the Mount was proudly in the window, along with the orgasm one and random sized outcries. Every time she left it, the fact it was facing the harbour meant he had given back her sighs of contentment. The days were fresh, a euphoric freedom resided and everything had changed from Musa's absence, especially the house. But there were still moments where she grieved for him, for what was. It was still love, after all, however much of a nightmare, the colour magenta reminding her of the knot that untied. She could still hear the crushing of his bones, wincing at the disembodied sound that squeezed her temples.

Her mother's letter, now dried up with smeared blue ink remained folded in a wooden box like an heirloom, one she had read at every available moment since. The letter that had thrown her into a new turmoil, just when she was getting over the last. She was on her way to the café, the 'Habibi', renaming it was her second mark and way of starting over. Max idled behind her, still a little sore around his middle.

The town lay in wait for Peter; its essence and soul. Every night the floodlights were set upon the harbour hoping to catch a glimpse of the thrashing tails of dolphins. The waters were eerily quiet, there had been no news, everyone just drifting through existence.

Layla, Akash and Hassan sat outside the Habibi chatting and laughing. The kids were happy, free. Hassan had closure but he was missing the father replacement he was promised, and he hadn't stopped thinking about it all, especially the letter. Samir's injuries meant he was stationed at the orphanage for most of the time. He had become the pillar of the parish, a hero in fact. Holding talks about the true love of Islam and fundraising for the girls and new arrivals from his night-time rescues. He still looked over his shoulder and it would take time to be totally rid of Janan's presence, feeling her breath on his neck on many occasions. The stone heart had become a tourist attraction and legend of the Mount, a little larger and darker than anyone could remember.

Esme kissed her strange little family on their foreheads, especially now Akash had been adopted into their lives. She couldn't imagine life without him, and his fierce presence made up for the missing pieces. Layla was in love and that was okay now, a lifted weight so great she felt lightheaded from the release.

Suzie came to the table with their orders, her back in half and feet swollen. 'Sit, I'll do the rest,' Esme demanded. Suzie only too pleased to adhere. The pregnancy was going well, albeit fast. The baby had doubled in size and she felt it. She never spoke about the rape even though it played over in her mind every day. It was the most traumatising thing her quiet life had endured. The lifeboat crew had been her support and saviours, feeling part of a highly protected community. They all said it, but never in front of Esme, Peter was needed to help raise the baby and to set it upon the right path.

The barista machine reminded Esme of Musa oddly enough, probably because he never knew how to use it, muttering and cursing while making an espresso. She wiped away a tear while she read Suzie's scribbled notes: two cappuccinos going 'max' with carrot cake, and a latte with a white chocolate flapjack. Inside was empty, everyone sat out front preferring to sup while taking in the atmosphere.

Banging the used grounds into the steel bucket, Hassan made her spill them when he barged in.

'Mum! Mum! Beaky's back!'

She dropped everything, the barista still steaming. Chairs were knocked over and tables strewn as everyone scrabbled to get to the railings of the harbour.

'Excuse me! Excuse me!' Esme pushed through, running down the harbour's slope, her toes pushed forward and squashed in her Crocs. The rib had entered the waters, circled by dorsal fins and tails. Max barking loudly at the arrival.

'Is it him?! Is it him?!' Esme shouted over the din. Beaky emerged squeaking and clicking, the rest of the pod solemnly moving through the shallows and between moored boats. The volunteers were hauling something in. '*Please*! Is it him?!' her mouth open and face frozen. Peter's body lay still in the rib, she didn't recognise him, half of what he was, lifeless. Akash waded in, his beautiful face spoiled by grief.

'No, please, no.' Esme whispered, cupping her hands over her face to stop the eruption.

'Has he, has he gone?' Hassan asked, his voice constricted, tasting a rush of salt.

'I don't want to believe it. God wouldn't be this cruel.'

'God isn't cruel, mum. People and flippin snakes are.'

Not wanting to succumb because this morning, happiness was just a breath away. She had been running to a light that sparkled with hope, only to be devoid of it. No farewell, no last condescending word, hurt the most. Holding the kids hands, saliva gathering from all sources as her intuition confirmed the worse. The three of them entered the water without due care, Esme's tears came from her veins, pleading for him to move. Peter looked rested. A relief etched on his face, curled up on his left side in his checked shirt and jeans that were barely filled. Linking her fingers in his, the Hamsa gone from his left hand, she brushed his calluses and fine splits with her thumb, holding the cold, rough skin to her lips.

'His wounds were passed saving. Nagini venom is too strong. Dolphins did all they could.' The volunteer said, while another comforted Akash's cries that turned into ear-piercing screeches of spurn.

The harbour and its occupants were still, heads bowed, lowed chatter and sporadic sobs. Denial swept sorrowed expression realising how much of Peter lived within them and the foundations of Saint Ives. How could he leave when they thought he was invincible? Accepting none of us were. God had spoken with the greatest wisdom, while everyone blamed and tormented themselves. The volunteer strode the rib, balancing while he silenced the crowd.

'We have indeed lost a great presence today! One that will be impossible to fill. A greater power and evil won this time, but not anymore!' There was air punching and vengeful responses from the half bloods. 'Death came to us, with its replacements...Harvey and Akash!' Cheers rang in his Hassans ears, the volunteer jumping in the water to be at his side.

'There will never be another Peter, but his replacements come with divine gifts and hope! Let's send them all back to hell if they dare come into our waters again!' The cheers and applauds deafened him, was he dreaming? His eyes overflowed, making it difficult to take in the tainted celebrations. A soft voice to his left just atop of the slope, bringing solace.

'How is my best student?'

Hassan ran to Samir, who grunted from the impact of his arms. 'Help me, Ustaz, I'm scared!'

'BismiAllah, Hassan. Be calm. I am here to help.' Samir's eyes were blood shot, grief sagging his facial muscles. 'Allah has showed us great loss, and who is in charge. But you must trust what that will bring. Better than we dare imagine. You know this, eh?' gently shaking Hassan to drum in the message.

'I can't, I can't do it! I need, Peeeterrr!' sobbing into Samir's tweed jacket.

'We have all lost a piece of our hearts today, dear Hassan. Time will not heal us, only acceptance. He will live on in our memories, inshallah ones that will bring a smile. Cry for as long as you need, but do not despair of Allah, death comes to us all.'

Hassan released his hold, convulsing as he wiped his face, his eyes the deepest amber they had ever been. 'I don't believe it! They're lying!'

'Go, Hassan, say your goodbyes and pray for his soul, and tell your mother I want to see her.'

Esme had to be prised from her grip on Peter, with reassurance from the volunteers that it wouldn't be the last farewell. Reaching Samir her grief erupted, prompting further tears from him. He placed his arm around her shoulders and led her away, 'this tragic loss will be difficult to endure, sister. With great suffering, comes great ease. Come, I have someone who wants to see you.'

Her belly buzzed and squelched not knowing how to prepare herself, or who it might be. Had Musa come back to life? Dealing with the prospect in her head, picking at her hands.

Samir stopped at the café's door, 'salaams! She is here.' he called to the someone who had been waiting in the kitchen.

Esme choked on her spittle as they emerged, her knees buckling at the sight of her mother. Triggers firing on all cylinders, their grudges aside as Esme blurted her joy and wasted no time in running to her. Back in each other's arms was surreal, she cried like a child. The emptying coming from her Crocs.

They looked at each other, the moment incredulous, hugging again setting everything aside, it was all water under the bridge. No words could be spoken for there was nothing that could articulate the reunion. Laughing and crying as they became embarrassed by their reactions. A pressing vibe suddenly breaking off the embrace.

'Hey now, c'mon. You'll ruin that lovely makeup o'yours,' wiping her daughter's face with her cotton handkerchief.

Laughing through her tears, the comprehend distant. 'I couldn't, I mean, I wanted to find you, but…' the whole experience flashing through her mind.

'Sshh. Come on, let's get you sat down,'

They pulled up a chair each, the wooden legs scraping the flagstone, the surprise arrival in the noise.

'I can't believe it!' Esme sobbed, 'do you know, I mean, do you know what's been happening?'

Her mother calmed her fussing hands, holding them tight. 'I know.'

Esme ran her puffy eyes over her mother's long, red greying hair. Her soul shining through her brown eyes. A wisdom had come to organise the chaos, put it straight. Esme felt something being injected into her, it was warm and filled the agonising gaps, dispersing resentment and self doubt, settling her heart and seating her gently in a belonging.

'I'm guessing you got the letter?' her mother asked.

Esme pulled her hands away, her back hitting the chair, eyes darting between Samir and her mother.

'In the most disgusting way, yes.' Everyone reflected with averted eyes. Esme's resentment wasn't done yet, pushing its way through the avoidance. 'Why didn't you make a bigger effort? Why did you just…give up?!' She threw up a little in her mouth, stepping away from the table, her face on fire while it all added up, pacing the floor. She mourned, Peter was still around, trying to imagine what he'd be saying right now, which raised a smile and lightened her heart.

'Why did you *do* that? Why make me think, make me feel… make me fall! God, do I feel super cringed out by that one!' Looking into her open hands, aching for him even harder, flinching when her mother came to console.

'I'm so sorry, more than you'll ever know. But they were never going to give up.'

'I, I see that now, I know, but, we could've gone somewhere, hid somewhere!'

'Musa was determined to find you, at all cost. I surrendered to it, hoping I could make you see. But you were so in love, so, engulfed in him, it wouldn't have mattered *what* I said! It was one of the hardest decisions I had to make. But there was no escaping it. Musa's spell was too strong. He was never letting you go.'

She was right, Musa had a hold impossible to escape from. 'Well, he's dead now, and I, I cut you off because, I thought, you hated me for what I'd chosen to be. But all the time, you were trying to *warn* me! I went to the ends of the earth to find my daughter! How can you just turn up here like you were here the whole time? And how come you know Samir? Were you in on it? Are you a Jann?' Did her mother even realise how much therapy she needed just from one decision?

'Just you hold on a minute! You have no idea what happened! Musa told me I was no longer allowed to contact you, and if I did, he was going to take you all to Riyadh and cut off all ties! I agreed, but wrote to you hoping you would at least see one of them. We were so close, Esme, I even tried telepathy because that used to work between us! Esme, please, look inside you.'

'Ugh! Peter kept telling me that! Look inside you, look inside you. At what? The trauma? The massive gap you left that I've been trying to fill ever since with expensive therapy!' Esme composed herself, her childhood memories flashing vividly across her mind. 'He saved me, didn't he? He saved me in the water when I was little. And now I've realised, he's gone!'

She sniffed, caressing her peach hijab and gently pulling it free. Her mother's heart leapt at the auburn waves she'd missed so much, stroking them and setting them into place.

'You don't have to take it off because of me, Esme.'

'I don't want to believe he's gone! He, he can't be! There must an antidote, or, or something! He always was a dinosaur! Being bloody stubborn, even now!'

Samir looked on with guilty eyes, nibbling on a Biscoff.

'I'm sorry you had t'go through all that to find me.'

'And I wouldn't have changed it for the world. I've had the best and worse time,' throwing her arms around her mother. 'Come and see your grandchildren, they've missed you so much. A day hasn't gone by when they didn't ask about you or wished things were how they used to be. Well,' she sighed, 'seeing you will hopefully put the nightmare behind us, Harvey is still having visions. Oh, and I've got a gallery! And did you know about the orphanage?' She chewed her mother's ear off as they walked back to the harbour, spewing all there was to spew because there was so much she'd kept by to say, just for her.

The seagulls cried out over the low murmurs and the bitter-sweet, as preparation began for Peter's pyre and a different Thursday night.

62

HOME

Arm in arm with her mother, they followed Peter's procession through the warrens, lined with dimly lit lanterns above them. Heading for Porthminster, flooding the narrow streets of Saint Ives, Akash and three other lifeboat volunteers were the pallbearers of the driftwood raft carried from Crow's Street. The taste of sea and mould lingering on Esme's tongue from the slither of seaweed Akash gave her, something "to calm her nerves" he said. Although she felt calm enough, letting go of the draining burdens was therapy alone. She was someone different, someone she didn't recognise. It was weird how many skins she'd shed, desperately holding onto the last skin of Peter, the one she really didn't want to release. Her mother kept her head down, but Esme watched him idly rock beneath the white muslin. She didn't care to carry such loss, void and confused, the memory of him stinging her frontal lobe. Frustrated with herself, and God, she absorbed the unconditional love coming from the little one's hand she held so tightly at her side, who had gotten a little heavier from her nourishment. Skipping and muttering to her imaginary friend in the English she had picked up. Everyone was there, even Margaret and Bill, the woman from the Rum and Crab shack and the artist. The cyclist and Suzie in love and adapting.

The girls were behind Esme, finding it hard to believe Saint Ives was real, in awe of the chocolate box setting they thought only existed in movies. The American was still coming to terms with her new surroundings, not the concrete and neon jungles she became accustomed to. She was spaced out for different reasons, liberating her numbed conscience. The people were exceptional and healed all the nasty internal scars and wounds, feeling sure she had died and gone to heaven. Perhaps she had, and this is what is was really like.

Hassan walked with solemn underneath the raft, just managing to support it with the tips of his fingers.

Layla beside Akash, her hand resting on his back. He needed her there to keep him steadfast and under control; burgundy emotions illuminating his exposed skin under the brightest stars.

The blood moon glowed like a giant peach, reflecting in the black sea. Lit torches, agitated by the sea breeze, lined Porthminster's shore. They carried Peter into the whispering tide, the men and Hassan stopping at their middles. Dolphins circled the raft, the trees behind the beach huts full of brooding crows. Samir stood back folding in his lips, he was asked to light the raft but he could not, it was forbidden. The thought of Peter burning could be felt on his own body.

Stood at her mother's side with Layla, Esme watched Akash pile seaweed on Peter, periodically looking in her direction. The cyclist pulled a torch from the sand, holding it aloft before handing it to Akash; like that night, the best night of her life. Her bottom lip in spasms at the memory of them sat outside the café, the portrait and his heroism she found in no other man. Akash looked at her again, making strange noises of victory as everyone held their breath before he lit the edges of the muslin, followed by gasps at the rush of flames.

Hassan opened a doorway to the Mount that sat on top of the waves, its light forgiving with mellow hues and fireflies. The pyre danced in the eyes of mourners as a collective vibe descended when the raft was respectfully pushed by Beaky and his companions, into the residual of a Marazion sunset. There he would rest amongst the gardens he loved, the succulents with their forever existence carrying Peter within symmetrical perfection. Max barked and whimpered as he observed from the shore with the girls, the little one reaching out and crying for him. Khadija watched with her parents, clutching her father's arm.

As Esme observed all around her, she took in others' emotions, their auras, disbelieving it. Each one with bespoke colours that danced around them, like the doors Samir opened. A sudden spark ignited in her stomach and then the rest of her, a rush of blood to her head. A heightened awareness witnessing the neurons firing up the cerebral; feeling nauseous as everyone and everything around her moved oddly with dispersing light. Her heart raced, she was afraid but couldn't stop the rush. Everything that was suppressed, came forth with lucidity.

'No! Wait!' she called, running towards the shore. 'Close it, Harvey! Close it!' Wading in, she tore away the outer layers, it was good to be back in the water without fear. 'Dad! Dad! Wait! I remember! Wait!' reaching the raft she used the Dolphins' backs as leverage, jumping on and unsteadying it. Esme's mother screamed from the beach, followed by other cries. Shielding her face from the flames, Beaky and the pod filled their mouths and began dousing Peter. Throwing off the seaweed and singed muslin, his checked shirt was intact.

'Peter Pascoe! Dad! Wait! I got it! No, no, you bloody wait!' Akash went in after her, his face beaming with a wide grin.

The flames dying, there seemed to be life in Peter's hair and beard where there wasn't in the harbour. Esme looked at her hands, turning them over and back. She rubbed her fingers together, they tingled. Flexing them she tore at Peter's buttons.

'What now?!' she asked Akash, treading water, Hassan front crawling to reach them.

'You know!

'I don't!' Pressing her stomach, 'what am I supposed to see?!'

'Look harder, Ma'am!'

Max swam out to them, barking frantically. Her mother stood at the shore's edge, a shift in energy erecting the hairs on her arms, the half bloods joining her and the rest of the mourners. Each of them took a torch and raised it, and started to sing Peter's shanty in gentle harmony:

"O'er the horizon, with eyes for thee. Ere I'll be waitin. Remember me. Be treading the path laden with gorse, there I'll be waitin. Remember me. Follow them crows, where theym settle, there, I'll be waitin for thee. And when you shine your emerald eyes, there, there you'll remember me."

Esme's skin prickled as she turned her palms to the night sky, a stirring beneath the raft. The moonlight penetrated, lighting up the jellyfish and neon shoals, forming shapes and darting in the shadows.

'Ya Allah, forgive me, I just wanna go home. Don't give up on me yet, I'll return, you know I will. But please help me get there.' She mouthed an 'Ameen' and wiped over her face, removing her peach hijab, letting the tide take it. The dolphins stopped dousing and retreated, their bodies merging with the water. It was time. Max reached her, circling, barking, wanting to get on. Esme pushed her open fingers through the black sea, her face alight from the blue luminescent plankton that swirled around them like a murmuration, illuminating her face. The haunting call of the whale, soft voices buzzing around her, sure she was growing. She could feel her bones reinforcing their position, her eyesight acute.

'Oh beautiful Marid, how magical you are. Greater than the largest devils on earth. I love you. I serve you. O' ruler of seas.' Her eyes turning the brightest emerald.

The dolphins moved aside for the rebellious, who began to gather around the raft making guttural noises of worship. Their webbed hands held the edges and respectful glances were exchanged between them and Akash.

'You will honour the half Siren. He is mine.' They bowed at her instruction, averting their eyes. 'Touch the Pascoe,' she commanded.

The waves ceased, the noise hushed, just the melodic voices on the beach and crows settling could be heard. The rebellious marid placed their hands on Peter where they could, skin fusing to skin.

'Akash, Hassan, you too.' They cautiously joined, Hassan screwing his nose up at the stench.

The melodies stopped when a white light emanated from Esme's palms. She placed them on Peter's wounds, channelling all she had through them, her wish for his return. Everyone held their breath, the raft in rhythmic motion. It frightened her, not sure how to control it or where it came from. The brightness intensified with her emotions and she joined Peter inside the shell of his body. The silhouetted moments, the chapel, propelling through the water with him, racing each other and collecting pearls, taken back to the moment she was rescued as a child, the shadow of her hero no longer obscured. Leading and pushing her through a golden tube of light at speed which stripped her of every condition and expectation, reaching the end in an explosion and rebirth. She was Marid, alive again, shedding the all the skins of Esme Kattan, growing a new one.

When she opened her eyes, Peter was looking back at her.

'You took yer blimmin time...maid,' his stature and demeanour restored. The three of them blurted their joy, waving arms towards the shore. Esme joyous through baptising tears. The rebellious released their hold and submersed, strings of green gloop stretching and dispersing like webs in the night wind. Akash let out a cry of elation, Hassan silent in his, gawping at this mother. Max still swimming, voicing the good news.

Esme's cheek squished against Peter's scarred chest. 'I'm home, Dad.' she said.

'Aye, that youm be, maid. That youm be.' Kissing the top of her head, the smell of her hair and scalp rekindling the bond. They could've floated forever, residing in cleansing relief and stability. Having his daughter and soulmate back melted his cold heart that held onto hope longer than anyone would dare comprehend.

Celebratory horns sounded from the highest points as they were pushed back to shore with everyone rushing to greet them. Esme looked wild, her hair in wet, tight curls highlighted in silver and fire. But it was her eyes which Layla kept staring at as she gracefully left the sea and received embraces. Her new mum, who briefly felt like a sister as garments clung. Esme caressed her daughter's face, their green eyes glistening.

'I have the coolest mum,' Layla trembled, a little nervous of her mother she felt she would have to get to know.

'And I have the coolest daughter. I'm not sure what we going to do with this change, but it'll make up for everything. We'll have the best times from now on. I'm sorry for being, well, y'know. Pathetic.' sniggering together, 'you're free now, my love.' They hugged, each a younger and older version of themselves.

Samir stood with grace and watched from a distance, wallowing in the glory of mercy and power in his creator. He may just have been the happiest to see Peter amongst them, a good sleep long overdue, discretely opening a circular shimmer to the Mount away from the crowd. As much as he wanted to stay, the rebellion still hung around Marazion and it will never be quite free of it. He wanted to get the girls back before a walk in the dark would become a treacherous one.

'Come on girls, it's getting late. Time for bed.' He said to them, all responding with pleas to stay a little longer. 'Please, girls, you can come back tomorrow inshallah. Every day in fact. Come,' he beckoned with an outstretched arm while the doorway fizzed like a Catherine wheel on the causeway. They waved goodbye to everyone, the little one hugging and kissing Max first, not forgetting Peter. She took Samir's hand and the girls entered one by one, the American giving Layla an extended wave who sealed their friendship with the peace sign and pout. 'I bid you all goodnight, the most precious of nights. Salaams,' he bowed, hand over his heart. Citizens aghast, they watched the doorway decrease and swallow them, Marazion projecting a gust their way before the circle popped as it closed.

Max dug random holes in random places around everyone, barking into them, hoping to find any bones. Sitting on the sand with mourners that were unsure where to place their emotions, feeling a little cheated after grief had paid a deceptive visit. They watched the raft rock with its singed remnants, Porthminster breathing its magic back into everyone. There were bursts of laughter now where there once were tears and disdain, the miracle dancing around them, tickling their noses.

Her mother and Peter made eye contact, reaching for each other's faces that glowed with long lost. His eyes wandered her freckled complexion and hair beautified by her age.

'Dydh Da, Claire Pascoe. Fatel os ta?'

'I'm well, my dearest Peter. All will be well, now.'

Peter wiped away her tear and licked it from his thumb, still a little frail but the welcome and reunion had thickened his bones. They fell in love all over again, euphoria erasing the years apart from the sacrifice of their child. Claire knew that she would die before him, which made her patient in the beautifully painful wait. The running was over, the, trying to make her stubborn daughter 'see', aided by the unseen with timely perfection. Saint Ives' foundations had been restored, but Peter accepted that he could only be saved once and the time would eventually come, for not even half Marids were immortal. His rekindled family, Akash and arrival of a new half blood from Suzie upholding his legacy.

Hassan and the other half bloods gathered around them with eyes amber, green and blue. Layla clutching her grandmother's arm for reassurance.

'Are you one of them, too?' she asked, feeling left out all over again.

'No m'love. It's you and me both. So no need to feel so deserted. They need us as much as we need them. But you'll have your very own half blood one day, won't ye?' she nudged and winked, looking in Akash's direction.

Layla found it difficult to live in the moment, disassociated with all she yearned for, with so much colour and clarity. Maybe it was granted because of the hijab, or her first prayer. But how could it just be hers when everyone else was praying for a release, for that break? All she knew, is that it took her mother great courage to step out of a toxic unit, held together by barbed wire. Promising never to doubt the love that was made up of her DNA. That there is so much more beyond our conditioning, beyond the stifling prisons of expectation. Control is a disease that has corrupted the human species, and the time has come to replenish our connection to the elements they try to shroud with numbing distractions.

Maybe then, we'll all finally find our way home.

The End
Khalas
Diwedha

Thank you for reading Marazion.
I hope you were paying attention.

If you enjoyed my novel, please leave a review on your preferred retailer or Goodreads. This helps all independent authors progress and sell their art. Thank you.

Follow me on Instagram for updates on my next books: @juliekabouya.writes

Acknowledgements

To Claire, the definition of a good soul.
To me, for striving to achieve something for myself.
To the cultures who helped me put this story together.
To the enrichments of family and friends.
To Cornwall for your magic which made this novel possible.
To the reality of the unseen.
To the Middle East, that shall soon become the world's focus.
To the Almighty.

And to you, for reading my books.
Go do that thing you've been dreaming of, it's never too late.

About the Author

Julie Kabouya, an only child, who never quite fitted into the academic side of life. English literature was her favourite subject, in the days where creativity was allowed to flourish. She left school as soon as the years were over, wanting to pursue a career in the office environment, where she succeeded making her way up to corporate establishments. Her experiences are reflected in her debut novel, HIMAYA, which she began to write when she left the office politics to become a freelance gardener, being a tree hugger and nature lover at heart. Julie lives in the UK and hasn't looked back since achieving her dream of working with the elements and becoming a self-published author. Stories influenced by her own extraordinary encounters and beliefs in supernatural phenomena, derived from her interest of paranormal perceptions within Arabic cultures, mythology and Islamic tradition.

Printed in Great Britain
by Amazon